About the author

Lisa Cutts lives in Kent with her husband. She has degrees in Law and Applied Criminal Investigation and is a serving police officer with Kent Police. *Never Forget*, her first novel, is the start of the DC Nina Foster series.

NEVER FORGET

LISA CUTTS

Myriad Editions

Published in 2013 by

Myriad Editions
59 Lansdowne Place
Brighton BN3 1FL

www.myriadeditions.com

3 5 7 9 10 8 6 4 2

A CIP catalogue record for this book is available
from the British Library.

ISBN: 978-1-908-434-26-5

Printed on FSC-accredited paper by
CPI Group (UK) Ltd, Croydon, CR0 4YY

For my husband, Graham –
all my love

1976

Later I would recognise the smell as blood. Much, much later. At the age of five, I had no idea what it was. The room was dark and I was scared. My sister wasn't moving but her face and clothes felt sticky. I suppose I was panicking, but at that age, with no frame of reference, I wasn't likely to know that.

Although I couldn't see anything, not even my own hand in front of my face, I could hear something. A loud cracking. It was followed by shouting and heavy footsteps, lots of pairs of feet, on the stairs.

Light was now coming from under the door. Shadows appearing within the sliver of brightness meant that someone was outside the room, waiting to come in.

'Nina, Sara, move away from the door.'

I didn't recognise the man's voice and couldn't decide whether his arrival meant good news or bad. I was on the far side of the room already; I couldn't have moved even if I'd wanted to. Another cracking noise and the door swung in, flooding the room with light.

I looked away from the open door, which was filled by the silhouette of a man. I couldn't make out his face but he was huge. Now the room was bright enough to see, I felt compelled to look round. She was my big sister and I couldn't help myself. I knew it wasn't going to be good. But the man was across the room before my eyes reached Sara. He scooped me up and hugged me to him. 'Nina,' he said quietly, 'I'm a policeman. I'm Stan. I've come to take you home.'

He was acting strangely. Few grown-ups had ever picked me up – parents, grandparents, the usual; not strangers. Somehow I didn't mind. I could tell he was there for the right reasons. Never underestimate a child's instinct.

'Guv,' whispered a woman I hadn't noticed before, 'let me take her downstairs.'

'No,' came Stan's abrupt reply. 'I've got her.' He began backing out of the room. It seemed strange at the time but at some point, years later, it became blindingly obvious. He backed out because, if he had turned around, I would have turned around. He wasn't about to risk me seeing my sister's bloodied body lying there on the bare boards.

When I grew up I wanted to be a policewoman. Not to tear around the streets trying to right a wrong that had happened to me and my sister twenty years earlier, not to be a one-woman crusade against the forces of evil, but because, from the moment Stan McGuire had picked me up, I'd been safe. What other profession cared so much? Well, I could have become a doctor, but that took years and I wasn't bright enough. Besides, it wasn't a team of surgeons or nurses who tracked us, kicked the door down, had a 'quiet word' with our abductor, and made sure he went to prison for a very long time.

Chapter 1

20th September

'Dozens of separate stab wounds and it appears that none of them would have killed her. It's possible she died because she drowned in her own blood… Come in, Nina. Welcome to Operation Guard.'

I hadn't even been aware that DCI Nottingham knew my name – but then, as I was the only one who hadn't made it to the briefing on time, I guessed he'd worked it out. The man wasn't a detective chief inspector for nothing.

About half an hour earlier, my detective sergeant, Sandra Beckensale, had called me into her office and, with her usual look of disdain, broken the news that I was to go and work with Serious Crime. 'You're to get yourself over to Divisional HQ as soon as you can. They want someone who can work long hours for the next couple of weeks and can be spared here. I told them that you're opinionated, loud, often aggressive, and that quite frankly I'd be glad to be shot of you.'

Cheers, you old hag, I thought to myself. Usually I would say it to her face too, but I wanted to avoid a row and get going. If she'd really said all that, it was a wonder they hadn't told her to send someone else.

'I did add, though…' she paused as if the next words were bile in her throat '…that you are a good worker, seem to get on with most people and can be relied upon to deal with anything competently, from mortgage fraud to our favourite shoplifter Joe. So you're to go, and I'll see you in a couple of weeks. Oh, and of course,' she added, rummaging through her handbag for a lighter to accompany the cigarette she was already holding, 'give us a call if you have any welfare issues.'

Not likely. The miserable cow didn't even look up as she said it. I went out into the main office and looked for my friend Laura. I wanted to tell her I wouldn't be around for a couple of weeks, and also to find out how she was fixed if it turned out that they needed any extra help. She wasn't at her desk by the window, so I scribbled her a note, grabbed my stuff and left for Divisional HQ.

On the way I thought about the defrosting dinner in my kitchen sink, the Pilates class I wasn't going to make it to and how I really hated getting to briefings late. It always made the boss focus on you, and that usually meant that a griefy job was more likely to come your way. I also thought about long-time criminal Joe Bring. Before my speedy departure had been arranged, I'd been assigned to interview Joe. He'd been arrested coming out of Tesco Express with three chickens down the front of his joggers. Tesco didn't want their chickens back. That had made me smile. It was the little things in this job that cheered me up. That, and of course walking down the steps of the Crown Court following a jury's guilty verdict. I'd been quite looking forward to asking Joe a few questions under caution. Although he smelt bad – as if he had poultry in his pants – he was actually quite a laugh. He never gave me a difficult time and usually didn't want a solicitor. There wasn't really much point when you'd been caught with food secreted in your underwear.

When I got to the conference room at Divisional HQ, it was already packed. There must have been sixty people there. Some I knew, but most I didn't. I'd never met DCI Nottingham but I had heard of him – it was hard to not hear of people in a force the size of ours. We were a county force, bordering London, but with our own crimes and problems keeping us as busy as the capital.

The room contained a handful of uniform lads and lasses – I knew all of them as they, like me, were local – but there were a lot of older detectives in the room too. As a group, I reckoned that we had over a thousand years' policing between us. Pretty scary when you put it like that.

As I squeezed my way to a space at the back, I spotted John Wing, another detective from my nick. I was pleased he was here as we got on well. He also had a few years' more experience than me in CID and had worked on a number of murders. I stood next to him and whispered, 'Fill me in later, Wingsy?'

'No worries, Nin.'

The huge white projection screen in the room was showing a map of the area where the body had been discovered.

'For those who have just come in, this is where our victim, Amanda Bell, was found.' DCI Nottingham pointed to a large green area on the map and explained that it was the site of an old hospital, recently burnt down, and shortly to be turned into a new housing estate. 'The body was here, behind some bushes, fairly well hidden, and was found by a member of the public, Graham Redman, who was out walking his dog.' The DCI pointed to a corner in the northwestern part of the site close to the edge of the green area. 'Mr Redman has been spoken to by local officers and his statement taken. Absolutely no reason to suspect him of anything at this stage. We haven't had the post mortem yet, but early indications are that death was some time before Miss Bell was found. I'll let you know more when I return from the PM.

'She was found at 7.45 this morning and patrols were called straight away by our witness at the scene, using his mobile. Nearest patrol was on the dual carriageway the other side of the old hospital site and took three minutes to get there. Crime scene investigators have taken photos and I'll show you where the body was found and images of Miss Bell's body in just a minute. Right – Kim, I know that you've had an update from Harry Powell, the family liaison officer who's with the family now. What has Harry passed on to you about Miss Bell?'

The DCI was addressing a woman dressed in a white shirt and crisp black suit, about thirty-five years old, blonde, and unfamiliar to me. She was sitting by the door and sixty or so heads turned to look at her as she spoke, amid a rustle of paper as notebooks were opened and pens poised.

'Well, boss, her full name is Amanda Janine Bell, born 19th July 1978, last known address of 127 Upper Bond Street, Berrybourne. She had no recent boyfriend or partner and has one young son, an eight-year-old boy, Kyle Bell, who lives with his dad. While that's unusual, from what I can glean it all seems to be very amicable, but I'll find out more later from Harry when I speak to him again. Kyle is understandably very distressed. The ex, James or Jim Hamilton, is on hand to identify the body as we haven't been able to locate any other relative nearby – but we're working on it.'

I was distracted by Wingsy passing me a piece of paper. It was a list of names and phone numbers, with DCI Eric Nottingham at the top, then DI Simon Patterson, followed by the details of everyone in the room, except the latecomers like me. I added 'DC Nina Foster', my phone number and 'Borough Staff'. Above my name was that of DS Harry Powell, presumably added by someone other than Harry, since he was elsewhere coping with the grief of an eight-year-old who was never going to see his mum again. Not the job for me. I could cope with the dead just fine, but the grieving were too much for me. Harry and I went back several years, professionally. Sadly for me, he was another happily married man. He'd been my first DS, and a more decent bloke you'd be hard pushed to meet. I hoped that I'd catch up with him at some point during the investigation.

Kim, who I learned from the contact list was Detective Sergeant Kim Cotton, continued with a very brief history of Operation Guard's victim. Amanda Bell had few relatives, a couple of close friends, and had been arrested on four occasions: once as a teenager for shoplifting, once as an adult for shoplifting, once for drunk and disorderly and the final time, a month ago, for assault. As a result, establishing her identity had been simple. Her most recent arrest had been by PC Ollie Murphy, who had also been the nearby patrol on the dual carriageway that had been called to the body at 7.45am. He had thought he'd recognised her but, because of the blood and the position of the body, he hadn't been certain. He hadn't moved the body or turned it over to identify her, as minimum disturbance at the scene of an obvious death was always the correct procedure; anything else might destroy evidence.

I listened as Kim explained that Amanda was known to have worked as a prostitute in the area and had mainly used the money to buy alcohol. Drugs, unusually, did not seem to be her vice of choice. Despite the four arrests, Amanda's police record consisted only of one caution for shoplifting and a marker for being on police bail for the assault. It wasn't much of a criminal record in the scheme of things. We did however have her DNA, photograph and fingerprints.

'Thanks, Kim,' said Eric Nottingham when Kim finished reporting Harry Powell's insight so far into Amanda Bell's life. 'Harry is, of course, getting the ex-partner's movements to rule him in or out.' He said the last to Kim, receiving an efficient nod in return, before continuing, 'Here are the photos from the hospital site, or scene one as it now is.'

The area had a bank of trees running along its perimeter, separating it from the dual carriageway on one side and school playing fields on the other. Amanda had been found several metres from the trees, hidden among low bushes and shrubs. Without passing by close to the body, it would have been unlikely for anyone to stumble across her lonely grave. The photos taken from the most obvious approach path showed her lying among the thorns. If she had been alive when thrown into the scrub, I could imagine her wondering if there was anywhere lonelier on earth. What an awful way to go.

Next, Amanda's face filled the screen. The crime scene investigator had taken a close-up of the head and shoulders. Her expression wasn't scared, at peace or terrified. She just looked dead. As the photos scanned out from the facial close-up they showed the broken, dumped body of a prematurely middle-aged woman, dressed in a dirty, tattered skirt which was raised slightly, caught on the low-lying branches. The thin, thorny extensions held berries coloured bright red, in stark contrast to Amanda's exposed flesh, her white legs, streaked dark with a mixture of dried, smeared blood and mud.

She was lying on her left side but with her right leg extended, as if to stop her toppling forward on to her face. Her left arm was out in front of her and her right hand tucked underneath her. It was as if she'd been reaching for something, with maximum effort, but then it had all became too much.

My thoughts were interrupted by Nottingham's voice as he said, 'The dark marks you can see here on her legs are stab wounds. They cover her body. It's difficult to see from the way Miss Bell is lying, but her navy blue top is open at the back. It would appear it's been cut with a knife as there's a single, clean slit. The CSI had difficulty taking photos from behind the body, as you can see, because of this very dense and spiky scrubland.'

By the time he'd finished talking us through the evidence, Nottingham looked energised, well up for the task. Solving murders had that effect. 'We have loads to do. I've declared this a Category A murder, and that means pulling out all the stops. Right now we believe we're dealing with a stranger murder, a body in a public place, which may either be the kill site or the dump site. However, I'm not ruling anything out at the moment. There is no obvious motive and we're talking multiple injuries so the press are bound to pick up on that soon; the media release from our press office is being put together. I'll leave Kim to assign roles and tasks to you all.

I've kept it short, as time is getting on and I want you out on the ground. We'll have another briefing in here at six. Either be here or call Kim with your updates and reasons why you won't be. Someone take the contact sheet and make copies for everyone, so we can keep in touch with you all. Thanks, everyone. It'll be a late one.'

We began filing out of the room towards fresher air, some people pausing to talk to those in charge, check details and submit paperwork.

'Wingsy, long time no see. How've you been?' I asked as I leant over to give him a kiss on the cheek.

'I'm good. Great to see you, Nin. How did you manage to get on this enquiry?'

'Right place, right time, I suppose. I was just off to interview Joe Bring when my DS told me to get to Divisional HQ to help out.'

'The great farmyard thief of the county. Nice one. See if we can work together, shall we? You can tell me all about that Portuguese bloke you were seeing.'

'He was Russian and also married. Oh, yeah, and a total wanker to boot.'

'You do pick 'em, Nin. Come on, let's have a word with Kim and see what she's got for us.'

Photocopying the contact list was my first job. I made seventy copies just in case, while Wingsy continued to wind me up. 'Well done, Detective Foster. Your first job in the murder investigation team and you appear not to have cocked it up. If only your love life was so easily solved.'

'Or this murder, you jug-eared halfwit.'

Chapter 2

'How long are we going to give this bloke to come home?' I asked Wingsy, forty minutes later. Our first enquiry had taken us to the registered home address of a vehicle seen travelling close to Amanda Bell's body. We were sitting in our unmarked car outside an attractive, well-kept detached house on one of the county's many new housing estates. The lights were off and it appeared to be empty. There were only a few other vehicles parked on the street: a painter and decorator's van about five doors away from our target premises, and a couple of other cars outside various houses.

'We've only been here twenty minutes. Stop being such a miserable fucking cow and have some patience. No wonder blokes keep chucking you.'

'I think you'll find, dickwad, that I finished with the last one.'

'What, the married last one?'

'Yes, the married last one. I've missed working with you, you know. Why'd you leave our team?'

Wingsy and I had known each other for about ten years and had a pretty good working relationship. You couldn't really call it a friendship as we never saw each other out of work, apart from the occasional leaving do, but whenever we worked together we got on well. It was just... easy being with him.

Wingsy let out a lengthy sigh. My attention had been focused on the house so I turned my head sharply to look at him and saw something flicker across his face: exasperation?

Annoyance? I waited for him to speak. When at last he did, it wasn't what I was expecting him to say.

'Remember Amber?' he asked. I probably looked puzzled, partly because I wasn't quick enough to stop my facial expressions reflecting everything I was thinking when I was in the company of someone I completely trusted, and partly because I really didn't know who this Amber was. I gave a small shake of my head rather than speaking; I didn't want to stop him from telling me something that was clearly troubling him. 'The PC who came to work with us for about two months in the summer? Pretty, redhead, well fit.'

'Oh, John, you didn't?' Wingsy was married with three kids; I hadn't had him down for that sort of thing.

'No, I bloody didn't. I'm not you, you old slapper.' I laughed, then punched him on the arm. 'No,' he continued, 'haven't got the fucking energy for an affair. I walked in on her and someone else. Someone else who should have known better. I immediately asked for a move. Well, not immediately, 'cos he still had his dick out at that stage.'

'Oh, crap, Wingsy. Would this person happen to be your father-in-law?' No wonder he'd gone so quickly and it had all been kept so quiet.

'Yep, Inspector Matheson. Makes family Christmas a bit awkward. But he did buy me a new golf driver this year. Definitely the most expensive present ever. Oh, and Mel doesn't know. Apart from an old schoolmate, me, you and the guilty parties, no one else knows.'

I watched Wingsy run his hands through his thinning, greying hair. He let out another sigh, then he seemed to pull down the shutters that twenty years of policing had forced him to acquire.

I wasn't really surprised that he had confided in me. I was used to hearing gossip and I never passed it on. I liked to hear juicy titbits of other people's lives, but I'd also done some stuff that I wasn't particularly proud of, and I always put myself in the position of the person being talked about.

To be fair, if you were embarrassed about something and didn't want others to find out, you shouldn't have done it in the first place. However, police officers were only human and that meant weakness. Chris Matheson was a pretty decent man. I'd worked for him from time to time and found him reasonable and approachable. A bit patronising, but fundamentally a decent bloke. Perhaps it had been a mid-life crisis, a one-off? I hoped so, as I didn't want to think about who else he'd been getting his nuts in with.

I caught a movement in the corner of my eye and glanced back at the road. 'There's a car coming,' I said. 'Seems to be slowing, too.'

A grey Ford Mondeo came to a stop outside the house we were watching. The driver was the only occupant, and he looked our way as he turned the ignition off. He didn't react to seeing the two of us feet from his front door, but got out of the car, shut the door and began walking up the path. Wingsy and I were both out of our vehicle by the time he'd taken two steps. As we headed towards him, Wingsy said, 'David Connor? Police.' He got no further than opening his warrant card when the man we'd come to see headed full pelt up the road in the direction he'd just come from.

It startled both of us. We were used to people running from us, used to people not opening front doors, used to people lying, but why pull up in front of your home in your car, see two suited people in a vehicle outside your house and then go to walk into it first? Still, if you were going to run from the police, clearly you'd done something wrong; the man had just upgraded himself from witness to suspect.

Fortunately, Wingsy and I were a bit quicker and fitter than him. He'd made a distance of about fifty metres from his driveway when Wingsy tackled him to the ground. I was a couple of seconds behind, and got there just as Wingsy was pulling his cuffs out from his harness inside his jacket and saying, 'You're under arrest for the murder of Amanda Bell. You do not – '

He was unable to finish the caution; Connor turned his now scarlet face to the side, saliva falling from his lips, and shouted, 'What the fuck are you on about? Who the fuck is Amanda Bell? Let me go.'

I came around to the side of Connor so that he would see me and tried to calm him, while Wingsy cuffed him with his hands behind his back. 'David Connor, we've arrested you on suspicion of a murder and so you're being handcuffed.' I knew that this would hardly stop him struggling, but at least it distracted him long enough for Wingsy to finish what he was doing. When he'd got Connor restrained, he looked at me and nodded. I called the DCI. He was on his way before I'd hung up.

By the time Eric Nottingham arrived, along with a van full of uniform PCs to search Connor's house, we'd got our number one suspect into the back of our Golf and he'd at least stopped foaming at the mouth and swearing. Following a quick search of his pockets in case of weapons or drugs, he'd been fairly compliant and even seemed to be finding the whole thing slightly amusing. 'A fucking murder,' he said – well, perhaps he hadn't totally abandoned the swearing. 'Who am I supposed to have murdered? I don't know anyone called Amanda.'

'David,' I said, 'you're under arrest and we've cautioned you, so we can't question you about the offence until we get you back to the nick. We've got your house keys from your pocket and, now that the other officers are here, we're taking you to the custody area and leaving them to search.'

I took my pocket notebook out and made a note of what he'd said. I planned to ask him to sign it later, as his hands were currently handcuffed behind his back.

While I was talking to the prisoner, I could see Wingsy updating the DCI. It was a short exchange as we hadn't much to tell – got to the house, bloke got out of a car, ran off, we nicked him. Then we'd waited for the search team and senior investigating officer to arrive. That was unusual in itself. SIOs were usually in meeting after meeting when something like this happened, so the fact that Nottingham had come out himself at such a crucial point in the investigation was intriguing.

'Nina, I want you to stay here with the search team and call DI Patterson with any updates from the house,' shouted Nottingham, before taking his phone from his pocket and answering a call. 'Hello, Eric Nottingham... Just on my way.' He walked away back to his car.

Wingsy came up to me and beckoned me away from the open police car window where I'd been talking to Connor.

'Why do you think this knobcheese ran away from us?' I asked him. 'He strike you as a murderer?' I just wasn't getting a feel for him. We'd only been told to go and see him because his car had been seen on the dual carriageway near to the body. He'd been a priority as the cameras had picked him up three times that morning half an hour before the body was found, twice northbound and once southbound. The pathologist still hadn't given a time of death, so, for all we knew at this point, he might have been driving along totally innocently, a clear twenty-four hours after Amanda was murdered. If he hadn't done anything wrong it seemed madness to have run from us, but then this job had introduced me to so many halfwits over the years that little about human behaviour struck me as out of the ordinary.

'No idea, Nin. Probably hasn't paid for his TV licence and is a bit nervy. DCI wants me to take him back with another PC –' he pointed at the van ' – and you're to stay here. I don't expect we'll be interviewing him. Probably a job for Serious Crime. Doubt you and I will get a look in.'

'But we nicked him.'

Wingsy just shrugged at me. Showing him my notebook, I told him Connor's earlier comments and we went back to the car. 'David,' I said. 'I've written down what you told me;

14

can I get you to sign this as an accurate account of what you and I said?'

'Sure, love, it'll pass the time.'

Wingsy recuffed his hands in front so that he could read and sign the notebook, while I passed the keys to the uniform PC who was taking him back to the nick. Wingsy asked the usual questions: whether anyone was in, whether there was any burglar alarm or a huge dog in the house that was likely to jump out and bite anyone. Once reunited with my notebook, I followed the search team to the front door. The only woman in the group, Lila Armstrong, was removing exhibit bags, labels and tags from the rear of the van.

'Wotcha, Bill,' I said to the sergeant.

''Lo, Nin. How you been?' he asked. Bill Harrison was six feet tall, well-built, with a bit of a soft heart – you wanted him on your side, as he could be pretty useful in the right situation. 'Any idea what's in this place?' He waved in the direction of No. 82.

'No. Dozy git just legged it when we said "police", and then you arrived.' I shrugged back at him. I'd always had a bit of a crush on Bill. I couldn't even tell you why, but I sometimes blushed like a teenager when talking to him. I had never worked out if he knew the reason or if he thought I just had high blood pressure. In fairness, either would have been a safe assumption to make, as I was no spring chicken and I did drink a lot.

To try to avoid eye contact with Bill, and in an attempt to stop myself blushing, I turned towards the house. I had the key ring in one hand and my notebook in the other. One of the two keys appeared to be a back door key and the other was for the front door. I unhooked the back door key from the ring and passed it to one of the officers heading for the side gate.

As Bill and I walked along the gravel driveway, I glanced up at the top floor of the house and ran an eye over each of the windows, then did the same for the ground floor and the glass-partitioned front door. No signs of movement; it looked as if the premises were empty. My heart was beating just a little bit faster. No, not Bill this time – this was in a professional context only. I was excited at the thought of who or what might be inside our murder suspect's house.

Bill peered through the frosted glass panel into the hallway. 'Can't see anyone in there,' he muttered.

I put the key into the lock, opened it with one turn and pushed the door inwards, shouting 'Police. Anyone home?'

'Police. We're at the front and back door,' bellowed Bill. The hallway stretched to the back of the house, where we could see into a vast modern kitchen. The two officers who had taken the back door key from me appeared in the kitchen. Bill and I made a cursory search of the downstairs in case anyone was at home but keeping very quiet about it, while the other two went upstairs.

'This bloke's got a couple of quid,' Bill commented as he looked admiringly around the front room. 'Huge wicker bar in the corner's a bit much, though. Just goes to show that money can't buy taste.'

'I've got one of them, Bill. Only stocked it with Baileys and Babycham before I came to work today,' I said, hands on my hips and mock indignation on my face. My cheeks reddened again. Now I was annoyed with myself in case he did actually think I was embarrassed because I owned such a piece of crap.

He was unable to answer, though, as one of his team from upstairs shouted, 'Sarge, up here. You'll both wanna see this.'

I followed Bill upstairs, trying not to look at his backside. What was wrong with me? I had serious work to do. I wasn't much of a women's libber but I made a note to insist that it be ladies first in future. Less distracting.

Once we reached the top of the stairs, Phil and Jerry, the other half of the current search team, confirmed that no one else was in the house but said again that they had something to show us. Phil, the taller one of the two, was standing in the doorway to the rear bedroom. 'Notice anything odd about this room?' He jerked his thumb over his shoulder to indicate the bedroom overlooking the back garden.

'Hardly, Phil, we're not even in it yet,' replied Bill. He spoke slowly and patiently to the young, clearly overexcited officer. In a kind and manly way, I thought.

'There's only one door into it, sarge,' gabbled Phil.

'Oh, right, good observation, Phil. Like most bedrooms, though.' Bill nodded encouragingly as he answered. 'What's special about this room?'

'It's two rooms and I think that someone's bricked the other doorway up. I noticed from the back garden that there are two windows up here but only one in this room. There's a wardrobe and another door behind it.'

David Connor had run from us as we identified ourselves as police officers outside his front door. Earlier that same day, his car had been seen on the road passing a disused site shielding the body of a murdered woman. The fact that he had a hidden room in his house looked very interesting. It was also disturbing; I wondered if there was another victim hidden behind the wall.

My personal mobile phone vibrated in my pocket. Bloody Russian moron, I thought; if that's you, I don't think much of your timing. The break-up had been straightforward: I'd just walked out one day and ignored him ever since. Even if he hadn't have been married, I hadn't been all that impressed with our 'early diners eat as many jacket potatoes as you fancy' dinner date. He hadn't exactly been an oligarch.

'Let's get in there, Bill,' I said, pushing past him. I found myself in a double bedroom with built-in wardrobes on my right-hand side. The doors of the wardrobe were heavy, solid wooden doors. Soundproofed, I thought to myself. I wondered if Connor lay in his bed at night with a dead or dying woman the other side of the door. That really would be perverted.

Bill opened one wardrobe door. 'There's another sliding door behind this one,' he said, loudly enough for the other officers to hear, and probably also anyone positioned on the other side of the chipboard door. The whole house was quiet as he slid it to one side with one hand, torch in the other. 'Bloody hell. Can't see anyone, but this man's a big football fan,' I heard him say, voice slightly muffled by the clothing he was shouting through. 'Phil, Nina, I'm going through. Clear the clothes and follow me in.'

Chapter 3

What I saw, on stepping through the opening, was a room filled from ceiling to floor with cabinets and shelves of football memorabilia, photographs, programmes and an impressive collection of weapons. Knuckledusters, flick knives, lock knives, machetes, batons, coshes, gas canisters and swords adorned the walls.

'Jerry. Get the camera in here,' shouted Bill. 'This is something else.' Then, in a much lower tone, 'I suppose this is why your man ran away, Nina.'

'To be fair, Bill, without a warrant or enough to nick him for murder and search his house, we would never have known about these,' I admitted. An enquiry to speak to someone regarding their location a mile from a murder scene didn't by itself give us the legal power to ferret around in their wardrobe. The law called the shots every time.

As if to remind me that my personal life was flapping around like a fish out of water, I once again felt my mobile phone vibrating. I must have reacted this time, as Bill looked at my pocket. For a moment I thought he might be looking at my crotch, but I told myself off. Of course he wasn't. It was only sad, desperate singles like me that had such thoughts. I really needed a date.

Phil came in and told us that the camera and operator were on their way and that we should leave the room if we didn't want to appear on the film. I went downstairs and headed outside to call Wingsy and let him know what we'd found.

Just as I got my work phone out to call him, it rang. The caller display showed 'Wingsy'.

'Nin, got your drawers on?' he asked with a smile in his voice.

'Yes, you pervert. Want to know something?'

'If it's the colour of your smalls, no, I don't. Got something to tell you, though, sweetheart. Our man Connor, he's only wanted. Football violence. GBH on a rival fan last month up north. The local police had him on CCTV and have only just identified him. Bloke's got a good job in the City, in a bank. Earns better money than you and me. Can you believe it? Why would he do such a thing? Sad bloody twat. They're gonna travel down to interview him, so once they get here we're working together again.'

That at least was good news. 'Well, his house is a regular armoury. Think he may be in just a little bit of trouble. We found all sorts of stuff. Just got a couple of calls to make and then I'll come back to the nick.'

I took out my own, less embarrassing twenty-first-century mobile and listened to my messages. Both were from the same person, but the content was completely unexpected.

Chapter 4

This was serious. The messages were from Stan McGuire, asking me to get over to his house that evening as he had something to tell me. I knew that it couldn't be good news.

We'd stayed in touch over the years, and he'd become a good friend. On the first Sunday of every month, I visited him for lunch and a session of putting the world to rights. He'd got older – hadn't we all? – but he was still a giant of a man and was a constant in my life. I always called a couple of days beforehand to see if he needed anything bringing over. He would tell me not to be ridiculous, he could take care of himself, and I would nevertheless take him a couple of bags of shopping and a liberal supply of alcohol. In all the years I'd been visiting him, only once, about ten years ago, had he called me. That was the day his wife died of a heart attack.

Waiting until that evening was not an option. I dialled his number. After just two or three rings, a woman answered the phone. From the single word, 'Hello,' I could tell that it was not Stan's daughter, Samantha. We got on fairly well but met infrequently. I couldn't tell whether this was because she didn't like me and thought I was muscling in on her old man, or – and this was more likely – she was actually a pretty decent woman who wanted to give me some time alone with Stan.

The woman talking to me now on the phone sounded much older than Samantha.

'Can I speak to Stan, please,' I asked.

'Not at the moment. Can I take a message?' came the curt reply.

I wouldn't normally be put off quite so easily, but this was uncharted territory. Not one but two calls from Stan out of the blue, and a woman in his house who wasn't a blood relative, or in fact me.

'Could you please tell him that his friend Nina called and I'll be there tonight at about 8pm,' I managed to say, without adding, 'And who the hell are you?' because, in fairness to Stan, if there was a lady in his life, it had been a decade since his wife passed away.

'Thank you for the call, Nina. I'll make sure he knows. Goodbye.' The call was ended without giving me any time for further comment or question. I tapped my mobile against my chin a couple of times while I thought over who the woman could have been. She hadn't exactly been impolite, but not overly helpful either. In a professional capacity I would have asked more questions and probed a bit further, but this was personal, not work, and that would have just been plain rude.

Still puzzling over Stan and his mystery lady, I was brought back to the house search, carrying on quite nicely without any help from me, by a shout from Bill. 'Any news, Nin?'

Walking towards him so that the neighbours wouldn't be able to overhear, I replied, 'The update is that our man is wanted for an assault.'

'Wouldn't be football-related by any chance, would it?'

'Blimey, Bill, you're good. Detectives from another force are coming down to interview him.'

I said my goodbyes, promised contact numbers for the other officers, waited until Bill turned around again to check him out a final time, and asked Jerry to give me a lift back to the nick to find Wingsy.

Chapter 5

Making our way back to the Divisional HQ took us past my own nick. The county had seventeen working police stations. Some were occupied twenty-four hours a day but some were satellite stations, used only during office hours and for the odd hour during night shifts for patrols to eat their grub without the public looking on.

As a police officer I was used to working from a number of locations. It wasn't unusual, although it was sometimes a bit unsettling to be away from your own station. It did at least allow us to get to know both civilian staff and officers from all over the county. The county town's main police station was situated in Riverstone's town centre, complete with custody suite, crime scene investigators and Major Incident Room.

Once Jerry had dropped me off, I went to find Wingsy, who handed me another pile of work for us to get through. He'd wasted no time getting us further witnesses to see. He told me what we had to do, having already efficiently researched each of the premises and people we were to visit. Breakfast was some time ago, so we opted to stop at a small sandwich shop around the corner and stock up on doorstop sarnies to eat in the car while we sorted out a schedule.

I felt much better after an egg mayo and cup of strong tea. Wingsy passed me the priority enquiry of the day. 'Interview and take statement from Belinda Cook, cousin of Amanda Bell. Already informed by police of her cousin's death,' I read from the enquiry sheet. 'Sounds pretty straightforward. I see you've even got a recent address, photograph and information on her.'

'Yeah – while you were poncing about looking in wardrobes and at Bill's bum, I was doing some work,' said Wingsy, downing the last of his tea from the polystyrene cup.

'I was not "looking in wardrobes", you saucy sod. I was going through the wardrobe to get to the hidden room.' I paused and glanced at my colleague. 'Do you ever tell your friends from outside this job what kind of thing you do all day?'

I saw him shake his head. 'Would anyone believe us half the time? And the other half of the time, it would just get lost in translation. I notice that you didn't deny the bum-gazing.'

I answered him with a grin.

As we drove to Belinda's house, we pondered what would happen to David Connor. Unlike Connor's house, which was in a decent part of the town, Belinda's was in one of the newer estates that already had seen better days. It was the type of area that wasn't exactly unsafe, but you wouldn't choose to live there if you could afford better. Not one person had come out to see what was going on when we'd nicked Connor and searched his house, either because the street's occupants were at work or were keeping a safe distance, allowing the police to carry out their duties. Belinda's street seemed the kind of place where the local residents would bring out deckchairs and a six-pack to watch the show.

'Someone's in,' murmured Wingsy, as I slowed the car to a stop outside number 112. It was a new-looking house: large driveway, token half-dead evergreen shrub in front of the lounge window. The plant might have begun its life as a rhododendron bush but was now serving as an eyesore. Immediately above the sorry-looking plant, I saw a curtain move and a woman's face appear at the top of the windowpane.

'Inside of the house must be more impressive that the outside,' I commented. 'Looks like she's cleaning the windows.'

The woman watched us as we got out of the car and walked towards her house. She remained motionless for three or four seconds before stepping down from whatever she had been standing on. Her pursed lips and frown gave me the impression of annoyance. I decided an apology would be my best course of action.

The front door swung in with speed. We already had our warrant cards held out for inspection. 'Sorry to bother you,' I began, 'could see you were busy, but we're here regarding your cousin Amanda.'

I saw the frown on her face disappear and the pursed lips relax into a smile. She looked from my eyes to the floor. 'You'd better come in,' she muttered, standing to one side.

'We just need to speak to you for a while, Belinda. As it's sensitive, is there anyone else at home?' I asked once we were all in the hallway and the front door shut behind us.

'No,' she said. 'My children are at school. Please come into the front room.' She led the way along the narrow corridor past a bookcase filled with hardback books. She paused as we entered the living room to pick up a discarded plastic wrapper from the floor, and, looking down at it in her hands, she said, 'Meant to throw this packaging away now the curtains are up.'

Despite the shabby front garden, from what I could see the house appeared spotlessly clean and was newly decorated. I turned to face the window and the heavy, plush curtains with a sheer new net behind, commenting, 'They're a great colour for this room.' I didn't want to overdo the interior design praise; we were here for a murder enquiry. I turned to explain to her why we were in her home.

'We realise that this is a difficult time for all of Amanda's family but we have to make sure that anything at all that can help us find her killer is being done.'

As I said this to her, I saw Belinda sag as if the fight was leaving her. She gestured in the direction of a three-seater sofa, and moved towards a two-seater opposite. She threw herself into the cushions, sending the remaining hooks and other paraphernalia from her curtain-hanging up into the air.

We perched on the edge of the sofa, leaning towards her, using open body language. Wingsy began, taking his cue from me as I opened my book to take notes. 'Belinda, I'm John and this is Nina. We're police officers and part of the team investigating Amanda's death.' He paused and Belinda nodded, her pale face framed by a black bobbed haircut. I continued to watch her as he spoke. 'When was the last time you saw Amanda?'

'About a week ago. I know that I should be with the rest of the family now, but after I took my children to school this morning I got a hysterical call from Jim, crying and shouting that Manda had been killed. I went over but there was loads of you lot there and I didn't have much to add. I was in the way, so I left my details and came home.'

I could see Wingsy nodding from time to time in agreement with Belinda. Nothing she had said so far was anything we didn't already know. We had got her details from Harry Powell.

'Such a shock.' Belinda's eyes filled with tears and she fumbled in her trouser pocket for a tissue. She held it over her eyes for a second before dabbing at the escaping cascade. 'She was always a bit – you know,' she continued with a little laugh. 'Well, you know about the prostitution stuff. All very unpleasant. I'm not making excuses for her, but if men are willing to pay for that kind of thing, and pay well, then there you go…' She trailed off, searching for another tissue and wiping her nose. 'Last time I saw her was last Saturday. She wanted me to have Kyle until Sunday morning. It was her weekend to have him. That poor bloody kid.' Belinda put her hands over her face and did her best to muffle a sob. It was a pitiful attempt. 'Sorry,' she sniffed. 'Meant to be helping you and I'm getting upset.'

'You've every reason to,' said Wingsy. 'Can you tell us how she seemed to you and if she was worried about anything?'

'She was a bit preoccupied. Said she needed to get some things done, go to the bank, that kind of thing, but it was unlike her to cut into her time with Kyle. Since Jim got custody of him, she really looked forward to having him. It was for the best for all of them when Jim took him, though. Up till then, Kyle was here about twice a week. I told her that I couldn't have him stay too often 'cos he ends up sharing with my Glen. Glen's six and likes his big cousin, but the house is a bit too small.' She paused again and looked at the tissue clasped in her hands. 'God only knows where he stayed when he wasn't here. Only reason I said yes to her was because she's got some nasty mates and I didn't like the idea of where Kyle might have ended up.'

'Belinda,' asked Wingsy, 'what made you think that she was preoccupied?'

Belinda stared into space, as if trying to remember.

'Her phone, now I think of it. She kept looking at it. Usually, for her, work was work, but when Kyle or other family were around her she wouldn't even have the phone turned on. She took it out of her pocket at least twice in the ten minutes she was here dropping him off. I told her he could stay for the day but she would have to collect him before his bedtime. She kept checking it when she collected him, too.' She gave a barely perceptible smile, as if satisfied with her answer.

After a few more minutes of talking, we took a detailed statement from her, then stood up to leave. As she saw us to the front door, I noticed a pair of men's shoes tucked under the coats on the rack. I guessed they were about a size nine or ten. They couldn't have belonged to Glen; he was only six years old. Kid was enormous if they were his.

'Thank you for your time, Belinda.' I smiled at her. 'You did say it was just you, your six-year-old son and seven-year-old daughter living here, didn't you?'

Puzzled, she tilted her head to one side and raised her eyebrows at me. I looked down at the shoes.

'Oh, those,' she said. 'They belong to my friend Tony. He left them here some time ago. Been here months, I think.'

'OK, well, thanks again, Belinda. We'll probably be back in the next couple of days,' I said, giving the impression she had given me a plausible answer.

Back within the confines of the car, I said to Wingsy, 'What do you reckon about her?'

'Good spot with the shoes, Nin. I thought that the drilled holes for the curtain rail looked new and there was no drill lying around. They were probably done by a man.'

'You sexist git,' I said. 'I'm capable of drilling holes in a wall, you know.'

'You may be, but a bloke would drill the holes, put the tools away and then, as in Belinda's house, leave the mess on the floor for the woman to hoover up. I expect that this friend Tony is a frequent visitor and does a lot of work around the place. We know she's been living there for some time but a lot of the stuff in there looked newly renovated or decorated.'

I considered this. 'Even so, why would she lie to us? We're investigating her cousin's murder.'

Wingsy and I were obviously thinking the same thing. Belinda had something to hide, and her friend Tony had something to do with her reluctance to tell the truth.

Chapter 6

Wingsy drove us to our next destination while we happily rowed about men and women using power tools to carry out DIY. I was convinced I was winning when his mobile conveniently started to ring. He appeared very keen to pull over and terminate our conversation. Wanting to give him a bit of privacy and stretch my legs, I got out of the car.

My attention was drawn to two women standing at the end of the short driveway of a mid-terraced house about twenty feet from our vehicle. I registered that it was probably an old person's house: the front garden was a mess, the once-white net curtains were a dirty grey, and the paintwork was chipping and peeling.

Instantly, I had a feeling that something wasn't right. The two women were standing looking up at the windows, one with a mobile phone in her hand. I was nosy and I liked to chat, so I walked towards them with my warrant card at the ready.

One of them, a pleasant-looking woman of about fifty, hair going grey in the front, said to me, in a voice with the hint of a Caribbean accent, 'Are you from the council?'

I'd been called worse. 'No, I'm a police officer,' I answered, warrant card backing up my words. 'Everything OK?'

'It's our neighbour's empty house,' said the older of the two. 'We were expecting the council to come back, but we've been worried about it for a while.'

The other woman, a few years younger, said, 'Delia, can I leave you here? I was running a bath when you knocked.'

I watched her walk away and go into a house two doors down. I wasn't sure what the issue was, but it was clear that something wasn't right, so I wanted to make sure I knew where she lived. Never let a witness leave without an address and phone number. I'd failed half of that, but I was too busy looking at the house in front of me.

'What is it that worried you?' I asked.

'Well, you see, it's just that, since old Mr Baker died, the house has been empty. Then, about a month ago, I started seeing someone hanging around. All different times of day, it was. Never got a good look at him, but, well, you know – what would someone be doing looking at an empty house? The last thing we need is kids getting in and messing about, smashing the place up. Or squatters.'

'Did you report it to anyone?'

'I was about to, love, really I was, but then this bloke turned up. Had a key, he did, and some papers. I asked him who he was and he said he'd been sent by the council, to see what sort of a state the place was in, tell them what work needed doing and all that. So I didn't worry any more. I thought, well, the place is going to be sorted out now, cleaned up and that.'

'And did you see anyone hanging around again afterwards?' I asked her.

She shook her head, curls bouncing. 'No, not a blessed soul. There was a bit of noise a couple of nights after that, just the once, but by the time I'd got out of bed and looked out of the window there was nothing to see. Probably foxes. They're dreadful round here; they make such a racket overturning bins and screeching like they're being killed. You do worry, don't you, what with those stories you hear of them dragging newborn babies out of their beds – '

'So,' I interrupted her – we'd be here all day otherwise, 'you weren't concerned any more – until today…?'

'Oh, yes, love, sorry. It was the postman, you see. Our normal one, he knows Mr Baker died and had no family to speak of so he doesn't bother to deliver next door; he just returns all the mail to where it came from. But he's on holiday this week – off to Bermuda, he was, something about his daughter's wedding...' She checked herself. 'Anyway, this one today was a temp, and he knocked on my door with a parcel for me – wouldn't go through my letterbox, you see – and we got chatting. He's not from round here, he said – comes from one of those new-fangled eastern European countries, used to be Russia... and anyway, he asked if I knew anything about the place opposite. "Why?" I said, and he told me he'd gone to deliver some mail there and he'd spotted a whole lot of insects at the window. Some dead, some alive, he said they were. I mean, that's not normal for a house, is it, empty or occupied?'

I stared at the windows. If I wasn't very much mistaken, an unusual number of flies were indeed bashing about behind the panes of dirty glass.

Wingsy, having finished his call and got out of the car, followed my gaze.

'Think we should knock, Nina.' It wasn't a question. He knew on instinct, as did I, that this was not looking good.

I went up to the front door, Wingsy just behind me. I banged a number of times on the door and the downstairs window. Wingsy did the same. Neither of us said a word. We had a good idea of what lay beyond the warped wooden front door of No. 17. Delia kept a safe distance on the pavement.

I looked through the letterbox. I could hear the faint buzz of flies, smell the unforgettable odour of a soulless shell. We each tried a house on either side but got no reply to our knocking there either. Resigned to what we were going to have to do, we telephoned DS Kim Cotton to tell her we planned to gain entry to the house.

We got ready to force the front door. We stood mentally preparing ourselves and squeezing our hands into white disposable rubber gloves. 'I still have a key for the front door, if that'd help?' said our helpful neighbour. 'Don't think they changed the locks.'

As she went back into her house opposite, Wingsy and I looked at each other. 'It could just be his cat or something?' he suggested. 'Or a stray that wandered in. You're not looking too convinced.'

'Way I see it, mate, we're gonna smell of dead body for some time. Last time I was in a situation like this was when I was in uniform. Had no qualms then about going home and burning all my clothes in the back garden. This suit is Next, you know?' I tried to make light of the situation.

'Yeah, but it's not this year's, though, is it?' said Wingsy.

'Piss off, you twat. I just – ' I broke off as I saw Delia coming back across the street towards us. As she gave us the key, I explained that she should go back home and we'd be across to speak to her later. Really I was stalling. I had no intention of leaving my friend to go into the house by himself, but I knew how unpleasant the next few minutes were going to be.

Wingsy turned the key with one hand and pushed against the cracked and peeling door with the other. As his left hand let go of the key, he wasted no time in placing it firmly against his mouth. The buzzing got louder. Two hasty flies flew past Wingsy's head.

'Bloody hell, even the flies can't wait to get out,' I said in a second attempt to lighten the mood. Still didn't work, of course. I followed Wingsy inside.

The hallway was dark. There was little natural light. The stairs were in front of us along the right-hand wall, one closed door to the left and one slightly ajar door at the back. The left-hand door was probably the lounge and the other the kitchen. For the second time that day, I heard myself shout, 'Police. Anyone home?'

While I opened the door to my left on to an empty room, Wingsy made his way towards the back of the house. The room I was standing in did at least have some light from the window. The unappealing grey net curtains hung dismally, the wire they were suspended from having long since lost its tautness and let itself go. There was nothing else to look at except bare wooden boards, a single light bulb in the middle of the ceiling and surprisingly fresh-looking blue wallpaper. I went to check on Wingsy, trying out the light switch on my way. To my surprise a dim glow showed me the room's full misery.

Wingsy was still in the kitchen, opening the back door. 'I've looked in that built-in larder thing and the other built-in cupboards. Not down here, then.' He slammed the wooden cupboard door shut. 'Only one thing for it.'

I should go first this time, I thought as I headed for the staircase, before I changed my mind and let Wingsy be the gentleman I knew he was. I didn't hurry, taking as many deep breaths of untainted air as I could. Thought about calling out 'police' again, but, if there had been anyone else alive on the top floor locked up with a corpse smelling this bad, the sight of me arriving was not going to do them any further harm.

Chapter 7

There really was no smell on earth quite like that of a decaying body. I moved along the landing towards the front bedroom, the boards creaking as I made my way towards the source of the stench and insects. I flicked on the light switch, illuminating the dingy area at the top of the stairs. Although there were three doors, my senses were making it quite clear which door separated us from a corpse. Bracing myself and making sure that my mouth was shut in case a startled bluebottle flew straight from the rotting flesh and on to my tongue, I turned the door handle. Wingsy said, 'Want me to go first, sweetheart?' I shook my head, mouth still shut, and pushed the door inwards.

The stench seemed to leap at me and attach itself to my nasal hairs. The air was thick with it; it had always reminded me of cheese past its best. My eyes, now accustomed to the dark, rested on a figure in the far left-hand corner. It was face-down, and from the size I guessed it used to be a man. Something seemed to be moving in the area that once was his right leg. Maggots crawled around the back of his thigh area. The man was naked, which was odd as there was nothing else in the room or, so far, anywhere else in the house.

I realised that I had been holding my breath. That now meant that I needed to take a lungful of rancid air.

The light came on overhead and Wingsy half shouted, 'Fuck me!'

I was thinking something very similar myself. 'Wingsy, do you think this bloke used to be white?'

'And he's stuck to the floor by the looks of it,' came the reply.

Angry-sounding buzzing was coming from the window, where the flies were hitting the glass, impatient to make good their escape. I looked up at the window, tearing my eyes away from the man on the floor. I noticed that there was a pathetic grey net curtain similar to the one downstairs, but that this one was pulled back across its suspension wire. The wire was taut, unlike the one downstairs and therefore possibly new. Why would someone replace the wire and rehang such a sorry item?

The sound of Wingsy calling the office to update them interrupted my thoughts. I moved closer to the body to see if I could make out any obvious cause of death beneath the decomposition and the maggots. Nothing looked suspicious, other than the naked, dead man on the floor of an empty house. I was relieved at not having to touch him and disturb the evidence. Besides, no action I attempted was going to help him. Under the circumstances, with the right side of his face disappearing into the living room ceiling, it would have been too little, too late.

I listened to Wingsy give details of what we'd found, and only interrupted to add that the neighbour, Delia, would need a visit. We were likely to be busy with our own statements. Then I went to check the remaining two rooms. The other bedroom was empty, barring the statutory once-white netting, and the bathroom contained a bath, washbasin and toilet but nothing more.

Downstairs we waited for the on-call DI and a couple of uniform officers to arrive and carry out scene-preservation. I checked the time: it was later than I'd thought. I'd only have a couple of hours to get my paperwork in order before the briefing at six. Staying late afterwards and missing my time with Stan was not an option.

Chapter 8

By the time we got back to the nick, driving the whole way with the windows open to lessen the smell on our clothes and hair, we had managed to make several poor-taste jokes to cheer ourselves up. We went straight in to see Kim Cotton to update her on our lack of progress on Operation Guard as well as our latest discovery. We then took ourselves off to a quiet corner to complete our statements. Making our way past the never-ending stream of workmen, who were improving the appearance of the old building with a lick of paint and repairing the crumbling older parts, we found an office with a couple of free computers.

No sooner had we got settled than Alf, the caretaker, came in.

''Ello, you two. Hiding away from work again?'

'You know me, Alf. Not one to meet a bit of graft head-on,' I answered. 'How's things with you?'

'Mustn't grumble. Only six weeks until I retire. Not that the pension's much to shout about.'

'What are you gonna do with yourself all day?' asked Wingsy. 'You're such a young man.' Alf was coming up to sixty-five but, in fairness, looked ten years younger. He was one of those people we all took for granted would always be around. The entire division knew Alf, and even those of us from other nicks were fond of him. He was always good for a brew in his poky little office at the rear of the station, where you could be certain no one of rank would ever venture. Nothing was too much trouble.

'Dunno. Bit of telly, read a book, visit my son Adam in Spain. Him and a mate have got a bar out there. He's doing very well for himself. Villa, that kind of thing.' Alf walked over to the window, opening and shutting it, peering at the hinges. 'Yeah,' he said, pretty much to himself, 'this is definitely broken. Get me tools. Later, you two.'

We had peace for all of about three minutes before Wingsy got a call from Simon Patterson, the detective inspector we'd seen at that morning's briefing. I heard only one side of the call but got the gist. The body we had found at Preston Road had been identified. I looked over Wingsy's shoulder as he wrote down, 'Jason Holland, 23/03/78'. Wingsy nodded as I indicated that I would put that into the system to see what came up.

While he got more detailed information on the phone, I got the lowdown on the deceased. He was not a nice person.

The screen in front of me showed an image of a well-worn white male, a tattoo of a swallow on his neck. Holland had been of a generous build when the picture had been taken, only three months ago. If he had been dead for three or four weeks, it was unlikely that he'd have lost much weight in between.

As if he read my mind, Wingsy leant over my computer, arm barely touching mine, and said, 'He's a big old lump. Can't see him being overpowered very easily.'

'Just what I was thinking, mate,' I said. 'Next briefing's when?'

'In an hour. Loads to do before then.'

Now I had a decision to make. The briefing meant that I would be cutting it very fine to get to my old friend's house by eight as I'd promised. But missing the briefing would not go down very well either. I would have to hope that it wouldn't go on for too long. Whatever it was that Stan wanted to tell me was clearly something that would impact on both of our lives.

Chapter 9

Once again sixty or so officers, plain clothes and uniform, squeezed into the conference room. The air already smelt stale. All the chairs were taken, so again I made my way to the back. It looked like much the same crowd as that morning. It crossed my mind that there should be more people here, but it would have been difficult to get anyone else in the room. As if in answer, the projection screen came to life, showing another conference room at Force Headquarters where a similar packed room of investigators waited. The noise level of conversation increased. Queries on how colleagues had got on with their own pieces of the puzzle were raised in the rank and file while the bosses gathered their notes and took last-minute phone calls on mobiles already set to silent mode.

I felt a blast of fresh air and relished the idea of standing near the open window. I made my way over to it just as the meeting was opened. I stood with my back to the blinds swaying in the early evening breeze.

'Welcome again, ladies and gents,' said DCI Nottingham. He looked less red in the face than earlier, but just as tired. 'You will be aware by now that there's been a second body, found by Nina Foster and John Wing today at 17 Preston Road. He has been identified as Jason Holland, born 23rd March 1978. We know a bit about him. Previous convictions and arrests for theft, burglary, GBH, indecent assault and several warning signs for drugs and child protection. He was last seen four weeks ago on the 25th of August. Reported missing by his long-term partner, Annette Canning.

'He was found naked and his clothing hasn't been recovered. It's early days yet to give you details about the cause of death but I can say that he suffered multiple stab wounds made by a similar weapon or implement to that used on Amanda Bell. We're linking the two murders, and I'll give you more details when I have them.'

He went on to describe Holland's lifestyle and the lives of his close family and friends. None except his other half had seemed too bothered that he had gone missing. They had previously been spoken to and the right questions asked, but few seemed all that troubled by his disappearance. The point was made to the crowded rooms of officers that it didn't seem as if there was a deliberate lack of co-operation, just that nobody seemed to care.

A noise in the office immediately behind the conference room caught my attention. Making an assumption that the window of the adjoining work space was also open, I craned my neck to try to peep into the next room. Bad timing. It was mine and Wingsy's turn to take centre stage. As he was nearer the front of the room, he relayed what we had found.

'Well, at least Nina was kind enough to stand by an open window. You stink to high heaven, John,' said Simon Patterson, who was two seats away from Wingsy.

A laugh went round the room, followed by a bizarre, slightly later laugh from those in the room at Force Headquarters.

I interjected with one or two points that Wingsy missed but he summed it up concisely. Once we had finished, each member of the team, no matter what their part or rank, contributed what they could to the information being amassed around the murders of Amanda Bell and Jason Holland. I scribbled notes furiously. The room was filled with the scratching of cheap black pens on paper and hastily turned pages of notebooks.

I glanced up at the clock above the DCI's head. 7.30pm.

Chapter 10

By the time the briefing had finished and I'd managed to call Stan it was after eight.

'Stan, it's me. Really, really sorry but I've been held up at work.'

'Saw it on the news about that woman. What time do you think you'll be here?'

I had never let Stan down before. I'd always turned up when I said I would, but he'd never asked me to come over, either. For the first time in over thirty years he was asking me for something, and he sounded desperate to see me. It made me feel uneasy. Well, to be honest, it made me feel grown-up. With being grown-up came responsibilities. I hesitated only for a second. 'It may be a couple more hours. Will that be OK?' I asked.

'If you're not finished by midnight, give me a call.' It was Stan's turn to hesitate. 'Nin, I have worked on murders, you know. I'm well aware of the hours you put in.'

With the last two sentences, I detected some of the old, tough DCI McGuire. His voice had sounded tired up until that point. No, not tired – resigned.

One thing was clear, though: he wanted me at his house no matter what the time of night, and I was anxious to go. Only Stan could make me feel like that – usually I'd be glad of a bit of overtime, as I was always short of money. My salary wasn't bad, but there never seemed to be enough once the essentials were paid for. And, of course, I ordered in my wine by the case. This was a costly outlay but cheaper in the long run and it meant I never ran out. I could do with a glass just about now.

Still standing with my phone in my hand, mulling over what was up with Stan, I saw Wingsy come towards me, with another man I'd seen at the briefing.

'Nina, this is Pierre,' said Wingsy.

Did we have an exchange programme running?

Pierre held out his hand and said in an accent similar to mine, 'Hello, Nina. We get to work together tomorrow.'

I shook his hand and said, 'Hello, Pierre. I thought that you were going to be F– '

'French – yes, I know. Get that all the time. Parents just had a sense of humour.'

I turned back to Wingsy. 'Where are you tomorrow, pal?'

'Crown Court. Last minute. But I may be back by lunch.'

Pierre was starting to walk away. 'Nina,' he said, 'I've got your number. See you after the morning briefing and we'll sort out a plan for the day.' He waved over his shoulder as he disappeared into a crowd of lively detectives.

I focused my attention on Wingsy. 'Why him?'

'Single.'

'Nice one.' Pierre was a bit easy on the eye, I had to admit. Good-looking, and I had got close enough shaking his hand to notice that even twelve hours into a shift he still carried a trace of aftershave and not sweat.

'Got a spare pen, Nina?' Winsgy asked. 'Wrote so much my pen ran out.'

I had a quick look in my handbag. 'No. The only spare I've got is blue. There's a stationery cupboard in the next office; we'll get a couple from there.' I hadn't said anything to him about the noise I'd heard from the adjoining room but I wanted to have a look in case anyone was still working in there. It had slipped my mind up until now.

The typing room contained six desks, all with computers and empty chairs. The windows were closed but the one nearest to the conference room was only inches from the

41

adjoining wall. This was a working nick; the building was never empty at any time of the day or night so the fact that someone might have been in the room was hardly unusual. I wondered if someone had been at the window, and could have been listening to the details of the briefing. But I was finding it difficult to comprehend why someone with access to a police station would want to listen at windows. Perhaps I was just tired and had my mind on other things. This was my seventh day on duty.

As Wingsy and I searched for pens in the typists' store cupboard, I said, 'Funny, you know, I thought I heard someone in here earlier during the briefing, Wingsy.'

'Probably just late-turn patrols raiding the stationery cupboard,' he said as he helped himself to three biros, a notepad and a box of paperclips.

I still wasn't totally convinced, but my friend had put my mind at rest for the time being.

Chapter 11

I pulled up outside Stan's house. It was a beautiful place. He loved his garden and, even at this time of year, hundreds of pink roses spilled across the porch roof. The scent hung all around me as I rang the doorbell.

On the way over I'd tried to work out what he might be about to tell me, but I'd been a coward and put it out of my mind. I'd rather face it head-on.

A light went on in the hallway and I heard footsteps coming towards me. Same footsteps as all those years ago; totally different circumstances. But this time felt just as terrifying, only now I had a frame of reference for it.

The door opened on an ashen-faced Stan. I dropped my handbag on the porch and put my arms around his waist. Stan started to cry. The tears were silent. He shook slightly as he tried to hold it together. After a minute he pulled away from me and said, 'I'll put the kettle on.' That was another surprise; he'd usually uncorked a good red well ahead of my arrival. I followed him through the hallway along its plush, heavy carpet, to his vast kitchen. I watched him walk over to the range and busy himself with tea, coffee, chocolate, sugar, sweetener. He fussed over arranging the mugs on a tray. I sat at the table. I'd deliberately chosen one of the chairs closest to the range – didn't want to put any distance between us. As a retired police officer, Stan was bound to pick up on that, but I thought that he would appreciate the gesture.

I waited for him to speak again.

'Sugar?' he asked.

I had never taken sugar and he knew it. I didn't answer. I waited for him to look in my direction. When he turned around to look at me, I simply shook my head. He didn't meet my eyes.

At last, he brought the tray and the superfluous sugar. He sat next to me on the corner so we faced each other but at an angle, not head-on. Less confrontational that way, just as we'd been taught over the years in interview training.

Stan placed his hands palms-down on the table, took a deep breath, and said, 'I have prostate cancer.'

I was out of my seat with my arms around him before I realised I'd done it. It was my turn to cry. I really tried not to. It wouldn't help Stan, it wasn't about me, it was about him, but what would I do without him? He hadn't just rescued me, he'd set me on a course for the rest of my life. I had a career, I had friends, a pension, a purpose. No Stan, no purpose. I had so many questions but I knew the answers might not be the ones I wanted. My mind was racing. Stan would not have been so insistent that I come over so late at night if this wasn't serious. Other than his face being pale, though, he looked just the same. I couldn't comprehend that he had cancer.

'Now, Nina. It's not that bad, you know. I need to have surgery and quite soon.'

'When?' I managed to say as I broke away from him. 'Need a drink, Stan.' I looked around at the wine rack built in to the dresser in the corner.

He got up and selected a bottle, taking an age to study the label. Just pour it, I wanted to scream.

Now that Stan had something to occupy his hands again, he seemed more comfortable talking about it. I let him carry on, as it calmed us both. Or it would calm me once he opened the bloody bottle.

'Next week,' he said. 'I have what they call "locally advanced prostate cancer". That means that the cancer has spread outside the prostate but not anywhere else. Surgery

44

should remove it, but there is the option of radiotherapy afterwards.'

Stan continued to tell me how he'd come to get tested, avoiding my eye when it came close to revealing anything too personal. He was my friend but still a bloke I respected, and some things really weren't for sharing. We talked about the options open to him, how long he'd known, what Samantha's reaction had been.

'Who was that woman who answered the phone earlier?' I asked.

'Deirdre. She lost her husband to prostate cancer and runs some sort of support group. She came round to see if she could help in any way.'

I grinned at him. 'You dirty old git.'

'Language, Nina.'

Chapter 12

21st September

Another hangover, another day at work. I'd stayed at Stan's until the early hours and, although while there I'd only had a couple of glasses of wine, I'd gone home and drowned my sorrows. It wasn't just the alcohol, it was the lack of sleep, and this was day eight on duty. I was already tired when I got to work.

I sat through that morning's briefing taking in all the information we had so far on the murders of Amanda Bell and Jason Holland, but distracted by the previous evening's events and the dull thud in the left side of my head. I didn't have much to add. The enquiries Wingsy and I had finished before we'd gone home yesterday hadn't moved matters on at all. Other colleagues had more important and relevant information to impart. I listened and made notes. An update was given on David Connor, who was being charged after the briefing with football-related GBH, plus possession of a few offensive weapons, but bailed regarding Operation Guard. It seemed we hadn't amassed enough evidence on him. The scale of work in store for the team was breathtaking.

An hour and a half later, when the briefing finished, there was the usual stampede for the toilets and tea machine. I found Pierre coming out of the kitchen with two mugs of tea.

'Made you one,' he said, handing me the cup. 'There's no sugar in it.'

'Thanks. That's good of you,' I said, thinking that he was pretty thoughtful as well as decent-looking. I hoped that my eyes weren't still bloodshot; that might put him off.

We took our drinks to a couple of spare computers in the middle of the Incident Room. The position was hardly ideal, but the room was full of DCs and DSs trying to gather their paperwork and sort out the logistics of their day.

Pierre told me a bit about himself and how long he'd been on the squad. He made me laugh a few times and I had to check myself to make sure I wasn't doing my over-the-top giggling. I didn't want to look like an idiot or far too keen. While we were chatting, Pierre passed me names and addresses to enter into the system so that we could research our witnesses for the day. Once we were armed with everything we needed, we gathered up our files and equipment and went in search of a car. That was our first stumbling block. Forty minutes later, having negotiated some keys from someone else, we made our way to the yard and found our newly allocated car for the day.

Our first visit was to see a woman called Josie Newman. She was an old friend of Amanda Bell's and lived about eight miles away from the nick. Pierre drove and I did a recap of what we had been able to find out about her. 'She lives with her mum and there's a suggestion that they were once a mother-and-daughter prostitute team. Previous for drugs, which would figure due to the prostitution. Nothing much else on them, though.'

We decided which of us would speak to the mum in case they were both at home, and ran over what we wanted to ask. With that out of the way, I started to pry into Pierre's private life. I thought I'd try a subtle approach to begin with, revving it up if the need arose.

'Had a bit of a late one last night,' I said as casually as possible.

'Oh, yeah. Did you go anywhere good?' he asked, glancing over at me.

'A very old friend needed a visit. It was great to see him but I stayed longer than I intended to.' Why had I said that?

'Lucky you, Nina,' came the reply.

'Oh, no. No, he really is an old friend. And he's old. Very old. We were just catching up. What about you? Did you get up to much last night or did you have a late finish at work?'

'I left at about eleven. Just went home and tried to get some sleep. It's going to be a very long couple of weeks.'

'Yeah. As great as it is to have a few extra quid at the end of the month, right now sleep seems more important.'

We were nearly at our destination and I still hadn't confirmed if he was single. I must be slipping. Eight miles used to be plenty to get a feel for a man.

At the address, Pierre walked beside me to the front door. I could smell his aftershave. He knocked and we waited. A woman in her mid-sixties came to the door. She was wearing a green velvet dressing gown tied with a gold cord, red lipstick on her lips bleeding on to her face, and a jet-black wig, which was wonky on her head.

Pierre said, 'Mrs Newman? Police.' We both showed our identification.

She didn't look down at the warrant cards, but walked back along the hallway, saying, 'Come in, come in.'

Pierre and I looked at each other and followed her inside. I noticed that on her left foot was a red slipper and on her right a green one. We hastened after her into the lounge, a pleasant if musty room. So far, she didn't seem too bothered about why there were two police officers in her house, but that could have been because she was crazy. As a police officer I wasn't qualified to make a medical or psychological diagnosis, but I wasn't about to turn my back to her.

She indicated that we sit on the sofa opposite the armchair she had just taken.

'Thank you,' said Pierre as we sat down. 'Can I just confirm that you are Mrs Newman, Josie Newman's mother?'

'Yes,' she answered with a nod. The wig inched forward. 'I'm Susan Newman.'

'Is Josie here?' asked Pierre.

'No, she's not. She lives abroad now.' Susan was sitting upright in the chair, leaning back against the headrest. 'She had to get away once little Josh died, things were so bad for her. She went to France with a boyfriend.'

'Josh...?' said Pierre.

'Her son, my grandson. He fell into the fishpond in the garden when he was two. He was only out of our sight for a minute.' Her mouth dropped as she said this, accentuated all the more by the lipstick. I'd found the Baby Jane impression pretty hilarious at the front door. It didn't seem so funny now.

Pierre and I persevered with our questions but after half an hour we weren't really sure that we were getting anywhere. Taking contact details for Josie and giving her our cards, we got up to leave.

Susan stood up too. Her wig remained in the chair. It must have been caught on the chair-back cover. She didn't seem to notice and we were too embarrassed to say anything. Her head was almost entirely bald. Just a few white, wispy strands remained.

As we walked back along the hallway, she said, 'Pierre Rainer. Are you French?'

We looked round at her and saw she was holding our business cards, one in each hand.

Pierre winked at me. 'Yes, Mrs Newman, I am.'

'Thought so. You have that garlic look about you.'

Chapter 13

Once back in the car, we set off for our next visit.
'Sad, a little kid dying like that. Wonder if she was barking mad before he died?' I said to my colleague for the day.

'Don't know but, as you said, it's sad. You got any kids, Nina?'

Here we go, I thought to myself: this might have just got easier. 'No, just me. No one to please or worry about. You, Pierre?'

'No. I do want kids but it's not looking likely in the near future. I split with my partner about two months ago.'

'You never know – you just have to meet the right person.'

'I thought I had, but it turned out he didn't want the same things in life.'

For crying out loud. I really was losing my touch. Might as well rip into the Galaxy bar in my handbag now.

I searched through my bag for the chocolate and offered Pierre a chunk to show there were no hard feelings. 'Were you together long?' I asked.

'Four years. We still speak but, you know…'

Yeah, I did know. Knew that the smell of his aftershave was getting on my nerves. I opened a window.

As we drove, I tried Josie Newman's number several times, but got no reply. Finally, towards the end of the afternoon, with several other dead-end enquiries out of the way, we got a reply. Pierre spoke to her on speakerphone as I wrote down the content of the conversation.

I got the impression that Josie had been expecting the call. I guessed that she'd already been warned by her mother, and Josie confirmed this was the case. She was in another country so there was little we could have done to prevent them contacting each other, which was a shame: it was always better to catch someone off guard if possible, as they were more likely to give something away, even if it was just the way they looked at you. On the phone, all I could glean was that she had a very soft lisp and was well-spoken. That revealed little.

'Mother has lost it a bit,' she said. 'She may have appeared to be somewhat, shall I say, eccentric? I gather that you were asking about Amanda. Such a shock. What can I help you with?'

'It's a bit sensitive over the phone really,' explained Pierre as tactfully as he could. 'We are aware that you, your mother and Amanda were all involved in prostitution. I know that's in your past but, as this is a murder investigation, we have to speak to those who may have information. Is there anything you can tell us that may help lead us to the person or people who stabbed Amanda?'

There was a short pause. Pierre and I looked at one another.

'Silly Amanda. She was such a bad judge of character. We did all work as prostitutes but I've not taken part in anything of the sort for a number of years. Neither has my mother.'

That at least was good news. I put my hand over my mouth to stop myself from laughing. From the shaking of Pierre's shoulders, I could see he was finding the thought of Mrs Newman and her wig turning tricks fairly funny too. Getting it caught on the back of a chair would be the least of her worries.

Josie, unaware of our silent merriment, continued, 'I left England some time ago and settled in the South of France six years ago. I've made a new life for myself. I'll help however I can but I haven't seen or spoken to Amanda since I left. I read about her online. Her little boy – he'll be about eight years old now, won't he? Is his father looking after him?'

'Yes, he is, Josie,' said Pierre.

We took the rest of her contact numbers from her, and requested that she call us if she thought of anything else at all, and then Pierre and I started winding down for the end of the shift. I'd enjoyed the day working with Pierre, despite my disappointment at the lack of progress in my love life. And that he kept eating my chocolate.

My headache had subsided and I fancied a drink.

Chapter 14

22nd September

I had offered to work on my rest day but, under the guise of health and safety, I was told to take the day off. The truth centred around an already overspent budget. Forensics alone was costing tens of thousands. I drank heavily, slept heavily and woke up feeling lousy. I drew up a list of chores I had to pack into one day off, before seeing an old friend in the afternoon and then heading off to meet Laura for a drink later that evening.

First, I worked my way through the jobs I could achieve without leaving the house. It made sense to prioritise telephone and internet tasks. Besides, I was probably still over the limit.

A couple of hours later, having demolished a pot of tea and a bacon sarnie, I got into my old, slightly worse-for-wear BMW and drove to the supermarket, where I bought the usual essentials for myself and a couple of bags of luxuries for my old acquaintance, Annie Hudson. It was difficult to describe my and Annie's relationship. I'd got to know her when I was working as a Metropolitan police officer in the area she'd lived in all her life; we'd met through some terrible domestic circumstances of hers. When I'd transferred to the neighbouring force where I now worked, although I'd moved home as well as changed job, I hadn't been able to leave Annie behind. I couldn't quite put my finger on why I couldn't shake loose of her. For over fifty years, Annie had barely been further than her estate or the local shops. Once a year she went to the out-of-town shopping centre for Christmas presents, and she had only been to the West End of London once in her life for a school trip to the theatre. She still referred to the play as 'a load of poncy shit'. Now and again, I would visit her and drop her shopping off, stay for an hour or so and listen to what she had to say.

Often the visits would leave me in a bad mood, other times grateful for the life I had. Stan's situation had made me feel more benevolent so I tried to convince myself that today Annie would be of use to me. She wasn't exactly a police informant; for a start, I paid her in coffee, butter and Italian meats. Sometimes she would pass on something of interest and I'd send it on to the relevant nick, marked 'source anonymous', but usually it was bored housewife drivel.

I parked around the corner from Annie's council house in my usual spot; she 'didn't want the neighbours to know the filth had been'. The street was well kept in parts, an embarrassment in others. Annie must have seen me coming: she opened the door and said, 'You've put on a bit of weight.'

I exhaled all of my benevolence on to the driveway. 'And your moustache is coming along nicely, Tom Selleck,' I replied.

She came towards me, took one of the bags from my hand and peered inside. 'Is there Parma ham in here? Not that own-brand stuff you got me last time.'

'Is the kettle on?' I asked. It was like this most times I called on her. I quite enjoyed it, to be honest. That was the thing with Annie: you got the truth. Whether you wanted it or not, there was no dancing around an issue; she gave it to you straight. Sometimes it was not what you wanted to hear or was hurtful, but it was usually the answer you knew was correct.

'You been on the piss?' she said. 'You look like something the cat dragged in.'

I followed her into the kitchen and set the second shopping bag down next to the one she'd put beside the fridge. Annie looked at me properly. 'Something troubling you, girl?'

I felt the tears welling up and tried to speak. 'It's Stan,' I managed to say. 'He's got cancer.'

She hugged me, and I hugged her back. Annie had never met Stan but I had told her bits about him over the years. I never revealed anything personal about him and I hadn't told her about my sister and me. She was, however, aware of the huge influence he played in my life and the total trust I had in him.

In the living room, we each sat on a sofa with our tea. I'd declined a biscuit, noticing that the cheeky cow was offering me a cheap own-brand rather than the deluxe chocolate ones I'd just handed her. My phone bleeped with a new message. I'd get it later.

Now my tears were dry, I didn't want to talk about Stan any more. Annie respected that and we caught up on what she and her family had been doing. As much as she'd want to share with a police officer, anyway. Some things I truly didn't want to know about. Annie's two sons doted on their mum and she on them. Their dad had been a very violent man and the burn on her face from a clothes iron still reminded me just how violent. It was no doubt a constant reminder to her, too, whenever she looked in the mirror, and to her sons when they looked at their mum.

'Those murders down your way were bad, weren't they?' she asked.

'Murders usually are bad, Annie, what with the dead people.'

'Alright, you funny mare. You know what I mean.'

'Sorry.' I let her speak. I didn't want to press her.

She sat forward as if she didn't want anyone else to hear, even though there was no one else present. 'I 'eard they was done by the same person because of all the stab marks.'

'Really? Where did you get that from?'

Annie gave me a look of disgust. 'Like I'd tell you that even if I knew. It's just talk. All round the estate. News travels fast, you know.'

I knew that this was highly unlikely. People did not discuss the specifics of who murdered whom thirty or so miles away. There was more to it, but I knew Annie well enough to say with some degree of certainty that she would not tell me where this information came from. From experience, I trusted that if she wanted to tell me more she would, but in her own sweet time. Any information she passed to me usually had some truth to it or I would have stopped passing it on years ago. I had a feeling there was more to come, but I would have to be patient and not rush her.

Chapter 15

When I left Annie's, I checked my phone and listened to the message. It was Wingsy, asking me to call him back. I returned the call.

'Hi, mate. How was Crown Court?' I asked.

'The usual. Sat around and then they didn't need me. Had a lovely bit of carrot cake from Jean in Witness Services, though. Anyway, you up for an early start in the morning?'

'Yeah. What time and why?'

'Get here for 5am; there's a team going out to nick someone. Can't say any more than that. I don't know any more than that. By the way, how did you get on with Pierre?'

'Did you know he's gay?'

Wingsy laughed so loud, I had to move the phone away from my ear. 'Didn't exactly know. It's not something you throw into the conversation.'

'You total git. You told me he was single.'

'Well, he is. Someone else told me his relationship had ended. Blimey, I was trying to do you a favour.'

'You mean that the manicured fingernails and Calvin Klein aftershave didn't give you any hints?'

'The thing is, Nina, I look after my fingernails and wear aftershave; it doesn't mean I'm gay. How was I supposed to know?'

I ended the call, got into my car and headed home. I thought it was better to have a drink earlier than anticipated if I was going to be getting up at 4am. I gave Laura a call to see if she fancied meeting me as soon as she finished work rather than the time we'd arranged.

At four o'clock on the dot, I was sitting in the Dog and Gun with a glass of red wine in front of me. Out of habit, I'd deliberately chosen a table tucked at the back but with a clear view of the front door. A gin and tonic awaited Laura on her arrival. When she appeared in the doorway, a couple of the old regulars at the bar turned to watch her walk across to where I was sitting. She was single, a stunner and they didn't stand a chance. She sauntered towards me with an air of confidence and gave me a quick peck on the cheek before removing her cashmere jacket and sitting opposite me.

'How's tricks, Nina?'

'Not bad, Lol. Things much the same as ever in the office?'

She rolled her eyes. 'You could say that. Too much work, and that miserable cow Beckensale has had it in for me since you've been gone. She clearly just needs someone to pick on.'

'Yeah, she gave me a speech when I left about how trouble-some I was and how she'd be glad to see the back of me. The feeling was mutual. I just don't get what her problem is.'

'Perhaps she needs a shag.'

'She's not the only one, but I'm pretty sure I don't go around talking to people the way she does. It gets my goat.'

Laura chuckled. 'Can't you just be single and happy?'

'I don't want to get married, just have sex.' I said that a lot louder than I'd meant to and the old boys at the bar looked round again. 'But not right now,' I added, looking in their direction.

'What's wrong with them, then?' asked Laura, inclining her head towards the bar.

'I've not reached the point yet where I'll settle for a man who doesn't have at least a couple of his own teeth.'

'You know who's single and has all his teeth?' said Laura. 'Alf, the caretaker.'

'Very funny, Lol. I think he may just be a bit too old for me.'

'Handy around the house, though. One minute he's in custody unblocking the toilets; the next he's fixing a flat screen telly to the wall.'

'Why didn't you say? My U-bend can be temperamental.'

'Mind you, Nin, you'll have to get in quick. He's going to live with his son in Spain. I was talking to him the other day when I dropped some files off at Riverstone nick. His son's loaded and owns a bar. And he's good-looking.'

'A bar, you say? I may have been too hasty.'

We hadn't been in the pub long before a familiar face showed itself. We'd just got our second drink, bought by Laura, who'd seemed not to notice the barman flirting with her. She slid back into her seat, temporarily blocking my view of the door, and, as she sat down, Joe Bring came into view behind her. He paused in the open doorway, eyes accustoming to the dingy light, then ambled into the bar. Something was wrong with his walk.

Bloody hell, I thought, if he's about to start selling knocked-off legs of lamb out of his gusset, I'm not going to be able to avoid nicking him. He'd walked into the pub opposite the police station where two officers he knew were watching his every move. This was my only day off in nine days and I was facing another six of solid work, starting in the morning at 5am.

Laura followed my gaze. We made up half of the customers in the pub. He couldn't fail to see us. He looked straight at me and something resembling fear flashed across his face. This was an unusual reaction. Being arrested and having your plans for the next twenty-four hours ruined was one thing, but being frightened didn't usually feature for a criminal like Joe.

'He got bail, then?' I asked Laura, watching Joe as he backed out of the pub the way he'd come in.

'Yeah. Went to court and gave it the usual about having a sick child, wife couldn't cope and it was all the fault of the system. Not a dry eye on the magistrates' bench.'

Another hour and a coffee later, I said that I had to get home as I had an early start. I also couldn't drink any more alcohol as I had the car, so we walked to the car park together and wished each other a good night.

Chapter 16

23rd September

I slept heavily but woke up refreshed and keen. Within forty minutes of the alarm jolting me into the day I was pulling into the nick's car park, already trying to guess what the day would hold. I hadn't been able to resist making a few phone calls the previous evening, I'd wanted to know what was happening today, but everyone I'd called had been tight-lipped. An arrest was imminent, but few knew the person's identity.

Swiping myself into the building, I made my way to the meeting room, which was more compact than the previous one, only capable of housing about twenty of us. I was one of the first, arriving at the same time as Bill Harrison. I hadn't seen him since he'd searched Connor's house with me a couple of days ago. He had his same team on their way and I could hear them noisily coming along the corridor, with Lila loudest of all. Jerry was making her laugh at something he had in his pocket. I was intrigued, but not so much that I could be bothered to ask him. Wingsy had already taken a seat, so I sat next to him. At one minute to five, DCI Nottingham walked through the door and shut it behind him.

'Are we all here?' he asked. 'I'm not going to risk waiting.' He made his way to the chair furthest from the door. 'Only a couple of us know who our target is today. I've got Bill and his team of six, Nina and Wingsy, myself, Simon and Kim here. Apart from us, only the Chief knows that our target is working on this nick.'

Stunned silence. Some uncomfortable looks were exchanged. I remembered the noises I'd heard on Friday evening, from the room next to the briefing room.

'It's not an officer; it's one of the contractors who's been on the site, painting and what not. That's another reason for it being so early: there are three contractors working here and the other two will be here at 7am. Kim's to go in the van with the entry and search team. She'll brief you on the way. You go in, do your thing, arrest him for the murders of Amanda Bell and Jason Holland, and then Nina and John will join you. The suspect's name is Gary Savage. Grounds for arrest are a DNA hit on Holland. Anyone have any pressing questions, as I'm handing you the warrant and leaving you in Kim's hands?' Without waiting for us to say anything, he got up and walked out, leaving the door open. We stood up, glanced at one another and left without a word.

In the yard a couple of minutes later, Wingsy and I watched our uniform colleagues piling into the van. We'd all made the workmen cups of tea from time to time. On several occasions I'd popped to see Alf and found him in his cubbyhole amusing at least one of the decorators with his navy stories. Last to get into the van was Kim, carrying a file and a notebook. As we approached, she was handing out photographs of Gary Savage.

'Sarge,' shouted Wingsy. She looked at him. 'Grounds for arrest are a DNA hit but what other details do you have?'

'A hair was found on Holland's body. You're not making the arrest so you don't need to worry about it.' She pulled the sliding door of the van shut and began her mobile briefing.

Wingsy was holding the car keys in his hand, pressing the remote unlock button, attempting to locate our car in the badly lit yard. 'Best get going, mate,' I said. 'We didn't even get an address.'

'Yeah, and that briefing was shite,' he said, marching towards the car whose indicators had flashed. 'Just what is going on here?'

Chapter 17

We stayed out of the way while Bill and his team entered Savage's terraced house. It was nothing out of the ordinary, though on the outside at least the decorator's house could have done with a lick of paint. The last one out of the van was Kim. She came over and got into the rear seat of our Golf, bringing the cold in with her.

Her first words to us were, 'One of Savage's hairs was found on one of Jason Holland's stab wounds. Holland had twenty-seven identifiable wounds inflicted on him but unlike Amanda, who drowned in her own blood, he would have died just from those. It would seem that he was left to bleed to death.'

A pause allowed this information to sink in. She continued, 'Not going to need you two for much, as the senior CSI is on her way. You're here only in case anything mundane needs doing.'

The interior light in the car came on as she got back out again. I looked over at Wingsy in the driver's seat. He was shaking his head as he watched her walk towards the house under the orange glow of the lamppost. 'Must be a full moon,' he said.

'Perhaps she's just not a morning person?' I said. 'Let's try not to rub anyone up the wrong way after just a couple of days.'

'Take it you didn't get three sheets to the wind last night or you'd not be quite so charitable. Who's that just come out of the house?'

I couldn't make out the figure clearly but could see the high-visibility part of a police stab-proof vest heading towards us. A few seconds later, I recognised Lila's cropped red hair.

Wingsy let the driver's window down as she approached. 'Hello, gorgeous,' he said. 'Are we needed?'

'Right, he's been nicked, and Kim, or Sergeant Cotton as she's told me she prefers, has asked that you two have a quick look in his car and his works van. Both are parked on the road.' She handed Wingsy two sets of keys and pointed with her free hand at some parked vehicles on the other side of the street. 'The white van and the blue Ford. Oh, and she said to tell you to wear gloves. And if you find anyone in the boot bleeding to death, be sure to let her know before you call an ambulance.'

'You're having a good morning too, then, Lila?' I asked.

We all looked up as car headlights came towards us. The senior crime scene investigator, Joanna Styles, pulled up behind us. Wingsy and I got out of our car. We waited beside our vehicle for the latest arrival to get out of her white van. She was met with a trio of genuine 'Morning, Jo' greetings and was filled in while we waited for the uniform officers to bring Savage out. She chatted to us as she sorted out her files, camera and equipment. We told her as much as we could, but it turned out that she knew more than us anyway. That didn't surprise us. Wingsy and I left her to it and returned to the task in hand.

'Ford or van?' asked Wingsy.

'You romantic. Mel's a lucky girl. Ford, just in case someone is in the boot.'

A cursory search of the Ford revealed nothing much, except the man's obsession with fast food and scratch cards. The transit van was a little more interesting. The rear double doors on the van were unlocked. Shining the torch over the floor showed little but a couple of dust sheets in the far right corner. A glint of metal stood out against the dirty white floor.

'Is that – ' I said.

'A knife,' said Wingsy. 'Better wait for Jo. I don't want to climb all over the back of this van.'

'I'll go and let her know,' I said. 'I can see them leading a bloke out of the house so she can't go in there yet. She may be glad to start out here.'

Jo was a CSI, which made her a civilian employee in our force. Being a civilian, she was never allowed to be the first through the door in a volatile situation, and from the noise Mrs Savage was making it was best that Jo gave the house a wide berth for now. From across the road I could hear Mrs Savage hollering something about someone hanging around the past couple of nights in the street near their car and how the police hadn't done anything to investigate it. Over the noise, I explained to Jo what we'd found and waited for her to get her equipment. She came back over to the van with me, shining her torch through the open doors.

'Best organise a recovery truck for this van,' she said. 'I can't risk getting in the back of it in an uncontrolled environment. I need to examine it under cover. The knife's covered in blood.'

Chapter 18

Suspect in custody, vehicle seized and the house searched, Wingsy and I went back to Riverstone nick and headed for the interview remote viewing room, equipped to allow us to watch Savage's interview, actually taking place in the ground floor custody area, from the CID offices on the second floor.

Pierre and another detective Wingsy and I didn't know had already started interviewing Savage. For a long time it was slow progress; often he gave only a slight nod of the head in answer to questions put to him. But then Savage seemed to go to the other extreme. He avoided Pierre's last question, not by refusing to answer, but by rambling on about his mum. As fascinating as it was to hear that the old girl loved a game of bingo but never went to the bookies, it wasn't what we wanted to know. DCI Nottingham, who was also watching the interview with us, didn't look too interested either. Several times he sighed, stopped writing and threw his pen down on to the desk.

'Gary, this isn't relevant. I'm asking you about Jason Holland,' said Pierre. 'I've told you that your DNA was found in the room where his body was discovered. Did you know Jason Holland?'

'No, officer. I didn't know him.'

'Have you ever been to 17 Preston Road?'

'Yes, I have.'

'When were you there?'

'I can't remember the date but the council sent me to price up a job. You can check with them. Some old fella had died and the place was a right mess. I was there for about twenty or thirty minutes and I cut my hand somewhere upstairs. May have dripped a bit of blood upstairs or down. I can't remember where. There was nothing in the house at all to stop the bleeding so I may have wiped the cut anywhere. Check with the council. Is someone talking to them? Bloke called Andy, Andrew Wells, I think. I've got his number in my phone, or just ring the council and ask for him. He'll tell you,' said Savage, red in the face. He appeared satisfied with his answer. We were not.

'How did you cut your hand, Gary?' asked Pierre.

'I caught it on a nail at the top of the stairs,' answered Gary without a second's hesitation. He nodded along as he spoke. 'See here?' he said, holding out his left hand towards Pierre. 'There's a bit of a scar here. You can still see it. I showed it already to that nurse in the cells. She marked it on a piece of paper.'

I thought Gary was going to laugh, he looked so relieved. It made no difference that when he'd been booked into custody the nurse on duty had marked his injuries on a body map diagram. He still had to explain his hair on a dead body, not his blood dripped on to the floor.

Wingsy leaned closer to me and said in my ear, 'Do you think Pierre's got much more to go before he challenges him on his hair and the knife?'

I was just about to answer when Pierre explained that the DVD recording the interview was about to run out and it would be a good time for a break.

'We can ask him in a minute,' I said to Wingsy. 'If he doesn't come up here, we'll go and see him in the cells. See if he needs us to do anything.'

As soon as all parties had left the interview room, Pierre called my mobile to find out where I was. By the time Nottingham gathered up his notes to leave, Pierre was making his way into the room to see us. He shut the door and sat down in the chair recently occupied by the DCI. Wingsy and I had been busy leafing through the information we had gathered on Savage, his wife, his home and his two vehicles. It hadn't taken long. We had three documents. The first was his Police National Computer printout showing that he had been arrested once for criminal damage, which was how we had his DNA on file and had been able to match him to the hair found on Holland's body. Secondly, there was 'stop check' information which showed that Savage had been stopped twice late at night in his van, returning from work around the Gatwick area. The checks carried out by patrols had shown that all was in order and he had been allowed to continue on his way home. The final piece of paperwork was a crime report of a burglary reported by his wife four weeks earlier. Some minor personal items including cash had been stolen while the Savages were having dinner at Mrs Savage's mother's house.

'At the moment, we have a hair on a dead body. The hair is Savage's. The body was in a room which Savage said he went into. The hair may have got there innocently.' Pierre looked from Wingsy to me and back again. As he continued to speak, his eyes rested on the crime report. I'd highlighted the missing property. One of the items was a hairbrush.

He sighed, avoided eye contact and said, 'The thing is that the knife you found was covered in blood. Even if the van doors had been locked, it might not be Holland's blood. Was there anything else that stood out to you about the van or car?'

'Not a thing, Pierre, not a thing,' I said, shaking my head. 'Is it looking like we're gonna have to bail this bloke?'

'It's not too good at the moment. We're waiting on Jo Styles' update but there's nothing else right now. She's gonna let us know if the knife was or could have been the murder weapon for Bell or Holland. She was meeting with the pathologist when she left Savage's.'

He stood up to go. Wingsy and I did the same. We walked to the Incident Room. The smell of paint was barely detectable.

Chapter 19

'You two,' said Kim Cotton to Wingsy and me. 'Need you to go and see someone. It's Holland's ex-wife.' She handed me a sheet of paper with scant details on, turned and stomped off across the Incident Room in search of someone else to patronise.

'I'm warming to her,' I said to Wingsy.

'Know what you mean,' he replied. 'I've just upgraded her to git status. What a miserable mare. Right, who we seeing?' He glanced at the paper then handed it to me. 'Check out this address,' he said. 'It's two doors away from Belinda Cook.'

On the way, we discussed whether it was a coincidence.

'It's likely that they know each other,' I said, 'but I don't know all my neighbours.'

'What we have here,' said Wingsy, 'is a woman who worked as a prostitute turning up with time unaccounted for between her last sighting and being killed. Her cousin saw her a week or so before we found her body, described her as preoccupied, and two doors away from the cousin lives our second murder victim's ex-wife.' He flashed a look at me. 'What do you reckon?'

'What do I reckon? Glad I'm not the DCI having to explain to the Chief why there are two mutilated bodies in my division and the only two nicked so far appear to be innocent men.'

'Yeah, and I can just see Nottingham explaining that the really bad news is that the nick's toilets won't get painted either.'

Belinda Cook's house was on a T-junction. I parked the car in the road leading to her house, about two hundred yards away. The house was clearly visible across a playing field.

'We getting a cab the rest of the way?' asked Wingsy.

'Funny, mate. Just thought that, as the ex, Chloe, is one side of Belinda's house, if we sit here for a bit someone of interest might come or go.'

A double-decker bus drove past us and turned right at the top of the junction, heading towards the town centre.

'Looked like Alf on that bus,' I said. 'Keep seeing him everywhere.'

'Perhaps he's the murderer,' said Wingsy. 'He cuts them up and puts them in his boiler.'

'First off, the victims haven't been cut up, and secondly, the size of the nick's boiler in this warm weather, it'd take him about three months. Place would stink.'

'Maybe he gets the bus all over the county and drops bits off in rubbish bins.'

'Wingsy, shut up.'

After a few minutes of not much happening, I was just about to suggest we walk over to Chloe's when the front door of the house we had worked out was hers opened, a man came down her driveway – and went into Belinda's.

'That looked as though he let himself into Belinda's with a key,' said Wingsy.

'Yeah, it did. Or else the door was left open. Either way, he's not just a passing acquaintance.'

Deciding against walking two hundred yards – as I said, it was a warm day – I started the engine and drove to the top of the road. We crossed to Belinda Cook's house and rang the bell. Several minutes later she answered the door, but this time she only opened it a fraction.

'Hello again, Belinda,' I said. 'Can we come in?'

'No, not at the moment,' she replied.

'We just have a couple more questions about Amanda,' I tried.

She hesitated, glanced behind her, then nodded and let us in. Once inside, Wingsy made a point of closing the door behind him so we could both clearly see the space the men's shoes had occupied.

'Tony came back for his shoes, then?' said Wingsy.

Belinda crossed her arms in front of her and shifted her weight on to one foot. 'What exactly do you two want?'

'Truth would be a start, Belinda,' said Wingsy. 'Help us to find your cousin's murderer instead of lying to us. Who else is here in the house now?'

All three of us turned to the top of the stairs as a voice said, 'That'd be me, mate.' Heavy footsteps sounded on the carpet, bringing the size tens towards us, bearing the enormity of Belinda's house guest who, fortunately at this stage, took his time to reach the bottom of the stairs, giving me and Wingsy a chance to react. Both of us were wearing equipment harnesses. The slow descent would give us time to reach inside our suit jackets if necessary.

'I'm Tony Birdsall,' he said. 'I asked Belinda to keep it quiet that I was here. I've got family around this area I haven't seen in a while and didn't want to spoil the surprise.' Tony's dark eyes looked from me to Wingsy, then settled on Belinda before crinkling at the corners. 'But thanks, Bel.'

Belinda blushed. Bloody hell. She was under this man's spell.

'Mr Birdsall,' I said, 'we need to get some details from you and ask you about where you've been for the last week or so.'

'Of course,' he said, waving us through to the living room. 'Please, let's sit down.'

Seated, cutting straight to the chase, Wingsy said, 'Did you know Amanda Bell, Tony?'

'Yes, I did. We used to go to school together many, many years ago. It was infant school, St Agnes, other side of town. My mum and dad split up and my mum took me to live with her. We moved away and I didn't come back here for years.

71

Think the last time I saw Amanda was over eight years ago. She was pregnant with her little boy – Kyle, is it?' Tony looked over to Belinda who nodded. He continued, 'Kyle is eight – saw that on the news, poor bugger – so she must have been just about to have him when I knew her. I've only been back in the country three days. You can check my passport. I flew from Malaga to Gatwick. You can check that, right?'

'Yes, we can, Tony. Can I take a look at your passport – get the number, that kind of thing?' I asked.

Tony turned to look at me and the intensity of his stare was overpowering. It wasn't so much that he was good-looking with piercing brown eyes; it was that he had such a presence. No, not a presence, more of a command of the room. He was a man used to getting his own way.

'Of course.' A smile and then, 'I won't be a moment.'

I listened to the footsteps make their unhurried path upstairs. 'How long have you known Tony?' I asked Belinda.

'Couple of years off and on,' came the reply.

'He come over from Spain often?' I asked.

'Well, you can find that out from his passport, can't you?' said Belinda. I doubted that we were going to get much more from her today.

Having got the details we needed, Wingsy and I made our way along to Chloe Holland's house. On the very short journey, I whispered, 'Couple of fucking weirdos, Belinda and Tony.'

'Couldn't agree more, duchess. He's a twat and she's a silly cow. How do you think Chloe's going to be?' he muttered.

'Not nearly as pleasant,' I said, moving aside to avoid a ripped black sack, full of used nappies, at the top of Chloe Holland's driveway. Wingsy gagged.

A warm breeze touched us as we made our way down Chloe's path. Someone nearby was frying chips; the grease hung in the air. Hope it's not coming from Chloe's house, I thought, as we rang the bell. It had taken two days to get dead man's pong out of my hair; I didn't want to be catching a whiff of chip fat for the remainder of the day.

Chloe opened the door. Great, I thought, a chain smoker – even better.

'Chloe Holland?' asked Wingsy.

'Yeah. You gavvers?' said the delightful Chloe. She took a drag of her cigarette and screwed up one eye while she exhaled the smoke over her shoulder. A toddler started to cry in the background. She turned her head further and said, 'Curtis, will you shut the fuck up.'

'Yes, Chloe. In answer to your question, we are police officers. We're here about Jason. Can we come in?' Wingsy said.

'What's that moron done now?' she asked.

'It really would be best if we didn't do this on the doorstep. It is serious,' Wingsy said. She paused to look at him. Some part of her brain was working as she wandered back inside the hallway, pulling up her baggy pyjama bottoms. I saw Wingsy hesitate as he went to step into the smoke-filled house. It made me think of an act with stage fright appearing on *Stars in Their Eyes*.

Our entrance into the living room disturbed a cat defecating on the shiny, threadbare carpet. Chloe stepped over the turd to turn the sound down on the forty-two-inch plasma television. 'Have a seat,' she offered.

I looked at the sagging sofa, piled high with clothes, an overflowing ashtray and another cat. You're a dirty, disgusting slag, I wanted to say, but instead I asked, 'We may need to write. Is there a table and chairs in another room?'

'Yeah.' She sighed. 'But the other room's a bit of a mess.' She sidestepped the turd again and took us to the kitchen, the place dirty plates went to die. Fag still in her mouth, she bent down to pick up the howling Curtis. 'Just going to put him down for a nap,' she said, disappearing towards the stairs.

'Gonna need to get all of my clothes dry-cleaned again,' I said to Wingsy when I was sure Chloe was out of earshot.

When she returned, she put the first cigarette out before lighting another and clearing some space at the kitchen table. The three of us sat down. Wingsy went first.

'Chloe, we have some bad news. Jason was found dead three days ago.'

She stopped puffing on her cigarette. 'Dead,' she said. 'What – an accident? A fight? I can't believe it. I used to see him in the shops, the pub from time to time. What happened?'

'We're not entirely sure, but his death is being treated as suspicious; a murder investigation has begun,' said Wingsy. 'When was the last time you saw him?'

'Dunno. Two weeks, three weeks? No, wait. Some police officer came round to see me 'cos he'd been missing for a few days. Tall blond bloke in uniform. Asked a couple of questions but, as I say, we split up a while ago now – years ago. He's been with Annette for about three years. I hadn't seen Jason for a while before the other copper came round.'

'Sure, Chloe,' said Wingsy, 'we've got a record here of what you said, but just in case you saw him after the police spoke to you but hadn't got round to telling anyone...'

She sniffed and inspected her dirty fingernails. 'I don't really talk to many people here. Don't go out much. I've only been here a couple of months.'

'What are the neighbours like?' I asked, thinking about Tony leaving her house a few minutes ago.

'Her up there's OK,' Chloe pointed her thumb in the direction of Belinda's house. 'Her cousin got killed.' Chloe sat back in her chair. A light went on somewhere in her head. 'You think they're connected?' Ash fell on to her lap. She brushed it on to the floor.

'We're not sure at this moment,' I told her. 'Why did you and Jason split up?' I wasn't trying to take the piss, genuinely, I wanted to know.

Chloe shrugged. 'He thought he could do better. She tapped the side of her head with her right index finger.

74

'He wasn't right in the head. Hung about with some weird friends. Had a couple of mates who gave me the creeps. Wouldn't have wanted to be alone with them, know what I mean?' She pulled her food-stained dressing gown over her chest. The chest that had been spilling out throughout the conversation until this point. When it came to filling in the boxes on her description form, I wouldn't need to ask Chloe what tattoos she had.

'Who were his friends?' I asked.

This was met with another shrug. 'You'd have to ask Annette. He was a bit secretive about them. He'd go off and meet them, not tell me where he was going or who with. Had a couple of rows about it but I never suspected him of cheating on me. Why would he?'

I ignored that comment. Instead I said, 'And the break-up between you was amicable?'

'Yeah, totally. He wanted to go and live abroad. I didn't. Dirty on the Continent.'

And you'd have built up a great germ resistance living here, I thought. There were probably stray dogs in Lisbon with better hygiene than this woman.

We had what we needed and my lungs had been punished enough. I got up to leave and Wingsy followed suit. 'By the way,' I said, 'how often do you speak to your neighbour, the one whose cousin died?'

'Belinda? Once or twice a week. Her bloke's been here today; you just missed him. He was offering to take some rubbish to the tip for me. Told him not to bother – that's what the council's for. Just an old sofa, fridge and some bikes. Hardly takes up any room in the front garden.'

'That was good of him,' I said. 'He pop in often?'

'No. That was the first time for a couple of weeks.'

Chapter 20

Wingsy and I mulled this information over as we walked back to the car.

'I think we'd better go back and pass this on,' he said. 'Might be relevant. Murder investigations always involve stuff that you and I won't get to know about, Nin.'

'Right, I get what you're telling me: pass it back and let the boss decide. OK. Let's go and see him, then.'

Eric Nottingham's face was difficult to read as he walked into the Incident Room. But he dropped a bombshell that neither of us was prepared for.

'Call just came in that there's been another body found.' Safe to say his expression was not so perplexing now: it was thunderous. 'I want this bastard found *now*.'

This meant that Gary Savage couldn't be considered the culprit for this latest murder. If the three were linked and he wasn't the offender, once again we had a lot of work to do.

Wingsy and I glanced at one another. He summed it up nicely by saying, 'Fucking Ada. We've got a nutter on the loose.'

'A third victim, boss?' I asked. 'Who is it?'

'A seventy-seven-year-old woman, Daphne Headingly. She was stabbed in her home by the looks of it. Neighbours across the street saw her at about 7am putting the dustbin out. The next-door neighbour later went to call on her around eleven and found her body. Savage was still being interviewed; you don't get a much better alibi than being in a police interview room with two of my DCs when the victim

76

was killed. At this time, we're treating all three of these as being linked. The stab wounds and injuries appear the same. We need to establish what connects these three. Full briefing at 4pm.' He put his head down and started to write in his notebook. It was a dismissal. We took the hint and left. Jo Styles passed us in the office doorway on our way out.

'What do you make of all that, mate?' I asked Wingsy.

'There's so much pressure now on this department, the senior investigating officer, the entire force. In fact, pretty much every one of us. Everyone's run ragged, Nina,' he said.

'If this is your way of telling me what a long day it's going to be, I don't know about you, but I'm going to need some grub. You coming?'

At four o'clock, we assembled again. There were the same people present, the same buzz of conversation. DCI Nottingham opened the briefing by thanking everyone for attending and praised those who been at work since 5am. He then got our attention as he said, 'As many of you know, something that's not all that unusual in extreme acts of violence is the presence of bite marks on victims. And in this case both Amanda Bell and Jason Holland had bite marks puncturing the skin on their left shoulders.'

I could bet that not a pair of eyes in the room strayed from Eric Nottingham at that moment. He looked down at his notes then up at us.

'Ultraviolet photographs of Amanda Bell and Jason Holland's bite marks indicate that they would appear to have been made by the same person. Your next question is probably what about the third victim, Daphne Headingly? It is unofficially confirmed by the CSI from examining the body *in situ*: we have a serial killer.'

Chapter 21

'I don't have to tell you that this enquiry is massive,' said Nottingham. 'Most of you will probably never work on anything like it again in your careers. You're here for the long haul; no one's leaving this operation without speaking to me. It'll be long hours, rest days worked through. We are splitting this into three investigations, one for each of our victims, but the overall name will be Operation Guard and you will talk to each other, attend all briefings unless you have a very good excuse, and report back anything of interest immediately.

'Let's start again with Amanda Bell.' Nottingham took his jacket off and hung it on the back of his chair. 'She'd been missing for a few days and her body had been open to the elements for some time. This significantly reduces the possibility of obtaining forensic evidence from her clothing. There are no signs of sexual assault. Who was looking into her last movements?'

'That was me, sir.' Everyone in the room shifted slightly to hear the detective who had just spoken up. He looked young: if he worked on a supermarket till and I was buying wine, I would have avoided his queue in case he needed adult supervision to serve me.

'Go on, Danny. What have you got?' said Nottingham.

'I looked at her bank details and found that she paid £1,600 in cash into her account in the town, in the morning. This was last Monday, four days before her body was found. We have the CCTV from the bank, as yet unviewed; a statement from the cashier who served her and remembered her; CCTV of her leaving the nearby car park in her Fiesta; and then nothing at all once she leaves town. The straightforward route for her to take doesn't go past any cameras. There is a speed camera but it wasn't working. Then there's nothing at all. No one saw her, spoke to her, she didn't telephone anyone, and her Fiesta was still on the driveway after she was identified as our first victim. The only thing outstanding is the result of the investigation into what was on her computer.'

Danny squirmed a bit in his seat and his face reddened slightly. He gave a small laugh, clutched his notes and said, 'She had a website and, er, operated under the name "Crystal". It's a bit sordid.' A few people tittered and Eric Nottingham raised an eyebrow. 'There's some stuff involving inserting stinging nettles and Deep Heat.' This was met with further mirth. 'Her price was £500 per go.'

A female Welsh voice announced, 'Got a bloody garden full of nettles, I have. What with the pension going to pot, might come in handy, mind.'

'Thank you, everyone,' cut in the DCI, before the sidetracking got out of hand. He summarised, 'Four days are unaccounted for; however, the post mortem showed that she was already dead when her body was dumped and it had been *in situ* for around three days. She may have been alive somewhere for a day with the murderer or, at that time, safe in her own home. We need to account for that time. It's crucial.' He glanced around the room, allowing it to sink in. Following a brief pause, he continued, 'And where did that £1,600 come from? Prostitution is the likely source, but paying it into her account? Find out if this was regular.' He aimed this last remark at Kim Cotton, who made a note of it.

'Anything else, Danny?' he asked.

'Yes, boss, one other major thing.'

All eyes turned again to the now glowing Danny.

'The search of her house found a receipt for currency exchange. She only had around a hundred quid in cash at home, but she had exchanged €2,000 into £1,718 sterling two days before she paid the money in to her own account. There's a good chance that that was the the money she paid in. I've looked into the *bureau de change* she used, in the travel agents, but their CCTV wasn't recording that day. Turned out that the robbery squad was there downloading footage from an armed robbery and so it wasn't working. Got the town centre CCTV, though. I printed off this still. It shows her with an unidentified white male going towards the travel agents.'

Chapter 22

It had been a really long day and I was tired. Looking forward to a glass of wine, a bath and a ready meal accompanied by a token bag of prewashed salad, I swung my carrier bag of food as I walked up the pathway leading to my front door, the movement setting off my security light.

I'd felt happier at the end of the last briefing. Something had been kept back, but for very good reason. Bag in one hand and keys in my other hand, I unlocked the door and gave it a push. That day's post seemed to be wedged behind it. Great, I thought – a hefty pile of bills. Another shove seemed to do the trick and the door inched open enough for me to get through the gap. I leaned across to put the light on and glanced down at the heap of mail on the floor.

I scooped up the seven or so items and headed towards the wine rack with them. Coat, bag and shoes deposited where they landed, I opened a bottle of Chilean Merlot. I didn't choose it for any reason other than that it was at the top of the rack and it saved me from stretching any further. I turned the oven on and leafed through the correspondence in my hands. Apart from the usual daily junk and bills, my attention focused on an A4 padded envelope. Sipping my wine, I ripped the end open and shook the contents on to the table. Photographs fell on to the table top. Each of them contained an image of me.

I froze.

I resisted the urge to touch any of them. The first one I saw was of me aged seventeen, dressed as a housekeeper in my school production of *Oliver*. I had kept a souvenir programme somewhere upstairs. The next was of me walking from my car to one of our regular haunts to meet Laura for a drink two weeks ago. I knew it was two weeks because the coat I was wearing in the photograph was my new winter one that I'd only bought the day before. That, and also the date had been written in black ink on the bottom left-hand corner. These snaps of me seemed to show totally random moments of my life, and someone had gone to the trouble of taking them, collecting them and posting them to me. My mind ran through a mental address book of friends, enemies, past boyfriends. No break-up had been that messy, I was sure. I simply hadn't known anyone other than family for long enough, and it wasn't something that anyone in my life would do. Who would have had done something like this, and why would they have done it to me?

It had been a very long time since I had felt out of control and I didn't like the feeling the photographs gave me. I refused to give in to fright, but this felt like a warning, and to ignore it would be very unwise.

There was only one thing for it: I decided to go and get advice from an untried source.

I turned off the oven, and put the pictures and the envelope into a carrier bag ready to go back outside to my car. I hesitated for only a second at the front door with one hand on the latch, then wrenched the handle and stepped outside. I glanced up and down the road looking for movement, unfamiliar shapes or anyone hanging around. Closing the door behind me without a break in the surveillance of my street, I made my way to my car, ensuring the back seat was as empty as I'd left it minutes ago.

I would usually run straight to Stan with any serious problem. His advice had never once failed me and I had relied on him increasingly over the years. Right now, though, I wasn't going to worry him when he was going through so much. However calmly he'd acted in the past whenever I shared a problem with him, I knew that any torment I had felt had played on Stan's mind.

Beckensale always stayed late in the office. If she was due to finish at 5pm, she'd hang around for at least an hour. If her finish time was later into the evening, it was not unusual to see her at her desk until the early hours. She never talked about her personal life except to say that she didn't mix work with pleasure. Every Christmas she came along to the office meal, washed her food down with lemonade and left straight after the speeches. One miserable woman. One trustworthy woman. She didn't socialise, mix or gossip. I'd never known her to slack off, get anything wrong or go out of her way to bring about someone's demise. She was my best hope.

As I let myself into the back yard of the police station, I held the carrier bag and its contents at my side. Whether or not I had correctly judged Sandra Beckensale was about to become clear. There was a risk that something like this could get me kicked off Operation Guard, the most exciting investigation I was ever likely to work on, but I didn't have a choice. I wouldn't raise the question of whether my role was compromised, and would have to hope she wouldn't either. That was my plan. It was poor.

I picked up two pairs of white plastic gloves from the store and climbed the two flights of dimly lit stairs to her office. A light was coming through the window. Pausing to catch my breath, I listened in case anyone else was working late. Not too unlikely in a twenty-four-hour police station. It was, however, that time of night when few CID officers were still working and the patrol officers were either in custody or out at calls. The building was quiet.

Sandra Beckensale looked up as I walked past the window towards her door. I knocked. It seemed the right thing to do even though she was looking straight at me. Her deadpan expression did not alter. She raised one hand to gesture to me to come in.

'Sorry to bother you, Sandra,' I said. The use of her first name probably alerted her to something out of the ordinary. That and my appearance late at night. I sat down, clutching my carrier bag. Realising what I was doing, I placed it on the desk. We both looked at it and then at one another.

'Got a problem and I could really do with your advice,' I said. A nod was my reply. She wasn't going to make this easy, but at least she'd not said anything negative either.

'When I got home today from work, these were waiting for me.' I tipped the contents of the bag out and tossed her a pair of gloves. We sat for a couple of minutes going through the photographs, holding them by their edges with our gloved hands. From time to time she glanced up at me. I couldn't read her expression.

At last she said, 'Any idea who could have sent them or why?'

I shook my head. I'd have liked to say her features softened, but there was no alteration in her expression before she continued, 'I'm going to log this, send them for fingerprints and get some enquiries under way to find out where and when they were posted.'

All of this I'd expected – you weren't a police officer for very long at all before you knew this stuff – but just having someone listen to me, take me seriously and help me, meant a lot. The relief was enormous.

She picked up the phone. 'I'm calling the DI – I want him to be aware of this – then I want you to go and get some sleep. You look like shit.'

I stood up to go.

'Why don't you stay at Laura's tonight?' she suggested. 'She's just about done here.' I hadn't realised that Laura was still on duty. Or that Beckensale actually cared.

Staying at Laura's would have meant telling her about the photos. It wasn't that I was embarrassed, though I did have a shocking Eighties perm in one or two of them; I just didn't want to involve her and put her at risk. As yet, I had no clue as to who could have done this or what motive they might have had. Who had a stalker for decades without knowing about them? I'd considered it being an elaborate prank by one of my friends, but the content of the photos was so diverse, and covered such a long period of time, that it was impossible for it to have been the responsibility of any one person I knew. My mum had burnt most of the family photographs years ago and had only kept a couple of me and my sister as kids. Even my own still intact collection did not cover the timescale. No one had immediately sprung to mind, from among past demons or new potential ones.

So I went home after seeing Sandra, locked the door, checked every window and cupboard, looked under beds, even took a torch up into the loft in case someone was waiting for me to turn out the light and go to sleep. I'd rather meet whoever it was head-on, I decided, than be woken at two in the morning with a hand over my mouth and a knife at my throat. I took one of my own kitchen knives with me on my check of the house. I wasn't a total moron.

Satisfied I was alone, I reunited myself with my Merlot. I took the glass and knife up to the bath with me. Granted, it was difficult to wash my hair with one hand holding an eight-inch steak knife underwater against my leg, but I wasn't taking any chances.

An uneventful bath and three units of alcohol later, I tried to get to sleep, but my mind was racing. Three murders in such a short time and so far they had nothing obvious linking them, except the killer. And now this.

Chapter 23

24th September

The next morning's briefing began with the usual banter, last-minute phone calls and general chatter of a room of very busy, focused investigators. The temperature was cooler so the room was a bit more pleasant than before. The DCI called everyone to order and an immediate hush fell.

'OK, morning, everyone. It's official today. We need this in the news for witnesses to come forward so we're launching a media appeal in relation to the murders of Amanda Bell, Jason Holland and Daphne Headingly. All three were stabbed a number of times, possibly with the same weapon. The knife that was recovered from Savage's van yesterday has been examined by the pathologist. He's not ruling it out as the weapon used on the first two victims. It's been sent off to the lab for prints and DNA.

'The cuts have been made with a straight-edged blade. Measurements of the width of the cuts are two centimetres, or three-quarters of an inch for those of you still old enough to use imperial. The deepest cuts are thirteen centimetres or five inches, indicating where the knife was plunged in up to its hilt. Some of the slashes and insertions have been made with the offender behind the victim; we're assuming this is where the offender was when he or she bit their shoulder. The odontologist will confirm this.'

This was clearly a man under pressure. He spoke firmly and calmly, but looked even worse than I did. I didn't know who was breathing down his neck but the deep lines across his forehead, bags under his bloodshot eyes and tie already loosened at 8am gave the impression of a worn-out man. The suit, shirt and hair were still immaculate, though – and there was not even a hint of stubble on his face. It wasn't a problem to appear on national television and look as if you were working all the hours possible, but the public expected a certain standard of its officers, even when looking for a serial killer.

'First off, the suspects so far,' continued Nottingham, surveying the room. 'Suspect One, David Connor. He's been dealt with for football-related GBH, charged and remanded. Difficult for him to have murdered Daphne Headingly when he was at Her Majesty's pleasure. Suspect Two, Gary Savage. He was being interviewed by two of our detectives at the time of Daphne Headingly's murder. Never known such good alibis.' He had the air of a very displeased DCI. 'All the same, Savage can't explain why he had a bloodstained knife in the back of his van, nor why his DNA was on a dead body. Savage is to remain on bail for the moment. Anyone got any good news for me?'

This was met with silence, so the briefing continued. By the time details of all three victims and any other information had been shared with all those working on the force's biggest priority, three and a half hours had gone by. We had stopped twice for breaks, which had led to stampeding to the kitchen and toilet and missed calls being frantically returned. My head was full of facts and my notebook needed replacing.

The vital information had been pinned up on boards around the room, and at the end of the meeting I stopped to look at the photographs of Daphne Headingly more closely. My mind fought down the recent memory of my own life in pictures delivered by my postman. As I was making the effort to concentrate on Daphne's problems, much more pressing than my own, Wingsy came up beside me.

'Why would someone do that to an old lady?' he said.

'Dunno, mate, but there must be a reason. There's always a reason, even if it's 'cos the bloke is an utter nutcase.'

'What makes you think it's a bloke?' he said. 'You heard what the boss said about keeping an open mind. May even be more than one of them.'

'I have my doubts about that,' I replied. 'If there's more than one, that means they're keeping each other's secrets. You know what people are like. It's difficult enough to trust anyone with harmless gossip, let alone a secret like this.'

'Nina, I think you're being naïve. Think about paedophile rings kidnapping and raping kids. Always more than one of them, by definition.'

Wanting to steer the conversation in another direction, I said, 'Let's go and find a couple of computers in the Incident Room so we can go through our work for the next few days.'

Wingsy and I had some information about Daphne, our latest victim, as some of her family had been found and spoken to, but it only scratched the surface. Each person's life was made up of so many factors: family; financial; educational; social. Each of those was a minefield in its own right and each of them was important, but, with no obvious suspect, one part of Daphne's life must hold the key to why she was murdered.

We found two adjacent terminals. Wingsy was checking his email while I waded through the paperwork, one hand gripping a Yorkie bar. I stopped mid-bite as he sat up in his chair and said, 'Fuck me,' a little too loud. A few people nearby tittered, while a couple tutted at his language. 'Look at this. Got some financial checks back and Daphne had £750,000 paid into her account two months ago. They've done some digging and she won it on the lottery. Lucky cow – or not so lucky, since she's dead.'

At that moment, Catherine Thomas came up and caught our attention. Well, Wingsy's more than mine. I thought about kicking him under the desk to stop his tongue from hitting the 'enter' key on his keyboard. 'Alright, you two?' she asked. She had a deep, husky voice which didn't quite go with her petite build. 'We haven't met properly so I've come to introduce myself. I didn't want to just hand you the work and send you off. Bloody hell, is that a Yorkie bar? Supposed to be on a diet but I could wrestle that right out of your hand. I'm Catherine, and I know that you've been here a while but come and let me know if you have any problems.'

'Thanks, Catherine,' I said, since Wingsy was finding it difficult to form words without closing his mouth. 'We've got Daphne's financial stuff through. I see that it was sent to you too. That's got to be worth looking into. Were the others lottery winners?'

'No, they weren't. That would have been too easy. Holland never gambled. Like your thinking, though. I'll be about if you need anything.' She bounced off in the direction of the DCI, who had just appeared in the doorway looking for her.

'She seems alright,' said Wingsy at last.

'"She seems alright"? Oh, please, mate,' I said. 'I was gonna offer you some chocolate but you've probably filled up on the flies you've been catching.'

'You jealous, Nin? Lay off the chocolate and you might have a chance of looking like that.'

'Really? So I can attract baldy wingnuts like you? I'm good, thanks.'

Chapter 24

There was only so much you could glean from paper and computers. Nothing could come close to meeting people and talking to them. Wingsy and I put together a plan and went out to meet Daphne's family. I braced myself for dealing with people in mourning again. It was inevitable in a murder enquiry. Talking to her family was going to be very draining, but that was police work.

As we drove out of the security gates, Alf, the caretaker, was leaving through the pedestrian gate. Wingsy pressed the window control, rolling the glass down. 'Alf. Want a lift?'

Alf stopped and leaned in the window. 'Nin, Wingsy. No, ta. I like the bus – good for listening to other people's conversations. Thanks all the same.' He straightened up and strode in the direction of the bus stop.

'Makes sense,' said Wingsy when Alf was out of earshot. 'He'll have another body part to get rid of on the number 27 by now.'

'Don't talk such rubbish. Concentrate on driving,' I replied.

Wingsy and I had made arrangements to see Daphne's sister, who lived only a couple of miles from her house, before visiting other members of the family. As he drove, I read out the family tree that had been put together so far. Daphne's maiden name had been Lloyd. Her father had died during the war and her mother had died of cancer in 1988. Daphne had married George Headingly in 1956, and seven years later they'd had a son, Scott.

'Where's the son now?' asked Wingsy.

'Died. Oh, sad. He hanged himself in 2004. Got to be pretty desperate to do that. It doesn't say why and there's no coroner's report attached. It shouldn't be too difficult to find out: he hanged himself at his mum's house. I recognise a couple of the names here who went to the call.'

'Is there much written about the sister?' said Wingsy.

'She's Diane Lloyd, seventy-one years old. She married but got divorced and he remarried. Changed her name back to Lloyd from Green. No children. There's a bit about Donald, the brother, but we'll see what we can get from Diane first.'

'What's the door number again?' he asked as he slowed the car.

'It's 52. Oh, here it is. Looks OK. Garden's neat, no car in the driveway, looks well maintained. It would suggest to me that it's not a lonely, childless seventy-one-year-old divorcee living here. Someone cares.'

'Or she's loaded.' We pulled up and made our way along the neat and tidy pathway, not a weed in sight.

I rang the bell and waited for my first view of Diane Lloyd. A smiling, grey-haired woman opened the door and I wondered for a moment if we had the right house. She was dressed in a yellow blouse and cream trousers – hardly mourning colours. Her upright, almost rigid posture did not suggest she was gripped by fear at her sister's murder, but that she was a woman who carried herself well. She glanced at our warrant cards and welcomed us in, repeating our names back to us as if she was learning them and didn't want to forget them later on. She stared at me and held out her hand to shake mine. Her hands were cold, unlike her eyes. She unnerved me a little, as she kept hold of my hand for longer than really necessary and barely gave Wingsy a glance.

As I seemed to be more of a success with her than Wingsy, he allowed me to do the talking.

'Ms Lloyd,' I said. 'Thanks – '

'Please, Nina, call me Diane. That's if it's OK to call you Nina – or Detective Foster if you'd prefer.'

'No, Diane, Nina is fine. Thank you for seeing us at such a difficult time for you.'

She waved my condolences aside and led us into a compact but tastefully decorated kitchen. 'I'll put the kettle on and show you to the conservatory while it boils,' Diane said. We glanced at one another and Wingsy gave a small shrug. I felt the same: she didn't appear to be at all bothered. But grief was a very tricky thing, with its own agenda.

Seated a few minutes later in her conservatory, we looked out over a beautiful garden full of jasmine and roses, the scent wafting in through the open door. The chattering of birds pecking at seed on the feeder halfway down the garden completed the peaceful setting.

'Diane, we explained on the phone why we wanted to see you. We're very sorry about your sister. We – '

'Hated her. She deserved to die. I understand that it was brutal.'

I searched Diane's face carefully. She looked me straight in the eye, and the previously warm gaze was now as cold as her hands.

Chapter 25

'My family ran into a few difficulties many years ago and I and my brother, Donald, had problems with Daphne. Donald stayed in contact, but I stopped speaking to her. Our main problem started with George. No one approved of their marriage, least of all my mother, but when Scott was born we thought that things would settle down. They didn't. They were constantly rowing – even separated a couple of times. She always went back, though.' She paused and took a sip of her tea and then, still looking solely at me, continued, 'The day Scott hanged himself, he was doing the world a service. Best thing that bastard ever did.'

Reluctant as I was to utter a word and interrupt her, I crept a question in.

'What did Scott do that was so bad?'

A loud ticking clock filled the silence. Wingsy and I kept as still as we could, willing her to go on.

'He'll be on the police records. He had a thing for children.' Her lips were barely visible as she said the last sentence. 'Disgusting creature. Suppose the bleeding hearts would say that it wasn't really his fault at all; that he was ill and needed help. Me, I think hanging was too good.' She paused and took another sip of her tea. 'Oh, I am sorry, I forgot the biscuits. How rude of me.' She was up and out of her seat. 'I definitely have some chocolate ones somewhere. Won't be a sec.'

'Bloody hell,' said Wingsy, keeping his voice down. 'Someone might have mentioned this to us before we left.'

I didn't get the chance to reply; Diane was back in the room. 'They're supermarket's own, I'm afraid. My nephew has a tendency to eat all the good ones when he visits.' She placed a flower-patterned plate down on the tablecloth. The plate held fifteen biscuits, neatly stacked one on top of the other in three piles. 'Have one, Nina.' It felt like an order. Hansel and Gretel came to mind. 'My nephew, Jake, he's been great to me. He's round here once a week helping with various jobs. Upkeep on this house would be impossible for me if it weren't for him.'

I knew my next question was likely to be entering dangerous territory. If she took offence at this, Wingsy would have to take over with the questions. I chanced it.

'Had Jake and Scott been close friends?'

The ramrod spine stiffened. 'No, Nina.' She might as well have added *you stupid child*, the way she spoke to me, leaning forward, her voice full of practised patience. 'Not when it all came to light. It took some time of course, and a lot of what he did was never proven.'

Wingsy and I leant forward in our chairs.

'Jake and Scott were fairly close when Jake was very young, despite the age gap. I never liked them playing together but Jake wasn't my son and Donald had always been the more trusting. Perhaps it's something to do with him being the youngest with two older sisters, I don't know. Anyway, he allowed Jake to associate with Scott, something he regretted in later life and no doubt still does. There was something about Scott's behaviour as he got older that seemed to get to Jake. He has never told me about it because I refuse to talk about Scott or my sister to him. You'll have to ask him yourself.'

'What was proven against Scott?' I asked. 'You said that a lot of what he did wasn't proven. Tell me what was.'

'He kidnapped two young girls.'

Chapter 26

Over the years I'd learnt to put my past behind me. It often felt as if I'd read about two girls being kidnapped in the paper, as if it had happened to someone else. Just a distant memory. I knew that Scott Headingly wasn't responsible. He would have been far too young in 1976, only thirteen, and anyway I was fully aware of who and where the perpetrator of my crime was. I needed sleep, a lot of it, and that knowledge kept me tucked up in bed for eight hours every night. He was out of my life.

I mentally drew a line under Diane's revelation and carried on listening to what she had to tell us. It was for the best. But, if truth be told, I'd been struggling to concentrate since seeing Daphne's photographs in the Incident Room. They'd brought crashing forward the thoughts I'd been trying to push aside. Why would someone be taking pictures of me? Just as importantly, why would they then post them to me? It was a senseless act. My old friend Rioja would no doubt pour a little clarity on it – but standing between me and a glass of red was the rest of the day working on a murder investigation. I was counting on Wingsy listening to Diane as intently as I purported to. I was battling to stay on track. I won, but then I usually do. My sanity couldn't afford weakness.

Before the Incident Room churned out the paperwork locating the two girls kidnapped by Scott Headingly, Wingsy and I needed to speak to the rest of the Headingly family. As Daphne's brother, Donald Lloyd would normally have been our next call after Diane. However, the deceased's brother seemed less important now that we knew that Scott, her son, had once been friends with Jake, Daphne's nephew.

We left Diane's, thanking her for her help and saying we would be back, possibly in the morning. Back in the car, Wingsy said, 'Jake Lloyd's next, then?'

'Yeah, just what I was thinking. Bloody weird family by the sound of it.'

'Kidnapping children – sick bastard. Bet you never get over a thing like that.'

I didn't reply. I had never told Wingsy about my sister and me. What was there to tell after all these years? Everyone knew I had a friend called Stan who was a retired policeman and looked out for me, but I guess they all thought I'd got nicked as a kid for shoplifting and he'd taken me home by the ear and watched over me ever since. Didn't bother me. I didn't want their pity and I'd never get their understanding.

'You alright driving, mate?' I asked, to change the subject.

'Yeah, it's only round the corner. This is the street. Diane said his was the last house on the right.'

As we pulled up outside a large detached house with a magnificent front garden, lawn like a bowling green, a man's head appeared from the other side of the hedge. As he stood up, I saw that he had a pair of hedge clippers in his left hand. He beamed a big smile at us. Well, at me really.

As we got out of the car, he rushed round the hedge, abandoning his gardening tools as he went, and grabbed my hand before I could say anything.

'Nina,' he said, speaking very fast. 'You don't know how pleased I am to meet you.'

What on earth was going on? I assumed this was Jake Lloyd: he had the same dimple in the chin that Diane had, the same colouring and good posture. He certainly seemed to know who I was.

Wingsy appeared by my side. 'Alright there, mate? Wanna let go of the officer's hand?' I was grateful to my friend for spotting that I had a look of surprise on my face. It was clear to him that I didn't know this man.

'So sorry, Nina. I didn't mean to startle you. My aunt called and said you were coming over and I was looking forward to meeting you at last.' Jake prattled on, still holding my hand.

I pulled away from him and said, 'Shall we go inside, Mr Lloyd?'

'Oh, yes, of course, Detective Foster.' He looked slightly crestfallen. His massive shoulders dropped forward slightly and he looked down, breaking eye contact with me. 'Please follow me.' He led the way past his beautiful garden and the highly polished grey Shogun parked in the driveway. He pushed open the front door and stood aside, welcoming us in.

In the vast hallway, the walls were adorned with large photographs of international landmarks. The vestibule must have been twelve feet wide; it had rooms leading off it on either side, and a central wooden staircase. I had to admit, I was impressed.

'What do you do for a living?' asked Wingsy, probably thinking the same thing as me.

'TV production,' he replied, glancing over his shoulder as he strode across the polished floor. 'The financial backing is not quite as it used to be but it allows me to pursue other interests. Please, please, this way. We'll sit in the kitchen. It's the heart of the house and the warmest room.'

We followed him to a snug kitchen. It was warm, but not as big as I'd been expecting. The noise of a washing machine spinning came from behind a closed door. Utility room, I thought to myself – that'll be why the kitchen's not as large as the house would suggest. I liked the house, though it was a bit sparse. It seemed to be missing a woman's touch. All that pointless crap we would buy: hilarious signs saying 'The cook's on strike'; candles that never got used; old, broken French clocks. I bought them all, silly cow that I was.

'Is anyone else home?' Wingsy's question focused me.

'No. Just me. I live here alone.' He looked straight at me as he spoke.

It was true, he wasn't a bad-looking bloke. At six feet tall he was about the right height for me, with greying dark hair but loads of it. He clearly had money, and his taste wasn't too bad from the looks of things. I could do a lot worse, and in fact frequently did. He was, however, out of bounds. The man was a witness and, oh yeah, seemed to come from a family of total nutters. Shame, because it was a nice house. I could see myself living in such a place.

'If you've spoken to your aunt, and she said that we were coming to see you, she probably said why.' Wingsy said.

'Yes. Please, have a seat.' Jake was standing beside me and pulled a chair out for me. He might potentially have been nuts, but he had manners. Wingsy pulled his own chair out, scraping the legs on the tiled floor. I got the impression he was a bit annoyed. All three of us sat down at the table.

'We're investigating your aunt Daphne's death. This is a murder investigation. Anything you tell us will be very useful.' I got my book out to start writing, as Wingsy was doing the talking.

Without warning, Jake stood up. 'I didn't get on very well with her. I used to spend a lot of time with my older cousin, Scott, when we were kids. The crazy bastard. Then I realised just how dangerous he was, and I cut myself off from him. Aunt Daphne too. I never really told anyone about it, though Aunt Diane knew more than anyone else.'

'Dangerous?' echoed Wingsy. I looked up at Jake, who was standing with his back to the window, knuckles white where he was gripping the edge of the sink behind him. The sun through the window lit him up from behind, making his features very dark and difficult to see. I could make out enough to realise that he was staring at me.

'Diane told you about the girls he kidnapped?' It was a casually asked question aimed, once again, at me.

'Yes, Mr Lloyd, she did. Our colleagues are looking into that aspect of the investigation.' I gave him my official response, and shivered despite the warm day.

'It's part of the reason that my current work project is focused on historic crimes. I take my work very seriously. Kidnapping is to be a feature-length episode,' said Jake.

I tried not to squirm. I'm not sure I managed it.

'I suppose that you're also here about Jason Holland?' he asked. Another casual question – so casual, in fact, that I almost missed its significance. Thankfully Wingsy was more on the ball.

'Jason Holland?'

Lloyd moved away from the window so I could now see his expression very clearly. 'Yes. Scott and Jason Holland were very good friends.'

Chapter 27

Hours later, after a lengthy statement completed in Lloyd's kitchen and several muffled calls to the Incident Room, Wingsy and I were on our way back to the nick. Our mood was euphoric: this seemed to be the biggest breakthrough yet. A link between Jason Holland and Scott Headingly was bound to have a relevance to the death of Daphne Headingly. The entire family seemed odd. Simon Patterson had mentioned, briefly during one of our phone calls, that the suicide of Scott might be looked into again.

To pass the time and stop our minds from racing, we engaged in the tried and tested method of ridiculous banter. 'Right, Wingsy,' I said, 'if you had to be a flavour, what one would you be?'

'Methane,' he replied.

'Is that your way of telling me to open the window? Look – over there. Is that Susan Newman waiting to cross the road?'

'Who's Susan Newman?'

'Sorry, mate, I was with Pierre when I met her. She's the mum of Josie who was friends with Amanda Bell.'

'Oh, the sordid stinging nettle thing. Is she wearing a wig? It's lopsided.' He started to laugh.

'Don't, Wingsy. She's a harmless old woman.'

'She may be our killer.'

'She can't put a wig on straight; it's unlikely that she murdered three people – four if you count Scott – and bit them in the process. I'm not even sure she's got her own teeth.'

Made me think, though. I'd made my diagnosis that she was mad. I'd seen one of the mutilated bodies myself and photos of the other two. The offender couldn't possibly be sane. The scariest part was wondering what could have driven someone far enough towards the point of madness that they would commit such brutal crimes – and whether the victims were chosen at random. We were just coming through the gate to the police station car park when I saw a figure walk out of the back door among the shadows thrown across the yard by the low sun. He was heading our way.

'There's Bill Harrison,' said Wingsy. 'He's a decent bloke. He likes you.'

My attempt at being nonchalant failed. 'Really? I don't know him very well. Is he single? And not gay.'

'Dunno. Shall I ask him?' He opened the window and yelled, 'Alright, Bill?'

'For crying out loud,' I pleaded. 'Don't mess this up.'

While Bill headed our way, kit bag slung over his shoulder, Wingsy reversed into a space and I jumped out of the moving car to distract him from Wingsy. 'Hey, Bill. How's things with you?'

Whether Wingsy chose that moment to help me out or genuinely had a call, I didn't know, but he opened the door and announced, 'Phone's ringing. Be with you in a minute.'

'I'm really good, thanks, Nina,' answered Bill. 'I'm glad I saw you. I've been meaning to ask you for a while if you fancy going for a drink some time.'

I'd have liked to think that my reaction was one of interest, but instead I must have looked either horrified or a bit simple, as he felt the need to add, 'With me... Some time... If you fancy... Not a problem if you don't.'

'Love to,' I managed to say. 'Apart from work, I'm not usually up to much.'

He produced a phone from his jacket pocket. I took this as my cue to leave him to it; I didn't want to get in the way of an important phone call. I made to back away.

'I'll put your number in here and then I won't lose it,' he said.

Such nice eyes…

Chapter 28

Skipping into the briefing would not have been appropriate, so I floated instead. Wingsy and I got a couple of 'well done's and 'nice one's for our discovery of the Scott Headingly and Jason Holland association. It was nice to be appreciated, but Jake Lloyd had offered the information to us and we had simply passed it on. It didn't stop either of us feeling a little bit superior at the same time. I didn't want to be modest; I wanted to stay on this enquiry.

'Evening, everyone,' said Eric Nottingham. 'Don't worry, the pizzas are in the building. I know it's been another long day.' The door opened and a stack of flat cardboard boxes entered the room, carried by the unsmiling Kim Cotton. The aroma of cheese, pepperoni and onion filled the room. Nottingham continued, 'Pass them round, Kim; we can eat and talk. Nina, you can go first. Tell us about Jake Lloyd.'

Cobblers – I wanted pizza. I tried to look interested and not hungry.

'Well, sir, Lloyd offered up the information freely,' I said, glancing down at the notes I had made to check a date. 'Holland and Scott Headingly met after both were released from prison in 1998. Holland was only twenty and by all accounts fancied himself as a bit of a big shot. Scott Headingly, having done time for kidnap, was someone for Holland to look up to. Holland had served a very short term for burglary. Jake Lloyd is not too clear on how or where they met, but he saw them together on a couple of occasions and later found out about Holland from his father Donald.'

I recapped on the family for my own sake as much as anyone else's. 'Daphne, our latest victim, has a brother, Donald, and a sister, Diane. The sisters didn't talk but Donald was more of a family mediator, by all accounts. Jake gave us the impression that he himself kept a close eye on Scott even though they no longer talked.' I looked from the DCI, at whom I had been largely directing my words, towards Wingsy, who was sitting on my left-hand side.

'Yes,' Wingsy agreed. 'It was only an impression but I agree with Nina.' He held a large slice of pizza in his hands. It was level with my nose. I thought about leaning across and ripping a big chunk out of it with my teeth. I restrained myself.

'We also got the impression that the "close eye" was more because he didn't trust his cousin rather than because he was looking out for him. Jake Lloyd is a bit odd. We've done the usual checks on him. He was cautioned a few years ago, in 2006, for theft. Looking into it, it was something to do with an ex-girlfriend and some property belonging to her. He said it was his. Later he admitted to taking it and so he was cautioned. Nothing else on him, just a bit of a feeling that something's not quite right but couldn't tell you what, sir.' I directed what I was saying towards the boss, watching him write down the salient points of our earlier encounter with Jake.

'Without speaking to Donald, the father, it is all a bit third-hand, 'cos Jake wanted to know who his cousin was mixing with, couldn't or wouldn't ask him himself, and went to his dad to find out,' I added.

Eric Nottingham put his pen down, leaned his right elbow on the desk and rested his chin on his fist. The other hand he ran through his hair from his forehead to the back of his skull. 'Why?' he asked.

'Why did he want to know who Scott was with?'

I was greeted with a slow nod of agreement. He stared at me. 'You got a feel for Jake and you've met Diane. We're running out of family liaison officers and no one's spoken to Donald Lloyd at length.' Nottingham straightened up, checked his watch and said, 'Go and see him tonight.'

Yeah, fine, but not without a slice of deep pan first. I stole a look into the pizza box just out of my reach. All that was left was an olive and the white plastic tower put into the box to stop the topping sticking to the lid. My day had nosedived since Bill took my number.

Next to speak in the briefing was Wingsy. Before he began, he slid a slice of pizza resting on a paper towel my way. Once more, life was good.

Chapter 29

Despite the lateness of the evening, I made plans to visit Donald Lloyd. Inwardly, I wanted to go home, open a mean red and glug away. But it would have to wait.

Wingsy had a quick word, explaining that Mel was getting a bit fed up with all the hours he'd been working. Before Operation Guard, he'd had a three-week murder trial at a Crown Court forty miles away and had worked sixteen-hour days without a break. I was tired and ready to call it a day myself, but thought it was best to visit Donald Lloyd as soon as possible. I was gathering my stuff, prepared to go to his house on my own, when Catherine came over with Danny. I had already decided that I liked Danny. He had a good attitude and made me want to go 'aah' when I saw him. He was a sweetheart.

'Thought that you and Danny could go and see Donald Lloyd and his wife June together,' she said. 'He could do with a break from CCTV and, from the sounds of it, the entire family's a bit mad. Just to be on the safe side.' She was distracted by someone offering to make tea, and made towards the poor sod buckling under the weight of a tray heaving with empty mugs.

'Don't know about you, Danny, but I'd love a tea,' I said. I thought about using my Aunt Lou's favourite expression when she was hinting for a cuppa – she loved to say, 'I'm so thirsty I couldn't spit on a sixpence' – but I doubted if Danny even knew what a sixpence was. 'Suppose we should get on with the enquiry, though.'

Danny was already tightening his tie and heading in the direction of his jacket, resting over the back of a chair. 'Couldn't agree more,' he said. 'Girlfriend's gonna do her nut with me being so late home again.'

Even if it hadn't been for my and Bill's romantic encounter next to the disused diesel pump in the yard a couple of hours earlier, I wouldn't have been too perturbed by Danny's admission of having a girlfriend: I put him at about fifteen years younger than me. Besides, I didn't own an Xbox.

Content that I could have a son of Danny's age, once we were in the car I shared a bar of Dairy Milk with him. One slice of meat feast hadn't touched the sides, so to speak. Danny was good company and surprised me by saying he had been a police officer for eight years. Never having worked together before, we formulated a plan, involving me doing most of the talking, as I'd met Jake. Like all police officers' plans, it was fluid. We dealt with people, and people were unpredictable, so over-planning could be pointless.

Outside the house a few minutes later, I called Catherine to let her know we had arrived. No sooner had I told her where we were than she asked, 'How would you be fixed for an overnight stay in Birmingham?'

'Can do,' I said. 'You don't mean tonight, though, do you?'

'No, in a couple of days, see,' she crooned. 'I'm calling everyone to check their availability for the trip. Had an update from Forensics re. the blood on the knife you and Wingsy found in the back of Savage's van. We've got a match to a fella called Benjamin Makepeace, but he's missing. Thought as you and Wingsy found it you might want to follow it up, but we'll let you know. Got to go, I've another call coming in.'

And she was gone.

Danny and I made our way up the pathway. The house was not as grand as Jake's, but it too was in a good neighbourhood. As we stood at the porch door and rang the bell, I noticed the curtain twitch in the bay window. A light went on behind the front door. Warrant cards at the ready, we stood and waited for our first glimpse of Donald Lloyd. The door was opened by a dull-eyed man in his mid-sixties. Despite the warmth and the lateness of the evening, he was wearing a shirt, tie and buttoned-up cardigan. Making the assumption that he was Donald Lloyd from the family dimple – that and the fact he was in Donald Lloyd's house and was too well dressed to be a burglar – I said, 'Mr Lloyd? I know that this is a difficult time for your family, but can we come in and speak to you about your sister, please?'

He gave me a lame smile and shuffled backwards in his slippers to let us into his home. As we stepped across the threshold, a woman peered around the doorway from what was probably the front room. Her smile contained both sadness and friendliness. I smiled back.

'I'm June,' she said with a soft Scottish accent. 'Donald, I'll show the officers in. Why don't you make us some tea?' I read her face as she looked back at me. A barely noticeable tightness around her eyes flickered there and then was gone.

Donald did as he was told and went in the direction of the kitchen, slippers dragging on the floor. June shook her head, watching him go. Seeing me looking at her, she said, 'Poor Donald. He's taken it hard. Please, come in and sit down.' June stepped back, giving us space. Danny stood aside for me to go first and I noted his manners. June indicated a couch and I sat down, Danny next to me.

Stealing another look in the direction of the door, June said, 'I wanted to speak to you without Donald. I can't really do so here; he'll be back soon. I wrote this when you knocked at the door. Here.' She pressed a piece of paper into my hand and covered the six feet to a vacant armchair in the blink of an eye. Adopting a more relaxed pose, she said, 'I hear you've met our Jake, then?'

'I haven't,' said Danny, 'but Nina did a bit earlier. A couple of things he told her are important, and we hope that Donald can shed some more light on them.'

I could hear china rattling on a tray as it was carried by the long-suffering Donald. He hesitated by the open door as if uncertain whether he should enter his own lounge.

'I'll get a table, Donald,' said June, jumping up to move a small occasional table into the centre of the room. Spurred on by his wife's words, Donald lugged himself, with the tray, towards the wooden stand. Setting the drinks down, he straightened himself up to his full height for the first time. There was a similarity between him and Diane but he didn't seem to have any of her self-importance. He lowered himself into an armchair then turned his attention to Danny and me.

'I was quite close to my sister Daphne,' he said, eyes closed. He tilted his head back and let out a sigh before opening his eyes, moist with tears. 'I really adored both of my sisters. They looked after me, you see. My father died during the war, before I was born, so the three of us were very close. You must know by now that it all went a bit wrong with Scott...'

As he trailed off, I followed his gaze to an old black and white photograph on the oak sideboard. It was of two striking young women, one of whom had a small boy on her knee. She was doing her best to hold on to him.

'That was us on our annual holiday, hop-picking in Kent. I have such fond memories of those times. Six weeks of fresh air and having my sisters all to myself.' He produced a white handkerchief from his cardigan pocket and wiped his eyes. 'Just can't believe she's gone. Who would do such a thing?'

'We're doing everything we can to find out, Donald,' I said, fighting an urge to put my arm around him. June leaned across and patted his hand.

Donald continued, pausing occasionally to fight back a sob. 'Daphne's neighbour, Mrs Turnbull, she found my sister. She told me that there was blood everywhere. This was the work of a madman. Daphne was a harmless old lady. Scott was another matter, but Daphne...'

When next Donald clenched his handkerchief to his mouth, I shifted in my seat to warn him that I was about to ask him a question. It seemed to have the desired effect, as he paused and waited.

'We are not ruling out the possibility of a link between the death of your sister and that of Jason Holland,' I said carefully.

Donald blanched.

'What can you tell me about Holland?' I asked.

He shook his head back and forth with increasing ferocity, as if his worst fears had manifested themselves on his pure wool carpet.

'This is all my fault,' he said. 'I should never have introduced Scott to Jason Holland.'

Danny and I gave Donald several seconds to compose himself again. He rubbed his hands over his face, then, dropping his arms on the arm-rests, told us through his torment how his nephew had met Jason Holland.

'It was Christmas 1997. There had been several burglaries in this street and nearby neighbours were telling us that the police were handing out crime prevention advice and leaflets, Neighbourhood Watch meetings, that kind of thing. You never think it will happen to you but I was sitting in this armchair one evening. The furniture was arranged differently then – this chair was over there with its back to the door.' Donald pointed to the spot where I was sitting. June leaned over to her husband once more and squeezed his hand.

'Thankfully, June was out at a church meeting and I was by myself. I was reading a book. The house was quiet. I was so engrossed in the book that I was only vaguely aware of a noise behind me. As I got up to look, a young man rushed towards me and punched me right in the face.' A hand went up to his right eye as the story replayed itself in his memory. 'He ran for the front door and out into the street. I called the police. They arrived and took fingerprints – well, you'll know what they'd have done. Anyway, some time later, they arrested the burglar. He had got in through an open window upstairs, come down here thinking no one was home, and I'd taken him by surprise. Can't really blame him for hitting me. I must have startled him.

'I wasn't really all that bothered about taking him to court. He was a young man who'd made a mistake. I had a black eye but I was fine otherwise. It transpired that his name was Jason Holland and he had been responsible for a number of other break-ins in the area, and he asked for them to be taken into consideration.' Donald swallowed, looked up at the ceiling, adding, 'I thought it would be a good idea to introduce him to my nephew. I thought, when Jason got released from prison after such a short time at such a young age, a shock would be the making of him. I wanted to show him that he needed to turn his life around. Show him what might become of him if he didn't mend his ways. We had seen eight years of incarceration turn Scott from a very outgoing young man with his life ahead of him into a shell of his former self.

'But my attempt at his rehabilitation failed. My great plan – ' he paused and let out a harsh laugh ' – was to make Jason see how he would turn out if he continued on the path he was on. What I hadn't foreseen was Scott and Jason becoming as thick as thieves. My tactics were incorrect. Instead of Jason being revolted by Scott, he wanted to be Scott.'

Chapter 30

By the time Danny and I had finished speaking to Donald and June it was very late. I made a quick call to the nick to say we were heading back with the paperwork and calling it a day. Alcohol was now in sight.

I checked my phone and saw that I had a couple of missed calls and a text from Laura telling me that she was joining the enquiry for a few days, maybe a week. More good news for me. She was great to work with, as well as a good mate.

In the nick's back yard, I told Danny that I would take the paperwork upstairs if he wanted to get away to his girlfriend. Then I thought about Bill and smiled. Hugging the statements and notebooks to me, I headed to the Incident Room.

At first, I thought that the room was empty, but I could just make out a head behind a computer screen in the far corner as I dropped off the paperwork.

'Goodnight,' I called.

The head moved, revealing the sour face of Kim Cotton. 'Night,' she said. 'Briefing's at 8am.' And then her bitter features moved back out of sight.

On the way downstairs, I listened to my messages. The first one was from Annie asking me to visit her. Probably run out of imported cheese. The other was from Bill. Stopping to catch my breath, I replayed the message asking me to call him if it wasn't too late and I wasn't too tired. He actually thought about my wellbeing before asking me to call him.

Searching in my coat pocket for my car keys, I found the piece of paper June Lloyd had passed to me. I took it out and read the handwritten scribble. *Parish Church of All Saints, tomorrow, 9am–1pm. June*

There was no suggestion that I would not be going to see her. It was a church, a public place, and she'd given me a window of four hours. I put the note inside my warrant card as I was guaranteed not to lose that, took my keys out and got into my car. I checked the back seat and the boot first. Never take chances.

Inside the car, with the central locking activated, I called Bill.

'Hello?' he said.

'Hi, Bill, it's Nina.'

'Hello. You just finished?'

'Yes, just about to leave the nick. Been another long day. How about you?'

'Not too late for me today. Caught up on a few things.' There was a slight pause, and I was about to speak when he asked, 'Still fancy going for that drink some time?'

'Definitely. Not sure when, though – we're working such long hours and you don't want me on my knees in front of you.' I slapped myself on the forehead as I said this. Never mind Wingsy messing things up; I was doing a great job all on my own.

Bill chuckled and said, 'I'm free for the next three or four nights but then I'm on late turn for a couple of days. You just let me know when you can meet up.'

'OK. I'll see what's going on in the morning and I'll call you tomorrow.'

'Sounds ideal, Nina. Speak to you tomorrow.'

'Goodnight.'

Throughout the drive home I planned where Bill and I might end up on our date. I didn't mind the cheaper chain pubs but even at the best of times the clientele did resemble the *Star Wars* cast. Bill didn't strike me as the wine bar sort either, so a quiet local pub would be my preference. I wasn't really paying attention to the journey, merely enough not to cause an accident. At some point, though, I realised that the car behind had been keeping up with me for some time. Annoyed with myself for not having paid more attention, I indicated right, took the turn and headed for the roundabout. The vehicle behind did the same.

Reaching the roundabout, I indicated right again, as did the driver tailing me. On the roundabout, I turned full circle to the fourth exit back to where I'd come from, forcing the other car either to do the same, or give up on me. He chose to take the third exit. Still unsure whether it was my imagination or not, I considered following the car and getting the registration number. But the thought of a glass of wine almost made me salivate, so I headed home instead.

Chapter 31

25th September

The day began with a promising blue sky, and could almost have been a summer's morning even though it was late September. That, at least, lifted my spirits. Despite sleeping well, I was feeling a bit worn out. I'd woken up with the sense that something was wrong, before calling to mind my mystery number one fan roaming the land with a camera sending me a potted history of my life. Oh, and I'd drunk a bottle of Merlot the night before.

I couldn't afford to feel tired. My days off were not even on the horizon, and that was if I didn't have to work through them. Making myself a cup of tea, I glanced out of the kitchen window at the garden. It backed on to a wood. Its seclusion was one of the things that had attracted me to the house in the first place, but the borders needed so much work to get them up to scratch, not to mention the maintenance. I never seemed to have the time to spend weeding and digging. I told myself it was a wildlife habitat. Even the shed seemed depressed. Dismissing any ideas of spending my next few days off pruning, I got ready for work and drove to the Incident Room.

Laura was in the meeting room when I got there. She looked poised and elegant in a black, well-cut suit, her mane of hair draped on her shoulders; even without any make-up she glowed. Just as well she was my mate or I could have taken a real dislike to her. Making sure she had a notebook and a quick rundown of where everything was, I took a seat next to her and we waited for the others.

Pierre was one of the first to wander in. He came over to introduce himself to Laura and sat the other side of her. If he hadn't already told me he was gay, I'd have really been hacked off; I could have sworn he was flirting with her. I decided not to let it upset me. Who was jealous of their fantastically attractive friend being spoken to by a gay colleague? That would be really childish. I decided that by the end of the briefing I'd be over it.

I was grateful for the brevity of the meeting. A number of officers had lots to say, including us, and we were told to keep it snappy. DCI Nottingham made it clear it wasn't because he didn't want to listen but if fifty people were each going to talk for twenty minutes, nothing would get done. In as few words as possible, everyone was brought up to speed.

Having recovered from my internal tantrum regarding Laura and Pierre, I was pleased to be told I was working with Wingsy again that day. We were to speak to Jake Lloyd straight after the briefing. First Danny and I told the packed room what we had learned from Donald and June, including Donald's sorry tale of his good intentions in trying to reform a burglar, that had backfired so badly.

'One other thing, sir,' I added. 'June Lloyd slipped me a note last night asking me to meet her at her church today. Can I go there first?'

'Yes, you can,' Nottingham said. 'Leave the details with Ray. Ray's joined us today for a couple of weeks.' He jabbed his pen in the direction of a man in a long-sleeved blue shirt, fiddling with the lanyard around his neck. Ray raised his hand a few inches from the table and smiled at the gathered mass.

Another few minutes and that morning's resumé of events was finished. Laura and I headed to the ladies'. After checking the cubicles were empty, I told her, 'I've only got a date with Bill Harrison.'

Her face broke into an enormous grin. 'He's such a nice fella, Nin. Where are you going?'

'Don't know yet. He's asked me out, don't know where or when. Said a drink somewhere. Bloody hell – he does drink, doesn't he? You don't think he meant a coffee?'

Laura threw her head back and laughed. 'I think everyone knows you like a glass of wine or ten. Don't think he would have asked you out if he was teetotal.'

'Perhaps it's a challenge for him – he may be trying to reform me. Be wasting his bloody time.' My turn to laugh. 'Listen, mate, catch up later – got to go to church then on to see Jake Lloyd. Take care.'

I left her in the toilets and found Wingsy, talking to Catherine and Ray. Catherine was running her hands down over her hips, saying, 'Well, I think I'll have to take the dress back. It's too revealing, see.'

Wingsy looked fit to burst.

Ray said, 'Don't be hasty, Catherine. We'll be the judge of that.'

'Hate to interrupt you all,' I said, 'but here's the address I'm going to. Wingsy, you coming with me? We can go straight to Jake's from there.'

At the church, I went inside, leaving Wingsy in the car. He was sulking after I told him I'd clocked him checking out Catherine's cleavage. Couldn't say that I held him fully responsible: she had been flirting with Ray, whereas Wingsy had seemed to be an innocent bystander. As innocent as a heterosexual male could be when confronted with an enormous bust.

The sun went in as I entered the church. Inside it was poorly lit, and the musty smell hit me as soon as I walked through the door. While I stood growing accustomed to the gloom, the sun came back out and shone through the stained glass windows. Particles of dust danced in the air.

The sound of footsteps on the stone floor made me look to my right. A smiling black woman in her early twenties was walking towards me. She held a large flower arrangement in her hands.

'Hello,' I said. 'I'm looking for June Lloyd. Could I speak to her?'

'Course you can,' she replied, putting the oasis down on to a nearby trestle table. 'She's in the office. Is she expecting you?'

'Yes, but we didn't agree an exact time,' I said.

'Follow me,' she said, leading the way to a wooden door, set in the recess beside the last row of pews. She put her head round it and said, 'A young lady here to see you, June.'

She opened the door fully to reveal June sitting behind a desk with a phone to her ear. June waved at me to join her. Thanking the flower arranger, I went into the office, closing the door behind me.

June was mid-flow and said into the receiver, 'I know that you've helped us out with the typing, but listen, dear, this new slogan from the church reads "I've upped my pledge – up yours". Listen, I'll call you back later, I have a visitor.'

June hung up and stood to shake my hand. 'Thank you for coming to see me, Nina. I've kept a secret for a very long time, but now I think the truth should come out.'

Chapter 32

Waiting patiently for June to speak, I stood completely still. But when she remained quiet I felt compelled to say something in case the intense stare I was giving her wasn't evidence enough of my interest.

'What truth, June?'

'There's really no point in asking that this not go any further, is there?' she asked.

'No.' I shook my head to underline the point. 'Not in a murder enquiry. What did you ask me here to tell me?'

'The night that Scott hanged himself – or maybe I should say the night he died – hours before we received the news, I had gone to Diane's house.' June fiddled with the notepad on the desk in front of her. 'She was burning clothes in her garden. Odd, don't you think? It was the middle of the day in the summer and she was burning clothes on her back lawn. I couldn't see whether the items were men's or women's – by the time I got there they were unrecognisable, so I couldn't tell you who they belonged to. It's the only time I've ever known her to have a bonfire. I wasn't sure what to make of it at the time but I dismissed it. Later that day we got the news that Scott had taken his own life.' June leaned across the desk, shoulders hunched up, and said, 'I know that Scott was a bad penny but, the way he ended up, that could just as easily have been my Jake. Jake's a lovely wee boy. Never married and I can't understand it. If Jake had been the positive influence on Scott we would have liked him to be, then surely both Scott's and Jason Holland's lives would have turned out differently.'

'That's something we'll never know, June. Did you ever ask Diane about the clothes she burned?'

'Only once. After the funeral. She claimed not to remember at all. I let it go.'

'Did you tell anyone else? Donald?'

'Oh, no. I didn't want to worry him. I just kept quiet.'

'Earlier on, June, you said "the night that Scott hanged himself" and then you changed it to "the night he died". What did you mean by that?'

Her blank stare initially made me think she hadn't a clue what I meant. But then she answered, 'Scott was murdered.'

'What makes you say that?' I asked.

'Isn't it obvious, dear? Diane murdered Scott, and now her own sister. She probably killed Jason Holland too.'

Was no one in this family sane? Hoping my face was still showing interest and not incredulity, I said, 'I need to check I have this right. You're saying that when Diane was in her sixties she was able to hang her own forty-one-year-old nephew; then, aged seventy-one, she stabbed her seventy-seven-year-old sister and overcame the twenty-stone, thirty-something Jason Holland.' Really, I did try to say this without sounding as if I was taking the mick. I liked June. She had until now seemed to be the only one in the family holding it together. Now she was coming undone. But, most importantly at this moment, she was trying to help me, help the police solve a murder. Sarcasm was not going to help.

'Aye, listen to me,' she said. 'I sound insane when you put it like that.'

'No, June, not insane, just someone who's worried about her family. The comments you've made about your sister-in-law burning clothes – I'm going to need a statement. That OK?'

She nodded. 'I'll put the kettle on. But please, ignore what I said about Diane being responsible. I don't know what I was thinking. I've never said those words out loud and, now I have, it seems ridiculous.'

'It's your statement, June,' I said. 'You have to be happy with the contents before you sign it.' It wasn't going to stop me passing the information on, though.

I explained that I was going to tell my colleague in the car what I was doing and get the correct paperwork. Outside, I stood in the sunshine, remembering how guilty churches always made me feel. Like I should have led a better life. Given more to the poor and less to the Wine Emporium.

Wingsy was on the phone, but he hung up when he saw me. Following a quick resumé of my conversation with June, I said, 'So that's the short of it, mate. Call the office and pass it on, but I can't see that Diane is physically capable of killing either Scott or Jason. If she did kill Jason, that means she probably was capable of killing her own sister and Amanda Bell. Can't rule it out, but Holland was a big old lump.'

I said I'd be back out when I'd finished the statement. As I walked out of the sunlight and into the church again, I felt a chill go down my spine.

Chapter 33

Emerging some time later, paperwork complete, June's mind put to rest and my mind already on the next task, I got into the car. Wingsy was eating a satsuma.

'Want one?' he asked, holding open a string bag of fruit.

'Shops run out of crisps?' I asked, reaching for one.

'No. It's Mel. She's put me on a healthy eating campaign.'

'Well, you look over the moon about it.' I said. 'You just tell her that chips and tomato ketchup, that's two of your five a day. Throw in a can of lemonade and you're almost there.'

'You tell her. Don't know what's got into her lately. She keeps telling me to play more golf or join a gym.'

'Perhaps she's sick of the sight of you.'

'Don't know how. I've seen more of you in the last week or so than her.'

'Going home early last night didn't work, then?' I asked.

'No. We had a row. Might as well have stayed at work and earned some money. Not like three kids ain't expensive.' He turned the ignition on and said, 'Let's go and see Jake Lloyd again.'

Jake was at home. It took him a couple of minutes to get to the door but once he opened it he beamed at me, welcoming Wingsy and me inside. Well, he welcomed me in, Wingsy followed.

A the kitchen table, Jake sat down opposite me. Trying to feel flattered rather than unnerved, I broached the subject of Scott's death with as much tact as I could manage.

'Jake, I realise that you spent little time with your cousin when you were older – ' I broke off and paused, interrupting myself. 'I can smell burning.' It seemed to be coming from the direction of the room that housed the noisy washing machine.

Jake waved my concern aside and said, 'I was just burning some old letters and correspondence before you arrived. It's fine, really.'

I looked at Wingsy briefly, but decided not to be sidetracked right now. 'As I was saying, when you were older, was there anything unusual about Scott's behaviour just before his death that you recall?'

'He was becoming more dangerous, more reckless and more obsessive,' he replied. He smiled at me as though this was all good news.

Attempting to break this down, I asked, 'Obsessive? Tell me about the obsession, Jake.'

'Obsessed with you and your sister, Nina.'

I went cold.

I could hear the confusion in Wingsy's voice as he said, 'Nina, what sister?'

I had always told everyone that I was an only child. I could hear a loud thudding in my ears, as if every drop of blood in my body was pumping through my head.

'He followed your every move on the news. The pictures of you when you were rescued, what happened to your sister – all of it. It took over his life. Being younger than him and looking up to him, I thought he was just interested. Clearly he wasn't. When he took those two girls, snatched them, I suppose it was an attempt at copying what had happened to the Foster girls. Sick bastard. I'm so sorry, Nina. I did what I could to stop him, but I was only barely out of my teens myself. You would never have come to any harm, though, I made sure of that.'

My work phone rang. Normally I would have ignored it, but I needed to look away from Lloyd's face. I could read something disturbing in it. I took the phone out of my pocket and read the word 'Beckensale' on the screen. What could she possibly want at a time like this?

'I have to get this,' I mumbled, getting up and muttering my name into the mouthpiece.

'Nina, listen. Just got a result back from Fingerprints about those photographs you were sent. The name Jake Lloyd mean anything to you?'

I couldn't speak. Managed to turn my back on Lloyd so that he couldn't see my face but stayed at an angle so that Wingsy could. Let him see the horror on it, I thought. Please, Wingsy, help me.

'Nina, are you listening? Where are you?'

'Enquiries at Jake Lloyd's house. Operation Guard,' I managed to say.

'Fuck. Who you with?'

'Wingsy. Kim Cotton sent us. Is it urgent, sarge? We can't really leave now.' It was terrible cover but my mind wasn't working.

I could hear her frantic shouting in the background and knew that she would be today's Stan McGuire.

'Listen to me. A patrol is on its way. Every spare man is coming. Keep him talking. Make out you're hanging up but leave the line open. OK?'

'Sure, sarge, got that, but we're likely to be here at Francis Street for about another hour or so. See you after that. Bye, then.'

Wingsy was staring at me. He knew something was up. I glanced over at Lloyd, catching sight of myself in a mirror on the far wall as I did so. I didn't have to worry about the blood in my head any more. I looked as if I'd come to haunt the place. As I sat back down, Wingsy took over smoothly. 'When was the last time you saw your aunt Daphne?' he asked in an even tone.

'I went over there four or five days ago. As I said, we don't have much to do with each other but her security light kept playing up. This time, someone had smashed it. She's still family so I went to have a look. Obviously her lottery win gave her enough to pay someone to fix it, but I thought I'd do the decent thing.' Jake stood up. 'Can I get you tea or coffee?'

'No,' I almost shouted. 'No, thank you. We just had one before we got here.' Last thing I wanted was him armed with a kettle of boiling water. If my friend had been in any doubt that I was acting oddly, this was concrete proof – I never turned down a brew and it had been hours since we'd had one.

Through the window behind Lloyd, I saw a marked police car make a hasty stop. I thought it through quickly – couldn't leave Wingsy alone with him to let them in, couldn't be alone with him if I sent Wingsy to let them in. The only option was to let Lloyd open the door.

The doorbell sounded. Lloyd looked slightly confused, but went off to answer it. I gestured to Wingsy that we should follow him.

We stood behind him as he opened the door to Bill Harrison and Phil Williams. Another police car pulled up across the driveway. The two occupants jumped out and made their way towards us.

'Jake Lloyd?' asked Bill. Lloyd nodded, looking from one officer to the other. Bill stepped forward. 'I'm arresting you on suspicion of harassment of Nina Foster. You do not have – '

'What are you talking about? She's in my house. How can I harass someone who comes to see me?'

I left Bill and Phil putting handcuffs on Lloyd and as soon as there was a gap to get past them I went outside into the fresh air. Wingsy followed me. Without a word, he unlocked the car and opened the passenger door for me. Two other patrol cars arrived as we left.

Chapter 34

We drove back to the nick in silence. The air smelt of citrus fruit from Wingsy's earlier snack. As we got to the car park entrance, waiting for the security barrier to open, only one question came from my friend. 'Wanna talk about it?'

I let out a breath. 'Don't really know where to start, mate.'

He reversed into a space, but neither of us made to get out of the car. After a couple of minutes, I thought that he was at least owed an explanation, although I knew for sure that, if I opened the door and walked away, that would be that. There'd be no pressure from Wingsy.

'Me and my sister were kidnapped when we were kids. It didn't end well for her. I never talk about it. A couple of days ago, a stack of photographs of me came in the post in an envelope. They spanned years – decades really – as if someone had been following me for years – '

'Bloody hell. Why didn't you say? You must have been terrified.'

'Which time?' I gave a small nervous laugh, which wasn't fooling either of us. 'I took the photos to Beckensale and she got them and the envelope fingerprinted. She called when we were at Lloyd's house to say the match was Lloyd. If his prints are on them, then the chances are he sent them.'

'Or at least had something to do with it. So when he...'

'When he started on about his cousin being obsessed with me, then the call came, you can imagine what I was thinking.'

'Actually, sweetheart, I can't. Tell you this, though: Beckensale did a good job. Who do you wanna see now? Nottingham? Kim Cotton? We'd best go speak to someone.'

'I think we'll try Nottingham. Before we do, though, Wingsy, I need to make a call.'

I got out of the car and called Stan. He had been admitted to hospital today for his operation and I was desperate to hear his voice. I didn't know if he'd answer his mobile in the ward, if he'd feel like talking or even if he'd be awake, but his voicemail was enough to get me through.

Eyes shut and clasping the phone to my ear, I listened to the recorded message of his deep voice telling me, *'This is Stan McGuire's telephone. I am not at present able to take your call, but please feel free to leave me a message and I will get back to you as soon as I am able. Thank you for your call.'*

I cried without making a sound.

Chapter 35

Wingsy told me he was taking me to the top floor of the police station, to a 'quiet office'. I took that to mean I was to be put into isolation. He obviously had strict instructions not to let me anywhere near custody, and I could well imagine that there had been whispered conversations about making me leave the building altogether.

I knew where we were going. The windows moved in their frames when the wind blew hard enough. I reckoned it was built as a tribute to the set of *Prisoner Cell Block H*. I mounted the nick's stairs in a state of indifference. From time to time on our short journey to my segregation we passed colleagues in the corridor. While the saner part of my brain knew that those I glided past couldn't know what the last half-hour had brought me, I concentrated on faded blue carpet tiles rather than their expressions.

The day was getting warmer – the sort of day when I would normally look forward to finishing work on time and sitting in the sunshine, picturing how my garden would look if I could be bothered. I made do with gazing out of the open window on to the yard below, watching patrol cars come and go on the tarmac. The docking area where Jake Lloyd would be taken from the police car to the custody holding area was out of my view. No one was taking any chances with that. I did hear a car pulling into the caged space where prisoners were unloaded before being taken through the gated door for booking in by the custody sergeant. A couple of minutes later, I heard the familiar sound of Bill's voice as he took Lloyd towards the metal door of the custody suite.

A noise behind me made me turn as Wingsy nudged the door open with his knee, carrying two mugs of tea.

'Blimey, Nin, it's cold in here, girl.' He put the drinks down and slammed the window. He positioned himself so that I had, out of politeness, to look at him and therefore away from the window when he spoke to me. 'The DCI's coming to talk to you in a minute. They just wanted me to check with you. They need a statement and want to know if you're up to doing it yourself or if you'd like someone you know – or someone you don't know – to write it for you.'

'Wankers. Course I can write a poxy statement. I've not lost the use of my arms. Sodding cheek.' I was aware how tightly I was holding the mug of tea.

'Alright, alright. The thing is, at the moment it's him sending you a load of photographs but...' Wingsy looked away, at a poster about forced and arranged marriages and who to contact for help and information. His eyes flitted over it, not really reading it, before looking back at me.

'But...' I prompted.

'The search of his house is taking some time. They've found some stuff.'

Eric Nottingham exploded into the room and slammed the door behind him. He picked up a chair with one hand and positioned it directly in front of me. 'John, I'd like you to stay, but Nina, if you have any problem with – '

'No, sir, I'd like him to stay. What do you want to know?' I saw Wingsy out of the corner of my eye pull up a chair and sit down just to the left of Nottingham.

His first remark surprised me.

'Know all about you and your sister from the Seventies.' I wasn't sure if my face reflected my thoughts or whether he thought that he'd better explain anyway. 'It's difficult to keep a thing like that quiet. Not many people do know but, even today, something like that is massive news.'

129

If this hadn't been enough to stop me in my tracks, his next declaration certainly was.

'You've a good friend in Stan McGuire,' said Nottingham, unblinking. 'We met some years back on an SIOs' course. We've kept in touch. You don't have to tell me all about your sister.' He blinked in rapid succession at the word 'sister'. 'Just tell us about the photographs and any connection to Jake Lloyd or Scott Headingly.'

'Never met Jake Lloyd until the other day, and as far as I'm concerned I've had no dealings with Scott Headingly at all.' My mind was attempting to process this information but failing. I tried to recall if I'd ever met anyone called Scott Headingly.

'You need to go home, Nina. I'm sending someone over to sit – well, to take your statement.' He'd been about to say 'someone to sit with you'. I wasn't sure whether I was worried or really hacked off by this. 'I've thought about using someone from a different division or force so you're speaking to a stranger, but I decided to opt for Catherine Thomas. Do you have any objections to her?'

Head in my hands, I answered, 'No.'

As he got to the door, I looked up and took a chance I would get a straight answer. 'Boss. I have a question.'

He paused, one hand on the doorknob, head turned to look at me.

'What have they found at Lloyd's house?'

He broke eye contact at my question and coughed. 'Early days yet. They've not finished looking.'

Chapter 36

All the way home, I thought about the photographs I'd received and whether they could in any way be connected with the three murders. I wondered whether the killing would end now, or if another living soul was to be stabbed to death in a frenzy. If that extra horror was to take place, would it be someone who was already a part of the enquiry or a totally unsuspecting victim? That petrifying thought foremost in my mind, I pulled up opposite my home. I was doing little to calm my own nerves. This was the place of sanctuary I'd lived in for seven years and always enjoyed coming back to. I never, ever took chances I was aware of, but I had never felt unsafe in my own home. Not until now.

A search of the house made me feel better but I couldn't shake the feeling that I wasn't alone in my home. I knew how irrational this thought was. Jake Lloyd was in custody.

Catherine arrived at my door an hour later. I had tried to eat but couldn't face food just yet. She'd thoughtfully brought a selection of sandwiches with her and insisted on making tea while I sat in the lounge. A few minutes later, she appeared with the sandwiches cut into fours, arranged in a neat row, and two cups of tea, all on a tray.

'Used to be a waitress, see,' she boomed, as she looked around for somewhere to put the food. I pulled the coffee table over and she thudded the tray down, spilling the tea. 'Don't worry, love, I'm a better detective than I ever was a waitress.' She laughed and I couldn't help but join in. I sat with my feet tucked under me and my jumper pulled down over my knees. It was my favourite one for lounging around the house and had been dragged out of shape over the years.

Two tiny triangles of cheese and pickle later, Catherine had made me smile a few times with tales of her exploits. Seemed like she, too, picked the losers when it came to men. Bill, I felt, was going to be my turning point. That was, if he wanted to stick around after all this. Catherine and I had a bit in common, especially a liking for wine. Her company was making me feel better than I had in days. That and a combination of sitting indoors and resting for a bit. I was struggling to remember the last time I had just sat and watched telly or read a newspaper.

But we both reached the point where we knew that the inevitable couldn't be put off for much longer and there was a purpose to her visit. I saw her reach into her folder and take out her notebook. She took a deep breath and sat forward in the chair. I tried to get comfortable but it wasn't happening.

'You just talk and I'll write, and we'll see how we get on.' Catherine sat with her book open on her lap, arms still on the armrests, pen in her hand.

I looked up at the ceiling and began to verbalise a five-year-old's nightmare.

It was easier not to look at Catherine while I told her about my sister and me. I didn't expect to see pity or horror on her face but I couldn't take the chance. I had tried hard not to let what had happened affect my life, and being so young at the time had its advantages. The memories were old and belonged in a child's head, not that of a woman. As a child, the ghost train was scary. Now it wasn't. It was simply a matter of putting the whole episode into the 'cheap fairground' file in my brain. Then it didn't occupy my every waking moment, and mercifully I could get on with something resembling a normal life. I had certainly tried my utmost to enjoy myself over the past couple of decades.

When I came to the stuff about the photographs and how I took them to Sandra Beckensale, I looked at Catherine for the first time in many minutes. My neck was stiff from holding my head at an angle to avoid her dark eyes, and I noticed for the first time the noise of her fountain pen as it scratched its way across the page. I could see she had been writing furiously to keep up with me.

'You know about as much as I do, Catherine, about the pictures. I couldn't begin to guess where they'd come from. They spooked me so much because, for them to be taken by one person, he must have followed me for years. I'm guessing that there was more to Jake Lloyd than meets the eye.'

I watched her take that practised pause when she couldn't or wouldn't be able to answer. For just a second she glanced down at her notes, and then she met my stare head-on. 'They're still searching his house.' It was the only reply she was able to give.

I believed her. I also understood that she couldn't tell me what they were looking for or had found. It was quite likely to freak me out and impact on anything else I might have to say. Whatever it was gave me a bad feeling. I could see another bath with a sharp knife for company coming on.

My landline phone rang on the table next to me. I glanced at the display and leapt for it when I saw the number. By this time, my legs had gone numb from sitting on them and I slipped off the edge of the sofa making a grab for the phone, thrashing around a bit in my anxiety to speak to Stan.

'Hi, Stan. How are you?' The words in no way reflected what I wanted to say or how I wanted to say them.

'Hi, Nina. It's Samantha. He's doing OK but he's resting. He wanted me to call you as soon as he came out of theatre. It all went well but he's probably not up to any more visitors today.' Stan's daughter spoke softly, and hesitated before adding, 'They would only let me in for a few minutes. He didn't say much, just to call you.'

Despite the pins and needles in both my legs, I managed to twist away from Catherine. She had the good grace to make out as if she was looking through her notes for something but

I could feel the tears returning again. Catherine was probably already thinking I was a bit unhinged; I didn't want to labour the point.

'Thanks, Samantha. I really appreciate your call. I'll be in tomorrow to see him,' I said, remembering to add, 'if that's OK with you.' I didn't want to step on her toes but, whatever she said, I was going.

Catherine busied herself writing her notes while I made more tea and prodded the sandwiches to find the least curly-edged of the bunch. My stomach was growling at me. I supposed I felt better now that I knew Stan was out of surgery and on a slow mend. I thought about cracking open a bottle of Chianti; that would definitely complement a round of Coronation chicken. As I reached for the corkscrew, though, I remembered that I was probably still on duty and should leave getting off my face until the DS in the living room had left.

As I walked back to her, I could hear her Welsh accent as she talked in the hallway. Despite her lowered voice, I heard the words 'shrine in the cellar'.

I was more heavy-handed than usual with the teacups. Catherine looked over towards where I was standing. Her usually smooth forehead wore a frown and her red-lipsticked mouth had formed a tiny 'O'. She dropped the expression instantly.

Ending the call, Catherine explained that Eric Nottingham was on his way. He wanted to speak to me in person.

Chapter 37

Now don't get me wrong, I was only too aware that senior officers frequently spoke to the public and often had to break the worst news to victims, families and sometimes their own staff. However, not usually staff who had just found out that they'd had a stalker for half their life. Throw in the stalker's cousin who kidnapped children and hanged himself, and add a good measure of the stalker's aunt recently being murdered, and no suspect in custody, and my level of concern went up a notch.

I put the kettle back on. The DCI was bound to want tea.

The sound of the doorbell brought me from the kitchen to the living room. Catherine was up and out of her seat and tottering towards the hallway. I wouldn't be able to walk in heels that high. I stood waiting, palms a bit sweaty and too warm in my jumper. I should have got changed, put something else on. I moved to straighten a photograph on the wall.

I could hear a whispered exchange but couldn't make out any words this time. Probably just as well. Perhaps I had misheard earlier and my mind was playing tricks.

The heavy footsteps of the DCI were interspersed with the tapping of Catherine's impossible heels. The door was pushed open.

'Nina. I've got a few things to tell you about Jake Lloyd,' Eric Nottingham began. I pointed to a chair and sat back down on the sofa. He sat, pinching the pleats of his trousers, gathering the material to prevent creasing. The slight shift in the material lifted the hems and revealed Mr Men socks. I loved that. I looked up at his face and he winked at me. 'My children bought them for Father's Day.'

I smiled.

'We can't tell you everything that's going on, as I'm sure you'll appreciate. Jake Lloyd is in custody and being interviewed. In his house, we found...' He glanced at Catherine. I didn't take my eyes off him. 'Well, we found hundreds of photographs of you. Some look recent but others not so recent. It would seem that he'd destroyed some of them just prior to your arrival with Wingsy. The arresting patrol could smell burning and tracked it to a room off the kitchen where they found the remains of some photographs. It's likely he was watching you for some time. There were a substantial number of press cuttings, too, about you and your sister.'

He paused. He seemed to be taking it worse than me. I watched him pull at the knot of his tie with immaculate fingernails.

'Can you tell me what he's said in interview?' I asked.

The DCI took a deep breath, blew the air from his cheeks and said, 'He's still being interviewed but Lloyd claimed that he was "only looking out for you". He followed you because he was worried about you. His even crazier cousin was fixated with the story of you and your sister but according to Lloyd this was more because he was fascinated with what happened to you both – how it...' Another uncomfortable pause for Nottingham while he fidgeted in his seat until he added, 'How you were both – er – abducted.'

I filled in the words for him. I liked him and didn't want to see him struggle on my account. 'How it was orchestrated?'

'Yes, yes. That's it,' he enthused. 'How it was orchestrated.'

I was glad to have helped out.

'Jake Lloyd maintains that he was watching out for you and not out to do you any harm. You had any threats, break-ins, that kind of thing?'

'No, nothing at all. Funnily enough, until yesterday not even the feeling that I've been followed, but I clearly have. Now I'm concerned that someone's been in my house. Probably my imagination.'

'Thing is, Nina…' One more pause, a bit more trouser-arranging and a flash of Mr Tickle. 'Thing is, without anything further…'

Again, I went to his assistance, poor bloke. 'What I think you're trying to say, boss, is that, unless there's any further evidence against him, you're going to release him.'

He responded by dropping his head further forward and shaking it slowly. 'We're doing all we can to establish any links between him and the murders, but yes, basically…' He lent his elbows on the pressed folds of his trousers. I fought the urge to warn him of the danger of creasing them after all that effort.

'I understand, sir,' I reasoned. 'You can't do any more without further evidence. What do you both suggest I do?' I looked from Nottingham's lined face to Catherine's. And they looked at each other.

Chapter 38

My parents' house was not an option. I'd brought them enough pain over the years. My mum usually averted her eyes from mine on the occasions we met. Bringing more trouble to her door wasn't something I wished to heap upon her. Stan was completely out of the running. I thought about friends from outside of work, then Laura; I even contemplated Annie. In the end, I settled on a hotel. Nothing fancy, obviously as the taxpayer was footing the bill, but something with its own bar, or a pub next door. I wasn't fussy.

I packed a bag, got in my car and, waved off by Catherine, left for a fifteen-mile drive to a modest en-suite double. Leaving my own home didn't really please me very much but, while neither Catherine nor Nottingham could insist that I did, I didn't feel like arguing. Besides, I had no food in the house and thought that a trip to the busy restaurant feet from my hotel room for a medium grilled steak and bottle of Rioja might cheer me up a bit. I had to say, it did exactly that.

Wingsy phoned my mobile as I got back to my room from the bar.

'Heard what happened, Nin. As it currently stands, they're looking at no choice but to let him out with bail conditions not to come anywhere near you.'

'Yeah, totally understand, but now I'm in a hotel room and don't even have a bloke to share it with.'

'Which one are you in?'

'Can't tell you that. Security risk.'

'The Premier Inn, then.'

To be fair, it was where we put everyone.

'I'm only here for one night. I can't live here forever but they're just being cautious. Totally understandable.'

'When are you back at work, honey?'

'The DCI insisted that I have the rest of the week off and come back Monday. Not too sure what to do with myself for four more days. I can hear your kids in the background, Wingsy. Sounds busy there.'

'You can always babysit at the weekend.'

'I'll pass on that one, thanks.'

'Listen – ' he lowered his voice and the sound of siblings rowing lessened as if he had moved to another room ' – I have something for you and need to drop it round. Your place about noon tomorrow OK with you? It's just some stuff you left in the car.'

'Oh, thanks, Wingsy. I'm always doing that. See you in the morning.'

We both knew full well that I had not left anything in the car.

Chapter 39

26th September

Following a very comfortable night's sleep, I drove home, looking out for a grey Shogun all the way. I didn't think that Jake Lloyd would be that stupid, but I had met some inept criminals over the last fifteen years. Joe Bring came to mind. Shoplifting joints of beef by putting them in his boxer shorts had been his trademark for a while, prior to poultry. At least it got one over on those who bought cheap 'ask no questions' joints of meat in their local pub – their Sunday lunch had left the supermarket rubbing against someone's genitals.

I stopped off to get some shopping and a card for Stan. I bought him a couple of magazines and some grapes. Predictable, but I figured Pinot Grigio was not a viable option. I then drove to the hospital, excited at the thought of seeing my old friend but determined to make the effort not to talk about the photographs I'd received or the man arrested for his obsession with me. Last thing I wanted to do was to worry him.

I checked my phone as I was rushing across the hospital car park towards the main entrance, and re-read Samantha's text giving Stan's ward and bed number. I even felt slightly nervous about seeing Stan. I could only put that down to not knowing how he was feeling physically and what my own reaction would be to that. What exactly did happen when those you'd always relied on needed you?

Glancing up as I got to the entrance, I saw Eric Nottingham coming down the stairs into the main foyer. He was looking directly down the staircase and I was a little to his right. It was a huge hospital with dozens of wards, thousands of patients, and, had it not been for his earlier revelation that he knew Stan, I would have put it down to coincidence. Regardless, I turned sharply to my left and ducked behind the pay and display machines. Keeping out of sight until I saw him through the window behind me on his way to the car park, I stood for a moment, wondering if he'd been to see Stan, and why I'd hidden from his view. I was being a bit of a silly cow. I liked Nottingham and should have said hello. I'd avoided him to sidestep talking about work or Jake Lloyd, though. I was here to see Stan. I wanted nothing to overshadow that.

Grapes and magazines in hand, I followed the blue line which the map promised would take me to Stan. Don't cry, you silly moo, I thought to myself, as I buzzed the ward's intercom. I paused once inside the double doors to cover my hands in the gel that was supposed to stop infection. A gel that stopped cancer would be more use to us all, but one thing at a time. I made a bit of a meal of the gel-rubbing and concentrated hard on appearing cheerful.

Deep breaths and confident walking took me to Stan's bed. He was propped up, glasses on, reading a tabloid newspaper.

'Come all this way and you look like you're on a spa break.' I feigned annoyance.

He dropped the paper and put his arms out. We hugged. Me less hard, as I didn't know if he was in pain.

'Nina, I hope you haven't taken time off work. I'm probably going home later today.' His face was pale but he had just the same alert eyes and strong grip when he embraced me.

'Like I wasn't coming to see you. I got you some grapes, a gardening magazine and one about which celebrities are sleeping together.' I put them down on the table on wheels beside his bed.

He peered over at the cover. 'Am I supposed to know who any of these people are?'

'No, the shop was out of the geriatric edition. How are you feeling – how did it go?'

'It went very well and I feel quite good. The food wasn't as bad as I expected. You look pale. Are you eating?'

'Never mind about me. You're the one in hospital. What did the doctor say?'

'He's very pleased and, as long as I can get about, I'll be home later today. Samantha was here this morning and she's staying to look after me.'

This annoyed me but ridiculously so; she was his daughter, after all.

'Oh, and I had another visitor. Left just before you got here. Eric Nottingham.' He let the information sink in, watching my face. 'He wanted to catch up, make sure everything was going well for both me and for you. He's a decent man, you know. He cares about his staff. A dying breed. He and I go back years. We got to know each other years ago on a course. We have a similar outlook on life.'

Then Stan's sudden change of topic caught me off guard. This was a trick I liked to use myself.

'I understand that you spent last night in a hotel. I think you should tell me all about it.'

Chapter 40

Happier now that I'd seen Stan and knew that everything that could be done for him was being done, I drove home with the window down, singing along to the radio. It was a clear, crisp day and I needed some fresh air after the stale atmosphere of the hospital.

Once indoors, with the shopping put away, I had a bit of a tidy-up for Wingsy's arrival. I even hoovered. Each time I heard a car pull up, I drew back the curtain and peered into the street. It wasn't that I was anxious for his arrival, but I felt slightly worried in my own home alone. I couldn't live in fear of Lloyd but he clearly knew where I lived, as well as where I shopped, drank, parked at work and even that I used to wear a trilby in the late Eighties. That was possibly the most disturbing part.

After peeking out half a dozen times, I finally glimpsed Wingsy's Honda pull up three doors away. I nipped to the front door. He paused at the gate, opening it with one hand, a bulging carrier bag in the other. I saw the outline of a bottle of wine through the flimsy bag. I grinned at him and welcomed him in.

'Result, having a few days off,' said Wingsy once we were in the kitchen, waiting on the kettle.

'I suppose so,' I replied, opening the milk he'd brought.

'Got you a present, Nina.'

'Red wine by chance? You know me so well,' I chirped as I poured boiling water on to teabags.

'That, and something for you to watch in private.'

I turned to look at him, a frown on my face. I saw him reach into the bag and rustle his way to the bottom before pulling out a DVD in a white cardboard envelope.

'Is that what I think it is?' I asked.

He nodded and placed it on the kitchen work surface, sliding it across to me. Hand still on the top of the envelope, he added, 'You've never seen this and I didn't make you an extra copy and drop it off here. I haven't even seen it all myself so I don't know everything that's on it.'

I snatched it up and slid it into the nearest drawer, hiding it among a pile of teatowels.

'Thanks, mate. I – '

Wingsy put his hand over mine as I slammed the drawer shut. He leaned in close to my ear before saying, 'Nina, some of it's a bit disturbing. I'm only giving it to you because I think you should be aware of what's going on.' He removed his hand and retreated a step. 'He's still in custody.'

'What?' I said.

'Jake Lloyd. He's still in custody. They were talking last night about a Superintendent's Extension on his original twenty-four-hour detention time. If the super granted another twelve hours, he's staying in until at least this evening.'

'Then why did Nottingham send me to a hotel last night? That makes no sense.'

'It was getting fairly late and they had to make a decision. They wanted to make sure you were OK so they stuck to a plan that ensured you were out of harm's way. I'm not sure what triggered the extension on his detention. Mel was moaning so I had to go home. And I missed this morning's briefing. Leave it with me. I'll try to find out.'

'Wingsy, thanks for coming over,' I said. 'Is there any news from the Incident Room about the murders? I've been so caught up in the whole Jake Lloyd thing, it's only now I've taken a breath that I've begun to think again about three people slain with no obvious motive or suspect. Could the killer be Lloyd?'

I peered at his face, confident he wouldn't lie to me. If Lloyd was responsible for the murders as well as for watching my every move, he'd been one busy bloke. Even so, I needed to know.

His answer did little to put my mind at rest. 'It's a possibility.' He kissed me on the cheek and made his way to the front door.

'Wingsy,' I said with my hand on the latch, barring his way. 'During the briefing following Lloyd's arrest, did much else come out about him? Catherine and Nottingham have told me they were still searching, but was there anything else?'

'There was a bit about his finances. He's in TV production, travels a lot but it seems that his company's going to the wall. He made a few bad decisions on the work front and with personal investments, that kind of thing.' He broke eye contact with me again. I was a bit disappointed with my friend's reply. Talking about money seemed a bit gutless when there was bound to be more depraved stuff.

'Anything else?' I tried one last time.

'He took five grand in cash out over the counter at his bank on 13th September. The rest's still being worked on.'

After Wingsy had left, I cleared the cups away, put some washing on and got the hoover out. My mind continually returned to the disc in the drawer. Impossible to ignore it. Twice I got it out and twice I put it away. As I plugged the vacuum cleaner in, I remembered that I had already done this once today. Perhaps I was losing the plot. I remembered my Aunt Lou telling me about some of her cousins who were sectioned under the Mental Health Act, or whatever they had in her day. One thought he was a dog and used to bite people when they came to the front door.

Banishing such ridiculous thoughts, I bolted to the kitchen, pulled open the drawer and rushed back to the lounge. I had to watch the DVD whatever the consequences.

Frustrated at having to locate the remote under the chair cushion for the second time that week, convinced that I hadn't left it there, I put the disc into the player and sat cross-legged on the floor in front of the telly. The screen came to life, showing me a view of a police station interview room, Jake Lloyd centre stage. The two police officers in the room introduced themselves as DC Daniel Clark and DC Mark Russell.

The view of the interviewing officers was not clear, but it wasn't supposed to be. The voice of Daniel Clark was familiar and I thought back to the earlier briefing regarding Amanda Bell's finances and our visit to June and Donald Lloyd. I thought of the fresh-faced Danny and how his mum must be so proud. He had a good manner about him in interview and handled Jake Lloyd, who was at least fifteen years his senior, very well. Mark Russell I had seen in the Incident Room but hadn't got to speak to. He was the squad's only black officer and was new to the investigation, having just returned from honeymoon.

The first fifteen minutes were taken up with introductions, cautioning Jake and other legal formalities. While I knew it pretty much word for word, having said it hundreds of times myself in interviews, I sat transfixed throughout, watching the suspect's face. He remained calm and nodded away, answering politely when required to. By the time Danny and Mark started to ask him questions, I was sure that my legs had lost all feeling from sitting on the floor. I thought about moving but I was spellbound.

Lloyd was facing Danny when he asked, 'What can you tell me about the photographs sent to Detective Constable Nina Foster at her home address?' Danny held up a package and I heard a rustling. I processed the thought that the photos were now in a sealed evidence bag. 'These are the photos and are exhibit SB/1.' Sandra exhibited them, I thought; that's good of her.

'The photographs were ones I had taken of her, officer, but I didn't send them to her.' There was a pause. 'I told her this morning when she came to my house that I tried to make sure nothing would happen to her.' Lloyd shifted in his chair and looked straight up at the camera, as if he was speaking directly to me. 'I've looked after her for years.' He smiled. I ran to the bathroom and threw up.

Breakfast, fortunately had been light and I'd not had lunch. A few minutes later, I returned to the lounge. The DVD was still playing. I pressed pause and went to get some water and headache tablets. If I was going to watch the rest of the interview, I needed to get a grip. I made myself a sandwich and took it back to the sofa to rewind the part I had vomited through.

Remote in one hand and lunch in the other, I prepared myself to listen to whatever else Lloyd had to say. The best way forward, I reasoned, was to be objective and listen as if I had never met the man and as if the plethora of snapshots being referred to were not images of me. That was bound to work.

Mind back on the task and sandwich untouched, I pressed play. It got worse, so much worse.

Chapter 41

'Nina requires looking after. She's a very special person, you know? About three years ago in Sainsbury's car park, an old lady dropped her purse as she got into her car. Nina ran so fast through a line of cars, grabbed the purse and ran after the old lady as she drove away. She was so grateful she tried to give Nina some money.' Lloyd jabbed with his index finger at the surface of the wooden table dividing him from Danny and Mark. 'Know what? She refused, of course. Not that anyone would have ever found out. They were talking for a couple of minutes before Nina finally accepted a Swiss roll from the old lady's shopping.' Lloyd threw his head back and laughed. 'What a sweetie.'

It had been a really good Swiss roll, too. Reminded me of Sunday tea at my nan's when me and my sister were still able to row about who got the biggest slice. I'd never declared that Swiss roll to my senior officer. I panicked momentarily, thinking back on it. On duty it could have constituted a bribe. Would I be in trouble for accepting a Swiss roll? But I remembered the day clearly, and I was definitely not on duty so I was off the hook. Oh, and then I remembered – I really didn't care.

Lloyd continued to boast to the officers about how his job gave him freedom to travel, allowing him to follow me, and how I hadn't suspected a thing. He was quite right about that. Somehow it was impossible to even feel that frightened, despite knowing the truth. I had dissociated myself so completely from Lloyd, I was beginning to feel as if I was in a trance. I began to wonder why a bell was ringing in the interview, then, back in real time, jumped when I realised it was someone at my front door.

I hesitated in the hallway, pondering whether I should get a knife or simply not answer it.

'Nina,' called a male voice. 'It's me, Bill. You OK?'

I was good at voice recognition. It was Bill. I glanced in the hallway mirror. I was no Scarlett Johansson, but after the week I'd had I doubted that Scarlett Johansson would look too sassy. To be fair, her breath probably didn't smell of puke even on her worst days. I ran my tongue around my teeth and opened the door.

'Hey, Bill.' I attempted a seductive greeting but it sounded like I had a sore throat.

He frowned, a glimmer of concern, and said, 'You OK?' He peered over my shoulder. 'Can I come in?' He took a step forward.

I was sure I smelt of vomit, so I didn't want to let him in. But Bill was probably genuinely worried about me, and he might have thought that I was acting oddly because I was being held hostage. Knowing what I did about him, if I refused to let him in he would most likely dial 999 and a van of burly men would arrive.

And my television screen showed a police interview. A police interview I couldn't possibly possess without someone's help. This was much worse than an unpleasant odour.

'Course you can, Bill, but I am a bit tired. It's been a long week and the place is a mess.'

'Doesn't bother me. Been a single bloke for so long now that I doubt it's any worse than I'm used to.'

There was something about his smile and the ever-so-slight tilt of his head. I failed to recall if I'd always liked men with dark wavy hair or if he was the exception. In my hand, I had the remote control. If I let him in, and walked into the lounge ahead of him, I could turn the television off as I entered and he wouldn't see the interview. I could then put the kettle on, go to the bathroom and clean my teeth for the second time since I'd sat down to hear what Lloyd had to say. My plan was foolproof.

I moved out of the doorway and muttered something about making tea. I managed to turn the screen off before he got in the lounge. I crossed to the kitchen, filled the kettle and called, 'I won't be two minutes,' before heading for the stairs. Then, satisfied that I had much improved breath, I returned to the lounge to find Bill in the armchair and two mugs of tea on the coffee table.

'Made yours with milk, no sugar. That's right isn't it?'

'Thanks, Bill. Great to see you. Don't think I've ever seen you out of work before.'

'I've seen you a couple of times,' he replied before picking up his drink. For crying out loud, please don't let him be another stalker, I thought, and it must have shown on my face. Realising what he'd just said, he blanched, put his cup down without taking a sip and ran his fingers through his hair. 'That came out wrong, I'm sorry. I've been in town and you've gone into a shop as I've been coming out, that kind of thing.'

'I know what you meant, Bill. Please don't apologise.' As if I could be annoyed with Bill.

'I just wanted to make sure that you were OK. You looked shaken up yesterday when we got to Lloyd's house. I would have called round last night but I saw that Welsh DS and she said that you were staying somewhere else.'

'Not a boyfriend's house,' I blurted out. 'The Premier Inn, just the Premier Inn. The Premier Inn, on my own.'

By now he had probably grasped that I'd stayed at the Premier Inn.

He winced as he drank his tea. Mine was still very hot but he seemed to be prepared to take the impending mouth ulcers and oral numbness – anything to get away. While he was getting some feeling back in his lips, I said. 'We used to bump into each other all the time when I worked in the office downstairs.'

'I'm glad I keep seeing you. I'm even more pleased that you don't have one of those wicker bars stocked with Babycham.'

'How do you know? You haven't been in the bedroom yet.' I blushed. We both looked at our drinks.

Bill stood up to leave. I seemed to be ruining my chances here. It had been easier to talk to him on the phone, though the last day or so might have played a part in the tension I sensed developing between us. He turned to face me and said, 'How about that drink in the next couple of days?'

'That would be great, Bill.' I grinned at him.

With his hand on the lounge door-handle, he paused and said, 'I'll call you in the morning.'

'Can't wait.' I followed him to the front door. As he opened it, he hesitated. I supposed it was difficult for men: if you tried a kiss at this stage, it might seem too pushy; if you didn't, it might be construed as lack of interest. He probably didn't want to come across as some sort of creepy weirdo turning up on my doorstep having found out about Lloyd's antics and then trying to snog me.

Turned out that wasn't the cause of his hesitation.

'This probably won't mean much to you right now,' said Bill, 'but on the way back to the nick Jake Lloyd kept telling me how he'd never hurt you. He claims everything he did was his deluded way of making sure you were alright.'

I could tell from the way Bill had started to move from one foot to the other that what he was saying was making him uncomfortable. I assumed he wanted to tell me without sounding as if he was condoning Lloyd's behaviour.

'Are you sure you're OK by yourself tonight, Nina?' He looked down at his feet. 'Sorry, that was forward-sounding, especially as I've probably scared you half to death. What I meant was, are you sure that you don't want me to drive you to a friend's or relative's house? Or – er – the Premier Inn?'

'Really, I'm fine. Put up with a lot more in the past.'

'In that case, goodnight, but call if you need anything at all.' He stepped out of my house. 'And we'll definitely go for that drink some time,' he said as he backed away down the concrete path.

I waved him off and shut the door on the world. As I paused at the hallway mirror, I said out loud, 'Top that, then, Scarlett Johansson. Don't know who you're going to the pub with, but I bet he's no Bill Harrison.'

Chapter 42

Smiling, I went back to the living room. The remote control was still on the coffee table. Of course – the interview. Surely even that couldn't ruin my present mood. Trouble was, I had no idea how much worse the content was going to get.

I sat back on the sofa and continued watching Lloyd tell all to Danny and Mark with hardly any effort on their part. Lloyd talked and talked. Most of it was about me and how he'd followed me home, especially on evenings when I'd gone out with friends and had a good drink. Turned out he was worried that I would meet someone dangerous when I was too inebriated to take care of myself. The story of the old lady dropping her purse in the car park was the tip of the iceberg. He knew just about every detail of my life: the part-time job I'd had when I was at school; where I went to the dentist; boyfriends I'd had, including the Russian loser, and that I'd tried ice-skating a few times but got annoyed when I'd continually fallen over and injured myself. His concern even appeared genuine when he recalled the time I head-butted the ice. There seemed to be nothing he didn't know about me. Throughout the interview, he maintained that he meant me no harm but had been watching over me.

Bill might have been right, but I still felt my flesh crawl at the thought of Jake Lloyd being my guardian angel.

According to Lloyd, it couldn't be harassment as I hadn't known he was watching me. Legally, he did have a point. Problem I had was that he had been doing it for over twenty years and I hadn't had a clue.

Four o'clock. Bit early for a drink.

Being at home by myself was unsettling. I still had a feeling of being watched but knew how little sense that made with Jake Lloyd still in custody. I glanced over to the windowsill at the old photo of my sister and me as kids, wearing our favourite outfits. Hers was a short-sleeved yellow sundress; mine was a white T-shirt underneath red dungarees.

The clothes we'd been wearing.

My mum never liked anyone wearing red and white together. She said it was a bad omen – blood and bandages. I often wore red and white these days. I liked to defy demons. Made you stronger, sometimes.

My mobile jolted me through three and a half decades to the present day.

'Hello, mate. What you up to?' I asked Wingsy, answering the phone.

'Just been speaking to the DCI,' he informed me. 'Your friend Jake Lloyd.' Wingsy paused. 'He's about to be charged with murder.'

'Murder? His aunt Daphne?' I was incredulous.

'No, not Daphne,' came the hushed reply. 'His cousin, Scott.'

'He hanged himself in 2004, didn't he? We read the report together. He left a suicide note and everything.'

'Listen, Nin, I can't say too much here. I've been advised not to talk to you – '

'Why on earth shouldn't you talk to me? I've done nothing wrong.'

'No, you have to understand, everyone is very nervous at the moment. The whole nick is tense. CPS authorised the charge minutes ago. There are still three unsolved linked murders and the only death we've detected was nine years ago, one that everyone thought was a suicide. DCI's doing his fucking nut.'

'Why is Lloyd being charged now, after all this time, Wingsy?'

'Got to go. Call you later. Promise.'

The line went dead. I slumped back against the sofa. I had to find out why Lloyd was charged with Scott's murder. It was unlikely that I would get any answers from the DCI. I thought about calling Catherine and decided that was unfair. If Wingsy didn't want to talk to me in the open, she'd hardly be prepared to.

Now it was half-four, I uncorked a bottle of red. Figured that letting my hair down was safe with my very own stalker remanded in custody. I looked through the news for an update, but I didn't really expect a press release yet. From what Wingsy had told me, it sounded as if the charge was being read to Lloyd at the custody desk as I channel-hopped.

Steadying myself for another dose of Jake Lloyd, I resumed watching the interview. From Danny and Mark's body language, I got the impression that they were fairly comfortable with everything he had said and were striking up a rapport with him. I sat transfixed as Lloyd said, 'Thank you, officers, but I have to tell you about the death of my cousin. It was all to protect Nina Foster, you know. By killing him I was doing the world a service.' Simultaneously, Danny, Mark and I all leaned closer to Lloyd, them on the screen, me on my sofa.

I pressed 'pause' and topped up my glass. Of course, alcohol solved nothing, but I liked it. The self-satisfied smirk on his face was too much. I'd briefly imagined myself living in the crazy bastard's house! I really did have bad taste in men.

Diane Lloyd had used the same expression – 'doing the world a service'. I tried to call Wingsy but now his phone was off. I chewed my lip. A terrible habit.

It was an unusual phrase to use but I mulled over the possibility that it was a well-used phrase within the family. The thought that members of the same family might have conspired to murder each other was fanciful, something I could not even comprehend. I was well aware how crime ripped a family's fabric at the seams.

However, I allowed myself the freedom to consider that, if the Headingly-Lloyds had been in on it together, Diane Lloyd could have murdered her own sister after all, despite the reservations I had had earlier when speaking to June. The nagging doubt then was that the three unsolved murders had been committed by more than one person.

I followed this line of thought like a detective. I glugged my wine like a woman with a stalker embroiled in a murder investigation.

Myself and Wingsy knew the words that Diane had used, but so much had happened, I couldn't remember if we had recorded them verbatim in our report of our visit to her. I paced my living room carpet, glass of dwindling wine in hand, weighing up how any of this fitted together. Chances were Wingsy could answer that. I tried his phone again. It was still switched off.

I pressed 'play'.

Lloyd initially sat very still, unblinking. After several seconds he said, 'Scott was out of hand. He was getting worse. He kidnapped two children. We spoke little then, but after he went to prison I had to ask him why he did it. You see, officers, it should have been enough to follow the Foster girls' case in the papers. There was never a need for him to try to re-enact it.' Lloyd's head moved from right to left as he searched the interviewing officers' faces for some kind of praise for his actions.

'Officers,' he said, 'I'm getting the sense that you don't appreciate what I've done. Scott was dangerous. Sooner or later he would have killed someone. I stopped him the only way I could. I'd done my research, you see. I even went to speak to Henry Bastow.'

At the mention of the name, I reached my trembling hands towards the remote once more. Had Jake Lloyd any idea what he was doing to my sanity? Just hearing his name gave Henry Bastow permission to invade my brain, my sanctuary, my soul. Lloyd had summoned up the devil. My devil, anyway. Fingers fumbling at the buttons, I stopped the DVD. This time I needed help.

Fighting to get my breathing back under control, I found the strength to move. There was only one thing for it: I was going to have to find out what was going on through official channels.

It would take all my willpower to pull myself together, to stop my voice from giving me away over the phone. I had to put on a braver front than I felt was possible: I couldn't know that Jake Lloyd's interview contained the two words guaranteed to render me useless unless someone had leaked the contents to me. Selling Wingsy out to Nottingham was not an option. But being a sitting duck wasn't an idea I relished either.

I called Catherine. I heard a male voice say, 'Catherine's phone. Ray Hopkinson speaking.'

'Hello, Ray,' I said, voice wobbling more than I'd have liked. 'It's Nina Foster. Is Catherine able to speak – or perhaps you can help me?'

After a very brief pause, Ray said, 'I can't see her. How are you?'

'Oh, yeah, I'm fine,' I lied. I hardly knew the man so I wasn't going to elaborate. 'I was just wondering what had happened with Jake Lloyd. I heard he was being released.'

'Hang on,' he said before I heard muffled speech as if he had put his hand over the mouthpiece. I could hear his voice and another very faint male voice, then the sound of the phone being handed over.

'Nina, Eric Nottingham here. How are you?'

'Hi, boss. I'm good, thanks. What about Jake Lloyd? Where is he?' I asked.

'Still here. He's been charged with the murder of Scott Headingly. I'm sending Catherine over to see you and explain. Are you at home?' asked Nottingham.

'Yes, I am.' I knew not to ask too many questions. But there was one thing I did need to know. 'Sir…' I paused, took a deep breath and, feeling someone walk over my grave, said, 'Could you check on Bastow for me? Make sure he's staying put?'

'Nina, I checked yesterday. He's not going anywhere,' said Nottingham. I hung up without saying goodbye, which I hated doing, but my tears were waterlogging the mouthpiece.

While waiting for Catherine's arrival, I called Stan. He was never out of my thoughts.

When he answered, 'Hello, Nina, how are you?' I choked back tears.

'I'm OK, Stan,' I said. 'Think I'm coming down with a cold. That's why I probably sound a bit funny. How are you feeling?'

'Very well, and very optimistic. The doctors are pleased with my progress and I have some further check-ups in a few days. Samantha is here tonight and said she would stay to look after me for as long as she can. But frankly, Nina, she's tired. Sorry to impose on you but any chance you could come and stay with me for a day or two? You don't need to do anything. It would just make her feel better knowing that you're here.'

'Course I can, Stan. Glad to be able to help,' I said. I didn't want to be alone but I wouldn't have dreamt of asking Stan if I could stay with him. Being asked to visit suited me just fine. 'I can come over tomorrow if that fits with you. I have a couple of days off. I'll be over some time after midday – I'll call you to tell you exactly when.'

'Thank you, Nina. I look forward to it,' said Stan. 'That cold of yours isn't sounding too bad.'

Well, it wouldn't now, would it? I'd stopped crying.

Chapter 43

Not long after I ended my conversation with Stan, I tried Wingsy's mobile once more, cursing him for not leaving it on. I was going to be having a few words with Wingnut when I saw him. I then busied myself waiting for Catherine to arrive by packing for a couple of days at my old friend's house.

I'd barely placed the basics into my overnight bag when the doorbell rang, and I ran downstairs to answer it. I heard two female voices on the doorstep.

'Nin, it's Laura,' said one of them.

I took the security chain off, opening the door to her and Catherine standing side by side. Laura reached forward, embracing me. I felt Catherine's hair brush my arm and looked up to see her glancing up and down the street.

'Please, girls, come in,' I said. Catherine was making me nervous.

I led the way to the living room after bolting the front door. Couldn't quite place my anxiousness. Once settled, I said to Catherine, 'Was it Ray Hopkinson, that new DS, who gave you my message, or Nottingham?'

'Both of them really,' she answered. 'Ray told me you'd called after Eric asked me to come and see you. I've known Ray a few years. He's a decent enough bloke. Anyway, we're here to give you an update on Lloyd.'

Laura and Catherine both held my gaze. Tough call for Laura, more so than for Catherine. As my friend it was an uncomfortable position for her to be placed in. No doubt she'd volunteered to visit me, though, no matter how it made her feel. Two intelligent faces, one story. Laura began.

'Jake Lloyd was going to be released from custody. When Mr Nottingham and Catherine came to see you that was the plan. That was why they recommended that you stay in a hotel.'

'Just so you know, you were never on your own,' Catherine added. 'We were going to follow him, to see if he came back here, and then arrest him.'

That didn't really make me feel all that much better.

'As the evening wore on,' Laura continued, 'as the interviewing officers were finishing up, Lloyd suddenly began talking about how his cousin died. He rambled on for ages. They'd almost given up on him but then he came out with how he murdered Scott. He gave details, lots of details, and spoke about the clothing he wore when he killed him. Lloyd told us that he took it to his aunt Diane's house and told her he'd spilled oil from his car on his top and jeans, and asked her to be so kind as to burn them.'

'Are we really going to believe him?' I asked.

Catherine shrugged her shoulders and said, 'Diane was spoken to and confirmed what he said. It's the DCI's decision not to arrest her.' I watched her repeatedly tap her pen against the notebook in her lap.

'But you would have nicked her?' I guessed.

'Boss's call on that one. That's why he's in charge,' said Catherine.

Laura was sitting back on the sofa, out of Catherine's view. I saw Laura nod and mouth the words, 'I would.'

To hide my smile, I put my hands across my face, breathing in heavily.

When I took my hands away, my words crashed out with my breath. 'What was in Lloyd's cellar?'

My sudden swerve of questioning had the effect I intended: they appeared momentarily stunned. The truth came from their eyes and manipulated their expressions. I

160

read repulsion, disbelief, wonder. Whatever Lloyd had been housing was obviously monumental compared to a couple of hundred photographs.

One of you speak, I thought. It really can't have been that bad.

They glanced at one another before Catherine placed her pen down and said, 'He had some of your belongings.'

I was only aware I was dangerously close to the edge of my chair when I felt my knees begin to ache. As I shuffled myself backwards, I realised that my mouth was hanging open. I didn't want to start dribbling; I might still end up in secure accommodation if I didn't pull myself together. All I managed to say was, 'Belongings?'

'Clothes. We know they were your clothes because they were the ones you were wearing in some of the photographs he had on the wall.'

At some point, I must have said, 'What?' because I heard myself say it along with a sniff from Laura as she wiped her eyes with a tissue. Catherine continued, 'We also found children's clothes, some of them identical to those you and your sister were found in. He had old photos and newspaper reports describing the clothing. Some of the items had traces of blood on them. We're testing it to see if it belonged to you.'

I managed to say, 'Are you telling me he actually had the clothes Sara and I were wearing when...' I put my hands over my face once more, I couldn't recall the last time I had said my sister's name.

'No, no, no,' said Catherine. 'It's likely those would have been destroyed along with everything else, other than the paperwork and forensics. They may be replicas. We're looking into it.'

'What about the other clothes?'

'We don't know. I'm sorry, Nina, but we just don't know. We think he's been in your house. We're not sure. We want to bring a CSI here, if you agree.'

'Fuck...' I found myself standing up. I wanted to shout at Catherine, call Nottingham, shout at him. None of it would help or give me the answers I needed. I went to make tea. Wine was never an angry option.

Having given me a minute to calm down, Laura and Catherine followed me into the kitchen. With my back to them as I filled the kettle, I said, 'Sorry. This is too much for me to take in. I have things to get done. I'm visiting someone this evening and staying at a sick friend's tomorrow. What do you want from me now?' I turned, searching both their faces.

Catherine said, 'We need a statement, but not necessarily right now. In the morning?' She knew that I'd do whatever she asked of me. It wasn't in my nature not to. Besides, I was still a police officer. I had little choice.

Laura stepped nearer to me and said, 'I've got my stuff in the car if you want me to stay over. Else you're welcome to stay at mine.'

I declined. Jake Lloyd, my only demon at large, wasn't going anywhere. And just the offer from her was enough to get me through the evening.

I showed Laura and Catherine out. Earlier I'd craved company; now I felt relieved to be alone again. Bereavement could do that to a person. My childhood was dead. I wouldn't allow it to haunt me.

So many questions were tumbling around in my head but I felt unable to cope with the answers. I promised to call them in the morning and I insisted that I would go to the nick myself the next day to make my statement. This would be my chance to get back to work, speak to friends and colleagues, generally be a nuisance.

Attempting to put all morbid thoughts from my mind, and my packing for Stan's complete, I took myself off to the supermarket to stock up for Annie. She'd left a couple of messages for me, full of swear words, asking where I was. The spelling in her text messages was dreadful but she always got the four-letter words correct somehow. I texted her to tell her that I was on my way. The reply was '*Bout fucking time. Fort u were dead.*' I laughed in spite of the turmoil I felt myself being drawn into.

Shopping complete, I drove to Annie's and pulled up around the corner away from her house, as was my usual drill. I was surprised to see a new BMW in the driveway. Annie couldn't drive and I'd only once before seen a car on her driveway: on the day her husband was arrested for attempted murder. My mind filled with hazy images of a marked police vehicle on the tarmac and an ambulance across the drive. I walked back to her house from my car with two carrier bags of quality foodstuffs, not at all sure what was coming next.

A man opened the front door to me.

Chapter 44

As I got nearer to the figure at the door, my mind carried out a speedy run-down of likely people. I figured it must be a relative or friend of hers. I tried to place her two sons. It was a number of years since I'd last clapped eyes on them. They were both local but kept out of trouble with the police, or managed to avoid arrest at least. One was twenty-five and the other was thirty-three. This one had to be the eldest.

'Nina. Long time, no see,' said the man. 'The old girl was worried about you.'

As I was about to reply, Annie's tiny frame appeared under his arm as it held the door open. 'Worried, bollocks. What are you telling her that for, Richard?'

Richard – of course it was: number one son. He rolled his eyes, opening the door for me.

'Hello, Richard. Good to see you,' I said. It was partly true. He was a kickboxer and welcoming me into his mum's home. This could only be good news for me. I had told Annie what time to expect me, so her son being here was no coincidence.

Premium delectables unpacked and put away, I made my way to the front room with Annie. She seemed a bit tense: she'd only taken the piss out of me once. Richard was already sitting in the armchair, hands in the pockets of his hooded tracksuit top, left knee jiggling up and down. I decided to prompt him. It seemed the decent thing to do.

'Richard, it must be years since we've met. How are things with you?'

'Thing is, right,' he answered, left knee motionless, 'you never got this from me. I'll deny talking to ya, seeing ya. Got it?'

'Yeah. Got it,' I said.

Richard glanced at his mum. Annie was inspecting her fingernails.

'Those three murders over your way... heard some stuff,' he said.

Interview trainers would call my reaction 'guggling'. Don't bother to look it up. It's not really a word. I just sat there nodding and making interested noises without saying a thing. It required no acting skill on my part.

It seemed to work as, after only a few seconds, Richard said, 'It's a foreigner. You know, like, not English. From abroad.'

'Richard,' I said, 'what makes you say that?' I really wanted to say, *I know what a bloody foreigner is.* The thing with sarcasm and police officers, though, was that we weren't supposed to use it. Not in front of the public anyway.

He glanced at his mum again. I continued to look at him, keeping silent.

'I've heard that some bloke from Europe's been killing people and slicing them up. Sick bastard. You know I wouldn't normally talk to the police. Murder's bad enough but this is out of order. I can't tell you where that came from. What I can tell you is that that old lady, Daphne, she used to do a lot of work in children's homes and stuff like that. Friend of mine knew her when he was a kid and said she taught him to read and write when the school had given up on him. Even helped him get his first job. You know, application forms and interviews and stuff like that.'

Richard paused. I wasn't sure if there was more to come, so I waited. After a few more seconds, I risked a question.

'How can I find out who this foreigner is?'

'Dunno,' said Richard. 'Only heard he was foreign, not from round here.'

165

'I appreciate what you've told me,' I said, 'but there are a lot of foreigners in and around the county. He may not even still be here. Do you know what country he came from?'

'France or Spain, I think – maybe Portugal,' Richard said.

Cheers, I thought, that narrows it down. For a minute, I thought that the task was impossible.

'Can you tell me who you heard this from?' I asked.

'No, like I said, can't tell you. It's just gossip, that part,' said Richard.

Annie stood up, muttering something about custard creams.

As soon as she shut the door behind her, I said, 'I need more than this to find him. If you're worried about talking to me, it can be someone else, you know. At another location, away from anyone who may know you.'

'Yeah, we used to call them grasses. Now they get a couple of quid and you've given them a fucking stupid name, trying to make them sound like anything other than a grass,' he said. I could see his knee begin to move up and down again. 'No, I'll tell you what I know now and that's the end of it. I heard that some fella's come over from France or wherever it was, killed them people, cut them up badly and may still be here in England. He's shacked up with some local bird he's been knocking off. Don't know why he's done it or if there's gonna be more. I really don't know any more than that.'

'What's your friend's name – the one that knew Daphne?' I asked.

For the first time since I entered the living room, Richard took his hands out of his pockets. He unclenched his left fist to reveal a scrap of paper in his palm and held it out to me. The paper contained the name 'Charlie' and a mobile phone number. While I was reading the number, checking for legibility, Richard stood up. 'See ya,' he muttered as he left the room.

'Thanks,' I said.

He paused before turning. 'Like I said already, didn't see ya and didn't speak to ya.'

The front door slammed. I heard the sound of the car on the driveway start as Annie came back into the room with a packet of biscuits, complaining about her heating and how it made a terrible noise. I took the cue that there was to be no more mention of her son who had just passed me a lead on a serial killer.

I spent another hour or so at Annie's listening to her moan about the weather and other trivia. She still made me laugh frequently, and the time passed quickly. As I was leaving, she walked with me to the front door. Annie grabbed my arm and said, 'Listen, Nina. You've always looked out for me; when my old man knocked me about, put an iron in my face, you tried to do what you could to keep my boys on the straight and narrow. Make sure you're careful. That's all I'm saying.'

'Thanks, Annie,' I said, placing my hand over hers, which was still gripping my bicep.

Chapter 45

27th September

At 8.30am on the dot, I left for the police station. I'd even managed to leave an open bottle of wine in the fridge the night before, so I wasn't hungover. It was a small matter but one that made me proud.

As I made my way into the yard, I passed Nottingham's car parked in the senior investigating officer's bay. I'd decided that I was going to speak to him about staying on the enquiry before writing my statement. I felt a bit strange letting myself into the nick and making my way to the DCI's office, but I had every right to be there. Technically I was doing nothing wrong. I wasn't suspended; I wasn't banned from the building. I'd merely been given a few days off because I had a stalker who was currently remanded for murdering his sexual deviant cousin. There was probably no precedent for such an occasion. The boss didn't really know what category to fit me into.

Any day soon I expected to be sent to work elsewhere, far away from this enquiry. Problem was – the DCI had said it himself – chances were that none of us would ever work on anything like this again. I didn't want to be back interviewing shoplifters when I could be working on a series of murders, and I needed to keep busy. I wondered if the officers who came looking for me and my sister in 1976 got the same personal satisfaction from a job well done? The likelihood was that they had. We were only human.

In order to avoid seeing anyone, I'd chosen the furthest, quietest corridor of the nick. The thoughts of my childhood rescuers had slowed my feet until I found that I had come to a stop outside Alf's room. I could hear his voice, and curiosity made me listen at his door. A second male voice was answering a question I hadn't heard. 'Not sure, Alf. Any time soon but it's looking like the next couple of days.' I'd heard that voice before but I couldn't place it. Something wasn't right. I felt the hairs on the back of my neck prickle.

Only one thing for it. 'Alf,' I called as I opened the door. Alf was standing next to the boiler, metal door open, throwing something inside. On the other side of the room, sitting on a wooden chair with one of its arms missing, was Tony, Belinda Cook's visitor.

'Nina,' said Alf. 'Come in. This is Tony. He's just given me a lift into work.'

'Hello, Tony,' I said, venturing into the room but still close to the door. I didn't feel threatened, since I was in a police station, but this was very unexpected. 'How do you two know each other?' I asked.

'Me and Alf go back years, don't we?' said Tony before Alf could say a word.

I directed my words to Alf but didn't take my eyes off his visitor. 'Tony and I have met. He's been interviewed as part of Operation Guard.'

'The murders? Have you, Tony?' said Alf. 'Didn't know about that.'

'Yeah. I've been staying from time to time with Belinda, Amanda Bell's cousin,' said Tony. He looked from Alf to me and said, 'Always happy to help. You're just lucky to catch me in the country. Anyway, it was great to catch up with you, Alf. I'd better be going.'

Tony stood up and Alf said, 'I'll see you out of the building.' He shut the metal boiler door and searched in his pocket for his keys. 'Better lock up while I'm gone,' he said, as a polite way of telling me to leave his office.

Still mulling over the conversation, I walked up the staircase towards Eric Nottingham's temporary office. Wingsy's words about Alf disposing of dead people in the nick's boiler came to mind. And there were those noises I'd heard in the office next to the briefing room last week. I dismissed the idea for a second time as it was totally insane. Alf was not a murderer. Why would he be murdering people and biting them? Why would anyone be murdering people and biting them?

Chapter 46

The door to Nottingham's office was open, the DCI sitting behind his desk. The sunlight showed up the grey in his hair. He glanced up as I appeared in the doorway, and smiled at me.

'Hi, boss,' I said. 'You OK? You look like you've been up all night.'

'Come in, Nina. Shut the door and have a seat. Yes, I pretty much have been. Anyway, I wanted to talk to you about Jake Lloyd. You're aware that he's been charged and remanded for his cousin's murder, plus charged with harassment offences against you? He's not going anywhere. I've no problem with you speaking to Danny and Mark, the interviewing officers. There may be some stuff they can't tell you, such as why he's still refusing to admit to posting those photos.'

'I was thinking about that. Crazy sod probably thinks he'll get more for some sort of postal telecommunications offence than for following me for decades,' I said.

This caused an uncomfortable silence between us for a couple of seconds until I continued. 'Boss, I've got loads I need to tell you.'

I watched him shift back in his seat and place his elbows on the armrests, fingertips together. His expression was neutral. An image of a television DCI came to mind, one who would swear, shout, tell their staff to get out of their office unless they'd just nicked the murderer. Maybe that was what he really wanted to do, but, all credit to him, the bloke hadn't slept yet here he was listening attentively to a detective he hardly knew. I sat in the vacant chair the other side of his desk, and pulled a piece of paper out of my handbag, realising as I did so that I'd been clutching my bag on my lap. I slid the paper across to him. He studied the handwritten sheet.

'I wrote this out last night,' I explained, letting go of my handbag strap to indicate the piece of paper. 'Someone stopped me in the street late yesterday afternoon. Don't know who he was but he must have known I was a police officer 'cos – as you can see from my notes – this anonymous source said that the murderer was from somewhere in Europe and is living with a local woman. Also gave the contact number of someone who knew Daphne Headingly.'

'You're telling me that you don't know the source of this information, Nina?' he asked.

'No, boss. White male, aged thirty or so, average height, average build, jeans, black jacket. He stopped me in Brewer Street yesterday, market day,' I said.

'Brewer Street yesterday, market day,' he repeated, a smile playing around the corners of his mouth.

I nodded. He knew as well as I did that it was the borough's notorious black spot known for its lack of CCTV. Cameras were planned for the next financial year.

'And you were both on foot?' he asked, with a hefty raise of his eyebrows this time.

'I'd driven to the town to go to the supermarket cashpoint. Then I fancied a walk, and that's when he stopped me and gave me that information and that phone number.' Leaving nothing to chance, I actually had gone to town on the way back from Annie's the previous day, in case they checked the cameras looking for my car. 'He was on foot. Didn't see which way he went when he left.' I let go of the paper.

'OK. Thanks, Nina.'

Then I hesitated. Not wanting to make trouble for Alf but feeling disturbed at having seen him with Tony Birdsall, I weighed up what I was about to say. 'One other thing, boss. Just saw Tony Birdsall in the building.'

Nottingham looked momentarily puzzled before saying, 'Amanda Bell's cousin's associate.' He was good. So far we'd traced and spoken to something in the region of four hundred people on the enquiry, and that didn't include the ones we were still looking for, but with only a second's hesitation he'd found the information as quickly as the HOLMES computer system could have.

I nodded. 'He was talking to Alf, the caretaker, in his office. They know each other. Don't think that Alf's up to anything. He seemed to be genuinely surprised that Tony had been spoken to by the enquiry team. Thought you should be aware.'

I examined the edge of the desk to avoid his eyes.

'There's something else.' He said this as more of a statement than a question.

'There is.' I peered up at him. 'You gave me a few days off. I'm grateful. But I'll be back at 8am on Monday.'

He repositioned his fingertips against his desk edge before saying, 'Don't be late. We've a stack of work, but I want you to speak to Ray about continuing to work on this enquiry.'

I exhaled a little louder than I anticipated, so I stood up, attempting to mask the noise. 'Oh, and Nina...' I froze, half-crouching above the seat. 'Give my best to Stan this evening.'

'Thanks, sir,' I said, heading for the door.

As I turned my back to him, I frowned as I remembered that I hadn't called Stan as I'd promised.

Speaking to the DCI had gone as well as I'd hoped but I still had to contend with Ray. I made my way to the Incident Room to catch up with Wingsy and Laura before fighting my corner with the DS.

As I entered the Incident Room, Ray Hopkinson was standing with his back to me. I heard him say to Laura, 'Come here, you saucy, goddess. How about I take you home and lock you in my basement?' Laura's face broke into a huge grin and the others nearby began to laugh. My initial reaction was to smile, join in as I normally would. Only the circumstances weren't normal any more. The instant Laura saw me, her grin was replaced with a sympathy smile. Ray moved to see what had drawn her attention, and the others who had gathered sloped off to do some work or turned in their chairs back to their computer screens. The only one who acted as if nothing was out of place was Wingsy.

'Nina, you old tart,' he said. 'Glad you could make it. What's with the jeans and Christmas jumper?' I could have kissed him. In fact, I did.

'Christmas jumper, you knobhound?' I said. 'It's cashmere.'

Ray, in a quick recovery or total ignorance, said to me, 'Ah, Nina. Perhaps you could help me out, I was just making a bet with Laura that we'll have these murders solved within a month. If I lose she gets to peek into my pants; if she loses, she has to get her bangers out.'

'Sounds like a win-win situation for Laura,' I said. 'You making tea, Wingsy?'

'Looks like I am,' he said, heading off to the kitchen. I indicated that I wanted Laura to follow us and the three of us piled into the tiny kitchen.

'How have you been, Nin?' said Wingsy.

'I'm OK, thanks, mate. Don't worry about me, I'm pretty tough, you know,' I said.

'Clearly you are,' said Laura. 'I had no idea about you and your sister. I'm not prying, but, for God's sake, when you got those photos through the post you must have been beside yourself.'

I felt exhausted suddenly, and sagged against the sink. 'It's the clothing, Lol. That got to me the most. I just need an explanation about how he got it, and if they're the original clothes we were wearing, or... oh, you know...'

'Wingsy and I will find out and let you know. It was good that you've come back in today to catch up with everyone,' said Laura. 'How about the three of us grab a beer tonight and we'll update you on any progress? Can't really talk here.'

Wingsy broke off from making the tea, saying, 'I'll check with Mel. I'm sure she won't mind if it's not a late one.'

'Good plan,' I said, 'I'm at Stan's for a couple of days but he'll probably be pleased if I leave him alone for a while.'

'I've never met Stan,' said Laura. 'Do you think he'll fancy joining us?'

'I can always ask him,' I said. 'Not sure he'll be up to leaving the house, but that's his call.'

When the tea was made, the three of us walked back into the Incident Room. I felt we'd given them all enough time to talk about me, warn each other not to make further kidnap-related remarks, and take down anything from the boards and walls I wasn't supposed to see. I risked approaching Ray, who was seated in a corner of the office on a bank of desks, to ask how much longer it was likely to be before the children's clothes in Lloyd's cellar could be authenticated.

'Might be a while. It's like this, sweetheart,' said Ray. 'Backlog at the lab, lack of funding, job's running over budget and staff going off missing for days on end – like you. When are you back?'

'Monday. Wasn't my idea. Rather be here,' I said.

'I'd rather you were here too, you little firecracker,' he replied with a wink.

God bless you, Ray, I thought to myself. Some would call it inappropriate behaviour on his part but I was feeling better than I had in days. There were several people sitting nearby and he was making no attempt to keep his voice down. At least, like Wingsy, Ray was treating me normally. Well, if you called sexual harassment normal.

'What am I going to be doing? Please don't stick me in an office. I'll do whatever paperwork you need but, just for a few days, let me get out and about,' I said. 'Catherine checked my availability a few days ago for a MisPer enquiry in Birmingham. That would do – and keep me out of the way.'

I wasn't going to grovel, but, if they didn't let me get out straight away, I didn't know that they ever would.

'Yes, that's right. A few of the team aren't able to go due to other commitments. I've checked with Laura and she's free. Perhaps you can go together and carry out enquiries around this Makepeace fella. Unless you hear otherwise, consider you're going. Tell you more on Monday.' He got up as his mobile started to ring, walking away while he spoke.

I saw that Laura was on the phone, scribbled her a note to say I'd call her about Birmingham and about meeting for a drink later, and went off in search of Alf. I really needed to talk to him. I had a feeling something was very wrong with our caretaker, now only five weeks away from retiring to Spain.

Chapter 47

Alf was unlocking his office as I turned the corner.
'Hiya, Nina. You stalking me?' he said as he pushed the door open.

'No, Alf. But can I have a word?' I asked while he put his keys back into his overall pocket. By way of answer, he stood back allowing me through the door. I felt the warmth from the furnace and figured it must be several degrees warmer in the compact room than in the corridor.

'Have a seat. I'll put the kettle on,' he said, turning his back to me at the sink for a moment. I'd known Alf for years, but still found myself looking around for a wrench or hammer. I'm sure that I'd read somewhere that prolonged stress led to anxiousness producing feelings of paranoia. Explained a lot.

Covering for my wandering eyes, I said, 'Usually a lot tidier in here. You having a clear-out?'

'Only got a few weeks so thought I'd better start.' He saw me apparently look towards a framed photograph face-down on the desk. I was actually clocking the claw hammer under it.

'That's me and my son, Adam,' he said. 'Didn't see much of him when he was a kid. His mum took him to live up north and later on he moved to Spain.'

'You mentioned you were going to visit him. How long's he been there?'

'Few years now.' Alf moved to the cupboard, taking out cups and a tea caddy.

'He come back often to see you?'

'Not really. Haven't seen him for three months now, but sometimes I get news of him from his mate Tony. Fella you saw in here.' He picked up the milk carton from the sink and sniffed the contents. Satisfied it was fit for now, he poured a generous splash into the mugs. 'That's how I know Tony – through my son, Adam.'

'Right, I see. Tony and Adam both live in Spain.' I remembered Tony telling us that he'd flown in from Malaga.

'That's right. Sugar?'

'No, thanks. Do they work together or…?'

Alf paused with his hand on the kettle and looked up towards the ceiling. 'Do you know, I'm not really sure how they got to know each other, but I think they had a mutual friend who ran a bar out there. Turned out they came from the same area, grew up near to one another, same schools, that sort of thing. They've got a bar of their own there now. Doing really well, too. They've just bought another one, Tony was telling me. My boy's got a villa with a pool. I'm so proud of him.'

I'd come to see Alf to tell him that the DCI would be sending someone to see him about his association with Birdsall, but it was becoming clear that he would have to be spoken to about his son too. Taking the mug of tea from Alf, I asked, 'You mentioned his mum took him up north. How old was he then?'

Perching on the edge of the desk as I had the only usable chair, Alf held his drink up to his mouth, paused and said, 'He was seven,' before taking a sip. 'It wouldn't have been so bad, but it's a long way from here to Birmingham.'

The word 'Birmingham' echoed in my brain. Something stopped me telling Alf that I was heading there in a couple of days. It was only a fleeting thought, then it was gone.

The police station tannoy summoned Alf to some sort of plumbing problem in the men's toilets. Not usually one to leave a drink, whatever its contents, I made to get up.

'S'alright, love, it can wait a few minutes. Let me show you a couple of pictures of me and Adam when he was growing up. I've got one of us in front of the children's home on the day I went and got him. Best day of my life – apart from the day he was born. I'd taken my camera along. Brand new, it was. Got all that digital stuff now. He was only there for a few weeks, then I heard what the silly bitch had done – sorry for the language, love.' I shook my head in dismissal. 'Went to get him and for a short while I had him at home with me. She got him back eventually… but anyway, enough of my life story.' He rummaged through a drawer and pulled out another framed black and white picture. It had faded slightly but showed a younger, grinning Alf with a young boy, gappy grin, terrible tank top, hair flying in the breeze. They both looked deliriously happy. The imposing Victorian two-storey building behind them, complete with turrets and a water tower, didn't conjure up images of groups of kids playing musical chairs and painting rainbows.

The tannoy once again announced that Alf was needed immediately – presumably before we all drowned, such was the urgency of the voice. I thanked Alf for the tea and, at the door, mumbled that someone would probably speak to him about Birdsall. Some days I was such a coward.

Chapter 48

Exiting the nick, statement completed, I let my head fill with the thought of seeing Stan. I called him to confirm when I'd be with him.

'Good morning, Nina. I'm looking forward to seeing you. How are you?'

I smiled at the sound of his voice. 'Never felt better,' I lied. 'I'll be with you in about half an hour. I'll unpack, we can have lunch and then see how it goes.' I didn't reckon my chances of getting out for a drink with Wingsy and Laura but was prepared to see how that went too.

As I said goodbye to Stan, I made my way across the yard. I was surprised to see Beckensale at the smoking shed, puffing away. She was looking directly at me. I waved. She remained motionless. Still a miserable cow, then, I thought.

Making my way the thirty metres or so to her smoky domain, I struggled to come up with what I was going to say to her. We hadn't spoken since the Jake Lloyd business. I started with a pleasant, neutral, 'Morning, sarge. What brings you to this nick this morning?'

'Nina. Heard you're seeing Bill Harrison.'

'Not exactly seeing him,' I mumbled, thinking that chance would be a fine thing. I changed the subject. 'Never got to say thanks for the rapid response and, well, everything you've done for me.'

Beckensale took another drag, then ground the stub against the base of the metal ashtray bolted to the lean-to shelter. Immediately, she opened her cigarette packet and lit another one. 'I like him,' she said. Momentarily confused, I opened my mouth to say something but she cut me off. 'Bill Harrison. He's alright. Someone like you could do a lot worse.'

That was as near to a compliment as I was going to get. I had become used to Beckensale and her ways. No one knew much about her. She liked it that way. There she stood, not a totally unattractive woman, intelligent and diligent, in a cheap, creased suit made from static-conducting man-made material, nicotine-stained fingertips and fingernails like talons. There was surely something for everyone. I'd tried and failed to gauge how she saw the world and what she wanted from it.

'Well, thanks again, sarge. I'm glad I saw you; I haven't had the chance to go over to our nick lately. Bye.' I hoisted my handbag on to my shoulder in preparation for my departure.

'Make sure you look after yourself. And tell Bill to keep an eye out as well.'

This was tantamount to caring. All I could manage was to wave at her before I headed for my car.

I pulled my mobile from my bag and pretended to check my messages. On reaching the electronic gate, I opened it with my access card, to be greeted by a marked police van, with six constables on board plus Bill. Caught up in phony message-checking and my escape from Beckensale, I hadn't heard the van approaching. Lila was driving and gave me a wave. Before I had a chance to put my phone away, it bleeped as a message arrived in the inbox. The text, from Bill, read, *'Was just thinking about calling you.'*

Not wanting to hang around the van like a sad police groupie, I stood to one side to let them through, but couldn't resist texting back, *'Will call you later.'*

I got to my car and drove to Stan's with the sun shining all the way, the radio on, enjoying a surge of pleasure from life.

Chapter 49

Stan's front garden looked immaculate when I pulled up on the driveway. Glancing up at the house, I also noticed that the top-floor windows were open slightly. I wasn't the only one who cared.

As I turned the engine off, the movement of the front door opening caught my eye. Samantha stood at the door. She came towards my car and I got out to greet her. Her face was slightly pale but her normal in-control poise, inherited from her father, carried her along the pathway to where I stood. I still had mixed feelings about her, but knew it was as ridiculous as being jealous of Pierre talking to Laura.

'Hello, Nina. It's lovely to see you. He's been asking if you were here yet ever since you two spoke earlier. I told him that you're never late.' She moved closer, lowered her tone and said, 'Thanks for helping out. There was not a doubt in my mind that you would, but I know that work's been crazy for you.'

'Hi, Samantha. You can say that again. They gave me today off so I'm here till Sunday evening or whenever he's sick of me,' I answered, then realised that the use of the word 'sick' was tactless. She didn't seem to notice.

We unloaded the stuff from my boot, chatting as we did so. It turned out that her husband had kept the gardening up, making a fantastic job of it as far as I could see, and Samantha had helped out indoors. She promised to give me a run-down on anything I'd need to be aware of, such as medication for Stan, once I'd seen my old friend, and then she'd clear out of the way.

Dumping my four bags plus groceries in the hallway, casting a glance at that day's local newspaper next to the front door, I followed her through to the garden room. Really, it was a dining room extension with big glass doors. My parents had never been keen gardeners so, growing up, I'd been in awe of anyone who had the time, energy and know-how to create something as beautiful as an outside room full of colour and life. The first time I'd seen Stan's garden it had been as if an extra sense had kicked in: my life had been in black and white until my eyes fell upon the cascade of flowers, every shade imaginable, the lushness of shrubs vying for attention.

Stan sat in an old-fashioned armchair, at an angle so that he could survey the evolving beauty of his garden but also see Samantha and me entering the room.

'Hello, Nina,' he said. 'You look well. Have you been sleeping?'

'I've not felt this good for a long time,' I said as I went over to him. I was relieved to see that he didn't try to get up. 'How about you? Samantha's gonna tell me what you can and can't do, so that you don't try to get one over on me while she's gone.' He was clearly knackered and couldn't overdo it if he wanted to, but I didn't want to dent his pride.

He smiled and took his glasses off now that I was standing next to him. I bent to kiss him on the cheek and squeezed his hand. He squeezed mine in return.

'Have a seat,' he said. 'I think Samantha's gone to put the kettle on.' I hadn't noticed she'd left us to it.

The breeze from the garden touched my cheek. I fought an urge to wrap him in the blanket, shut the door and turn the heating up. I was clearly going to have to chill out or get on his nerves with my fussing. 'Warm enough, Stan?' I said.

'Yes, thank you. It's a beautiful day. Tell me about the murders,' he said.

My eyes darted to the direction of the kitchen.

'Not now, perhaps,' he added. 'Later, when you've unpacked. Tell me about your new boyfriend instead.'

My mouth opened, but I failed to find the words for a second or two while his eyes twinkled. Wasn't much that got past Stan, even after a hospital stay and copious medication.

We continued to chat long after we'd had tea and Samantha had left us to our lunch. I told him about Bill, of course. Why wouldn't I? Then we moved on to the business of murder. At this point, I made an excuse to shut the door in case we could be overheard. I was worried he was cold, but I was sure he knew the real reason. Sure he humoured me. Stan's nearest neighbours, even if they had been standing at the fence with listening devices, would still have been about one hundred feet from where we were talking. The chances of them overhearing were minuscule.

Over a fantastic crab and prawn salad, eaten on our laps, I told Stan the whole story, from murder one, Amanda Bell, prostitute, to murder two, our discovery of Jason Holland, missing person, through to murder three, Daphne Headingly. I filled him in on the photographs taken by Jake Lloyd and Lloyd's confession to the murder of his cousin Scott who had also kidnapped two little girls. Stan put his knife and fork down at this point but continued to listen without comment. I outlined the encounters I'd had with Belinda, Birdsall and the ex-wife, Chloe. When I mentioned that I'd seen Birdsall in the nick with the caretaker, he put his knife and fork down once more. Still no comment. I ended with my upcoming trip to Birmingham and threw in that the caretaker's son had been living in Birmingham as a child in a children's home. I wanted to see how Stan reacted.

Once more, I heard Stan place his cutlery on to his plate. This time he had finished eating. I was still only halfway through, I'd been so busy chattering. I watched him slowly chew the last morsel of his meal, pondering his first question or comment. Whatever it was, I would hang on every syllable.

When he had swallowed the last mouthful, he said, 'And you think the fact that Alf's son – a friend of a potential suspect – was in Birmingham in a children's home is more than just a coincidence? It doesn't seem like much to go on.'

'I know, I know, but Birmingham keeps coming up, and I wonder if there's more to it…'

'And you didn't think to talk to anyone about this?'

'How daft would that be? The trouble I've caused, if I told them, they'd put me in an office and send someone else.'

He laughed, then he closed his eyes, resting his head back against the cream and blue upholstery of the chair-back. I took charge and said, 'Samantha warned me that I wasn't to let you sit there. I've a schedule for you to follow. Afternoon nap is next on the agenda.'

'And what about you? Young woman like you is bound to have something to do this weekend. Especially with a young man on the scene.'

'"On the scene"? You're gonna use the term "courting" or "walking out together" in a minute. I haven't even got a date with Bill arranged. People getting murdered keep holding up the romance. A couple of friends asked me out for a quick beer tonight, that's all.'

'Wingsy and Laura, I assume,' he said. 'I've an idea: ask them here. I'd love to meet them.'

I was a bit surprised, but flattered and pleased to think that my friends would be under one roof. I allowed Stan to get himself up, and followed him upstairs at a distance, but not so far that I wouldn't be able to spring into action if needed. Before I went about about making the necessary calls and arranging a small gathering at Stan's in a few hours' time, while he slept, I stole down to the hallway to read the newspaper I'd seen there earlier. All thoughts of whether I should invite Bill along too, and wondering if Stan would find it too much, were pushed from my mind as I picked up the paper and read the front page. It hollered its headline at me: 'Crazy Knife Killer Claims Third Victim'. It went on to describe how seventy-seven-year-old Daphne Headingly had been savagely murdered. Reading through the article,

185

I could only agree with what it said about the police: we were indeed 'baffled'. At the part that described the second suspect's detainment in a police cell while Daphne was being slaughtered, I could only nod my head in agreement. I was mulling over the crassness of the word 'slaughtered' when my eyes flitted to the article on the opposite page.

This headline wasn't hollering; it was screaming in both my ears. It read: 'Arrest of Murder Victim's Nephew for Stalking Detective'.

I dropped down on to the bottom step of the staircase. Heart hammering, I read on. The article named me. It actually named me as 'Detective Constable Nina Foster' and went on to describe Jake Lloyd's obsession with me spanning decades. His arrest had been made, it said, while I was at his house conducting an enquiry into his aunt's murder.

Clutching the paper to me, I sat on the stairs to regain my composure. His bail hearing following his arrest and charge had been reported from an open court. The press and members of the public were free to come and go; I could have done nothing to stop it. But it was my name for all to see.

All I'd ever wanted to do was to keep a low profile and merge into the background. I had no idea who would read this. No one at work had warned me but then I should have seen this coming. I was angry with myself for not expecting it.

I couldn't let Stan see this – it would upset him. From the uncreased, immaculate fold of the pages I could tell that I was the first to read it. I ran upstairs and hid it in my suitcase. Then I got on with the job I had to do. I had a gathering to organise.

As the evening passed I felt more and more mellow, shelving all thought of the article. My three friends hit it off. Despite Laura's abstinence (she was driving), drinks were consumed and food disappeared as soon as it emerged from the kitchen. We all took it in turns knocking up snacks and dishes, some more successful than others.

My turn came and I opted for a lazy dish of nachos with cheese and dip. As I came out of the kitchen with the tray, the conversation stopped and all three of them stared at me from their seats at the dining room table. I read Laura's look as embarrassment, Stan's as annoyance. Wingsy just looked awkward.

'What's wrong?' I said, halting, allowing the melted cheese to solidify.

'Laura was just talking about the bloodstained clothing found in Jake Lloyd's house,' said Stan. 'You didn't tell me about that.' Even though he spoke with a calm and even voice, I knew he was angry with me.

'I didn't tell you because, if it's the original clothes I and my sister were wearing, then I'm practically saying that someone on your enquiry team lost them or gave them away.' Truth was, it wasn't so much about criticising Stan, but I hadn't wanted to worry him. 'Come on, you lot, eat these nachos. I've excelled myself with this signature dish.'

As I put the cheese-topped snacks down, Stan leaned across, placing his hand on top of mine. I steeled myself for whatever he was going to say.

'Nina,' he said, forcing me to look away from the hardening cheddar to meet his eyes, 'I destroyed the clothes myself. Process was a lot less sophisticated then, but I burned them. I wouldn't lie to you.'

That was good enough for me, and it confirmed what Catherine had told me about the likelihood that the clothes at Lloyd's house were replicas. I let go of the dish and picked up my wine. Wingsy leaned across to help himself as Laura gave me an empty smile.

Wingsy didn't stay too late, as Mel was still giving him some grief. He alluded to her wanting another baby but then shied away from talking about it. Laura left a couple of hours after him. We were both looking forward to going to Birmingham on Monday for a trip neither of us knew much about. I feigned tiredness to get Stan to go to bed.

I climbed into the cool sheets of the guest bed, feeling sleep reaching out and grabbing me, content to let it pull me towards an easy slumber. As I closed my eyes, my final thought was of the children's clothes that had been plaguing me. I was relieved to finally put to rest the issue of their authenticity. Stan's word sealed it for me.

Chapter 50

28th and 29th September

Saturday and Sunday were as relaxing for me as they were for Stan. I made sure the television was turned off so that he didn't see the local news, telling him it was distracting. Although I made sure that he rested, Samantha had been so diligent in taking care of all our housekeeping needs that, apart from cooking and clearing up, I had little to do. I read a novel for the first time in months, even called my parents. It was a quick call. I didn't have much to say.

Sunday afternoon came round soon enough. We ate a roast beef dinner, and I cleared away and then called Samantha as I'd promised. Packed and ready to leave, I prepared myself to part without a show of emotion. During the visit I'd felt useful, as if somehow I was making Stan better just by being there. Once I walked out of the door, I couldn't help him, and I couldn't wish the cancer to be gone with the same degree of success. I stood helplessly in the hallway, bag at my feet, thinking about placebos. They worked even when the patient knew they were placebos. Why couldn't Stan just will the cancer away? My face was wet. I was crying again. 'Please don't leave me, Stan,' I whispered.

The rustle of a magazine from the garden room warned me of movement. I ran upstairs, shouting, 'Just remembered, left something in the bathroom.'

After ten minutes, I re-emerged from the bathroom, all indication of emotion and worry washed away.

As I came down the stairs, Stan was letting Samantha into the house. After a quick hello to me, she headed towards the kitchen. I stepped over my bags to hug Stan goodbye. 'Thanks for letting me stay, Stan,' I said into his chest as we embraced. 'Exactly what I needed. I'll call you when I get back from Birmingham.'

He held me at arm's length, examined my face and said, 'I'm worried about you. The photographs from Lloyd were upsetting. You and Laura take care in Birmingham. Do not take any risks. Serial killers don't usually stop until they're caught.'

We hugged. I left. I cried all the way home.

Chapter 51

To begin with, I couldn't get hold of Bill. When he answered, late in the day, he sounded tired.

'How was work?' I asked.

'Another late one. Not been out of bed long.' I heard him yawn. 'We were kept on for a call to a rape. A fifteen-year-old girl was raped in her own bed, feet away from her parents in the next room. The offender had been released from prison three days ago.'

'Was he inside for sexual offences?' I asked.

'Yeah. His rehabilitation is in doubt.'

As I listened to him, I padded my way over to the fridge and took out a chilled bottle of beer, phone tucked against my shoulder. I had a bottle opener fixed to the counter for just such an emergency situation. In one swift move, the top was off. 'I have to go in to the nick first thing and then me and Laura are going to Birmingham for a couple of days.' I took a swig of beer.

'Sounds like you're drinking,' Bill said. 'Fancy some company?'

'That would be good,' I said. I opened the fridge again. 'I have some sort of pasta thing in the fridge. Fancy dinner?'

'I'll see you in half an hour,' said Bill.

I slung the phone down on the side, putting the bottle down with a bit more care, before running upstairs for a shower. Not to mention some serious flossing and hair removal. I didn't want to presume anything, but it was better to be prepared.

Thirty minutes later, I wandered back into the kitchen and busied myself with cutlery and glasses at the kitchen table. As I picked up my beer bottle, I saw that I had a text on my phone. I didn't recognise the number. The message was one single word: *Spain*.

The knock at the front door focused me and I went to answer it. Bill stood at the doorstep, smiling. 'What's wrong?' he said. 'You look worried.'

'Just had a text message,' I said. 'Come in, I'll tell you all about it.' And I did. The only part I left out was who had given me the information. It wasn't that I didn't trust Bill, but we were police officers, supposed to pass everything on. I had a loyalty to Annie and Richard; Bill did not.

The only question he raised in relation to the source was to ask me if I trusted the person. This was difficult to answer without giving too much away.

Sitting at the table with a bottle of beer each, a bowl of crisps between us, I said, 'I have no reason not to trust them and it's not as though they've given me a name. I do have a phone number of someone who knew Daphne Headingly. I've passed that on to Eric Nottingham. If I had a suspect's name, address or anything more solid, I'd have gone to see him by now. Oh, by the way, the pasta thing I promised you has gone out of date.'

We both regarded the snack bowl on the table with equal indifference. 'No matter how much I spend at the shops, I only ever seem to have wine and detergent. How about a takeaway?' I suggested.

'How about the pizza place in town? I did ask you out for a drink, and so far we've not made it within half a mile of a pub.'

'I'd like that. I'll get my bag.' This cheered me up. I couldn't remember the last time I'd been out for a meal with anyone whose company I really enjoyed. I'd walked out on the loser Russian on our last dinner date. I couldn't think of any reason why tonight wouldn't be a total success.

We walked from my house to the restaurant, chatting amiably on the way. It wasn't a bad area to live in. I'd chosen my home very carefully; it was important for a police officer. The choice was trust your neighbours or keep yourself to yourself. I managed to keep a low profile and had chosen to live far enough out of town to avoid the problems that towns sometimes brought, though I still lived close enough to a couple of decent local bars and restaurants. All in all, I enjoyed living in my leafy suburb with its 1930s-built semis, mobile library at the local community centre on Saturday mornings and lack of teenagers hanging around. When the mood took me, I even ventured for a stroll into the woods at the back of my house.

The walk to the restaurant took about twenty minutes, and the time passed very quickly. Bill had always seemed a bit of a shy bloke, but, apart from being easy to talk to, he seemed to be a gentleman. I hoped not too much of a gentleman.

From the street, I could see that the restaurant only had a few customers. As Bill held the door open for me, the smell from the pizza oven wafted my way. A waiter hurried over to us, menus in hand, and we chose a table in the window and sat down. Running an eye down the food choices, I ruled half of them out because of their garlic content. Well, never assume but remain optimistic.

Bill said, 'Order a bottle of wine if you like. I'm driving and only having one glass.'

That sentence spoke volumes: either he had no intention of staying the night, or he wanted me to think he had no intention of staying the night; if he did stay, he intended to be sober; and, just as important as everything else, he was certain I could polish off the rest of the bottle and had no problem with it.

The wine and pizzas were perfect, as was the company. The evening had already been drawing in by the time we'd got to the restaurant, but the atmosphere inside was relaxed, lights bright enough to see the food but soft enough to make us both very mellow. A double decker bus pulled up on the opposite side of the street, illuminating the pavement outside. Alf flitted through my mind. For a second I thought I had seen him again, walking past, but then I realised that it was someone else I knew. My mind had inexplicably linked them. It was Joe Bring.

He didn't see me. I probably wouldn't have seen him if the glare from the bus hadn't lit up the street just at that moment. He was walking past, talking on a mobile phone. Actually, it was more like shouting. I could pick out the swearing without any difficulty, plus the words 'not enough. It's out of order', then he was gone.

Bill's attention was drawn in the same direction as mine and I just about heard him say, 'Joe Bring. What a superstar.' I looked back at Bill as he continued, 'He was one of my first arrests. Sad story really. His dad used to inject him with heroin when he was a kid. Never stood a chance.'

Going out with police officers could kill any romantic moment.

'How come you ended up in CID?' he asked, reaching for his glass of water.

'Wasn't ever really cut out for uniform,' I answered. 'Got fed up with chasing loose horses down dual carriageways and back into fields at three in the morning, going to nightclub fights in the early hours, that kind of thing. All seemed like a lot of grief and it wasn't really what I wanted.'

Bill topped up my wine glass.

'Thanks,' I said.

'No problem. I can't drink any more anyway.'

'I didn't mean for the wine. Well, I did. The wine, the meal, taking me out and not asking endless questions. I've had a great time.' It was true. Until Joe had showed up, I'd forgotten all about Jake Lloyd and Scott Headingly and work in general.

'My pleasure. I'll get the bill and we'll go back to yours. Oh, not like that! I mean I'll walk you back to your house.'

His hand was resting on the table. I put my own over it and said, 'I know what you meant.'

The bill settled, we walked back to my house. I put my arm through Bill's, not quite believing my luck. This one was definitely a keeper.

At the front door, I got out my keys, hoping for a sign that he wanted to come in. When I didn't get one, I asked, 'You have time for a coffee?'

'I really should be going. Any chance that when you get back from Birmingham we can go out again?'

'Without a doubt,' I said, not even attempting to play it cool and aloof. 'I'll be there for a night or two. I'll give you a call when I get back?'

'Sounds good to me. Goodnight.' He moved towards me, caressing my face with his fingertips, his mouth meeting mine. We kissed. He lowered his hands to my waist and pulled me tight to him. I felt my knees begin to buckle.

Bill loosened his hold on me. 'Take care in Birmingham,' he said, before stepping back, and watching me go inside.

Chapter 52

30th September

The next day, I met Laura in the back yard at the nick. On our way up the stairs, I asked her if she'd mind driving first so I could read up on the enquiry's latest developments. Truth be told, I was tired. A couple of days of worrying about Stan, plus a night spent thinking about Bill after he'd left, not to mention working on three linked murders and having a stalker, and I was beginning to crack.

'Sure, Nin,' said Laura as we made our way to the detective sergeants' office, 'happy to.'

Ray was sitting in the office stapling papers together when we walked in. He glanced up, set the stapler down and said, 'Fantastic: a blonde and a brunette. Always handy if you two want to make a porno. Lets the viewer know who's who.'

'What have you got for us?' I asked. 'And keep it clean.'

He chucked the paperwork across the desk. I picked it up. Laura was trying to read over my shoulder.

Ray said, 'That's a Missing Person report from West Midlands Police. It relates to Benjamin Makepeace. He went missing just under six weeks ago. No sign of him since. Initial enquiries were made, and then he swiftly became another of the two hundred thousand people who go missing every year.

'As you can see, a bit like Amanda Bell, he was last seen on CCTV, believed to be heading home. No use of his mobile or bank accounts, car hasn't moved, no word to family or friends. All very odd, but if you flick to the final page of the report you'll see that we have a DNA hit.'

I turned to the final page. The noise of Ray moving in his chair caused me to glance in his direction. 'Catherine mentioned that. It's to do with Gary Savage, isn't it? Second bloke we nicked for murder?'

Ray nodded. 'That's right,' he said, 'The knife you found in his van had Makepeace's blood on it. As a missing person, Makepeace's DNA was taken from his toothbrush and loaded into the MisPer Database. As you probably know, the blood from the knife was checked against the National DNA Database then the Missing Persons Database. The bloodstain profile took a couple of days to come back. When it did, it matched Benjamin Makepeace's profile. Get yourselves up there, speak to Robin Cox in Intel; his number's on the first page. See what you can find out about Makepeace. They're sending some officers down to us here at some point, probably once you've been up there, I'm not sure when, but this may now be the start of a countrywide investigation.'

As we went to leave his office, Ray said, 'Oh, Nina. You may want to see this.'

He pushed further paperwork across the desk. It was the newspaper article about Lloyd stalking me, shouting the same heading I had read at Stan's. Someone had cut it out of the local paper and stapled an 'Other Document' Incident Room sheet to the top. 'Relates to Op Guard so it's a part of the unused material,' Ray told me. As if to pacify me that it was routine, he then added, 'All items from the media get logged as ODs and reviewed by the disclosure officer for murder enquiries.'

I glanced at it, pushed it back across the desk and tried to banish it from my mind. I would never know who else had seen my name associated with Jake Lloyd.

Laura had the good grace to avoid talking about the newspaper article. For that I was grateful. We spent the next couple of hours making calls, researching what we were embarking on, drinking tea and packing up the car. Satisfied that we had everything we needed, we shouted our goodbyes to the others still typing and reading in the Incident Room and set out.

Laura drove first. 'Where are we staying?' she asked.

'Somewhere right in the middle of the bars. Got a recommendation for a fantastic curry house, too.' I flicked through the paperwork supplied by Ray. 'Laura, how do you think this guy's blood turned up in Savage's van?'

'Dunno,' she said. 'We know that Savage's van hasn't been to Birmingham from the Automatic Number Plate Readers on the motorway. Could the van have been on false plates?'

'Yeah, possibly, but it seems that the vehicle hasn't even been out of county for weeks. Last time was that sighting near Gatwick two months ago. I remember that from the work around Savage when he got nicked. Makepeace has been missing for less than six weeks. Can't be that. Gatwick, though?' I mused. 'Tony Birdsall said he flew in to Gatwick a few days before we saw him last week.'

Laura took her eyes off the road for a second to look at me.

'Think they're connected to Birdsall, Nin?' she asked.

'Too much of a coincidence not to be?' I said. 'Anyway, Lol, thanks for coming with me. I think I owe you an apology too?'

'What for?' she asked, frowning.

'I do know that I'm being sent to Birmingham to keep me away from the Lloyds. Keep me away from the Lloyds, you keep me away from the heart of the enquiry. I appreciate not being kicked off it. If this was a single murder enquiry, I'd have been sent back to Beckensale by now. Boss is only tolerating my presence because he's really short-staffed.'

'Do you reckon?' said Laura. 'I think he genuinely likes you, and you've worked hard on this job, in spite of the personal stuff.'

'Yeah, but he still doesn't need the grief I bring. Anyway, let's formulate some sort of a plan.'

I spent the rest of the journey making calls to the officers we were supposed to meet with. We made good time, only taking about four hours to get to our destination. The hotel was a pretty miserable affair. The taxpayer was once again footing the bill, so enjoying our stay was out of the question. My single room contained a tiny bed with a frayed tartan cover, badly hung tartan curtains that didn't meet in the middle and a broken tartan lampshade. Could have been worse: at least I wasn't Scottish; I'd have really been insulted. I did have a kettle and tea tray. Oh, and shortbread.

We drove to the nick. The security was very tight; it took ages to get parked and into the building. We had a quick meeting with an overworked DS. He was very pleasant and offered any help he could. He introduced us to the intelligence officer, Robin Cox, who couldn't do enough for us, researching anything we requested. Armed with everything we needed, including contact mobile telephone numbers for his staff, we set off for the home address of Benjamin Makepeace.

His ageing mother was his only living relative. Fortunately for Laura and me, local officers had already told her that her son's blood had turned up a week ago in a van hundreds of miles away. At least the poor woman had had some time to adjust to this latest news. Not knowing what had happened to your nearest and dearest must rip a soul apart. I knew only too well that grief played tricks: a face in the distance fleetingly morphing into the one whose company you craved, until disappointment and reality would break through. What must uncertainty do to the mind?

Mrs Makepeace opened the door. She was broken.

'Mrs Makepeace,' I said. 'I'm Detective Nina Foster. This is Detective Laura Ward. Can we come in and speak to you?'

She nodded, moving back into the gloom. She probably would have agreed to anything.

The house smelt musty. Dust jumped in the sunlight bursting through the open door. We followed her into the dining room, where she sat down at the glass-topped table. Its entire surface was covered in Benjamin memorabilia: photographs, school certificates, swimming badges, a lock of hair in a frame. My eyes were drawn to a small plastic pot with a screw-on lid.

She caught me looking and palmed the pot, holding it to her chest. Closing her fists around it, she said, 'Benjamin had his appendix out when he was eight. These were the stitches.' Now I knew what this was doing to her mind. Making it crazier than it had already been. Grief magnifies the person you already are, I thought. We all revert to type.

Laura began. 'Can we talk to you about Benjamin? We know that you've been told we've an indication he may have been in the south of the country. We haven't found him, but anything you tell us may help.' Laura continued speaking but to be truthful I wasn't listening. I was staring at a photograph on the wall. A black and white photograph of a much younger Mrs Makepeace with her son. They were laughing, hair blowing in the breeze. They were standing in front of a two-storey Victorian building. Complete with turrets and a water tower.

'Where is this place?' I said, already knowing the answer.

The old lady turned her head to where I pointed.

'Oh, that's the children's home at Leithgate. Used to be a mental asylum but they shut it down. Used it as a children's home instead.' She got up and staggered to the wall as if every step was agony. She stroked the boy's hair in the photo, and a tear rolled from her eye. 'We had a few problems with Benjamin, and he went there for a couple of weeks to give us a break.'

'When was this photograph taken?' I asked.

'When Benjamin was seven years old – 1985,' she said, running her finger along the outline of her son's image. 'Want to see his room?'

Without waiting for an answer, Mrs Makepeace moved around the table, leaning on the glass top for support on her way to the door. Laura and I exchanged looks. The progress along the corridor was slow: our guide paused every couple of steps, withered fingers grasping door handles, the banisters, anything for support. The mental torture she must have been going through was matched by physical pain, if her ascension of the stairs was anything to base a judgement on. Her son was missing and it was crushing her. From the notes we had, Mrs Makepeace was in her late sixties, but she moved like a woman much older.

We reached the top of the stairs and entered the bedroom of a child. The single bookshelf contained football annuals, an atlas, board games, puzzles; the bed was draped in a Birmingham City duvet cover. Whatever I'd been expecting, it wasn't this. I searched for something to say that wasn't too critical of why a man in his thirties would be living like this.

I began with a non-judgemental question, 'Benjamin is a Birmingham City fan?' Pretty obvious thing to ask, but I was pulling words out of a mental tombola.

Mrs Makepeace looked at the bed. Laura looked at the bed. I joined in. No one spoke. I thought for a moment I was the insane one. I stole a look at Mrs Makepeace, who was biting her lower lip.

'Yes,' she said. 'He's a Birmingham City fan. I'll put the kettle on. Please have a few minutes in here. I haven't moved anything since the last time he was here.'

Laura moved to one side to let our host out of the room. My friend raised her eyebrows at me once we were alone, listening to Mrs Makepeace hobbling down the stairs. I opened the wardrobe, largely because I just had to check there wasn't a school uniform or a Boy Scout outfit. I was relieved to see that it contained normal men's clothes. A cursory glance at the labels showed me that he took a sixteen-inch shirt collar, size Large for T-shirts and jumpers, inside leg was thirty-two, thirty-four-inch waist, and size nine shoes. He shopped largely in M&S, had one good suit, and middle-of-the-road taste. I made a note of what I'd found out. It was probably not going to be relevant but you never knew.

Laura joined me in leafing through the garments. 'This has all been logged with the initial local patrol who came out and took the Missing Person report,' she said. Lowering her voice, she added, 'This is a very strange set-up for a grown man. There's nothing to suggest he had any kind of social life or hobbies outside of football.'

Other than the wardrobe, bed and bookshelf, the room contained an empty bedside cabinet. There were no magazines, newspapers, handwritten notes or sign of a mobile phone. That at least couldn't be correct; we'd been told that his mobile phone records had been checked for recent contact. We made our way downstairs to speak to Benjamin's mother. There were a few things we wanted answers to.

We found her in the kitchen filling up the salt cellar. 'Mrs Makepeace,' I began. She continued to pour salt into the bottom of the overflowing pot. She watched the white grains spill on to the table for three or four seconds before abandoning her chore. Her dull eyes focused on mine. 'Are there any of Benjamin's belongings anywhere else?' I asked. 'A mobile phone? Personal items?'

'No,' she said. 'He didn't have a mobile phone. We didn't like them. All of his stuff is in his room, apart from his certificates and photographs. You've seen them in the dining room.'

'Is there any other family?' asked Laura.

The lifeless eyes roamed in search of the speaker. 'My husband died,' she said. Adding, 'He was killed on his way home one night. Drunk driver.'

'That's terrible, Mrs Makepeace. Is there anyone else that visits you or pops in from time to time?' asked Laura.

'No,' she said to the floor. 'My sister died from cancer a couple of years ago. She was the only other relative I had. Just me and Benjamin. Now just me.'

'What about friends?' I asked.

This was met with a shake of her head encasing a brain riddled with sorrow. 'Lost the few I had over the years; they either died or we drifted apart. Always knew I had Benjamin so I didn't need them.'

'Benjamin's friends?' I asked. 'We have the details of the library where he worked, but the Missing Person report stated he didn't have any friends or a girlfriend.'

Her head snapped up, eyes opened wide as she said, 'He didn't need a girlfriend. Women are trouble. He was clever enough to know that.'

I was getting a bit of a different picture of this whole scenario. The house was smothering me and I'd only been there for an hour. How Benjamin must have felt being brought up by a Brummie council house Miss Havisham was anyone's guess. More than likely he'd killed himself, or my favourite theory was that he'd had enough and legged it. Didn't explain the bloodied knife hundreds of miles away, however. We said our goodbyes, left our numbers and asked that she call us or West Midlands police if she heard anything.

'Right, well, she was hard work,' I said to Laura as we got into the car. 'I'm gonna call the Intel bloke we spoke to at the nick, find out if he has any Social Services contacts we can meet with about the children's home.' I glanced at my watch. Time was getting on. If they agreed to see us, it would probably be in the morning.

'Children's home?' asked Laura, shifting in the passenger seat to face me. 'That was over twenty-five years ago. What's your thinking?'

'Thing is, Lol, last week at the nick, I spoke to Alf in his office.'

'Yeah, you told me. Tony Birdsall was there too.' Her delicate features were weighed down with a heavy crease mark across her forehead.

'What I didn't tell you,' I said as I searched my paper-work for our Intelligence link's phone number, 'was that in the 1980s Alf's son was taken into a children's home in Birmingham.'

'I'm still not following. You think they're connected?'

'It's the same home. The photograph she had on the wall back there – ' I jerked my thumb in the direction of the Makepeace house ' – it looked as though Benjamin and his mum were standing in exactly the same spot in front of the building that Alf and his son had done. It was almost the same pose, same location, and most definitely the same building behind them.' I stopped talking and read the look of concern Laura was giving me. I realised that I was slightly breathless, having not paused for air. I concentrated on getting my breathing back to normal.

Why all this was taking such a toll on me, I could only guess. I was pretty sure I knew the reason, but I had taken Eric Nottingham at his word about making sure my sleep wasn't disturbed. It had been an unusual few days to say the least. I should probably cut myself some slack.

'OK,' Laura said after a few seconds' thought, 'you call the Intel man and I'll give the library a call.' Taking her notes out of the passenger door's side pocket, she climbed out of the car, adding, 'You use the car's hands-free kit. It's all set up. I'll get out of the way.'

My mind wrestled paranoid thoughts: Laura could have waited until I'd made my call, then made hers. Why the disappearing act? No, that was nonsense. I was going to have to stop thinking that way about my friend. Still, I tried to hear who she was talking to and what she was saying on her mobile as she walked up and down the pavement beside the car. Stalling as long as I could, I called the Intel number we'd been given in case we needed any further information or help, put in my request for Social Services to call me, and waved Laura back into the car. She got in, making arrangements for us to attend the city's central library to speak to Benjamin's supervisor. Who else would she have been speaking to?

Chapter 53

We drove to the city centre, parked and made our way on foot to the library. A cheerful-looking middle-aged woman greeted us at the enquiry desk, where we introduced ourselves and asked for Linda Hussain. After a very short wait, a white woman dressed in trousers and a navy blouse, hijab covering her hair, hurried towards us, holding out her hand in greeting.

'I'm Laura. We spoke on the phone. And this is Nina,' said my friend, shaking Linda's hand.

Linda greeted me and said with a slight local accent, 'You've come a long way. I hope I can help. Come with me to my office.' We followed her through a door marked 'Staff Only', and along a short corridor to her office. The three of us barely squeezed inside alongside the three chairs and the desk, which took up most of the space. Linda had to shut the door before Laura or I could sit down as there wasn't enough room to do so otherwise. Clearly, this local council couldn't be accused of squandering taxpayers' money on decadent library facilities for its staff.

'Can I get either of you a tea or coffee?' Linda asked. Personally I didn't want one, based largely on the fact that it would involve another furniture shuffle. Besides, three cups of boiling liquid in the room would further increase the temperature. The window didn't look as though it had ever been opened. The heat didn't seem to be bothering Linda or Laura. Both Laura and I declined her offer.

I began first. 'Thanks for seeing us, Linda.'

She smiled at me. Her eyes were blue. I wondered what colour her hair was.

'I know that police have been here before and spoken to you and your staff. I can't go into details but we have reason to believe that Benjamin has been in or around the Home Counties since he went missing almost six weeks ago. Laura and I are part of the investigation team making enquiries for three linked murders we've had in our area. Please don't think that Benjamin is in any way involved or has come to harm. We're simply here double-checking any leads and trying to jog people's memories for new information.'

Linda reached to her left and opened the desk drawer, moving to her right as she did so, to avoid being hit on the knee no doubt. She took a black mobile phone out of the drawer. 'You'll be wanting this,' she said, placing it down on the ink blotter in front of her. 'It's Benjamin's, I think. We emptied out his locker for the police when they were here the first time. Then we had a temporary member of staff replace him and gave him the locker below Benjamin's. Yesterday, he found this wedged at the top, right at the back. He's here if you want to speak to him.'

Laura and I peered at the phone in wonder, as if we'd never seen such technology before. I pulled a pair of disposable rubber gloves and an evidence bag from my folder.

'Sorry,' said Linda, 'I didn't think about fingerprints. At least two of us have handled it.'

'No, it's OK,' I said. 'Your fingerprints on it aren't a problem, but mine are a different matter. My boss won't be too pleased if I get mine on it. They're on the fingerprint database, along with my DNA.'

'I'll show you the locker,' said Linda. 'Then I'll get Mike in here. He was the one who found the phone. I don't think there's much else we can help you with. We've already given copies of Benjamin's files to the police but we're happy to supply anything again that you think may be useful.' She stood up and hesitated. 'Listen, I'd like to be present when you speak to Mike. He's quite young and only been here two days. As I said, he was only assigned the locker yesterday when he found the phone. I've not had time to contact the local police. Then you called to say you were coming. Problem is, we won't all fit into this room.'

My mobile started to ring, showing a Birmingham dialling code. 'I think this is the call I've been waiting for,' I said to Laura. 'You have this room. Is there somewhere else I can take the call?' I asked Linda, as we rearranged ourselves and the chairs.

'Yes, next door,' she said.

I answered the phone as we left the office. By the time I'd stepped into the room Linda showed me to, the caller had introduced herself as Judith Hazlewood from Leithgate Social Services.

I could hear Laura and Linda talking as they walked in the direction of the locker room. This office was even smaller than the one we'd been in previously. It housed only a desk and one chair. There wasn't even a window. I sat at the desk, notebook open.

'Thanks for calling me, Judith. I'm from Riverstone police station, investigating a series of murders, and enquiries have led me to Leithgate. I was wondering if I could talk to you about the former asylum in Leithgate which was later used as a children's home?' I asked.

There was a pause and, when she spoke, her voice was no longer clear. I pictured her on the other end of the line with her hand over the mouthpiece, shielding the words as she whispered them so they wouldn't go astray. 'I'll talk to you,' she said, 'But not on the phone. We'll have to meet. Tomorrow. Can I see you then?'

I put my hand over my other ear to block out any background noise. I felt I couldn't risk missing a word of anything she said. 'Tomorrow's fine,' I said. 'What time and where?' The sound of Laura, Linda and a man, presumably Mike, striding back along the corridor to Linda's office covered some of her words. I asked Judith to repeat what she'd said.

'Ten o'clock tomorrow morning in the Bullring. There's a café there called the Cup of Coffee. I'll be sitting outside.'

'Judith, it's not a problem for us to come to your place of work, unless you don't want us there,' I said.

There was another brief hesitation before she replied, 'I'd just feel happier talking to you out of the office. The whole children's home thing is still in a lot of people's minds here. Some can still be very touchy about it. I don't want to upset my colleagues. When a child is murdered, even years later, it can still touch a nerve.'

Wondering now if I'd heard her correctly, I said, 'Did you say a child was murdered?'

'Yes. At the home. That's the main reason they shut it down.'

'I'm guessing that the staff were suspected?'

'No, no. Not the staff, the other children. Have to go. See you tomorrow.'

For some time after Judith hung up, I sat with my phone in my hand, staring at it. I could hear muffled sounds coming from the adjoining office. Knowing that Laura would be taking a statement about the finding of the mobile, I snapped into action to make use of the time while she worked. I called Ray to tell him about the phone. As I suspected he would, he told me to let West Midlands download any information that was on the handset and that I should take a copy of the information, leaving the phone with them, as it probably wasn't relevant to our murder investigation. I didn't tell him about the children's home in case he stopped me from looking any further into it. I did tell him that we had a meeting in the morning with Social Services. That was at least truthful.

Next I telephoned our liaison man to ask for anything he could tell us or find out about a child murder in the 1980s in Leithgate children's home. Even as he was telling me that he'd find out what he could, it dawned on me that the best place on the planet to conduct research was a library.

I knocked on the door of the occupied office and through the inch-wide crack between door and frame told Laura that I was going to look something up in the public part of the library. Laura turned in her chair to look at me as I peered in at her. 'Don't worry, Nina, I'll finish up here and see you downstairs.'

Having found a computer with internet access, it took me little time to come up with the basic facts: the former mental hospital had been turned into a short-term children's home while another was being built following on from a non-suspicious fire at the city's largest home. Initially Leithgate had only been intended to accommodate a handful of children, as it was deemed unsuitable. However, this was quickly forgotten and up to thirty children were placed there at any one time. The staff were mostly from the fire-damaged home, while the children were taken from various homes as only the older, more settled children were uprooted, or those intended to be 'short stays'.

The home was shut down shortly after the death of nine-year-old Peter Woods. He had been found hanging by the neck in one of the disused parts of the former hospital. There was no mention of its having been a murder. It was a huge, tragic embarrassment for the local Social Services, who were mercilessly berated for allowing a former mental home to be used to house children, but it was deemed to have been simply an awful accident. Neither the local nor the national press articles shed much more light on it, other than Peter's mother coming forward and telling the world that she'd left drink and drugs behind and found Jesus. According to the tabloids, Mrs Woods had been days away from collecting her treasured son, regretted how she had previously lived her life and was now a God-fearing woman. For some reason, she had decided to tell the world this over a double-page spread in a newspaper while lying down wearing transparent clothes,

Bible in hand. Copies must have flown off the newsagents' shelves. Clearly this was the Eighties, before the press cleaned up their act.

Still I failed to find any mention of murder. Pondering whether Judith Hazlewood could be mistaken, or even if I had heard her correctly, I flicked from article to article, so engrossed that I didn't notice Laura and Linda approaching.

Laura placed her hand on my shoulder, making me jump. 'Sorry.' She laughed. 'We've just finished. What are you looking at?'

'It's Leithgate children's home,' I said, directing my words at Linda. 'Benjamin was once there.'

She frowned and leaned towards the screen. 'He never spoke about it,' she said, 'but I do seem to remember some sort of scandal there when a child died. He hanged himself, I think.' She straightened upright, staring down at the floor while she tried to recall what she knew. 'No, can't remember anything else,' she said, shaking her head, her hijab brushing against her shoulders as she did so.

'Well, thanks, Linda. We've taken up enough of your time, but we're here for another day or two so we may come back or call you if there's anything else.'

The three of us shook hands, then I said, 'If you don't mind, I just want to stay here for a bit longer to show my colleague what I've found.'

'Take as long as you need. It was good to meet you.'

When she was out of earshot, I brought Laura up to speed on the children's home.

'This hanging is a bit of a coincidence, don't you think?' she asked.

I chewed on my bottom lip for a couple of seconds before I said, 'Well, there's no suggestion at all that the Lloyds had anything to do with the place. From all that I've read, it seems that little Peter Woods' death was just a very sad accident. We'll know more when we get the paperwork from the local nick and then meet Judith tomorrow.'

'Don't know about you,' said Laura, 'but I'm knackered. Shall we call it a day and head for the bar?'

'Best idea you've had all day.'

We left the library, got the car and made our way back to the tartan palace.

What the hotel's rooms lacked in style and presentation, the bar more than amply made up for. The bar staff were helpful and friendly. The criteria for getting a job seemed to be being young, beautiful and Asian. Giggling after my second glass of wine, I decided we should go out and eat before I got too plastered. I was drinking alone, as Laura had a headache and wanted to take it easy given that we had to be at the nick by 8am, get the necessary information, give ourselves time to read it and get to the Bullring for 10am. At least one of us was being sensible. I'd ploughed my way through enough working days in the past with a hangover to even accept it as the normal way to feel at work.

Before I knew it I was back in the Scottish nightmare again. I slept badly, dreaming I was being chased by a haggis. I wasn't even really sure what a haggis looked like, but it could race along when provoked. Rubbing my eyes next morning, I tried to remember what I'd done to goad the haggis into chasing me but couldn't. I texted Laura to make sure she was up and got ready to find out whether the local police had found anything suspicious about the sad death of little Peter Woods.

Chapter 54

1st October

Back at the local nick, we found Robin Cox, our liaison. Once I was settled in his office, he handed me the pile of paperwork he'd been able to put together since I called him the previous day. He had gathered a lot of information in a short space of time.

'I've managed to track down the post mortem photographs if you want to see them, too,' he said. He carried on without waiting for a reply; I was considering whether seeing photographs of a nine-year-old's body would carry us any further forward. Probably not. 'They're in storage, but someone can get them out later today if you need to see them.'

'Thanks, Robin,' I said. 'Why are there post mortem photographs if there wasn't a police investigation?'

'Oh, but there was an investigation to start with.' He blinked three or four times, took his glasses off and laid them on the desk. 'It was a suspicious death in the beginning. After a few days, when all of the staff and kids had been spoken to, bit of digging about into what an inquisitive sort of child Peter had been, ligature marks examined, that kind of thing, the incident was shut down. It was before my time. Haven't had a chance to read through that lot.' He pointed at the three-inch-thick bundle of paper I was holding. He picked his glasses up and put them back on.

'How about we go and read through this in the canteen, give you a shout if we think of anything else?' I suggested.

As I said this, a police officer in uniform came in to speak to Robin. I got the impression he was reluctant to do so in front of me and Laura. He was clutching his paperwork to his chest, eyes flitting in our direction. Robin was already engaged in conversation with the newcomer as we stood up to leave.

Reckoning we had about an hour until we had to drive to our next appointment, we sat in the canteen, split the paperwork in two, and attempted to find something to link the children's home to Operation Guard. For the first twenty minutes or so, we read the odd line out to each other but nothing of great importance was jumping out. Laura grabbed my attention when she said, 'Bloody hell. I've just got to the witnesses' accounts. These names ring a bell? Benjamin Makepeace, Anthony Birdsall, Adam Spencer?'

'Tony Birdsall was here? I thought he was from our neck of the woods.'

'He is, but so is Adam Spencer and we knew about him. That's Alf's son, isn't it?'

'We need to see Judith this morning and then make some calls. This isn't right.' We were running out of time before we met up with her. Ordinarily we would just visit her a second time, but she had sounded on edge as it was, so the more we were able to ask her now, the better. As I talked to Laura, I fanned through the remaining pages I hadn't got round to reading. 'If you drive, I'll read the rest of this.'

'Nina,' I heard Laura say, 'You look terrible. What's wrong?' She leant across the table and uncurled my fingers from the creased sheet. Feelings of sadness were engulfing me. I felt very sad for the loss of life, especially the life of a little boy. I found myself wondering if his death all those years ago really could have been an accident. If it hadn't been, then it forced me to accept that the child had been murdered. We'd left three corpses behind in our own force and had been met with another unexplained death here in Birmingham. I was finding the thought of what could drive a person to mutilate another living human being, and watch their life blood drain away, more unsettling that I'd imagined possible.

I was struggling to think clearly. Judith had mentioned something on the phone about the children being responsible. Three decades on and those children were grown men. One was missing, possibly living a stone's throw from all three murder victims; another we knew was staying in the same area as the victims; and the last one was the son of the local police station's caretaker.

I feigned pulling myself together. 'Let's go see Judith. We can make some calls on the way,' I said to Laura.

'You really look ill, you know?' she said.

'Knew I'd brought you along for a reason,' I said, forcing a smile. 'I'm OK. Come on. I'll even let you drive.' I took the car keys out of my pocket, slid them across the canteen table to her and stood up, making an extra effort not to allow my knees to let me down.

During the journey, I tried and failed to clear my mind and focus. I could feel a terrible burden pushing down on my shoulders. You know when you get that 'can't quite put my finger on it' feeling? That was what I had.

Chapter 55

I kept my feelings to myself. I had a job to do. After Laura parked, we found our way to the Cup of Coffee café using the map at the entrance to the Bullring. As we got nearer, I saw a woman of about fifty-five perching on the edge of a metal chair outside the coffee shop. Although five of the six tables were occupied, I spotted her at once: she was alone, and continually glancing from left to right. She watched us as we walked towards her, and smiled tensely at me as I said, 'Hello, Judith. I'm Nina and this is Laura.'

'Hello,' she said, relaxing her shoulders and loosening her grip on her handbag. She settled back into the chair, crossing her legs.

'Are you OK talking here?' I asked. It was busy in the coffee shop as well as on the shopping centre concourse. Once Judith agreed to staying put, Laura went to get us some drinks and I pulled another two chairs closer to the table.

'Thank you for meeting with us, Judith,' I began. Just as I was about to say that we'd wait until Laura returned, she narrowed her eyes and beckoned me closer with a nod of her head. I perched on the edge of my chair, moving towards her. I got the impression that she was about to say something I couldn't miss, and I teetered on the chair to hear her.

'Stan McGuire told me I could trust you. That's good enough for me,' she whispered.

Unable to utter a word at this revelation, I sat back into the cold metal chair, snapping to it when I heard the sound of Laura approaching with a noisy tray of ceramic cups and saucers. Laura handed out the drinks, sat down and drew her coat around her. I saw her shiver and pick up her cup, placing both hands around it.

'We waited until you came back,' I said to Laura, to convey to Judith that I had no intention of mentioning my old friend Stan. I turned my attention back to Judith again. Her face was now relaxed, no sign of the earlier eye-narrowing. 'Where do you want to start?' I asked her.

She moved her chair closer to the table. Laura and I did the same. Judith spoke quietly.

'Back in the mid-Eighties a local children's home burned down. Some of the children and staff were accommodated in other homes but places had to be found quickly. The old asylum at Leithgate had only just been closed so it was fully functioning, albeit unsuitable. After a few weeks, the home was holding a number of children, some on a short-term basis.' Judith paused, cleared her throat and moved a hand towards her coffee cup before changing her mind and continuing, 'Peter Woods was placed in temporary accommodation at Leithgate. He was quite a difficult boy. He used to wander off all the time, get lost, up to no good. A cat was found drowned in a barrel. It was thought that Peter had done it. Some of the other children had seen him playing with the cat, then it turned up dead with a piece of wood over the top of the barrel. He was unpleasant. Sorry, sorry, know that I shouldn't talk about a little boy like that who died so horribly. The other children didn't like Peter, and the staff didn't care too much for him either. I was never happy that it was an accident.'

The noise of the two young girls from the next table getting up and scraping their metal chairs on the tiled floor, giggling with each other about some private matter, caused Judith to pause. This time she reached for her cup and took a sip.

'There is a possibility it was an accident, but how a child falls through broken floorboards, hanging himself as he goes, is beyond me.' Judith closed her eyes. 'It's beyond me,' she repeated.

'You must have worked for Social Services for some time,' I said, after she had remained silent and unmoving for a few seconds.

She opened her eyes, nodded weakly and said, 'Yes, some years. Before that I worked at the children's home. That's how I know so much about it. I remember how scared little Adam was when Peter died. Thing was, Adam was such a lovely young boy, and he was... well he was the one who found Peter's body.'

Judith broke off at this point and wiped at the end of her nose with a tissue she fished from her pocket.

'He was in a terrible state afterwards. He couldn't speak for a while. It really got to him. Probably still haunts him to this day. Well, it would, wouldn't it? It's something you'd never forget. He seemed afraid of everything at one point.

'He was about to be sent off to a short-term foster home when his father came for him. That just seemed to snap him out of it. He seemed to go back to being the same lovely little Adam. The change back was remarkable, and rapid. I remember him clearly because, apart from being the one who found Peter, Adam and another boy, Anthony, weren't from round here. They had southern accents, like London accents. Well, like yours.'

'Do you remember their surnames, Judith?' asked Laura.

'Adam Spencer and Anthony... no, I can't remember his surname. Think it began with B. They spent quite a lot of time together but they weren't there for long. Anthony left shortly after Adam but I don't recall where he went. I left too, soon after that.'

All the time Judith had been talking, I had been listening intently but also wondering why she hadn't wanted to meet anywhere official. She hadn't told us much more than we could have found out by reading the police reports and statements. I was beginning to wonder if we were talking to someone who pictured themselves at the core of an investigation but in reality was nothing more than a bit-part witness. She knew Stan, though, so I was prepared to cut her a bit of slack, see where she was going with this.

'Thing is,' she said, glancing left and right, 'what seemed to unnerve little Adam more than anything, even more than being the one who found Peter hanging, was one of the other members of staff. She was at the home only briefly, before Peter died. Then she left the area.' Judith stared down miserably into her empty cup.

'What was the member of staff's name?' Laura asked.

'Daphne – Daphne Lloyd,' came the reply. 'Adam seemed to be determined to avoid her and he wouldn't say why. She was very strict with the children. She always, as my mum used to say, "had her landlady face on". People said she had a son of her own somewhere but no one knew much about her. She did seem to really care about the kids, but the thing with Peter didn't sit right. Adam found Peter's body, and he later told me that Daphne was already in the roped-off area when he found him. But then he clammed up and wouldn't say another word about it. Who knows what actually went on.' Judith glanced down at her wristwatch. 'Is that the time? I've been going round the gasworks.'

'Would you recognise Daphne if you saw her again?' I asked Judith, rifling through my paperwork for a photograph of Daphne Headingly.

'Probably yes,' she said. I held up the photograph of Operation Guard's last victim. Judith leaned across and took it from me. She held the picture for a short time before answering, 'She's aged a bit but yes, that's her. That's definitely Daphne Lloyd.'

Chapter 56

Euphoric wasn't the word. In my mind I was doing laps of the Bullring while air-grabbing for emphasis. This was the link. No coincidence could be this massive.

Now I had to call Ray, or probably Eric Nottingham, and tell them all about the children's home. I fumbled in my pocket for my mobile to call the DCI, make his day with news of this breakthrough. The suspect line-up now clearly consisted of Tony Birdsall, Adam Spencer and Benjamin Makepeace.

I thought about whether, despite his disappearance, Benjamin Makepeace should be just as much of a suspect as Birdsall or Spencer. Birdsall and Spencer lived in Spain. And 'a foreigner' had done it, Richard Hudson had told me. According to enquiries, Makepeace didn't even have a passport. And why Daphne Headingly had been working in Birmingham under her maiden name while still married was anyone's guess. I didn't let these complications worry me too much, though. There was an entire team of dedicated investigators working on this. I was never alone, never without support.

Laura explained to Judith that she had just identified a murder victim hundreds of miles south as her former colleague, and the massive implications this had on everything she had told us. The last thing either of us wanted to do was to cause her more anxiety than she was clearly experiencing; however, we badly needed what she had told us in writing. A murder investigation depended on it. I was itching to call the

DCI. It would have been good to actually see his face when I told him the news, but then he'd go loopy that I'd driven all the way back from Birmingham just to watch his facial expression. I couldn't leave it a minute longer, so I stood up with my phone in my hand and said to Judith, 'I have to call my boss. You can trust me.'

'I know,' she said.

I winked at Laura, she nodded to tell me she'd stay, and I knew that she'd explain to Judith what needed to happen as I hastened off as far from the shopping crowds as I could manage. I dialled as I strode.

'Hello, Nina,' Eric Nottingham said as he answered. He'd put my number in his phone's memory. I liked that.

'Boss,' I said. 'Me and Laura have uncovered some great stuff here in Birmingham. Daphne Headingly used to work up here in a children's home in Leithgate. A little boy was hanged while she was here. Also here at the time were Anthony Birdsall and Adam Spencer, Alf the caretaker's son, as well as Benjamin Makepeace.'

He listened, he asked questions and he took notes. I could hear the pages turning. Some of it he read back to make sure he'd recorded it properly. Now it was his call whether he arranged an arrest and search team to trace Birdsall, put in progress locating Adam Spencer as a suspect, and did any further work around Benjamin Makepeace's disappearance. I made a couple of suggestions regarding things that Laura and I should do before heading home. He made a couple more, including that we should stay another night. I hoped it was for welfare reasons and not because he didn't want me back in his Incident Room.

'Oh, and Nina...' he said as I was about to disconnect the call. 'Well done to you both.' I soared. 'We'll talk about why you were investigating a children's home from the 1980s when you get back.' I plummeted.

I'd work it out. Benjamin Makepeace was sure to get me off the hook on that one. Back at the café, as I approached the table I heard Judith say, 'Benjamin? No, sorry, I don't recognise the name. Doesn't mean he wasn't there after I left, or maybe I've just forgotten him.'

'Judith,' I interrupted, 'I've just spoken to my boss. We need to arrange getting this in a statement. He's sorting out the necessary data protection forms so that we can see any files you still hold. He's also going to make a call to arrange for us to visit you officially at work.'

With some reluctance, she agreed to see us at her office at one o'clock. As we walked away from her at the café, I glanced at the couple at the next table. The woman laughed at something the man sitting next to her said as he held her hand up to his lips and kissed the back of it. I hadn't spoken to Bill since I'd left. I got my phone out to call him.

Laura was tactful enough to stop and look in the nearest shop window, appearing genuinely interested in making her own toy bear.

'Hey, you,' I said as he answered the phone.

'Hey, Nin,' said Bill. 'Been thinking about you since you left. How long are you likely to be away for?'

'Don't know. At least one more day.'

'Anything interesting happening?'

'Not really, just paperwork,' I lied.

'Well, you girls be careful. I'll call you later tonight. And, er...' He paused and coughed before adding, 'Still looking forward to another date.'

'Me too.' I blushed and ended the call.

When I looked over to where I'd last seen Laura, she was watching me with her phone to her ear. I hadn't realised that she was making a call too, being preoccupied with my own. As I made eye contact with her, she disconnected, dropping her phone into her handbag in one swift movement.

'Alright, Laura?' I asked.

'Yeah, fine. How was Bill?'

'He's good.' I grinned. 'Was that the office on the phone?'

'No, no, it wasn't. I need to find the ladies' before we leave,' she said, heading in the direction of the store locator map.

A few minutes later we were on our way back to the car, planning how we were going to make use of the time. We devised a plan to split the making of calls, writing up our notes and returning to see our intelligence liaison for further information as a result of police checks made on the staff at the children's home at the time. Most of what we wanted was already in the paperwork he'd given us, though. It was a question of sorting through it all.

That done, it was soon time to head to the Social Services offices. The building was an unassuming 1970s concrete structure close to the town centre. Once past reception, we were led along the corridor to a meeting room to await Judith's arrival.

She came in carrying a box of paperwork and wearing a frown. She dumped the box down, muttered something about tea and left. A couple of minutes passed before she returned again, closing the door behind her.

'I've got you everything you should need there,' she said, pointing towards the cardboard box she had deposited on the table. 'I have this room for the rest of the day. I know that you want a statement from me and that, of course, is fine. I'm sorry if my demeanour seems somewhat off. We co-operate with the police but there was always an uneasy feel about Peter Woods' death. Even though it was supposed to be an accident – ' as Judith stood there, her left hand fluttered up to her throat, and she stole a glance towards the closed door ' – something wasn't right. You asked me earlier at the Bullring if there was anyone else who might know more.' Judith was looking straight at Laura as she spoke now. 'She's on her way with the tea.'

I saw how tired Judith looked. My first impression of her was superseded by this new one; the hesitation to talk had been replaced by nervousness. 'I'll just see where she is,' said

Judith as she reached out and opened the door. Laura and I found ourselves looking into the corridor at a black woman of about sixty years of age, holding a tray of cups, tea pot and sugar caddy.

'This is Mary Williams,' said Judith, and we all politely said hello to each other. Mary placed the tray down with more precision than Judith had displayed with the box. 'Can I leave you to talk for a few minutes? She can help you. She also knew Daphne Lloyd.' Judith retreated from the conference room, leaving Laura and me in suspense.

Mary walked to the other side of the table and sat down. 'Shall I be mother?' she asked, taking charge of the tea-pouring.

Laura glanced at me before saying to Mary, 'Anything you tell us would be really helpful. I don't know how much Judith's told you, but we're investigating three linked murders and it's led us to Leithgate children's home. One of our victims worked there – Daphne Lloyd.'

I studied Mary's face as she mulled this information over. She pursed her lips and gave a tiny nod. It was so fleeting, I wondered if I'd imagined it.

'I never talk about Daphne, she said. 'I know about that little boy dying because Daphne was lodging with me at the time. My mother had just died and left me and my brother her house. He wasn't looking to hang around and I didn't fancy living in that big draughty place alone, so I decided on a lodger. Well, Daphne arrived, she hinted at husband troubles, moved in and a couple of weeks later that little boy was dead. She didn't stay around long after that.'

I had so many questions, but began with, 'What did Daphne tell you about Peter's death?'

'Tragic, really tragic,' she answered. Her mass of black curls bounced from side to side as she appeared to be shaking memories from her mind. She turned her attention back to the tea, but then a thought struck her and she stared past Laura and me as she spoke, 'Can't say I've thought about this in a long time. Daphne came home that day very late – your lot kept her late. She was very upset and kept saying, "That poor boy, that poor boy." I said to her, I said, "Daphne, it's so sad but at least he's at peace, he's with God." Then she said the strangest thing.'

Concentration wrinkled Mary's face as she fought to recall a conversation from so many years ago. She closed her eyes, which seemed to switch off the part of her brain that told her she was holding a teapot. It clattered to the table.

'She said, "He'll have to live with it; things will never be the same again."' Mary stared straight at me. 'How could he live with it if he was dead? She didn't mean Peter Woods, did she? She meant some other boy.'

Laura and I continued to ask Mary about Daphne, whether she could recall any more of the conversation with her, any other detail such as why Daphne's stay in Birmingham was so brief. She helped as much as she could, we took her statement and she left us to send Judith back.

Left alone, Laura said, 'Can't believe on the way here you apologised to me for getting us sent up here.'

'Seems like we've been very lucky. Do you want to call Nottingham this time?'

As my friend went off to make the call, I handled Judith. She came back into the room, taking Laura's empty chair beside me.

'Thanks, Judith. I know that this has been difficult for you. One thing I have to ask is, how do you know Stan McGuire?'

A mischievous glint in her eye caught me off guard. I hoped I had misinterpreted it. Really, I didn't want to think of Stan like that. But I'd asked the question; now I had to take the answer, whether I liked it or not.

'My husband was a policeman. He joined the Metropolitan Police, went to Hendon and met Stan there. They were in the same class, became really good friends, but John, my husband, missed his family and Birmingham. He decided to come home, transferred and we met, got married.' As she told me this, she relaxed completely for the first time in my presence: the hand-clenching and unclenching stopped. I was also more relaxed. The association was innocent.

She continued, 'John and Stan still speak from time to time. Before Stan's Angela died, the four of us would often meet up, have a drink, put the world to rights. Stan told me that you were heading up this way. He called me on Sunday, said that you were working on an enquiry and might end up needing help from Social Services. That's why I called you.'

I intended to verify this with Stan. It wasn't that I didn't believe Judith, but I liked to double check where my friends were concerned. I had been thinking about Stan on and off since leaving him on Sunday. I didn't know Judith, but she had known him a lot longer than I had. I didn't want to talk about him with her any more.

'Have you been asked about Peter Woods in the last few years?' I asked.

'No, I haven't, and there's no way of checking if anyone has looked at the paperwork records unless they added a note. Some of it was on computer but the system wasn't sophisticated enough to log all enquiries.'

I got down to the official business of taking a statement. I explained that it was to record her identification of Daphne Headingly from the photograph I'd shown her, and that I was seizing a box bursting at the sides full of paperwork from a child's death in 1985. I gave the box a quick once-over before opening it. Musty paper scents seeped out. Not as strong as they would have been if the box were the original. The pages felt slightly damp when I lifted a handful out, but were in good condition. I'd sorted through enough police paperwork stored in garages and unheated outbuildings to know that the immaculate cardboard box before me had not spent over a quarter of a century with its contents.

As we were finishing, Laura returned to join us. We left further contact details with a promise of an update for Judith as soon as we could, before heading out of the building with our stack of paperwork to add to the files we already had from West Midlands Police.

Safely out of anyone else's earshot within the confines of the car, I turned to Laura as she fastened her seatbelt in the passenger seat and said, 'Three questions, Lol. One, who do you think is the offender: Adam Spencer, Tony Birdsall or Benjamin Makepeace? Two, what did the DCI say? Three, can we eat? My stomach thinks my throat's been cut.'

'Fast food, sandwich or pub?' she said.

'Pub. There's one on the way back to the local nick. We can park easily.' I drove towards the car park exit as she told me she had about as much of an idea of who the culprit was as I did. Fortunately, we had to locate the evidence to make our decision for us.

'So what did Nottingham say?' I asked as I reversed into a parking space outside the pub offering '2 for 1 on all main meals'. The loser Russian I'd dated sprang to mind, rapidly replaced by thoughts of Bill.

'What are you smiling at?' said Laura, turning to look in the same direction as me. 'The special offer?'

'Sorry, mate. Don't know why I was smiling.'

'Were you thinking about Bill?'

Poxy detectives. Always so smart. I was just about to say something witty – not sure what, though – when her phone started to ring. She took it from her handbag, and, on reading the display, held it close to her chest and asked me, 'Can I catch you up in a second? I want to take this call.'

I left her the car keys and went inside to order a soft drink, hesitating only a second at the wine list. Still on duty. I ordered a lemonade, started a tab and sat myself down with two menus.

The table I chose was one of many empty ones in the pub, but this one faced the car park. I watched Laura's face as she talked on her mobile; she seemed to be speaking quite fast and at one point paused, looked in my direction and covered her mouth with her hand. That seemed unnecessary, as I didn't remember telling her I could lip-read. I squirmed a bit in my sturdy high-backed chair. It didn't budge under my weight, purchased no doubt by the pub chain in an attempt to stop drunken customers throwing them about in fights at last orders. Then the thought struck me that a lot of pubs probably didn't even have last orders these days. Showing my age again. I was old enough to remember when orange juice was considered to be a starter in restaurants.

So engrossed was I in thoughts of the days when pubs were full of overflowing ashtrays and in a restaurant it was a lottery whether the entire meal could be consumed without the person on the next table lighting a cigarette before the bill came, I failed to register that Laura was standing at the end of the table. When I realised she was there, I held out a menu to her. 'I'll go back and order,' I said. 'I've started a tab. What do you want to drink?'

Once I'd ordered and got her the coffee she wanted, I asked again what the DCI had said.

'Well,' she began, stirring her cappuccino, 'he's mulling over making all three of them suspects.'

'Makes sense,' I said, considering this idea. 'At this stage, if we nick one of them, we nick them all. Could be a bit harsh if Benjamin Makepeace turns up dead as victim four and he's wanted for murders committed after he died. Still, can't see how Nottingham can make one a suspect and not the others at this stage.'

Laura was about to say something when I spotted a waiter heading our way with a plate in each hand. I jerked my head in his direction, causing Laura to pause. Once the food was in front of us, we were quiet for a couple of minutes.

'He wants us to be at the nick for three o'clock,' said Laura in between mouthfuls of ciabatta. 'Wants to have a briefing with us listening in on speakerphone.'

'I wonder if the system's compatible for a video conference,' I said. 'Hope not; I don't have to do my hair for the phone.

Doubt we'd be able to set it up in time anyway.' I paused for air in my haste to eat chips so hot they were stripping the skin from the inside of my mouth.

'Said he'd give us a couple more things to sort out before we head home, too,' said Laura.

'Yeah, he mentioned that earlier. Wonder what I'll dream about tonight? Being chased by sporrans... drowning in porridge...'

The bill settled, we drove back to the nick to find a room for a conference call and find out what progress the Incident Room had made in finding Adam Spencer, Tony Birdsall and Benjamin Makepeace. At least one of them was looking likely to be the killer.

Chapter 57

Tucked away in a room far removed from the main CID offices and uniform officers running in and out of the building, Laura and I sat with our paperwork in front of us. The only noise came from the telephone's loudspeaker bringing us the rustle of dozens of investigators entering the conference room and finding a seat. We could hear clearly but still sat as near as possible to the phone, hunched over in case we missed one single word. Introductions made, it was soon under way. Laura and I had a starring role. No one said a word until we had imparted all the information we had so far amassed.

Nottingham cleared his throat. Laura and I were motionless, staring at the handset. 'I've made a decision,' he said. 'I've updated the policy file and suggest that you all read it. We've already had two in custody for Operation Guard, David Connor and Gary Savage. HOLMES will always show them as suspects one and two. My decision reads that Adam Spencer is now a suspect. That makes him suspect number three. Anthony Birdsall is a suspect. He is suspect number four.' Furious writing both ends of the line.

'I have not made Benjamin Makepeace a suspect at this time. He is a missing person. We have his blood on a knife. How that blood got into Savage's van has still not been established. It is a priority that he be found. Once he's found, I'll reassess, but for the time being take it that he is to be traced, interviewed and eliminated from this enquiry. Nina, Laura, while you're in Birmingham, can you go and visit

Makepeace's GP in case something's been missed?' We agreed that we would.

Half an hour later, we were done staring at the telephone. Instead we stared at a list of outstanding enquiries which needed actioning before we could call our work in Birmingham finished. Incident Rooms were run on the allocation and completion of enquiries recorded on action sheets. Their range was far-reaching, varying from locating witnesses, then taking statements, to scoping for CCTV and its seizure. Laura and I spent the rest of the day completing calls, doing paperwork and knocking on doors following up on Benjamin's disappearance, though there was little to go on. We spent a great deal of time pestering local officers to carry out checks for us on their computer system, as security didn't allow us direct access.

Laura managed to speak to Makepeace's GP on the telephone and made an appointment to see him at the end of the surgery's hours, by which time we hoped our other enquiries would be finished. The surgery had previously been contacted by local officers in case staff could shed any light on their patient's disappearance, but they'd had little to tell. Benjamin Makepeace had only been to see his doctor on a few occasions and for nothing of note. This information, of course, had all been cleared via Data Protection. Even then, Dr Phillips informed Laura on the phone, before agreeing to an appointment, that he was reluctant to tell us anything relating to his patient's private records. The medical profession was helpful to a point in investigations, but, for very good reasons, they did not want to be seen as assisting the police beyond their legal requirements. This was completely understandable, but we were attempting to establish if the man could have taken his own life or was a danger to himself or others. After arguing this through on the phone, Dr Phillips agreed to see us.

We arrived for our appointment ten minutes early. It didn't pass us by that we had parked about five minutes' walk from the Makepeaces' house with its Benjamin memorial. This street was much more pleasant: the houses were spaced further apart and the Wayside Medical Centre was one of the largest. The structure had been added to over time, with an extension to the side and a disabled access ramp at the front. Laura and I made our way to the front door, pausing for a young woman of about twenty-five to struggle out of the double door with her pram. Laura held the door for her.

Inside, we made our way to the receptionist, carefully cocooned within her domain by a large glass screen with a hole cut out for verbal communication. These used to be confined to Underground Station counters and bookies, but clearly the wait for a doctor's appointment was proving too much for the clientele.

Once we'd been introduced to Dr Stephen Phillips, a small, slight man of about forty, and got settled within his office on uncomfortable plastic chairs, Laura explained again why we wanted to see him. She began with, 'The reason we're here speaking to you is that, when the local police first came to the surgery, the Missing Person enquiry was moderately fresh. No trace of Benjamin was found for some time. Just over a week ago, however, carrying out a warrant, we found traces of Benjamin's blood. This was hundreds of miles away in Riverstone, so we're making sure that nothing has been missed.'

Dr Phillips looked surprised. That might have been because he genuinely felt it, or he was used to appearing that way for patients when they imparted news to him.

'Well, let me see. I don't really have much else to tell you. You told me earlier that you have a copy of the Missing Person report, and everything medical about Benjamin was passed on, which was very little. He hardly came here to see me. I was on holiday when the local police arrived asking to speak to me. A colleague, Dr Darr, provided what information he could about Benjamin, but he's quite new and I don't think that he ever saw him as a patient. The last time Benjamin was here, it was several months ago, for a cold he couldn't shift. Oh, and, while he was here, I signed his passport application for him.'

Both my and Laura's heads snapped up at this information. 'Passport application?' Laura asked.

'Yes, I'm sorry, I realise that this information is very important to a Missing Person enquiry but, as I say, I only returned from leave some time after Dr Darr sent you the notes,' said Dr Phillips in an even tone. I got the impression he was trying to summon up the right 'don't blame me' tone.

'We were told he didn't have a passport and never went abroad,' Laura said.

'According to Benjamin, he was looking forward to his trip to Spain to visit a couple of old friends who had a bar out there,' said the GP.

'Did he happen to mention who these friends were?'

'No, sorry. To be honest, I wasn't all that interested,' said Dr Phillips.

We asked a few more questions before deciding that we weren't getting any further, wrote the obligatory statement, thanked Dr Phillips for his time and returned to the privacy of the car. Back within the vehicle, we stared at each other before I said, 'I thought that passport checks were done for Makepeace?'

'We probably assumed they were done because everyone said he didn't have much of a life outside of his mother and the library,' said Laura as she tapped her fingernails on the steering wheel. 'Looks like a couple of lucky sods from the Incident Room will be getting a trip to Spain out of this. Want to make the calls and then we'll drive back to the hotel, see what else is in the paperwork?'

Task completed, we headed for the Scottish nightmare for a shower and change of clothes before settling down to start reading our stack of paperwork. I lay on the floor, surrounded by the paperwork we'd divided in half as Laura sat on my bed, leaning back against the wall.

'Lol,' I said, gazing up at her, 'these murders won't stop, will they? Not until we find him.'

'We've got a link now,' she said, clasping the papers in her hand towards her. 'And a list of suspects.'

'But we don't have any idea who may be next,' I said. 'It might even be one of the other boys from the home. They're all going to have be traced and interviewed.'

My work phone started to ring from the bed where I'd left it before flopping to the floor. Laura handed it to me. I registered a flash of annoyance on her face.

'Hi, there, Ray,' I said.

I found her expression interesting.

'Nina, have a bit of news for you. We've got Makepeace's passport details. Seems that he flew from Malaga to Gatwick in August. He flew back on the same plane as Jason Holland.'

Now I was staring straight at Laura as the words registered in my brain. 'Hang on, Ray,' I said, 'Laura'll want to hear this too.' I hit the speakerphone button and placed it on the hotel carpet among the messy spread of paperwork. 'Say that again, Ray, for Laura to hear.'

'OK, Cagney and Lacey, listen up.' I laughed; Laura scowled. 'It seems that there was an application for a passport check on Makepeace when he went missing. However, it was still being processed. We did it on the hurry-up after your meeting with Dr Phillips today. He flew out of Gatwick after he went missing. He flew to Malaga on his own, as far as we can establish, and back again on 22nd August. He was on the same flight as Jason Holland. There is no activity on his bank account so we're still working out how he booked and paid for the flights. Anyway, we're looking into whether he travelled with Holland or on his own. Well done, girls. This is one of the best bits of information we've had yet.'

Feeling pretty pleased with ourselves, we packed the paperwork away and made plans to head to the bar again. Truth be told, we should have saved our celebrating and finished reading. But we were exhausted.

Laura wanted to nip back to her room to grab her handbag and change her shoes so I took the opportunity to call Bill. His phone was switched off so I left him a message, wandered around my room for a bit, tried to get the broken lampshade straight and then, figuring I'd given Laura enough time, I went off to get her.

I walked along the mercifully tartan-free corridor to her room. As I lifted my hand to knock on her door, I heard her say, 'No, Nina doesn't know. No reason for her to find out, either.'

I stepped back, uncertain of what to do. I wasn't sure whether to confront her or pretend I hadn't heard. Giving myself time to make up my mind, I tiptoed back to the sanctuary of my room. I sat on the frayed bedspread, which the cleaner had insisted on putting back on the bed, despite my attempt to hide it in the wardrobe. I thought rationally about the snippet of conversation I'd overheard. Firstly, it wasn't meant for my ears. Secondly, it could have been about anything at all, so why was I being so paranoid? For now, I wasn't going to mention a thing, just see where the conversation went that night. Mind made up, I wanted out of the room, so I stood up to leave just as a light knocking on the door told me Laura was ready too.

The evening was pleasant enough, but in the back of my mind I kept replaying the part of my friend's conversation I had heard. I wanted to ask her, but didn't know how I would feel at outright denial. Besides, I kept telling myself, it might not have been anything to do with work. We chatted over dinner at a busy steak restaurant recommended by the hotel's receptionist. Neither of us ordered steak. The force's budget couldn't stretch to it.

Once the chicken and pasta were paid for, we headed outside to wander back to the hotel, in time for the rain to start.

'One for the road?' suggested Laura, jerking her head in the direction of a seedy boozer on the corner.

Personally, I loved seedy boozers. I'd spent a lot of time working in one before I joined the job. It was a fantastic chance to meet blokes with names like 'John the Gas', 'Pete the Milk' and 'Harry the Butcher'. Harry was actually a butcher, not someone who hacked people to bits. I'd loved it at the time but seldom went to such places since becoming a police officer. Being offered joints of beef which had been liberated via jockey shorts was always a problem when I had a warrant card in my pocket and was under oath to the Queen.

We went in via the door that promised a Saloon Bar. It failed to deliver.

Six old men well past their prime greeted us inside. They all stopped talking and stared. I went up to the bar and spoke to the young, smiling barmaid. Wine was not a wise choice in such an establishment; we took our bottles of beer and found seats in the corner, away from the pub's few customers, who had returned to their conversation.

'How's it going with Bill?' asked Laura.

'OK,' I said, taking a sip from my beer to mask the smile that was forming. I didn't want to share too much at this stage and there wasn't much to say, only a good feeling I got whenever I thought about him. 'Much happening with you, Lol?'

A shake of the head as she swallowed some of her beer. 'Not much.' She didn't meet my eye, but played with a soggy beer mat instead. Changing the subject, she held the wet cardboard coaster up and said, 'Banned these in a lot of places, you know. They were being used to mix drugs up.'

'Really?' I asked. 'How bloody sad. That why I end up with my drink dripping into my lap – 'cos some arse wants to stick cocaine up their nose?'

'What are we doing tomorrow before we head back?' she asked.

I exhaled, examined my beer bottle and said, 'Mrs Makepeace, pick the rest of the paperwork up at the nick and get back to the Incident Room.'

'Good plan. '

It was a good plan, too. In the morning, after another night of Highland night terrors, we checked out of the hotel, saying we had had an enjoyable stay due to the terrific service in the bar. This was somewhat discreet and a little spineless. Then we headed off to see Mrs Makepeace one last time.

Chapter 58

2nd October

En route to Mrs Makepeace, Ray Hopkinson called to give us the latest from our county's serial killer enquiry.

'One in custody for the murders of Amanda Bell, Jason Holland and Daphne Headingly,' said Ray as I answered the call on the car's hands-free.

'Laura had a fiver on the first one being Tony Birdsall.'

'You'd better get to the cashpoint, then, Foster. Birdsall's waiting to be interviewed by John Wing and young Danny.'

'What did he say when he got nicked?' asked Laura.

'Not a word,' came the reply. 'You'd think being lifted for the murder of three people would make him say something, even if it was just "bollocks".'

'Is Wingsy there with you?' I asked.

'No, he's off preparing for interview with Danny. Try his mobile,' offered Ray.

The sounds of someone trying to get Ray's attention, plus a phone ringing and the tannoy, gave an indication of how busy it was there. I knew to keep it short.

'Ray, one other thing. We're on our way back to see Mrs Makepeace. Can we mention Birdsall to her? So far we haven't given her specific names but as he's now been nicked...'

'I'll check with Eric and let you know.' He ended the call.

By this stage, we were in Mrs Makepeace's depressing road again. One or two of the house owners had tried to cheer the place up with windowboxes of flowers or hanging baskets. The still grey sky was doing little to enhance the overall impression of the place. It didn't seem to be a bad area; it just felt as if the whole street was sulking.

'I want to call Wingsy before we go in,' I told Laura as I scrolled through my contact list for his number.

'Hi, hon,' he said when he picked up. 'Been behaving in Birmingham?'

'Course, mate. Listen, I hear that you've been a jammy so-and-so and got the job of interviewing with Danny.'

'Think Nottingham must be mellowing towards me; he didn't want me anywhere near David Connor. Shame you weren't here – could have done this together, duchess.'

'Yeah, I'm gutted – but listen. Something's been on my mind since that day we spoke to him at Belinda's house. Remember she was hanging curtains?'

'I know what you're getting at, Detective Foster, and I'm all over it like a rash. When he was nicked, search team did their thing and took the curtains and all the paraphernalia. Got that senior CSI to look at the lot. She's going to see if the curtain wire from Belinda Cook's house matches the curtain wire from the room we found Jason Holland's body in. Listen, gotta go, solicitor's just got here. Bye, doll.' And he was gone.

'Curtains?' said Laura.

'Yes, I'll tell you in a bit, but, talking of curtains, just saw someone at the window at the Makepeaces' house. Let's speak to her first.'

We crossed the road to the terraced house with its dirty, mud-splashed front door and knocked. We both heard the shuffling Mrs Makepeace long before the door opened. When it did, she looked just the same as on our last visit: crushed. There was no recognition or movement in her eyes. As I was about to reintroduce us both, she muttered, 'Come in, officers,' turned and shuffled back to the dining room.

We followed her along the passageway. Back in Mrs Makepeace's own Incident Room for her son's disappearance, the paperwork and keepsakes of her child's life were neatly stacked in piles on the tabletop. A sudden flash of sunlight did its best to light up the room, but had a fair amount of grime to penetrate through the narrow window.

'We wanted to see you before we left Birmingham,' said Laura. 'In case there was anything else that you've thought of since we were here the other day.'

My work mobile bleeped as a text message arrived. I read the message as Laura was talking. It was the go-ahead to ask her about Tony Birdsall.

My friend waited for Mrs Makepeace to answer. She remained silent, poking at one of the neat piles of photographs of her son.

'Mrs Makepeace, we need to talk to you about Leithgate children's home. It's important,' I said. 'I think we should sit down.' I made to move towards the dining table. I watched her pull out a chair with slow, agonising movements. I waited until she was seated, sat next to her and waited for Laura to go to the farthest side of the table to take her seat. It felt important not to flank her on either side and also not to both sit facing her as if this were a job interview or another equally nerve-racking situation. It no doubt did nothing to put her at her ease. This woman was truly on the edge, if not freefalling over it.

'Do you remember a little boy dying at the children's home around about the time that Benjamin was there?' I asked.

Her eyes turned towards me at a speed I hadn't been expecting. They had probably been very pretty green eyes once; soft lines around them gave an indication of thousands of smiles over the years – all, I expected, as a result of some miracle Benjamin had achieved, such as learning his two times table. 'He was hanged. Terrible, it was. Place was in uproar. We were due to collect Benjamin anyway so we went and got him. Upset, he was, even though he didn't really know the boy.' She started to drift away, not really aware of us. Laura and I exchanged glances across the table. I gave it another try.

'Do you remember anyone at the home called Anthony or Tony Birdsall?'

'No, no,' her soft reply came. 'He hasn't been to see me.'

Spoke volumes, that answer. I changed tack. 'Who has been to see you, Mrs Makepeace?'

'The other boy. Well, not a boy now, is he?' She gave a small hollow laugh. 'Friend of Benjamin's, he said.' All three of us sat still. The only sound came from the traffic driving past the house. 'What was his name?' she muttered, bowing her head, chin touching her chest. Another mutter, barely audible.

'Sorry, Mrs Makepeace. What did you just say?'

Lifting her head high, she said, 'Adam... Adam something. Something to do with a shop. Was it Woolworth's? No, they've shut down, but something like that. Morrison's? No, no.' She shook her head.

Say Spencer, I willed.

'Spencer. That was it,' she said.

'When was he here?' I asked. Laura was making notes.

'Let me see. A week ago, perhaps two. Wanted to speak to Benjamin.' Her liver-spotted hand went up to her mouth, fluttered there and returned to the table top. 'Can't remember much else about him, but he knew my Benjamin, he said, from the home, and wanted to look him up. He said it was urgent and he had to speak to him about Peter.'

'Did he leave a contact number or address?' I asked.

'Yes. I have it here somewhere.' She pushed herself up from the table and began opening drawers in the dresser behind where I sat. She found it in a surprisingly short time: a scrap of paper with the word 'Adam' and a phone number. I took it from her and placed it into the evidence bag Laura had already pulled from her file in readiness.

'What else did he say to you, Mrs Makepeace?' Laura asked.

'Nothing I can remember. He was only here a minute. Didn't know that Benjamin had been missing. He seemed surprised, even a bit – what's the word? – well, annoyed.' She went back to the dresser and began straightening ornaments, photo frames, embroidered placemats.

With her back to us, Laura wrote on a piece of paper '*Not happy to leave her here*' and held it up to me. I nodded, thinking of our conversation about who might be the next victim. I made the universal sign for telephone call with my hand. She nodded in agreement and got up to make the call out of Mrs Makepeace's earshot.

While she was gone, I continued to ask Mrs Makepeace about Adam: what he looked like, clothing, how he'd got to her house, why after all these years he had turned up on her doorstep, but she remained evasive. It was as if I was talking to her in another room, sealed off from everyone else. This went on for several minutes until Laura returned.

'Local neighbourhood officers are on their way,' said Laura. I understood this to mean that no one wanted to risk Mrs Makepeace being found dead with dozens of stab wounds. 'Have you got somewhere else you can stay tonight?' asked Laura.

'I can't leave here,' she said, turning to stare at us both, mouth hanging open, holding a framed photograph of Benjamin as a toddler on a tricycle, huge flared trousers grabbing all the attention at the bottom of the picture. 'What if he comes back and I'm not at home? Where will he go? He'll be frightened. He'll want his dinner.'

'We are worried about Benjamin,' I said stepping towards her, 'but at the moment we're more worried about you.' I pointed towards the photo she was now clutching to her. 'How old was he in that photo?'

'Five,' she said, crinkles around the green eyes reappearing. 'That was before he went to Leithgate.'

A knock at the door drew my attention from Mrs Makepeace. Laura went to open it to the two uniform officers. They introduced themselves to me and Laura, but spoke to Mrs Makepeace as if they knew her. She didn't seem to have a clue who they were. After some persuasion, she agreed to stay in a hotel. I was tempted to suggest Tartan Towers but thought that, as she was a harmless, if slightly deranged old lady, I shouldn't be so cruel. There was no way we could force her to leave her own home, but if Adam Spencer returned and he was our man, or in league with the others, I didn't fancy her chances one little bit. Leaving her here to meet an unpleasant fate wasn't an option.

'How long will I have to leave for?' she asked, blinking a number of times before her eyes came to rest on PC Sam Gordon, one of the West Midlands officers.

'Pack for a couple of nights for now,' he said guiding her by the arm to the stairs. 'And we'll be talking to these lasses here when they have any news.'

She started her ascent. We all watched her, no doubt each of us thinking that this might take some time.

'Panic alarm's being fitted here this afternoon,' Sam told me and Laura.

The other PC, Alan Parker, answered his mobile phone and, following a swift conversation, added, 'She's booked in for two nights at a nearby hotel. Can you girls take her? Be more subtle. We'll stick out like a sore thumb.' As if guessing my next question, he added, 'Someone from our Serious Crime Directorate will be on their way to the hotel soon to stay overnight in the next room to her. Understand that you girls are needed back down south. Your DCI's been on the phone.'

That was settled, then: Laura and I had been won back in the staffing war by our own force. We were needed in our own Incident Room and that suited me just fine. It was time to return to our force and help establish how the three victims were linked together, and discover the motive for their deaths.

Chapter 59

It took some time to get Mrs Makepeace and her suitcase down the stairs, then another age to get her in the car. Once we were all inside her room at the hotel, two West Midlands DCs arrived to look after her. We told them as much as we knew and that we had already set the wheels in motion to get them a recent passport photo of Adam Spencer in case he came calling. As it had taken so long to get Mrs Makepeace to the hotel, the two local DCs already had the picture, handing us a spare copy. They also handed us mobile recording equipment, complete with DVDs.

Laura and I had discussed at length what we should do with this very important piece of evidence from Mrs Makepeace. She wasn't exactly firing on all cylinders following her son's disappearance. Getting her to sign a statement didn't seem right, and taking her to a police station witness room and recording her evidence, in light of what she'd told us, was impractical. Record her here for all to see, make sure we hadn't told her what to say and let a court see her reaction, that was our decision. We ran it by the boss too. He agreed, but we left him little option – he wasn't here, we were. Our call, and he seemed to trust our judgement.

We sent the local DCs off to unpack while we talked to Mrs Makepeace in as much detail as we could about her visit from Adam Spencer. She could add little but, for what it was worth, we committed what she said to DVD. We got her to look at the passport photo for the first time. 'Yes,' she said, nodding, 'that's the boy who came round to see me. Said his name was Adam, Adam something, and that he was in the home at Leithgate with my Benjamin.'

'Earlier today at your house, you gave me a piece of paper with a telephone number on it. Is this it here?' I held out the paper in the evidence bag.

'Yes, I do remember giving you that. Adam gave it to me. He was a nice young man. Wanted to see my Benjamin but I told him he'd gone missing.'

'How did he react to that?'

'Looked surprised, bit annoyed. Said it was very urgent that I call him if Benjamin did return. It was all a matter of life and death.' She giggled. My blood ran cold.

'Did he use those words: "a matter of life and death"?'

'Oh, no, but that was how he seemed to me. Kept looking over his shoulder, he did. Said the bit about speaking to Benjamin about Peter. No idea what he was on about. I thought he might have been crazy.' She giggled again, putting her hand over her mouth.

'Do you remember him from Leithgate?' I asked.

'No, love, no. Don't remember any of them kids.'

'Any of the staff, do you remember them?'

'No, love.' She went to stand up.

'Mrs Makepeace, could you stay sitting down, please? Laura is videoing you with the camera there. Remember? We explained this at the beginning. If you move around, she can't follow you.' I gave it another try. 'Did Benjamin ever mention that he wanted a passport?'

'No, no, he didn't. Why would he want to go abroad? He had no need for one,' she snapped back.

I had been thinking long and hard about how to question her about this. She wasn't likely to be too pleased to find out that he'd planned to leave the country and therefore his mother too. At any moment I expected Nottingham, if he hadn't already done so, to declare Makepeace a suspect. All we needed was proof that it was actually he who had used his passport and that he was very much alive, and I could anticipate him becoming suspect five. 'Mrs Makepeace, I went to see Benjamin's GP today, Dr Phillips.'

'Oh, lovely man. Been our doctor for years.'

'He signed a passport application for Benjamin a few months ago.'

Her face went scarlet. 'He had no right to do that. What on earth has he done that for?' she shrieked.

'Please sit down.' I tried once again. 'Have you any idea where he was planning to go?'

I was now getting no reply. She sat back down again and rubbed one hand with the other time and time again, biting on her bottom lip. I was just about to ask her if she was alright when she said, 'I won't talk to you any more. You're a liar.'

Shortly after that, we ended the interview. I was loath to call it giving up. It wasn't my finest work, but we had got what we came for – continuity of our evidence to locate Adam Spencer via his phone number and a record of our conversation with Mrs Makepeace.

It was hardly an emotional goodbye: Mrs Makepeace was ransacking the tea tray, eating the bourbons, and barely glanced up as we left. We told her we would be in touch. Neither of us was sure if she registered our departure.

I shut the hotel room door behind me. Laura looked at her watch. 'Much later than we should be now, but I can't see what we'd have to gain by staying another night.'

'Couldn't agree more,' I said. 'Only thing that would change my mind would be if the old girl – ' I indicated towards the hotel room ' – had something else to tell us about Spencer's location and it was in or around Birmingham. Plus a hotel room with radically different décor from the last one we stayed in.'

'Let's get back, then. I'll drive, you make calls,' said Laura, yawning.

'Thought for a minute we might get back at a reasonable time, but it's already half-four and once again I'm hungry.'

'Yeah,' she said. 'I just about kept a straight face when your stomach growled in the interview. Be funny if that gets played in court.'

Chapter 60

Homeward bound, I called Ray and gave him a summary of the interview with Mrs Makepeace.

'Also,' I said, 'any update from Wingsy's interview with Birdsall?'

'He's denying it, in a nutshell. Says he has alibis for two of the murders, including being out of the country for Amanda Bell's. His passport's been checked and it would appear that he was in southern Spain.'

'And the curtain suspension wires?' I asked. Laura looked over at me. I'd not told her about the wires. It had slipped my mind.

'We've had them examined and they're possibly from the same batch of wire but the ends have been compared and we don't have a mechanical fit. In other words, inconclusive.'

'Bollocks,' I said, 'Thought I had something there.'

'Right, then. I'll see you girls at 8am for a briefing. Drive carefully.'

I needed to fill Laura in on my theory, albeit one that hadn't been any help.

'When me and Wingsy found Jason Holland's body in that house, the whole place was empty, apart from the net curtains hanging at the windows.'

'Yeah.'

'Well, all of them were droopy, as if they'd been there for years. All of them, except the one in the room where the body was.'

'Yeah, I follow you so far, Nin.'

'The day that me and Wingsy first went round to Belinda's house, she had just hung some new curtains. We figured that a man put them up.'

'Why?'

'A woman would probably have cleared the mess up. Men are too busy arsing about with power tools.'

'And there was brick dust on the floor, so it must have been a man. I'm totally with you on the mess part, but it doesn't make Tony Birdsall a serial killer because he won't hoover. Half the fellas in the country would be banged up.'

'Yeah, but it was a good theory. And it still doesn't explain why someone would rehang a curtain when they've just dumped a body. Only reason I can think of is the curtain came down in the struggle and the killer rehung it to stop the neighbours from noticing anything odd. Anyway, as you heard, the ends have been examined and there's no mechanical fit between them. Doesn't mean it didn't come from the same batch of wire, though.'

We carried along in silence for a couple of minutes until Laura said, 'Two ideas. One, we stop to eat, and two, after that, you drive. I'll start reading the file from Social Services.'

The prepacked sandwiches on the motorway held no surprise – they were terrible. The file, however, was a different matter.

Laura leaned towards the box on the back seat from time to time, grabbed more papers and read the odd passage out to me. Now and again we'd both comment but she pretty much summarised the documents with practised efficiency. The journey was starting to get to me. Several times Laura was talking and I wasn't concentrating. Wasn't even listening.

Forcing myself to pay attention to the road, I found I could only do so by naming each of the three lanes either Adam Spencer, Tony Birdsall or Benjamin Makepeace. Each time I switched to another, fresh thoughts flooded my mind about the part each of them could be playing in this most horrific of crimes – murder. There was no coming back from the dead. The rules were simple: you ceased to be, and everything you left in your wake would never be the same again.

'This is Benjamin Makepeace's birth certificate. It says that his mother is Maureen Makepeace, same as our woman back there. But it says "father unknown". Bit odd, no?'

She laid the birth certificate on her lap, turning in the seat to look at me.

'You're right. Mrs Makepeace said her husband was killed by a drunk driver. She didn't say "Benjamin's father". Have you found anything in there to show that he was adopted, or documents in another name?' I asked, glancing over at the stack of paperwork next to her feet in the footwell.

'No, I haven't, and I don't see why she wouldn't have told us,' said Laura. 'I'll call West Mids and get them to ask her.'

Desperate as I was to read some of the documents myself, in truth, Laura's grabbing of random documents from the box was starting to grate on my nerves.

'Lol,' I said when I could take no more, 'is there any chance you can stop doing that? It's like a really, really shit lucky dip.'

She obliged.

'I don't get it,' I said, slowing down due to sudden inexplicable queues in all three of lanes Spencer, Birdsall and Makepeace. 'It was a children's home, not a daycare centre. You can't book your child in and out of one, simply because he's been out late with his mates or thrown stones at the neighbour's greenhouse. There must be more to it. I'm hoping the answers are in that box.'

'If they're not, the only other person who may be able to tell us is Benjamin Makepeace himself.'

We couldn't drive all the way back without several phone calls to Ray and Catherine. Both were working on various aspects of the investigation that Laura and I wanted updating on. We were police officers at the end of the day. Nosy creatures. It hadn't gone unnoticed by me that Laura seemed very keen to make the calls to Ray. Often I read too much into situations, but I thought that Laura might have taken a liking to him. He seemed a bit of a fool but fundamentally decent. In my opinion she could do better, but you couldn't choose your mates' boyfriends. That in itself was lucky, 'cos undoubtedly I would have chosen her a total tosser if my track record was anything to go by.

Ray told us that Tony Birdsall was talking but still denying any involvement. He seemed to be giving checkable facts, causing a stream of detectives to run around southeast England, parts of London and a couple of airports. Belinda Cook had sworn her way through a day with Mark Russell and Pierre while they took a statement from her. Lucky fellas.

Several hours later, we finally got back to the nick, parked and carried the paperwork up to the empty Incident Room, ready to head for home. I couldn't speak for Laura but I'd developed a headache on the M25 and it was only going to get worse. A glass of something chilled would kill or cure it. Temporary panic gripped me as I couldn't recall whether I'd drunk the last of the Sauvignon Blanc from the fridge. I calmed down when I remembered there were two more bottles behind the out-of-date coleslaw and potato salad.

We were both very weary but glad to be back. A large note on the office diary informed us that the next briefing would be at nine in the morning, rather than 8am as Ray had told us. We'd already updated the team, but no doubt there would be more from the rest of them.

Laura shivered as we walked back out of the Incident Room. 'It's cold in here,' she said, touching the corridor radiator as we approached it. 'Heating's not on.'

'Oh,' I said, 'we didn't ask about Alf. If his son's going to get nicked for three murders, it's hardly likely that he'll be allowed to wander around a nick that's full of evidence against his own boy.' I felt bad. I liked Alf. Whatever his son had or hadn't done, I couldn't see Alf having anything to do with it.

'God, yeah,' agreed Laura, 'Alf probably won't be here. Hope he's OK. They would have looked after him, wouldn't they?'

'I don't know, Lol. Really hope so, mate. He's worked here longer than we have. He retires in a few weeks.'

'I bet he's going to miss it,' she said. 'Working, I mean. I'd always find it funny when he'd come into an office and open and shut all the windows looking for something to fix.'

This made me feel even worse about the accusations I'd made earlier, suspecting Alf of listening at windows.

We chatted as we walked down the stairs, curiosity taking us past Alf's office. It was locked, though we'd expected nothing more. My final thought for the working day as we wandered towards the car park was that Alf's retirement to Spain supping on San Miguel was looking to be in jeopardy.

Chapter 61

Laura and I said goodbye in the car park, dragging our overnight bags to our respective cars. The car park was deserted but well lit. I unlocked my car, activating the button to remotely pop the boot. At least putting my case in there meant that I could check the space. Really, I was too tired for all that. Caution was exhausting.

I heard Laura's case as she dropped it into her car. By the time she was about to drive away, for some inexplicable reason I had an urge to stop her. That feeling I sometimes got kicked in, the one that urged me to take stock, slow myself down, trust my instinct. The worst that could happen was that I was wrong.

I ran towards her car as she drove past my parking spot. She had already put her hand up to wave at me but stopped as she saw me bolt in her direction. She braked and opened the window, concern on her face. 'You OK, Nin?' she asked.

Bollocks: now I felt stupid.

'Oh, yeah, just wanted to say, that – er – thanks again for coming with me. Appreciate the company.' How feeble was that?

'OK. Thought you were going to tell me something major then. Well, sleep well and see you in the morning.'

I stepped back to let her drive off. I'd achieved my aim: there was no one on her back seat.

I checked my own before getting in and heading home.

The streets were quiet. The temperature had dropped somewhat, and a chilly midweek evening with the threat of rain was enough to encourage most people to stay at home. Even the traffic was light as I drove from the nick out of town towards home, mulling over the events of the last couple of days. I opted for the shortcut through the industrial estates, a favourite route at peak times, but my decision was based entirely on speed. I wanted to get home.

As I pulled into my road, I wondered whether I was going to find a parking space anywhere near my front door. My only regret when I'd bought my house had been that it had no driveway or garage, causing a problem whenever I came home with shopping or suitcases.

I managed to find a spot on the opposite side of the road, about four houses down from mine. I turned the ignition and lights off and sat in the dark pondering whether I should take my case in now or come back out for it. The rain made my mind up for me. As I sat there, I watched two or three spots fall on to the windscreen, making me jump out of the driver's seat, grab my handbag from the seat beside me and run to the boot. I tried to locate my house keys with one hand as I lugged the case out by its handle, slamming the lid shut all in under five seconds. I hauled the case across the road to the pavement, locking the car and activating the alarm with the key fob as I went. The rain was now starting to come down harder. I felt pretty pleased with myself, as I was now at my next-door neighbour's gate with my luggage and without getting soaked. Possibly at this stage my hair hadn't even started to curl.

I opened my gate, running an eye over the front of the house. It looked exactly the way I'd left it. I took a couple of steps towards my front door and stopped.

Something wasn't right.

I heaved my case to my right-hand side, as far off the path as I could. That gave me enough room to go backwards or forwards in a hurry. I couldn't hear anything but I couldn't see much either. That was the problem. The security light wasn't working. It should come on when anyone or anything came this far along the path. It had been working when I'd left.

And, when I'd left, the glass casing housing the light hadn't been smashed all over the steps leading up to the house, either.

The rain was coming down now. I was getting soaked to the skin. Neighbours with more sense than me were indoors. I glanced up and down the street. Nothing stirred.

My options were either to go into my house on my own, call someone and go in with them, or simply leave. I couldn't call anyone without sounding deranged and I didn't fancy the Premier Inn, even though it was a huge improvement on Tartan Towers. I decided I would go in armed with my keys and a can of hairspray. If I had to spray it in anyone's eyes, I'd just tell the patrol it had been in my pocket when I went through the door. I hadn't armed myself with it, merely used what was to hand to defend myself. They were bound to believe me. Probably.

I made my way, now drenched through, up the steps, avoiding the broken glass. I put my key in the door as quietly as I could, fumbled in my handbag for my mobile and travel hairspray. I unlocked my phone, dialled 99 and gave the can a good shake. Then delayed reaction to what I was about to do hit me full on. This was madness. I was about to do a very stupid thing. I'd been stalked, possibly had my house broken into by Lloyd and I was working on a series of unsolved murders.

I took my key back out of the lock and backed down the steps. Moving my case as far out of the rain as I could, I headed back to the car, calling Bill as I crossed the road. I felt a surge of relief on hearing his voice as he answered.

'Hi, hon. Are you home?' he asked.

Soaked to the skin, I got into the car and slammed the door. 'Hey, Bill. Would you be able to come over?'

Immediate concern ran through his voice. 'What's wrong?'

'Probably nothing, but I've just got home from Birmingham and the security light's smashed.'

'You in the house?'

'No. I'm in the car – '

'Good – stay there. I'll be five minutes. Lock the door.'

The siren on his police car sounded in my ear, just before he hung up. He arrived in less than three minutes. His marked vehicle pulled up outside my house, blocking the pavement. I was glad he'd turned the siren off before getting to my road.

I got out of the car to join him, leaving the hairspray behind. I put my door key into his outstretched hand, pausing to smile at him, and added, 'Thanks.'

I followed him back down the pathway. In the swiftest of movements, he turned the key, pushed the door and shouted, 'Hello. Police. Let's not mess about.'

Silence. I couldn't tell if anyone was in the house, but no noise or movement greeted us. I decided to leave the front door open, and stood still as Bill ran straight upstairs. I saw his right hand move towards his baton. I stood motionless but my heart was still pounding. I could hear him going from room to room. He ran back downstairs. He went to the kitchen next, then into the living room.

'Nina, did you leave the television on?' he shouted from the front room.

One thing was for sure: I had been right to worry. I definitely had not left the television on. As I joined Bill in the living room, I saw something else that was out of place. I had not left the DVD interview of Jake Lloyd on the coffee table either. At the same instant that I clocked the out-of-place DVD, another sense registered – an unpleasant musty aroma. Like something was festering in my living room.

Hands shaking, I picked up the DVD and slid it under a magazine. No need to let Bill know I had it. He was looking at the television set. 'If you didn't leave the telly on, we should get a CSI here to take prints,' he said, about to transmit a message on his personal radio.

'I can't remember, Bill, to tell you the truth. I may have done. I've had a lot on my mind. Besides, after Lloyd getting nicked, a CSI was supposed to be coming to dust for prints anyway but I've not been here to let them in. Can you wait here while I have a look under the beds, in wardrobes, that kind of thing? I'll sleep better if I do.'

'Nina, I'm off in two hours. I'll come back and stay the night in your spare room if you want me to.'

I ran an eye over him. That was a very tempting offer, I'd be a fool to turn that one down, but I didn't want to look needy.

'Thanks, but really, don't worry. I'm overreacting. Been a bit jumpy, that's all. But thank you.' I managed to smile at him as I walked him to the front door.

'I'll go and do a more thorough check upstairs while you get your case in,' said Bill.

I tried to get myself together. The front door was still open and my case was probably waterlogged by now. I went back down the steps to get it. As I did, car headlights came on to my right. I heard the noise of the engine as the car pulled away at speed. I couldn't see the make, model or even the colour. Maybe it had nothing to do with me. I stood in the rain watching it make its rapid departure before lugging my drenched case into the house.

By the time Bill descended the stairs again, I'd unzipped the soggy case and was in the process of carrying the contents to the washing machine. He touched my shoulder, acting as though he was about to kiss me, but then changed his mind, saying, 'Lock the door when I'm gone. I'll call you later.' His radio came to life as he walked away from the house, sending him off to another call.

As I carried on unpacking, I mulled over whether it was my imagination or whether I really had left the television on. I was pretty sure I hadn't left a DVD on show that I wasn't supposed to have. There were no signs of forced entry anywhere; nothing was missing and nothing damaged. I'd checked the front and back doors twice after Bill left. I'd stopped short of going out into the garden, but I closed the kitchen blinds for the first time in months so the darkness of the woods couldn't reach me.

My phone rang, jolting me back to reality. It was Bill.

'Hey. Only calling while I can to make sure that everything's OK. I'm probably not going to finish till a bit later than I thought. Some bloke's threatening to throw himself off the multi-storey car park in Woodford. The world and his wife are here.'

'Sounds like you're busy, then.'

'Yeah. We're waiting for the on-call negotiator to arrive. It's Kim Cotton. Do you know her?'

'Yeah, I do. Poor bastard's likely to jump when that miserable cow starts talking to him.'

'Sorry, Nin, I've got to go.'

'See you later, Bill.'

'You too, sweetheart.'

I put the phone down and picked the corkscrew up. I'd decided to wait up for Bill to speak to him before I went to sleep. I already had bags under my eyes from Tartan Towers; another hour or two wouldn't hurt.

Chapter 62

3rd October

Following a late night waiting up for Bill to finish work and call me, I returned to work to see what it held in store for me. The Incident Room was already filling up with DCs drinking tea and logging on to computers. I said hello to those around me and took myself off to find a desk.

No sooner had I sat down and entered my password to gain entry to HOLMES than I was approached by Catherine. 'Nina,' she said, 'can you go and see Eric in his office? He said it was important.'

'Yeah, sure,' I said.

'Wait a minute.' She pointed at my computer screen, just coming to life with the words 'Home Office Large Major Enquiry System'. 'Don't leave that unlocked.'

Thinking I was about to get my knuckles rapped for security reasons, I hastened to lock the keyboard. 'Sorry, Catherine, I wasn't thinking,' I said.

'No, it's not that, see. There are some very juvenile people around here. Did the same thing last week. Went for a pee and in my absence someone sent three emails from my computer. Apparently I can't stop thinking about the DCI in his Mr Tickle socks, I want to run away with the fella who fixes the photocopier and I would like nothing more than for Kim Cotton to slather me all over in chocolate. I'm supposed to be on a bloody diet.'

'Right. Thanks for the warning.'

'It's the stress of it all. It gets to them.' She fluttered her hands in the direction of the desks at no one in particular.

Having locked my terminal, I went to find the DCI, who was sitting in the office opposite the superintendent's. Nottingham had been forced to find another office, as the superintendent had returned from the Caribbean early and was rumoured not to be amused with events. His door was shut; Nottingham's was open.

'Morning, sir,' I said to Nottingham from the doorway.

'Morning, Nina. Come in and shut the door.'

That wasn't a good start. I'd been thinking since Catherine had told me the DCI wanted to see me whether I should start with an apology about the children's home or just play dumb. I technically hadn't done anything wrong, I'd just gone with the investigation. I wanted to stay on the enquiry more than ever now.

As I closed the door, I tried to arrange my facial features so they wouldn't betray how on edge I was feeling. I allowed myself to smile at him, a smile that hopefully oozed 'trust me, I'm a capable detective', rather than a maniacal grin that shouted 'I'm mentally unhinged, watch my every move'. Not sure of how I looked or what he thought, I watched his permanently neutral face.

He pointed at a chair opposite his desk. As I sat down, he said, 'You and Laura did well in Birmingham. Was the hotel OK?'

'If you're a Bay City Rollers fan, it was just the ticket.'

'That's good. We have a briefing at 9am.' He continued to stare straight at me, unflinching. 'I thought that you should know that, in your absence, Mark Russell and Pierre have spoken to Carol McNamara and Jillian Spora.'

I remained perfectly still. The names meant nothing to me. I nodded, showing my interest even though I didn't have a clue what he was telling me this for. His mobile phone on the desk in front of him started to ring. He glanced down at the display before hitting a button that put an end to the sound. Someone walked by the office door, causing him to look over my shoulder in the direction of the corridor.

'They were the two girls, now women of course, that Scott Headingly abducted. The ones he went to prison for.' He let this sink in for a couple of seconds. 'The rest of the team needs to be updated on what they've said. Come to the briefing by all means, but if you want to give it a miss Danny's a bit behind on CCTV, you can help him.'

Not bloody likely, I thought. I did appreciate the heads-up on the content of what I was going to hear, though. I'd sit, listen, take notes, ask questions and carry on as always. It was a matter of behaving as if everything was normal. There was so much I'd missed while I'd been away. I knew how important it was to get back into the enquiry and make myself pivotal.

'That's very kind, boss, but I would like to attend. I have a couple of things to add and don't want to lumber Laura with everything.' I made to get up.

'I understand. There is one other thing. You've probably not been told that Jake Lloyd said in his interview that the children's clothing we recovered from his cellar came from his work: they'd been made by a costume department at his request when he was working on a drama. We've also had an update from the forensic lab.' He paused again but this time he didn't need to let the information sink in; he had my undivided attention. Lloyd was even more twisted than I'd imagined. 'I'll let you read the report. Get a copy from Catherine. The traces of blood on the children's clothing aren't a match for your blood.'

I took this in, feeling an enormous wave of relief from both bits of information, but thinking there was more to come. I wasn't wrong.

'There was also a small amount of blood on a man's shirt. That has been identified as your blood. I'm sorry, Nina, it's very difficult to age blood so there is no way of knowing with any degree of accuracy how old the blood is. Speak to the forensic scientist who carried out the examinations. Her name's Freya Forbes. She can explain it fully when you've read her report.' Nottingham looked beyond me again to the corridor. Perhaps he was hoping someone would interrupt us and end this uncomfortable conversation. No one came to his assistance and I didn't feel like helping him out today.

All I managed to say was, 'DNA?'

'We've tested for your DNA. That wasn't...' He cleared his throat and looked down at his mobile again, fiddled with the perfect knot on his tie. 'That wasn't the difficult part. You're a police officer so your DNA is on the National Database. That was how we were able to match your DNA to the shirt. Apart from blood, the lab looked at contact fibres, hairs. They found a hair belonging to Jake Lloyd on one of the items.'

I decided it was best if I thought that this was good news. 'That's a good piece of evidence, then.' My mouth had gone very dry. It felt as though my top lip couldn't find it within itself to meet my bottom lip. I forced my mouth shut to stop myself saying anything else. It had got warm in the room with the door shut so I got up to leave, failing to remember having sat back down again. 'I'll call the scientist after the briefing,' I said, making a move for the door.

I went the long way round to the Incident Room, deciding I wanted a couple of minutes to think about what I'd been told. Lloyd must have gone to some trouble. He'd even been to visit Henry Bastow. He'd said so himself.

I hardly dared to allow myself to register this thought. It would consume me.

I found myself wandering in the direction of the office without meaning to. I took a deep breath and went in through the door. All the seats were taken as the enquiry team were busying themselves with last-minute paperwork for the morning briefing.

Ray was once again in the centre of a small group of officers, all laughing at something he had said. 'But that wasn't the best thing,' I heard him say. 'The funniest thing of all was that I was dreading this fella "Kong" coming back to the house because I pictured this really huge bloke. When he turned up, he was puny. I had to ask "Why do they call you Kong?" He took his shirt off and showed me his hairy back and said, "'Cos with my clothes off I look like a silverback gorilla."...'

I made my way over to the desk I'd left my stuff on. Grabbing my notes, I headed to the conference room but was stopped by Wingsy halfway along the corridor.

'Hello, duchess. You OK?' he asked.

'Great.' I gave him a smile. 'Off to get a good seat early. How are you getting on with Birdsall? Heard we're going for extra time from the Magistrates' Court to keep him in.'

'Listen...' He leaned in towards me. 'They're gonna talk about the two kidnapped girls this morning.' He said it in an almost comical way, talking out of the side of his mouth.

I wanted to stop myself smiling at his expression, so I did a kind of crazy half-laugh, as if it was all too much for me. Really it was to give myself time to chase the happy from my face. I didn't want him to think I found this at all funny. 'Thanks for the warning, but Nottingham told me a few minutes ago. He said I could sit this one out but I want to stay. I like it here. I like this enquiry.'

'Alright,' he said, backing away in the direction of the Incident Room, 'but I'm keeping an eye on you.'

'Yeah, right. I know. Keep 'em peeled.'

I went and took my seat. Waited for the information barrage to begin.

Several minutes later, once more the packed conference room held everyone on the enquiry, from the DCI as senior investigating officer to the Incident Room HOLMES staff and many in between. A slight buzz in my head forced me to concentrate more than usual. I was still tired from the trip. I promised myself I would take some headache tablets as soon as we were finished.

'Morning, everyone,' said Nottingham from the top of the table. 'Once again, lots to get through.' He straightened his papers while he spoke, before opening his notebook and writing the date at the top of the page. 'Before I start with Birdsall, I can confirm that I have declared Benjamin Makepeace a suspect following Nina and Laura's good work in Birmingham, discovering the existence of his passport. More on him later. Now I want to concentrate on Birdsall, as he's in custody. The interviews are carrying on today. We had a summary late last night. He's talking and, so far, we seem to have nothing on him linking him directly to the scenes. We're waiting for forensic results to come back.

'Once his twenty-four hours' detention period is up later on today, we're going for a twelve-hour Superintendent's Extension which will expire late tonight. The likelihood is that we're going for a Warrant of Further Detention at the Magistrates' Court, so that needs to be done today. That will also eat the custody time up. My main reasons are that, even though we have two other suspects, Spencer and now Makepeace, plus little directly linking Birdsall to the murders, we can't get what we need in a day and a half. Firstly there's Birdsall's association many years ago with two of the victims, plus association with the cousin of one of them; he's lied to us about his recent whereabouts and there's a great deal to put to him surrounding the three victims around the times of their deaths. I've justified my reasons, but, even though we had enough to nick him, there's not enough to charge. We need to do a vast amount of work before we even contemplate releasing him.

'We're using up the custody time so Wingsy and Danny may get more out of him this morning and we'll go to court later on today. Kim's going to speak to the clerk of the Magistrates' Court this morning and pave the way.'

Nottingham leaned back in his chair, palms up and surveyed those in the room. 'Anyone have any other ideas?'

A few heads shook but no one said anything.

'Anyone disagree or want to give me something I've missed?' he said.

Mark Russell was the first to speak. 'What sort of timescale are we talking for forensics and what's been sent, sir?'

Nottingham sought out Karen Pickering, a civilian police employee who was handling the exhibits from the enquiry. I'd had little to do with her but I'd heard her chatting in the office and knew her name. I had to see her about the stuff we'd brought back from Birmingham, to ensure we recorded who'd had it and when for continuity purposes.

'Not much has gone off at the moment, Mark,' she answered him, peering around another officer, who had been blocking her view slightly. 'We sent some shoes off that possibly had blood on them and Birdsall had a zip-up jacket with what looked like hair in the bottom of the zip. Don't know how that got jammed in the waistband area.'

That caused a juvenile snigger from those in the room. Even Nottingham smiled.

'Oh, and it doesn't look like it's Belinda Cook's hair. It's the wrong colour,' continued Karen. 'Birdsall had no precons so we've sent his DNA to the lab and have kept his hair, blood, etc. here in the freezer. Belinda Cook consented to give her DNA as well. Understand she was more of a problem than the prisoner.'

I saw Mark roll his eyes. Clearly Belinda's patience with the police was all used up.

'I sent it all on a premium service,' said Nottingham. 'It's going to cost thousands but there you go. If he's not our offender, we need to rule him out and be ready when the other two come in. Wingsy and Danny are cracking on with the interview this morning.'

He glanced at his watch before continuing.

'Right, let's move on to telephony. We've had masses of phone work completed, some in quick time and some not so. We've had trouble locating all the phones and numbers of our three victims but we're building up a very clear picture, via the work of the analyst, of who called whom, at what time, and where they were when they made and received calls.' He looked around the room at the assembled crowd, squeezing in for space around the table, spilling into the extremities of the room. His eyes came to rest on a young male DC. 'Matt,' he began. 'You're doing the phone work. Any significant update regarding our three victims? Let's start with Amanda first.'

'Sir, I've looked through all the numbers Amanda called, or was called by, from one month before she was last seen alive until the day her body was found,' said Matt. I hadn't expected him to speak with a South African accent. This sidetracked me briefly, putting me off what he was saying and making me pay more attention to how he was saying it, like listening to a TV weather girl with a lisp. Matt continued, 'There are few numbers not accounted for. The numbers belong mostly to family, friends and the odd punter. One, however, has only recently been identified. It has been cross-referenced on HOLMES and the analyst has put this phone number down to Adam Spencer.'

A quick glance around the room at the faces of my team members told me that they weren't too happy at this news. A couple of them glanced down, one or two shifted in their seats, and Mark Russell tutted and raised his eyes to the ceiling.

'There are several calls, but the time of the last one from Spencer to Amanda was 10.12 am on the 16th.' Matt glanced down at his notes and added, 'That was four days before her body was found. Spencer's number had also called her two days before that, an hour before she went to the travel agents with an unknown male. There are no outgoing calls after 10.12 hours on the 16th and the only calls coming in were either of a very short duration or went to voicemail.'

Nottingham pointed at Matt from across the table. 'It looks as though she didn't make or receive any further calls after Spencer's one.' He looked across to Danny. 'Any luck enhancing the stills from the town centre CCTV of Amanda and the unidentified male?'

Danny came straight back with his answer. 'No. They're no clearer even with a lot of help from our technical support. Even if we think it's Adam Spencer, we can't do facial recognition because there's no good shot of his face. It's just the back of his head.'

'OK,' said Nottingham. 'Before we move on to the telephone work for Jason Holland and Daphne Headingly, how are we evidencing that the phone number we're saying is Adam Spencer's is actually Spencer's?'

'Myself and Ray dealt with Alf Spencer,' said Kim Cotton. Lucky old Alf, I thought to myself. If it's not bad enough that everyone thinks his son is a serial killer and a lunatic, then the county's most miserable bitch turns up on his doorstep. Talk about kicking a man when he was down.

'After a great deal of decision-making and policy file entries by yourself, sir – ' she directed a smarmy smile and flutter of her eyelashes at the DCI ' – we went to Alf's home address. He gave us a lengthy statement and spoke openly about his son Adam, detailing his time in a children's home in Birmingham.' Her unflattering smile didn't extend to me as she sought me out around the table. If I'd been in possession of a mirror, I would have held it up to avoid looking directly at her. 'Adam had made no mention to Alf about the child dying at the home, and soon afterwards he went back to live with his mother. Alf can confirm, though, that the number he has for his son is the same as the number Matt's referring to. It's the number ending 837. Adam also gave the same number to Mrs Makepeace in Birmingham, which Nina and Laura have.

'Alf has frequently called his son or Adam has called him from this number. It was registered in Spain in 2005. Now we have the number, Matt's doing some more work around it.

'The last time Alf said he saw Adam was about three months ago, when he was home in England for about three days. He hasn't seen him since, or spoken to him for about two weeks. That's not unusual, and he doesn't think that he has any plans to come back to the UK, as Alf is planning on staying in Spain with his son for the winter.'

Kim continued to talk about how Alf had been affected and how he couldn't believe that his son could possibly have murdered three people. My head was beginning to hurt, largely because I was tired. I put my pen down and rubbed my temples. It didn't seem to help in the slightest.

I felt a kick under the table. I sought out the source of my sore shin. Pierre was pitching across the table towards me. I saw him mouth, 'You OK?'

I nodded, tapped the side of my head and mouthed back, 'Headache.' Kim was still droning on so I tried to block out her voice while maintaining a façade of interest. I'd already decided that after the briefing I would locate Alf's statement and read it for myself. Her voice was beginning to sound like someone was rubbing a kitten up and down pebble-dashing.

Before I knew it, we were back with Matt. There had been no update regarding Holland. His phone had already been looked at as part of the Missing Person enquiry, so, other than cross-referencing phone numbers to make sure none had been missed, there was nothing further regarding him. Daphne Headingly didn't have a mobile, so Matt had little more to add other than landline calls, which took us no further. There had also been nothing interesting or significant in relation to Benjamin Makepeace's newly recovered phone, which was a bit of a disappointment.

Then it was Mark and Pierre's turn. I concentrated again. It was nothing personal. So I told myself.

'We went to see Carol McNamara first,' said Mark. 'Nice woman, lives in Surrey now with her husband, a doctor and their two children. She told us what she could remember about her kidnapping. Even though she was only five at the time, she remembered a lot of detail.' Mark pulled at the side of his shirt collar. He ran his tongue across his top lip. Perhaps I should have stayed away. He was more pent-up than I was. At least I was hiding my discomfort. He continued, 'Carol had read about the murders in the paper and, when she saw the name Headingly, she thought it would only be a matter of time before we approached her. In terms of Scott Headingly, she described him as…' he glanced down at some photocopied notes, parts highlighted and quoted '…"a sick, twisted, depraved bastard". Carol has not been contacted by anyone out of the ordinary, definitely not the Headingly family, has no ties with Birmingham or children's homes and was sorry not to be of more help.'

Pierre then took over. 'We next went to see Jillian Spora. Quite a different story there. She took some finding. We tracked her to a hostel in Hackney. She's a drug addict, had her two children taken away from her, series of violent relationships. She lives a pitiful life and didn't want to talk about what happened to her and Carol. She said no one had dropped in on her lately from her past or unexpectedly. Wanted to put the whole thing behind her, hadn't heard about the murders, didn't know where Carol lived and had made no effort to contact her. Being so messed up by heroin, she didn't have much of a clue what was going on. Her being kidnapped as a child may have had an effect on her turning out the way she did, but Carol is doing well for herself, and so is Nina.' Pierre turned his head in my direction as he said his last words. I had been looking at him anyway but the mention of my name brought me to full alert. 'You're alright, Nina.'

My headache seemed to be lifting and I was back to paying full attention. I was aware that most people in the room were looking at me, although one or two stared down at the table.

'That brings us nicely back to Nina,' said Catherine. 'The telephone number of unknown Charlie that you gave to Mr Nottingham before you went to Birmingham – we've found out where that phone was registered to.'

It took me a couple of seconds for the penny to drop. It seemed like a lifetime ago that I'd handed the DCI the number from the slip of paper Annie's son had passed me from the pocket of his joggers.

Catherine added, 'Get the details from Matt, and then you and Pierre go see the subscriber this morning. Pierre's got something more pressing that needs to be done first, but it shouldn't take you all day. I'll give you the relevant action for the enquiry before you go.'

It suddenly dawned on me that Laura was not in the briefing. I searched the faces around the room but couldn't see her. I thought it was strange. She hadn't told me that she wouldn't be able to make it.

Chapter 63

Half an hour later, we piled out of the conference room, spilling in the usual directions of the loos, kitchen and quiet corners to return phone calls.

Laura was coming out of the toilet as I went in. 'Hi,' I said. 'You OK? Missed you in there.' I thumbed in the direction of the conference room.

'Yeah, had a couple of calls and stuff to make. Did I miss much?' she asked, pausing with her hand on the door.

'A couple of things. I'll let you know in a minute. Got some stuff to catch up on myself,' I said before heading into the ladies'.

I thought Laura's behaviour was odd. She'd seemed to enjoy being on the team, being a part of the murder investigation, so I couldn't fathom out why she'd missed the briefing. I wasn't at all concerned from a work perspective that she wasn't present – I'd covered our updates – but she should have been there for her own sake rather than mine.

When I went into the Incident Room a short while later, she was not in there. I headed for Ray and Catherine's office to get the report from the forensic scientist.

Catherine was already on her way to me. We spoke in the corridor, and she handed me the forensic report as well as the 'Charlie' telephone enquiry.

'Thanks, Catherine,' I said. 'Is it OK if I call Freya Forbes from your office? It'll be quieter.'

'Absobloodylutely,' she purred. 'Though I doubt it'll be quieter with Ray in there. I'm off to get some breakfast.

I'm bloody starving.' She wiggled away, all high heels and curves.

As I turned the corner to the section of the corridor where the DSs' office was, the door opened and Laura catapulted out. We almost collided.

'Sorry,' she mumbled. 'Didn't see you.'

'You sure you're OK?' I asked.

Her face released the tension it had been carrying before she said, 'I'm fine, just didn't sleep all that well.'

'You and me both,' I said as I headed for Ray's office.

'Nina,' she called after me. I turned. I thought she looked pale. 'Meant to say to you that West Mids got back. Mrs Makepeace hasn't yet been asked about Benjamin's father. Robin Cox thought the answer was in the paperwork somewhere. I'm going to look for it.'

I gave her a cheesy thumbs-up and turned back towards the DSs' office. I stood in the doorway watching Ray try to open the window at the rear of the room. He had his back to me.

'Can I ask a favour? I said. He looked round. 'Could I use your office for a couple of minutes to call the scientist? I won't be long.'

'Course you can. I was going to get something to eat anyway.' He walked out, closing the door behind him.

I took a deep breath and called the number at the top of the report. A female answered with a light, almost breathy, 'Hello, Freya Forbes.'

'Hello, Freya,' I began. 'My name's Nina Foster. I'm a detective working on – '

'Oh, Nina, I know who you are. We can talk on the phone, but I'm at Riverstone Crown Court today if you want to meet up?'

'That would be great, if you have the time. Does 3.30pm sound OK?'

'It does. I'm in Court Seven. I'll see you outside the court then.'

We ended the call and I went off to find Pierre. He was already armed with all the information we needed to speak to Charlie, as well as directions for finding his house.

Chapter 64

Pierre and I set off a few minutes later, in a worn-out Citroën begged from another department.

'This car's a tip,' I said, glancing down at the empty crisp wrapper, apple core, crumpled tissues and other debris in the passenger seat footwell. 'I dread to think what's in the glovebox.' Curiosity got the better of me. 'Oh, a box of tampons. Result.'

Pierre laughed and said, 'Shall we agree that under no circumstances do we open the boot.'

'Agreed,' I said.

'OK,' he said. 'Right, then, before we go and see Charles Bruce, the subscriber for your telephony action, I have an enquiry that's closer to the nick and more urgent. It's a result of something that came out of Birdsall's interview that needs checking. We'll see how we get on for time.'

'Sounds reasonable to me,' I said. 'What you got?'

'He changed his alibi late last night and claimed that, on the morning Daphne Headingly was murdered, he was with a woman called Sophie Alexander. Her address is on that printed sheet on top of my file on the back seat.'

I stretched over to pick the paperwork up. 'Bit worried about what might be back here,' I said. 'Anyone missing a cat?'

'Birdsall claims he stayed at Sophie Alexander's overnight, leaving about 11am on the 23rd, which is after Daphne was killed. I went to see her last night to verify it but she wasn't in.'

'Right, so, if she verifies this, that alibis him out for number three, plus number one, as Amanda was killed while Birdsall was abroad, but not for victim number two, Jason Holland.'

'True but he didn't know Holland as far as we know, unless the Malaga connection means anything, so at the moment we have no motive or anything linking him to his death.' As he spoke, he turned to look at me as we waited for the gate at the nick's yard to open before returning his concentration to his driving. 'Let's go and see what Sophie has to say to us.'

'Much else come out of the interviews yesterday?' I asked Pierre when the car was clear of the nick and traffic.

'Not really. Everything he said about being out of the country between when Amanda was last seen and her body turning up has been verified. He didn't have much to say about Holland 'cos he was in England at some point when he was missing but that's very vague. Right at the moment, he's not looking like the guilty party here.'

'You got a theory or favourite out of the three of them, Pierre?' I asked.

'No. No, but I wonder if we've been looking in the wrong place all this time?'

'Where do you think we should be concentrating, then?'

'The Headingly family. Everything always points back to them. They're such a strange bunch. I saw you made it into the newspaper. That must have been unwelcome attention. Want to talk about Jake Lloyd?'

'I don't know what to say about him, really. To be truthful with you, I've tried not to think too much about it, but...' I was conscious of Pierre pulling the car over into a car park marked private next to a small block of flats, set back from the town's ring road. 'We here?' I asked him. 'We could have walked this distance.'

'No, I've stopped because I thought you might wanna talk for a minute.'

Initial feelings of invaded privacy gave way to a rush of relief at being able to talk about Jake Lloyd. It wasn't that I didn't have anyone to turn to, but there was no one I wanted to burden. Talking it through with Pierre felt different; I hardly knew the bloke for a start and that helped, but also I knew that, being a police officer, he'd follow what I was about to say with his capacity to understand as an investigator, remain impartial, and pack no punches in telling me how it really was.

I took a deep breath.

'Why did Lloyd leave it so long before sending me the photos he'd been taking for years? Why after all this time? And why be stupid enough to leave his fingerprints all over them?'

Pierre used his fingers to count the points off as he made them. 'First and second, the important fact isn't that it was years but that the timing of sending them to you was right in the middle of a murder investigation involving his aunt. Thirdly, his fingerprints weren't all over them but were on the envelope, inside and out. And what happens then? Police arrest him, search his house, find the stuff in the cellar, he's banged up and out of the way.'

'Hold on, Pierre, go back a bit.' I rubbed my eyes as I spoke. 'If someone else sent those photos to me using an envelope Lloyd had already handled, that means that whoever sent them knew Lloyd was following me, got him to put his fingerprints all over the envelope and then did a good job of stitching him up.'

'Precisely,' said Pierre. 'Though there are a couple of issues with all of that.'

'Yeah, I know – such as who would want him out of the way and why?'

'And why, after all this time, would he confess to the murder of his cousin?'

I was aware how many unanswered questions I had surrounding Jake Lloyd and his stash of disturbing snapshots of my life, but this was getting in the way of my part in the investigation. I was grateful for the chance of talking it over with Pierre but figured we'd spent enough time picking apart my problems. Last thing I wanted was for him to return to the office and say I got in the way of a fast-track enquiry chewing over my own issues. Even if he didn't put it quite so blatantly as that, it could get misconstrued.

'Let's get on our way to see Sophie before she goes out for the day,' I suggested. 'We can talk on the way.'

Another thing had just crossed my mind too. If someone had wanted Jake Lloyd out of the picture, there had to be a reason. Lloyd had been watching me – or watching out for me, as he put it. He was no longer keeping an eye on me, but someone else was. They'd been in my house. They'd turned on my television.

Chapter 65

'We're here,' said Pierre. 'You OK? You haven't said a word in ages.'

'I'm fine,' I said. 'Looks like someone's in. There's a car on the driveway.'

I perked up as I looked up and down the street. I had a feeling I'd been in the road on another occasion, which wasn't unusual in itself, as that happened a lot when you were dealing with criminals: you tended to end up in the same streets and houses. This wasn't one of our usual haunts. It was a fairly wide avenue, trees on either side, room for long driveways complete with off-road parking and not a speed hump in sight. Not many of them left in the southeast. Every tiny plot of land had at least two semi-detached houses squeezed on to it; every reasonable-sized house within two miles of a town centre with a London train link was converted into flats. That was what it often felt like. The race was on to force people to live within an arm's distance of each other. It wasn't healthy – unless you were the one selling the land or the houses.

'I think I've been in this road before, Pierre,' I said as I opened the door. 'Can't think why I was here. It'll come to me later.'

We made our way to No. 86, admiring the gleaming black Audi with personalised numberplates feet from the front door. The upstairs windows hinted at two front double bedrooms, and the whole house gave the impression of being pretty well kitted out inside, too. I was forming a picture of

Sophie Alexander in my mind, and wasn't disappointed when she opened the door to us.

'Can I help you?' she asked, one hand on the side of the door, the other on her hip. A gold charm bracelet dangled from the arm poised on her tiny waist. Other than that, she was very plainly dressed in a white fitted shirt and black jeans. Her understated mode of dress served to accentuate the fact that she was a very attractive woman. Her hair seemed to do as it was told, unlike my own, which was still protesting at the soaking it had got outside my house on my return from Birmingham, despite having been treated to salon shampoo and conditioner that morning. How could hair sulk? Mine seemed to be managing it very nicely.

'We're police officers, and we need to come in and talk to you about Tony Birdsall,' said Pierre.

'Anthony?' she said. 'You'd better come in, then. Is he OK?'

Without waiting for an answer, she padded along in her bare feet, leading us into an impressive room at the rear of her home, which seemed to span half the width of the house. The windows overlooked a neat, if in my opinion very boring garden consisting mostly of lawn and fence. The focal point of the room was a grand piano. As if to invite comment, in case we missed it, Sophie stood with her back to it, gold-adorned arm resting lightly on its top. Just to make a point, neither Pierre nor I said a word about the elephant in the room – well, the bits of its anatomy hacked from its dead face, anyway.

'Tony Birdsall, or Anthony as you call him, is a friend of yours?' Pierre asked.

Sophie gave a silent laugh. For some reason, that annoyed me. 'We go back years. I used to sing in one of his clubs in Spain.' She walked around the piano and stood behind the stool.

Fucking hell, don't sing, I thought. This enquiry is already weird enough.

'When was the last time you saw him?' Pierre continued, not at all put off by the theatrical neck- and shoulder-rolling going on before our eyes.

'Let me see. He stayed overnight. I think it was a couple of weeks ago now.' Her hands went down to her sides, smoothing her flawless shirt over her hips. 'I can check my diary, if it would help.' She crossed the room and bent down to pick up an expensive-looking handbag from the floor. It was probably worth more than everything I was wearing, including my sister's St Christopher. I watched her rummage for a couple of seconds and then pull out a small red pocket diary. Her red-polished nails whipped the pages over until she found the date she was searching for. She shot a dark look at Pierre and said, 'Here you are, officer. 22nd September. "Anthony 7.30pm".'

My colleague reached out and took the notebook from her, reading the words aloud once more while nodding in agreement. 'Can I ask why you would write down when Tony visits you?' Pierre asked. I already thought she was a prostitute, I had to admit. She gave the impression of spending all day draping herself over the furniture – the very expensive furniture – and she kept a written record of when men stayed the night. Unless she was keeping a tally for some reason, I couldn't see why she would make an appointment.

'We have a very casual relationship,' came Sophie's reply, a coy smile creeping its way across her lips. She moved around the piano towards the window, pausing with her hands on her hips, turning so that her profile was illuminated by the sunlight.

If I'd known Pierre better, I would have told the silly preening cow that she was wasting her time – both Pierre and I preferred fellas. I didn't want to embarrass him, though, so I said nothing.

'Can we sit down?' said Pierre. 'It would be easier to talk.' I translated this as his way of saying he'd had enough of her dramatic wanderings too.

Sophie glided over to a white leather armchair, perching on the edge, hands on her knees. We took our seats on the matching sofa.

'What kind of casual relationship?' I asked.

Her eyes flickered towards me, before returning to Pierre. 'Just because we have a son together, it doesn't mean that Anthony and I have to live in each other's pockets.'

I did a mental double-take. 'You have a son with him?' I asked.

She continued to direct her answers to Pierre. 'Yes, Joel. He's seven years old. He lives here with me and Anthony comes over from Spain to see him six or seven times a year. He's at school at the moment, of course. That's why I make a note of Anthony's visits: so that Joel and I don't make any other engagements.'

The room we were in was adorned with photographs of Sophie. She was in every one of them and I estimated there to be about twenty-five strewn on the piano, tables, walls, everywhere I looked. Some of the pictures contained images of her with another adult, usually male, but there was no hint that a child resided anywhere in her house, or her heart.

'Did you and Anthony go out at all over the evening or night of the 22nd of September?' Pierre asked.

'No, no, we didn't. It was about eleven the next day when he left. I remember that because he had to meet someone at noon and he was running late. Before you ask, I don't know who he was meeting or where he went.'

'Is there anyone else who can verify that you were both at home on that evening?' Pierre asked.

'Joel, of course, but he went to bed not long after Anthony arrived. And there's the security system. It records anyone going in or out of the front, rear and garage doors. The windows are alarmed so, before I go to bed, I set the system. I seem to remember we went to bed quite early. We hadn't seen each other for some time.' She put her hand up to cover her mouth, I suppose in an attempt to appear embarrassed.

Bit late for that. She should have shown more humility when it came to poncing about at the piano.

I left her flirting mercilessly, not to mention pointlessly, with Pierre while I made a phone call to technical services at police headquarters to see if someone could come out and download the hard drive of her complicated security system. Short of seizing the whole thing, Pierre and I couldn't copy the footage we needed without risking wiping it clean.

One thing was for sure: if the CCTV was genuine and showed Birdsall arriving at 7.30pm on the 22nd and not leaving until well after the time of Daphne Headingly's death on the 23rd, coupled with a download from the security system proving the windows were locked and alarmed all night, he was out of the running for this murder.

I still had a feeling, though, that Birdsall was not a totally innocent man.

Chapter 66

Downloading the CCTV and the information from the security system had taken all morning. By the time Pierre and I had got away from Sophie with all that we needed, taken the footage back to the nick and begun to watch it, I had little time to get to my meeting with Freya Forbes. I wasn't too sure what she'd be able to say to put my mind at ease over the whole sorry saga, but it felt like an unresolved issue that needed putting to rest.

As I packed my stuff to leave the office, I put in a call to Wingsy. 'You alright, Wingnut?' I said, 'How's the interviewing with Birdsall going?'

He took a deep breath before saying, 'Slow. I'm cream-crackered 'cos I didn't get a lot of sleep. Poxy prisoner got his eight hours but I'm done in.'

'Never mind about you. Working restrictions mean nothing to us, so shut up and listen. We've been to Sophie Alexander's place. What a dozy tart she is.'

I heard Wingsy chuckle. 'You hit it off, then?'

'I let Pierre do the talking. He's a lot more tactful than me. Anyway, the point is, not only does she alibi him out, she's got some all-singing, all-dancing security system. He's on the CCTV coming and going at the times he said. We still need to check he didn't leave at some point in between. Sorry, mate, but it's not looking as though he murdered Daphne Headingly. More to do, though.'

The line went silent.

'Wingsy?'

'Nin, there's something else.'

'Go on, mate.' I detected a shift in his tone.

'I'm just stepping out of the office to speak to you in private.' The sounds of hurried footsteps and a creaking door implied he was on the move. 'After the last interview with Birdsall, I couldn't find a jailer to put him back in his cell so I took him down the corridor myself.' His breathing had got faster. I was having to put my free hand up to my other ear to block out any other sounds. 'Thing is, doll, as I went to leave him in the cell, he turned to me and said, "Nina Foster ever wonder why Jake Lloyd left it so long before he sent her those photographs?"'

Was there anyone in England who didn't know something personal about me?

'What did you say to him?' I asked.

'When I asked him what he knew about it, he said it was in the local *Echo*,' said Wingsy. 'Nina, are you still there?'

'Yeah, yeah, sorry – just trying to make a connection between him and Lloyd. Other than the three dead bodies, I mean.'

'Listen, Nina, I've got one more interview to do with him and then our PACE time with him is gonna run out. He'll be off to the Magistrates' Court for an extension on his custody time. Before that happens, in case it's not granted, I'll ask him about the photos and if he had anything to do with them being sent to you. His brief may object, but I've put a note on his custody record about what he said to me off tape, so I'll give him a chance to comment on it. You know, the usual bollocks to show he was given a fair opportunity to deny it. I'll let you know what he says.'

'Thanks, you're a mate.'

I hung up and threw my mobile up and down a few times, catching Pierre's eye. 'You OK?' he asked me from the alcove housing the viewing equipment. He had paused the CCTV footage to observe me wandering between the deserted desks of the Incident Room.

'Was thinking I should get down to the court to see Freya Forbes. I have a couple of questions for her about something.'

'You want me to come along? I could do with a break.'

I shook my head and reaching for my bag, said, 'No, cheers. Won't be long.' I glanced at my wristwatch. 'Should still have time to go to Charles Bruce's house on the way back.'

'Ring me and I'll meet you there,' he said tilting his head to one side. I clocked him glance down at my hands. I'd come to a stop behind an office chair, grabbing its back so tightly my knuckles were white.

Releasing my grip, I made towards the noticeboard where the car keys were kept. The empty hooks adjacent to the list of car registration numbers indicated a lack of vehicles.

'No job cars so I'll take my own,' I said as much to myself as to Pierre.

'Then come back here before you go to Bruce's. Don't use your personal car to go to his house,' warned Pierre.

'I appreciate your concern, Pierre, but it's not as if I haven't been followed for most of my life and have God knows who coming to my house – ' I broke off, realising what I'd said.

'Who came to your house?' He put the remote control for the monitor down and stepped around the desk separating us.

'No one. When I got back from Birmingham the other day, I thought that someone was watching me and a car drove off. It could have been anyone at all. With everything that's happened, I guess I'm overreacting.' I paused, taking in his expression. 'You don't look as though you believe me, Pierre.'

'I think that you ought to report it.'

'Report what? A car drove past my house. It's a fairly busy road. It doesn't make rush hour a crime spree. I'll call you when I'm done at the court. But thanks.'

I walked out and left him standing in the office in front of a frozen image of Sophie Alexander in her own hallway, long lacy nightie billowing behind her. Stupid cow.

I made my way towards the town centre to meet with the forensic scientist. I would happily admit to myself that I'd pinned all my hopes on her telling me I had nothing to worry about. Deep down, I knew that my fears were not going to be laid to rest.

Chapter 67

I drove through the busy lunchtime back streets to the front of the Crown Court, an antiquated building of historical importance but in practical terms able to deal with very little the modern world had to throw at it, such as how to get more than two people through security at a time. Not an easy task for the security team first thing in the morning, or after lunch when the jury, witnesses and legal teams returned en masse.

Walking towards the building, I felt a sense of dread, threatening to knock me further out of kilter than I'd thought possible. I'd tried to block Jake Lloyd and his twisted behaviour from my mind. Easier said than done when I knew that some of the blood on his clothing had been identified as mine, and that he'd somehow got hold of exact replicas of the items my sister and I were wearing at the time of our kidnap. I had been trying to push the thoughts down as they'd risen up in my mind but sometimes they managed to clamber over the edge of the pit, heading for daylight.

As I made my way up to the main doors, a huddle of six people came towards me. It was made up of two women in their early twenties, one woman in her late forties and three men of approximately fifty years of age. The two young women were clasping each other's arms and crying, two of the men were speaking in hushed tones to each other, and the older female was shaking her head in disbelief. They had all the hallmarks of half a jury.

Sauntering down the steps behind them was the unmistakable form of Harry Powell, my former detective sergeant and the family liaison officer for Amanda Bell's loved ones. At six foot six, with a shock of red hair on top of his rugby player's build, he would never have made a surveillance officer. As he ambled down the concrete steps, hands in his pockets, he saw me looking at him. He broke into a grin – a grin minus a top front tooth.

'Harry, good to see you. Long time no see,' I said. 'I didn't get the chance to catch up with you on Op Guard.'

He stopped in front of me as I began to mount the steps. Then he seemed to realise that standing three steps or so below me would benefit both our necks, and moved down a few steps until we were at eye level.

'Nina, how are you? Looked out for you but our paths didn't cross,' he said.

'That jury from a job of yours?' I asked tilting my head in the direction of the disappearing six.

'Yeah. They found the defendant guilty of murdering his wife. Took them three days. Then they found out he tried to strangle a former girlfriend too and heard all his previous convictions for violence, having sex with his own daughter, that kind of thing. Judge took a majority verdict of ten to twelve in the end, before they knew all this, of course. Can't have the truth getting in the way of the English justice system.'

'Who do you reckon the two were that doubted his guilt?' I asked, having a good idea myself anyway.

'I'm going with the two sobbing women, but I could be wrong.'

'You weren't near Court Seven, were you? I'm due to meet a forensic expert in there.' I ruled out Harry as having been in Court Seven, since his jury had been out for three days.

'I was in Court Eight but I've got no idea if they've finished for the morning. Are you meeting Freya Forbes, by any chance? Only ask because I saw her earlier.'

'As it happens, I am.'

'She's great. She gave evidence on a job of mine a couple of months ago. She wiped the floor with the defence. Heard you're seeing Bill Harrison, by the way. Good one.'

'How on earth can you possibly know that? And, changing the subject, how did you lose your front tooth?'

'Rugby.'

'Playing or watching?'

'Playing, you cheeky cow.' He laughed, running his tongue into the gap. 'Got to go, Nina. Promised the kids I'd take them to the cinema tonight. It's my eldest's birthday and this is my twelfth consecutive day on duty. Trial over-ran and I had to work the weekend. Take care.'

'You too, Harry.' On another occasion I would have taken the chance to ask why the defendant in Harry's trial hadn't had his previous convictions brought up in the court as part of the bad character evidence. This was the part where the jury got to hear about what a loathsome shit the defendant actually was and how we'd all danced this merry dance with him before. I made a mental note to email Harry and ask. I was a nosy sort. It went with the job. I also wondered why he hadn't been wearing a mouthguard, but that was Harry's problem.

The momentary distraction had taken my mind off my meeting with Freya. As I made my way to the main court entrance, my mobile rang. I paused at the door to answer it, waving at the security guard as I did so. He waved back. We'd gone out for a drink once. I couldn't remember his name. I always called him 'Handsome' whenever I had to go to court. Laura always found it hilarious.

'Nina,' said a voice I recognised as Freya's, 'I'm by the entrance.'

I squinted through the ten-foot-high, thick glass door. Handsome caught my eye and winked at me.

'I'm out here, Freya,' I almost shouted, partly in panic because I really didn't want her being intercepted by the security guard, and partly because I didn't want to go in there either. I didn't need it today.

'I can see you,' she said, and a petite blonde woman came into view. I saw her wave at me with her free hand, struggling to keep her briefcase shoulder strap in place. I heard her say goodbye to Handsome as she emerged through the tinted glass doors.

'Nina. Great to meet you,' she said extending her hand to shake mine.

'And you too, Freya. Have you time for a coffee or a drink?'

'Tea would be great.'

A few minutes later, we were seated at an oblong wooden table, on cheap plastic chairs, gripping mugs of weak tea.

'It's horrible in here,' I said, glancing in the direction of the gurning fat man behind the counter. I was grateful that the till blocked my view of whatever part of his lower region he was fondling.

'Yeah, it's dreadful, but thanks for the tea.' Freya smiled at me. 'Right, where to start? I've examined the clothing. The authenticity of it is being researched by your own department, as you're probably aware.'

I wasn't aware of this, but I let it go. Clearly we weren't taking Stan's word for the destruction of the clothes after all.

She continued. 'The traces of blood on a man's shirt were your blood.'

I must have made an involuntary sound, as I was aware that someone in the deserted café took a sharp intake of breath and it hadn't come from Freya or from the same direction as the behind-the-counter scratching. She studied me for a couple of seconds before picking up her tea, then changed her mind and put it back down again. She leaned closer across the table and said, 'In theory it's possible to age blood but, in practice, it's not so easy. Ageing blood is like the Holy Grail of forensics. Blood appearing dark or ingrained at a crime scene is thought of as "old blood", if you see what I mean?' She nodded encouragingly at me before adding, 'But blood on clothing is even more difficult. Research has been done into the ageing of blood, and for relatively fresh blood there have been some results. However, when we go into decades, then these ideas aren't any use, as they're untested.'

I watched Freya glance down at her cup and then in the direction of the bloke behind the counter, who was now picking his nose. I was glad we'd decided not to eat here.

I gathered from her change in eye contact that something else was to come. Something I probably wasn't going to like. I was correct.

'Nina, the blood came from you, within the last ten years or so.'

I sat still; only my brain was moving, and even that very slowly. 'Where would he have got my blood from?' I said, and began thinking about ridiculous scenarios such as my doctor taking a blood test and Lloyd getting a job as a surgery courier to take it to the hospital; or Lloyd breaking into my house, drugging me and taking a blood sample in the night. Crazy theories which made no sense.

'It is just traces – not a significant amount. Ever cut yourself badly in public?' Freya asked. 'Or had a nosebleed?'

I started to shake my head but then a memory came into my mind of falling on my face at the ice rink some years ago. I'd kept falling over and finally called it a day when, after one particularly violent fall, I'd thought I'd broken my nose. At the time I had been seeing stars, so I couldn't recall who was there but several people came to help as there was so much blood. I had heard Jake Lloyd say himself, in his police interview, that he knew I'd gone ice-skating and had seen me injure myself.

'About eight years ago I fell on my face while ice-skating and my nose exploded,' I muttered, more to hear the words out loud than to inform Freya. I remembered it was eight years ago because I'd been dumped by a Bacardi Breezer rep. Not only did he walk out on me, but the break-up ended my relationship with discount alcopops. I took solace in ice-skating for about five weeks until I met a plumber.

The sound of chairs being scraped across the lino flooring and the faint whiff of body odour indicated that the owner was moving around in preparation for closing up his eatery.

'Nina, court's adjourned for the day. I have to get the train home soon but I'm here again tomorrow; the defence may want to ask me some questions before the trial continues. Feel free to call if you want to meet up again or ask anything else,' Freya said.

'Thanks very much. I'll walk with you to the train station,' I replied, pushing my untouched drink to one side and putting my jacket back on. I followed her outside, listening to her chatting about train times and the rising cost of tickets. I thanked her for seeing me and waved her off in the direction of her platform, shivering in my unsuitable summer jacket on the way back to the car.

October had brought with it a drop in temperature.

Chapter 68

I had a sudden urge to visit Stan. I nipped back to the office to tell Catherine I was exhausted and ask if I could do the Charles Bruce visit in the morning instead.

'Sure, Nina, it doesn't sound that urgent,' she agreed, 'and anyway, you've been here since before eight. Call it a day.'

'Thanks,' I said, and went to explain to Pierre that there was a change of plan. I found him still in front of the screen, running through the film in its entirety to prove Birdsall hadn't gone out and back in again. His bored expression made me think that there was an absence of anyone crossing the threshold overnight.

'Pierre,' I said. He turned and looked over his shoulder at me. 'I've had enough. I'm gonna leave on time today and see Bruce tomorrow. That OK?'

'Good idea. I'll carry on and finish this, then. See you tomorrow, Nina.' Pierre turned back to his viewing duties.

Making my way to Stan's house, having phoned to say I was coming, my mind raced through the evidence so far, preparing to talk it over with him.

When I pulled up outside his house on the driveway, I had the now familiar feeling of sadness. The roses around the door were dying, the petals littering the driveway. The branches hung heavy with the weight of the wilting flowers. It made me want to cry.

The front door opened, scaring my tears into hiding. I couldn't let him see me upset. That wouldn't help. I turned the ignition off and pushed open the car door, waving at the emerging figure with more enthusiasm than I felt. My gesture was returned, visible despite the dusk.

'Everything OK, Nina?' he asked from the step. 'I was starting to get worried.'

'Sorry I was longer than I said, Stan. I nipped home first to get changed, sat down on the bed and fell asleep for an hour. Dead to the world. How are you feeling?' I asked as I hugged him.

'I'm very well. You still look tired. Hope you can stay for dinner. It's lamb.'

'Great, I'm starving.' We pulled apart and I followed him into the kitchen where the table was already laid for dinner, complete with a fine bottle of uncorked Chianti.

He made his way towards the oven, calling out to me, 'Pour the wine and you can tell me what's on your mind.'

I took my jacket off and hung it on the back of the chair before reaching for the bottle. The scent of the roasting lamb reached me from the cooker, growing stronger as I heard Stan open the door and set the pan on the side to settle before carving.

'What makes you think something's on my mind? I could just be on the scrounge for a meal and glass of red,' I said as I took our drinks over to him.

He glanced up from the contents of the saucepan he was about to transfer into a serving dish.

'Or I could simply be checking on my old friend,' I added.

'I'm guessing that you're doing all three.'

I was salivating as the roast potatoes were taken out of their pan. I went to help him carry the dishes to the table, sniffing the food as I went. I was certain that the last home-cooked meal I'd had was eaten at Stan's. I turned back towards Stan to find him watching me.

'What?' I said, standing still.

'You reminded me of a dog we once had.'

'Thanks very much, Stan. You're full of compliments today.'

'The way you keep sniffing the air. It's very comical.'

'Glad you're enjoying yourself.' I changed the subject. I didn't like being compared to a pet, especially a dead one. 'I wanted to ask your views on more than one person being involved in a series of murders.'

'You mean a conspiracy?'

'That is a better way of putting it. If you had a suspect who was most definitely alibi'd out of one murder, couldn't possibly have done another of them, but was a strong contender for all three, where would you track back to?'

Stan took a sip of his wine before reaching for the carving knife. 'I take it you are talking about Tony Birdsall and his security system alibi.'

'How can you know that?' I thought I knew the answer before he gave it.

'Eric Nottingham popped round earlier. You only just missed him. I offered him dinner but his wife already thinks he's a missing person, so he declined.'

'Bloody hell, he didn't waste much time.' I dropped down in the chair, prodding the dish of green beans.

'Language. Anyway, he said the same as you. He's not happy either.'

Stan strode over with two plates, large slices of roast lamb covering half of each. He sat down opposite me, bowing his head. For a minute, I was taken aback; I thought he was saying grace. Not that I had any problem with anyone wanting to give thanks for their food, but I'd never seen Stan do it before. I was busy thinking that a health scare could change a person... perhaps he'd found God. Then I realised he was wincing.

'You alright, Stan?' I put my knife and fork down, ready to go to his side.

'I'm fine, just moved a bit quick.'

'I tried that once. It's not good for you.'

'I forgot the mint sauce.'

'I'll get it,' I said, walking across the kitchen to seek out the jar. I took my time with my head inside the fridge, to give Stan what I estimated was enough time to recover his composure. As I sat back down, I said, 'This dinner is fantastic by the way.'

Brushing my comment on the food aside, Stan paused, his fork in the air, and said, 'Tell me what else is going on. How is the investigation going? I know that Birdsall was arrested but it doesn't seem as if he's your man. Not from what you and Eric tell me.'

'We can't find the other two, Stan. We're working on it.'

'I'm sure you all are, Nina – but let's hope it's before someone else gets stabbed.'

Chapter 69

4th October

'How did Birdsall react when we were granted another forty-eight hours by the Magistrates' Court?' I asked Wingsy the following morning in the Incident Room.

'Resigned to it. No doubt his brief had warned him he was being interviewed for three murders and it was almost certainly going to happen,' he replied. 'He kind of threw in the bit about being with Sophie Alexander at the end of the first day, and kept saying, "You'll have to go and ask her why I was there." He didn't seem very worried or anxious for a man who'd been nicked for something so serious.'

'I'm guessing either one cool psychopath or simply an innocent man,' I said. 'Innocent or not, though, I heard that the proverbial hit the fan when Sophie Alexander turned up at court at the same time as Belinda Cook.'

'Yeah, it was pretty funny. Come on,' said Wingsy, 'let's get a tea and you can tell me what you've got to do today.'

We wandered off to the crowded kitchen while I explained about the subscriber check that had been carried out on Charles Bruce and my imminent visit to him. Squeezing into the tiny room, we waited our turn at the hot water dispenser, clutching our mugs. As I took my turn in line, I watched Ray take the milk from the fridge, unscrew the top and sniff the contents. 'Fuck me,' he said, screwing up his eyes at the rancid smell. 'Anyone for yoghurt? That is rough.'

'I'll leave it,' I said to Wingsy. 'I'll get a cuppa on my way out. Good luck with Birdsall today.'

I still had to see Charles Bruce. I went to find Catherine or Ray, or, if my luck was really hitting an all-time low, Kim, to let whichever person of rank I could locate first know what I was doing. I saw Ray first.

'Ah, Lolita,' he said on seeing me in the DSs' office doorway. 'Have an urgent enquiry for you this morning.'

'More urgent than Charles Bruce?' I asked.

'Yes. Can you go and see the scorned Belinda Cook as soon as possible? She called Danny first thing this morning and started ranting and raving about Birdsall. Seems that, since the Warrant of Further Detention at the Magistrates' Court yesterday, she may have tumbled that she was not the sole object of Birdsall's affections. She was hollering at Danny but he's got to carry on interviewing. Clearly he can't leave him in the cells while he speaks to Belinda. Go and see what her problem is.'

Speaking to Belinda was possibly going to be fairly entertaining. I'd seen total adoration in her eyes when Birdsall had fixed his stare on her a few days earlier. That was before she'd found out he was making excursions to the Alexander household. Hell hath no fury and all that.

I weighed up who I should carry out the enquiry with. Wingsy and Danny were busy interviewing. Mark Russell had seen her previously with Pierre but I couldn't find either of them. I would have taken Laura but she seemed to be a bit preoccupied. After careful consideration, I opted to go alone. I couldn't see the harm in it.

I pulled up outside Belinda's house. The curtains were missing from the open living room windows. I'd momentarily forgotten that we'd seized the new soft furnishings. I supposed she couldn't even rehang the old ones, as we had her curtain wire too.

Previously, I'd seen grief, disbelief and idolisation on her face. I now expected anger. Sometimes my job didn't disappoint. The Belinda who answered the door to me was livid. She was not to be placated.

'Hello, Belinda,' I said.

'Come in,' she spat. 'Lucky for you I've calmed down.'

I walked through the entranceway. She slammed the door behind me. 'Go through,' she instructed me.

I didn't think I'd be needing any of my protective equipment, but I'd checked that I had what I needed, including my cuffs and spray in my harness under my jacket, before I'd left the nick. Best to be on the safe side.

Belinda took a seat on the same sofa I'd watched her sit on only two weeks ago, but this time she didn't throw herself on to it. She positioned herself on its cushions, all the while staring at me. The look was pure malevolence. I was glad it wasn't me she was annoyed with. This woman was in for the kill.

'I'm going to tell you exactly what Tony bloody Birdsall's been up to,' she began.

I nodded my understanding.

'He's backwards and forwards to Spain dealing in stolen passports. Probably other stuff as well. I've heard mention of drugs but I can't give more details. You want to write this down? I'll sign it.'

Course I wanted to write it down, but I also wanted to watch her face with its mask of hatred. I held up my book momentarily and guggled at her again.

'He used to hide the passports here. He was on the phone to someone the day before you nicked him and I heard him use the word "blackmail" and something about a boat in France somewhere.'

It wasn't that Belinda's comments weren't both useful and fascinating, not to mention hilarious now that Tony was out of the picture, but I needed details or this was all pointless.

I began with, 'When did you see the passports?'

Her face dropped before she bared her teeth at me again. 'I didn't see them. Tony told me about them.'

'Where did he keep them?'

'He wouldn't tell me. Said it would be for the best in case he got arrested.'

This was no use to me at all. I carried on along the usual line of questioning. Eventually, I said to Belinda, 'I'll take a statement from you, Belinda, but all of this is your word against Tony's. I'll get a couple of colleagues round and with your permission we'll search your house and garden, but without finding any passports or such items I'm not sure how useful this will be.'

I was about to add my thanks for her calling us when she grabbed my attention by saying, 'Doubt there'll be anything here now. I think he'd already got rid of most of them and his mate Adam took the last one. That's what Tony told me, anyway.'

'Adam?' I asked. 'When was Adam here?'

'He came round the day before Tony got arrested. He and Tony rowed in the hallway. I heard shouting and a couple of thumps. I went to see what they were doing. Tony had Adam in a neck-hold up against the coat rack behind the door. Tony's much bigger and stronger than Adam so it didn't last long. Tony made some comment like "Have the passport, then".' Belinda looked off into the distance as if she was trying to recall the scene. I made a note to ask her what coats had been hanging up. I reckoned I might have nicely put in place how Adam Spencer's hair had got caught in Birdsall's jacket zip.

Without turning to face me again, Belinda continued. 'Tony let go of Adam and he fell to the floor. He threw something at him. It looked like a passport.' She now stared over at me. 'As he dropped the passport, Tony said to him, "If you go to the police now, they'll think you're involved and they'll think I'm involved. I've invested too much in this deal to get caught now. No one likes a grass, Adam." Before you ask me, officer, I have no idea what the deal was. You ask Birdsall.'

Belinda was as helpful as she could be in her lust for retribution. There were a couple of problems with it, of course. She was scant on details for starters and, despite my calling for another couple of DCs to search the house with me, we found nothing. The search still took hours. We hadn't expected to find much, as the house had already been searched immediately after Birdsall's arrest, and since then he'd been at Riverstone nick and the local Magistrates' Court. Still, it needed doing. The final problem I had with what she'd told me was that any defence barrister worth a jot would wipe the floor with Belinda in court. She'd be made out to be the wronged woman, hatching a plot to bring about Birdsall's demise. That, in fairness, was true. Still, there was no other option, so I spent the rest of the day with her, gaining little information but that was the nature of my job: you had to take the ups with the downs. I really didn't fancy too many more downs.

Chapter 70

Friday night, and I got to spend it all on my own. It didn't bother me and never had but lately I'd been coming home, locking the door and shying away from looking out into the dark. The nights were getting longer. The shadows cast by the trees were invading my kitchen earlier in the day than I would have liked. I'd taken to closing the kitchen blinds, something I'd never bothered with previously, as the only eyes I had thought were likely to peek into my domain from the garden were those of a bird or nocturnal creature.

As I was coming to the end of my first glass of wine, Laura telephoned me.

'Hi, honey,' I said.

'Hi, Nina. I've got some news,' she said.

'Good or bad?'

'Kind of good.'

'Go on,' I said. By this time, I'd sat down at the kitchen table.

'I know I've been acting a bit weird lately. You must have noticed?'

'No,' I lied, tucking the phone against my shoulder so that I could free up a hand to top up my wine easily.

There was a pause as I pictured her trying to put something into words for me. 'Well… it's that I'm pregnant.'

I was stunned enough to stop pouring claret. I wasn't sure if this was good or bad.

'It's early days yet, so keep it to yourself,' she gushed. 'It felt so odd keeping it from you, but now I'm glad you know.'

'Well, congratulations, Laura. I'm really pleased for you. Let me know if you need anything. Do many other people know? Such as the father?'

'Well…' Another hesitation. 'I've only told a couple of people and no, the father doesn't know.'

'Do you want to come over here tonight? I'd love to come to you but I'm probably already over the limit.'

'That's some going, Nin – you can only have been home forty minutes. No, I'm having an early night but I'll see you Monday.'

I stared at the phone next to my diminishing bottle of wine. I was about to quaff my third glass in one go when my phone rang again. The sight of the one word 'Wingsy' in the display made me smile.

'Hi, Wingsy,' I said.

'You still in the office?' he asked.

'No, I got home two glasses ago. You OK?'

'Yeah, I'm fine. Nina… don't worry about it, but Birdsall's being bailed.'

'I wasn't worried about it until you told me not to worry about it. Now I'm worried.'

'Why are you worried?'

'Because you just told me not to be.'

'Women and their logic.'

'Wingsy, why wasn't there enough to charge him?'

'Everything he's told us regarding where he was and what he was doing was checking out. Part of the reason we got the detention extension in the first place was because a lot of stuff was coming back from Spain. We're hopeful we're getting Spencer in soon. You on your own tonight?'

'Yeah. Why?'

'No reason, Nin. Just… just call if you need anything.'

He ended the call. I sat stock still at my kitchen table, holding the phone to my ear. I would have felt better if he hadn't called.

Chapter 71

5th October

A fitful Friday night's sleep was followed by a working Saturday. Always a useful time for police officers to visit people who were unavailable during the week. I had tried to visit Charles Bruce with Pierre before going off duty the previous evening but we'd got no reply. Personally, I'd been grateful, as I'd wanted to get home, but I'd promised Pierre I would see to it first thing in the morning. It couldn't be put off any longer.

In the office, I found the paperwork where I'd abandoned it next to my file. As Wingsy and I got into the Golf to drive to the location, I saw him throw a carrier bag on to the back seat.

'That looked suspiciously like a bag of your five-a-day in there, mate,' I said.

'Yeah, Mel's got me on that poxy diet again this week.'

'Clearly it's doing you good. Your mood's improving. Shame it's not making your hair grow back,' I said.

The address we had for Charles Bruce was fifteen miles away, in a fairly decent part of the county, on another new estate in Woodford. As we drove along the main through-road for the estate, the sprawl of immaculate three-storey townhouses ran out somewhere near to the children's play area, and the social housing began. This was where we pulled up to hear what Charlie had to tell us.

'Before we go inside,' said Wingsy, 'tell me where you got this bloke's number from again.'

'OK. I'll be upfront with you, you know that. It was given to me by an old acquaintance's son. He won't have anything to do with the police. Lifetime of mistrust won't go away because I take his mum some biscuits now and again. He told me that this fella Charlie knew Daphne Headingly and said she was a pretty decent woman. Taught him to read when others had given up on him. He considered her to be a harmless old bird.'

Wingsy didn't look bowled over by what I was telling him.

'I've done the checks on him and this house,' I said. 'He only has a caution for possession of cannabis when he was a lad. I'd never walk us in here blind.'

'Bloody hell, Nin, I trust you, girl. Let's say hello.'

We stepped out of the car and made our way towards No. 27, our target address. We were barely a few feet from the kerbside when the front door opened to reveal a bald white male I could only describe as a man mountain. He stood on the doorstep, watching us walk towards him as he folded his arms across his chest, vest top begging for mercy across a gargantuan torso.

'Fucking hell, Nin,' said Wingsy in tones as low as he could muster, 'the trust I have in you may just have been kicked in the nuts.'

Despite walking towards a pretty hacked-off-looking bare-knuckle fighter, I had to suppress a laugh.

'Mr Charles Bruce?' I began. This was my enquiry, after all. 'I'm Detective Nina Foster, from the enquiry into Daphne Headingly's death. Can we – ?'

I had rarely seen such an immediate shift in facial features. His cheeks sagged and his eyes lowered for a second. Then he was back.

'Better come in, then, love. And your mate,' he said, in Wingsy's direction. 'Don't know what the world's coming to, killing an old lady.' He moved back to allow us in. He was surprisingly light on his feet when he moved.

In the kitchen, I watched Charlie glance at the water level on the electric kettle, switching it on to boil before turning and saying, 'Take it you two want a brew?'

'Yes, thanks,' I said. 'How did you know Daphne Headingly?'

'Daphne was alright. Used to be that a kid like me – shit, useless family, filthy dirty all the time, getting into fights, didn't want to be at school, picked on 'cos I was always trying to act hard – well, there was a time when kids like me dropped out of the system. Couldn't read and write, so they called you thick.' He reached towards the neatly lined-up row of mugs on the window sill behind the sink, stopped with his hand around one and said, 'To be fair to the teachers, I was a right little fucker.'

'And when did you meet Daphne?' I asked.

'I was about nine, or was it eight?' He put three mugs on the work surface and dropped teabags into them while he considered this point. 'Hadn't long been at primary school anyway, when I was sent out of class, yet again, for fucking about.' He poured hot water into the mugs, set the kettle back on its stand, and rubbed his hands over his bald head. 'She was some sort of school governor, and she saw me standing in the corridor waiting to go see the head teacher, Mr Cuthbert, the miserable old bastard. Anyway, she asked what I was doing, I told her, and do you know what she said to me?'

Wingsy and I clearly didn't or we'd have solved these murders by now with our fantastic insight into what conversations had previously taken place when we weren't present. We shook our heads.

Charlie gave a small laugh and said, 'She only fucking asked me why I'd been pissing about in class. And that wasn't it. When I said, "'Cos I was bored shitless." she said, "Why were you bored shitless?" No one had ever asked me why I couldn't concentrate, do the work. I'd done everything under the sun to hide not being able to read. She saw straight through that and said, "Can you read?" I'll never forget her standing there in front of me. She bent down and said. "I'll see you here at 3.30pm. I'll let your mother know you're helping me with something and we'll get cracking. It's a disgrace this school didn't see this." Bollocks, I'm out of milk. Hang on, I'll nip to the shop. You two have a seat.'

As Charlie felt in his pocket for money, I said, 'One of us can go and get the milk.'

'No, you're alright, love. It's only up the road.'

And he was gone, leaving us alone in his house.

'Well, he certainly has a lot of time for Daphne,' Wingsy said. 'I take it he lives here alone?'

'Dunno,' I said. 'We never got that far, but the voters' register only had him on it when I ran some checks. I'll shout up the stairs in case we scare the living daylights out of someone in bed.'

I made my way back towards the front door and stood at the foot of the stairs, hollering up to the next floor just to be on the safe side. I got no reply, as I'd expected, and I turned to rejoin Wingsy. As I did so, though, something drew my attention in the front room. Out of the corner of my eye, I saw an old black and white photograph on a side table. It showed a Victorian two-storey building, complete with turrets and a water tower. In the foreground were a young smiling boy and an older woman. Walking towards it, I saw the similarities between Charlie Bruce and the young lad's face. A full head of hair was throwing me off slightly but it was undoubtedly him. I continued to stare at the picture until Wingsy's voice behind me brought me out of my reverie.

'That looks like Charlie and Daphne Headingly. Where was it taken?' said Wingsy.

'This is Leithgate children's home in Birmingham. But he's got a family. Why was he there?'

'Looks like he's coming back. We can ask him,' said Wingsy looking in the direction of the lounge window. The bulk of Charlie was crossing the road towards us, a two-pint plastic milk carton hanging from his right hand. It looked tiny against his fingers, let alone the rest of him.

'Big bastard, ain't he?' I said to Wingsy.

'Yeah, he is. You ask him.'

Both of us stood in the living room facing the street. Charlie opened the door and, with one foot inside his house on the green carpet and one on the step, paused and said, 'What the fuck's wrong with you two?'

'Charlie, can you tell us about this photo?' I pointed vaguely to where the table housed the snapshot without taking my eyes off Charlie. I didn't have a feel for him being a murderer, but with biceps bigger than my thighs – and I had some flank on me – I was taking no chances. I should have given my Pava Spray a shake while he was out of the house. Or was it CS gas you had to shake before use? I could never remember, as I'd never used the bloody thing; a biro and a smile usually stopped me getting a hiding. I hoped my luck wasn't about to run out.

'The picture of me and Daphne, do you mean?' He walked towards the kitchen, unscrewing the green plastic cap from the milk. 'Fucking tea'll be brewed to bollocks now. Shit. I'll put the kettle back on. Fucking waste of bastard teabags. Sorry about the language, love. It's just that I hate waste.'

'That's OK. Even I swear sometimes,' I said. I avoided Wingsy's eye as I said it.

We had followed Charlie into the kitchen, where he set about making fresh tea. He explained as he busied himself with the drinks.

'I found that picture in the back of a drawer. Almost forgot I had it but got it out again when I heard she'd been killed. When I met Daphne, she told me if I got to a certain level with my reading she'd take me on a day out. I'd never been to Birmingham and she was going for a job interview at some kids' home.' He waved the teaspoon in his hand in the direction of the photo. 'It was only a day trip, nothing fancy, but my parents couldn't have given a fuck what I was doing so she took me with her. It was a great day. She tested my spelling, grammar, that sort of thing, all the way there and back.'

He added milk to the cups. 'Come upstairs, I wanna show you something while the kettle's boiling,' he said. We glanced at each other, then followed him up the narrow staircase to the small box bedroom at the front of the house. The room was about six feet by eight and contained an armchair and lamp in one corner next to the window and about four hundred books. The walls were covered floor to ceiling with shelves and bookcases. Where there was no wall space remaining, Charlie had arranged the books on the floor in neat piles.

I watched Charlie pick up a hardback book from the grey seat of the chair. He held the book in one of his massive palms and ran the fingers of his other hand across the cover. '*Rebecca* by Daphne du Maurier. You read it? It's fucking brilliant.'

Temporarily speechless, I regained my composure before replying, 'No, I haven't, Charlie. Have you read all of these?'

'Most, yeah. My point is, I'm a carpenter. It's a good job, pay's OK and all that. If it weren't for Daphne, I wouldn't be able to read. Not only would not being able to read make life difficult, but I wouldn't have got to read *The Great Gatsby*, *The Pickwick Papers, Jurassic Park* – way better than the film – anything by Stephen King. Get what I'm saying? Let's have a cuppa and you tell me how we find this sick bastard.'

The whole time he was speaking, Charlie continued to caress the book, as his face grew darker and his frown deeper. He put the book back down, straightened it on the cushion and headed back to the staircase.

Settled in the front room with the children's home photograph on the coffee table in front of us, we went back over the details with Charlie about when he went to Birmingham and how long he was there for. Very little new information was forthcoming beyond what he had already told us. He had been a very young child at the time of the day trip. He could hardly have known that, decades later, his day out would become part of a murder investigation.

Every avenue of possibility was exhausted in relation to the Leithgate home when we changed tack to the mobile phone number we had for him.

'Someone gave me your phone number, Charlie. The same person said it was a foreigner committing the murders,' I said. 'Who gave us your number isn't important, but what you know is. Do you know anything about this foreigner? Did that information come from you?'

Charlie sat across from me, staring straight at me. His arms were resting on the sides of his chair, his fists clenched, legs still, knees at right angles to the rest of him. For some inexplicable reason, I thought of a bear hiding inside the skin of a bald, fat bloke. Bears don't usually sit in recliners, I thought, but there you go.

He didn't say anything for several seconds, simply stared unblinkingly at me. Then he leaned towards me, big bald head looming closer. He scratched his chin before placing his enormous hand on his thigh.

'Truth be told, love, I wouldn't have contacted the police direct to tell you that I knew Daphne years ago. It didn't seem relevant but you're here now. All I know is what I've told you.'

'Was there anything else?' I tried.

'No, love. Nothing at all. Can't be of much help, but find whoever's killing these people, will you? She was an old lady,' he said through his downturned mouth.

'Whatever it takes, Charlie, whatever it takes,' I told him as we gathered our paperwork together to walk out of his front door. I had no idea, at that time, just how much it would cost me.

Chapter 72

Back at the Incident Room, I did my best to avoid Matt, who was still taking care of the telephone enquiries.

'I've been told this is now a priority,' said Matt, raising his eyebrows as I tried to make my way past him. 'Like it wasn't before. Don't know what they thought I was going to do with it. Bloody fools. Of course I put the application in and of course I asked for it urgently.' He walked away from me, still mumbling about how telephone enquiries took time, the results weren't instant, he was working as fast as he could, it wasn't the TV, he didn't have direct access to all phone records in the country...

Pierre sidled up to me and said, 'Ignore him. He's always like that when he's given phones to work on. It is a pig of a job. There's endless applications and justifications to get the data. Come on, let's grab a cuppa while we wait for instructions.'

As we made our way in the direction of the kitchen, Matt returned, still sporting an angry expression. He hurried towards me, so I steadied myself for another tirade on the subject of how hard done by he was, having to fill in telephone request forms to the Single Point of Contact for telephony work, or SPOC as it was shortened to. It never failed to make me smile at the thought of a fella with pointy ears sitting in an office somewhere reading all the applications. I might have mentioned before how it was always the little things in this job that amused me. Right now, I needed some light relief.

'Nina, meant to say, been looking at your man Jake Lloyd's phone work too. You any idea who's been calling him from France? Somewhere down in the south, in the St Tropez region?' said Matt.

Pierre and I paused while I took this in. 'St Tropez, you say?' said Pierre.

I shrugged, but said, 'It was a foreigner, someone from Europe.'

'But Adam Spencer and Tony Birdsall live in Spain,' said Matt. 'Still Europe, though...'

As I was thinking about what Matt had said, Eric Nottingham walked in with a satisfied look on his face. He stopped for a second and surveyed the room, cup in his right hand. He paused to take a sip, cleared his throat and, when he had the undivided attention of all of us in the room, seemed to take great pleasure in saying, 'Fantastic news, everyone. Adam Spencer has just been stopped trying to buy a ticket for a flight to Spain with over £6,000 in cash on him.' He looked at his watch. 'I need to get Ray to call everyone who's free into the Incident Room. It's likely to be another long day. I'll be back in a minute to let you all know what I know. For now the update is scant. Spencer made some comments on arrest but I don't have them verbatim.'

Nottingham walked off towards his office while a buzz of excited conversation took over the room, as we carried on working. Those who needed to busied themselves tying up loose ends before we were sent off to respond to anything coming out of the operation's latest arrest. I looked across at Wingsy, who was at a desk in the corner. He winked at me. I grinned back. We now had Spencer. Whatever he might have to say for himself, that only left Benjamin Makepeace.

My glowing inner thoughts were interrupted by another exasperated member of the investigation team making a fair amount of noise. Matt was back at his desk, shoulders hunched, banging the keyboard with his fingers. Preparing for another rant, I approached him to ask a question.

'Matt, do you know how many calls were made to Lloyd from St Tropez?'

'About twenty over a period of six weeks, starting just over a month before Amanda Bell's body showed up,' he said without looking up. 'Oh, this bastard computer; it's lost my application. I was almost done and it's gone. If you want to check the results, the analyst's done a spreadsheet. It's saved on the shared drive.'

I left him shouting and threatening to kick the living daylights out of his computer and went over to Wingsy. He'd been listening to my conversation with Matt – it wasn't too difficult to be alerted to Matt's pain by the number of times he shouted 'bollocks' at the screen – and had already called up the spreadsheet. As we studied it, we muttered behind our screen about the newest arrest and what a relief it was that Spencer had been nicked. I kept my voice low as I said how comprehensive the telephone results were and how user-friendly the spreadsheet was. One of us pointed now and again at the length of a call or the same number appearing time and time again. We hadn't realised that Matt was listening to us despite our hushed tones, until he called out, 'That telephone number you're looking at, the one that made several calls, has been identified as a telephone kiosk on the seafront at St Tropez. It's marked up at the foot of the spreadsheet.'

I glanced down the list of times and dates. Something about them caused me to stop in my tracks. I wasn't sure what it was, but some of them were so recent. I was trying hard to focus on what was niggling in my brain. I ran across the office to get my notebook which I'd left lying next to the office booking diary, almost colliding with Nottingham as he came through the door. I flicked through the pages until I got to the date I was after. Taking it back to Wingsy, I said, 'Look at this. Do you think this is a coincidence? I'm not sure that I do.'

I showed him the time and date I'd recorded in my book when Pierre and I had gone to see Susan Newman, and the subsequent phone calls we made to her daughter Josie in France. I pointed to the spreadsheet. The calls made from a St Tropez phone box to Jake Lloyd's landline were five minutes either side of Pierre's conversation with Josie Newman.

'You have to allow for the hour's time difference,' I said, 'but whoever made these calls made them minutes either side of our call.'

Nottingham had put his notebook down and walked around the desk to stand the other side of Wingsy. All three of us peered at the times and dates on the screen.

'Sir,' I said, 'I know that this means little at this stage, but something has always bothered me about Jake Lloyd.' Nottingham's head turned from the direction of the screen to meet my eyes. 'Apart from him being a total headcase who kept vintage children's clothing and... well, you know the rest.'

He nodded.

'What I mean is that, after all those years, he or someone else sent me photos in an envelope with his fingerprints on it. I know that he always admitted taking them but not sending them. The thing is, if Lloyd didn't send them to me, who did?'

'And why was someone in the South of France calling him?' asked Wingsy.

An unpleasant thought occurred to me. I said, 'Jake Lloyd took five grand out of his bank account. Boss, you said that on arrest Spencer had thousands on him. What if Spencer was blackmailing Lloyd?'

'That's one hypothesis,' said the DCI. Inwardly, I smiled at the word. It was used to show the police had thought of everything by 'hypothesising' about likely scenarios. The bollocks we had to do. The public had no idea.

Nottingham's phone began to ring. He read the caller's name and said, 'That's Simon Patterson. We should be getting an update from Stansted.' He took himself and his notebook and went back in the direction of his own office.

I moved an inch or two closer to Wingsy and said, 'Thing is, mate, what's worrying me quite a lot is why someone sent me those photos? The only thing I've come up with so far is, somebody wanted Jake Lloyd out of the way. And, again, I can only come up with one reason for that. Jake Lloyd was watching me; now he's not because he's in prison, awaiting trial. Terrible truth is, I was probably safer before Lloyd was locked up.'

Chapter 73

As we waited for our DCI to return and tell us what was happening with Adam Spencer, we made calls home to say we'd be late, grabbed last-minute cups of tea and mentally readied ourselves for what was coming our way.

At last, Nottingham came into the Incident Room. All those assembled stopped what we'd been doing. He stood just inside the doorway and relayed the conversation he'd been having with his deputy SIO, Simon Patterson. All eyes were on him.

'Adam Spencer is, as you know, in custody. The forensics are being taken care of in Essex before he's conveyed back here. He was intending to travel under a stolen passport in the name of Timothy Anderson, but was fool enough to drive to the airport in a vehicle his father, Alf, told us he stores between UK visits at a friend's garage. The ANPR picked him up on the M11, local police were alerted and then he was arrested approaching the ticket office at the terminal. We assume he was planning to buy his ticket at the airport, as he didn't have one with him on arrest.

'Once he was nicked for the murders, his reply after caution was – ' Nottingham held up his notebook at this point ' – "I didn't kill anyone. This isn't what it seems. I should never have got involved with her plans".' He lowered the notebook again.

'Once they've finished doing what they need to do at Stansted, Simon will sort out Spencer's transportation back here. His vehicle is being brought back too. In the meantime,

Pierre, I'd like you interviewing tomorrow. You free for the next few days?'

'Yes, boss,' said Pierre. 'Who am I working with?'

'Danny's in tomorrow. Give him a call and warn him. As for you two, Wingsy, Nina, can you ring Kim and see what else she needs doing this evening? She has a grasp of things here and we want the three victims' families told in person tonight before it's on the news. I'm going to update the Chief. See you all tomorrow.'

I didn't fancy calling Kim Cotton but one of us had to. I threw myself on my sword and rang the lemon-sucker.

She answered with, 'Hello, Nina. Wait. I'm talking to someone.'

I thought about hanging up but decided against it. I saw Wingsy grinning at me. He said, 'Your face's a picture. Lucky she can't see the expression on it. It's loaded with contempt.'

I was about to say something witty and scathing when a voice in my ear reminded me we were still connected by the wonder of technology. 'Right, Nina. Mark Russell is going to see Alf and Catherine's gone to see the Headinglys. That leaves both Amanda Bell's family and Jason Holland's. Harry, the original FLO for Amanda, is still on duty so he can take care of that one. I'll send you over to Holland's girlfriend's – Annette Canning. There's not much else for you to do. Make sure you ask her about Benjamin Makepeace, since he was on the same flight as Holland when he last left Spain. Go and do that with Wingsy, then call me and I'll let you know if there's anything else before you go off duty. All clear?'

'Yeah, got that,' I replied, sticking two fingers up at the phone. She disconnected without saying goodbye. I hated that.

'You're very childish, you know,' said Wingsy. 'No respect for rank.'

'I can't help it,' I said. 'She's a great big bastard.'

'What is it with you and women DSs?' he asked. 'I think you're sexist.'

'And I think you're a baldy wanker. Now drink your tea while I look up Annette's address. We get the pleasure of telling her that Adam Spencer's been arrested for her partner's murder. Also, Sergeant Menopause reminded me that Holland flew back from Spain on the same flight as Benjamin Makepeace. She thinks it's a good idea we ask Annette about that too. If only I'd thought of that.'

Wingsy and I exchanged a few more insults, got the information we needed, said goodbye to Pierre, Mark and Matt and drove to Annette Canning's house.

Chapter 74

The journey took us through a couple of decent new estates, past my own road and on towards the rural part of Riverstone. We found ourselves in a street dotted with houses on one side and a field on the other. Some of the houses were very grand with long driveways and lots of land. Others were more modest. We pulled up outside one of the smaller ones, well maintained if the outside was anything to go by, with a very neat front garden. I'd been reading out to Wingsy on the way over that the house was owned by Annette's father, who had worked for an airline but had been retired for some time. He lived there with his wife and their disabled son and had temporarily taken in their only daughter after the disappearance and then murder of her long-term partner, Jason Holland.

'Nice place,' said Wingsy as we prepared to get out of the car with our paperwork. 'Reckon even the smaller places like this are worth a few quid around here.'

'No doubt. Right, then, who gets to tell Annette the update?' I said as we made our way towards the front door.

'I'll allow you the pleasure,' said Wingsy.

My knock was answered by a small, grey-haired woman in her sixties wearing a raincoat. A man of about forty in a wheelchair was behind her in the hallway.

'Sorry,' I began. 'Were you on your way out? We're police officers and would like to speak to Annette if she's here.'

'Yes, she's in. We've just got home so your timing's good. Please come in,' she said. 'I'm Annette's mum and this is

318

her brother, Alan.' Introductions made, we were shown into the dining room to wait for her. I hadn't expected such a breathtakingly beautiful woman to walk into the room. Annette was tall, slim, elegant, well-dressed and had a self-assured air about her. The only clues to her misery were the bloodshot eyes and the presence of a tissue clenched within her fist. This she moved to her left hand before extending her right to me in greeting. I'd seen the photos of Jason before the flies took hold and bits of him started to morph with the floorboards. It didn't seem possible that a woman like her would be interested in a man like him.

After we'd introduced ourselves, I took a deep breath and watched her face for any changes as I said to her, 'We've made another arrest this evening in relation to Jason's murder.' She twitched at the word 'murder'. I continued, 'We've arrested someone called Adam Spencer.'

Annette gasped and clamped the tissue to her gaping mouth. 'But Adam... He was... I know Adam. He wouldn't hurt anyone.'

This I hadn't expected. The DCI had taken the decision not to publicly name Birdsall, Spencer and Makepeace prior to their arrests. It had made total sense as, although it was not uncommon to release a name, often with a photograph, if someone was sought in connection with a serious crime (and they didn't come much more serious than this one), in this unique situation we had three names. To have released to the media the names of two suspects and a missing person all sought in connection with the enquiry, later changing it to three suspects, would have caused uproar. It would have seemed as if the police were pulling names out of a hat. People were not named as suspects lightly, and the decision not to tell the families of the deceased was also a wise move. Journalists trying to find out anything of interest would not pass up the opportunity to turn such information into a story. We couldn't risk one of the nearest and dearest of our victims passing on something before we were ready.

So Annette had had no idea that the names Tony Birdsall or Adam Spencer or, more recently, Benjamin Makepeace, were those of the suspects sought for her partner's death. We had always intended that the first she would know of it was one of the county's officers – in this case, me – knocking on her door and telling her that one of them was in custody.

Giving Annette a second to compose herself, I asked her, 'How did you know Adam?'

'I met him around three years ago through a friend of a friend, on his boat down in the South of France, in St Tropez. I already knew Jason vaguely at the time although we weren't in a relationship. Jason and I had met at one or two earlier social functions in London. Adam then reintroduced us to each other at a party on his boat and we hit it off. It seemed very romantic.' She sniffed delicately, dabbed her eyes with the scrunched-up tissue and continued, 'I didn't mention it before when police called and took the Missing Person report because it didn't seem important. The police asked me how I met Jason, but, as it wasn't our first meeting, Adam's party didn't seem to be relevant. There were lots of other people on the boat too. It would never have entered my head to list them all and, as I've said, the police have never questioned me about it. I'd liked Jason, but always thought he was a bit, erm – I'm embarrassed to say, I always thought he was a bit rough around the edges.'

I tried to look surprised by this but think I failed to pull the necessary facial muscles into place, largely because I'd seen his list of convictions printed from the Police National Computer. He had basically been a violent criminal. My thoughts were interrupted by Alan Canning, who said, 'I told her he was an obnoxious individual who probably had a criminal record.'

Annette looked across at her brother, smiled and said, 'He did have a criminal record. He told me all about it.'

Her father had said little up to this point but felt the need to make some sort of contribution. 'I thought he was a bad sort too. When your colleagues were here when Jason was first found, they alluded to as much without actually saying so. I'd had my suspicions but you have to let your children do what they see fit to do with their own lives. Annette's an adult, so there was nothing I could do to stop her anyway.'

Annette told us how she'd initially met Jason in London, introduced by a mutual friend, but all of this had already been covered in her original statements when his body had been found. The mutual friend had also been spoken to by officers and alibi'd out of the enquiry by her passage on a non-stop Southampton-New York-Southampton cruise for most of the relevant times. The only information that was new was the bit about Adam Spencer. No one had known anything about his part in it all. Annette explained that the same seafaring friend who had introduced her to Holland had invited her to the South of France to a villa for a week, celebrating the birthday of a casual acquaintance. Once in France, the acquaintance had taken her guests to meet up with her friend Adam Spencer, who had sailed his boat from Spain to join them in St Tropez. He had invited her and the others from the villa aboard the boat for the evening.

'Much to my surprise, there was Jason, on the deck, pouring champagne for the guests. We got talking and arranged to meet up when I got home. Our relationship went from strength to strength and within six months we were living together,' said Annette.

The whole time she was talking, I nodded and uttered the odd, 'oh' or 'right', all the time thinking that Annette could not have been more of a contrast to Chloe, Holland's ex-wife. I failed to see what she could have seen in him.

'I expect you're wondering what I could have seen in him,' she said.

'No,' I lied.

'He was funny and kind and he didn't take life too seriously,' she replied. He wasn't likely to, I thought, with a wealthy, beautiful girlfriend he'd met while pouring champagne on his rich friend's yacht. I would probably find life a breeze too, in such circumstances. Holland probably counted on being set up for the rest of his life. And I supposed, in a way, he had been, short as it was.

'Can you tell us the names of anyone else at the party on Adam's boat?' Wingsy asked.

'Well, there was his girlfriend, of course, Josie Newman,' said Annette.

Both Wingsy and I took this massive news on board without alerting her to the significance of what she'd told us. Our faces didn't change. We didn't react in any way. Not on the outside. On the inside, it was a different story. Annette rattled off more names of those who'd been present. Some had been spoken to already but we took details again anyway. All of the twenty-two people she named would need to be re-interviewed now, following both Spencer's arrest and the naming of Makepeace as a suspect.

'Tell us about Josie,' I said.

Annette smiled and said, 'Josie and I got along quite well. Jason and I went to several more of Adam's yacht parties once we were together. Adam had his bar in Spain, but he used to sail down whenever he could, to see Josie. She told me that she came from this area and had friends around here. I heard her and Adam talking, actually, at the last party, about an old friend of Josie's who still lives here with her young son. Adam was planning to visit her and say hello. You know – check on her, that sort of thing.'

Again, I refused to allow myself to appear too eager. 'Can you tell us the friend's name or any more about her?' I asked, as casually as possible.

'No, sorry. I was on my way to get myself a drink at that point. I don't know if you're familiar with the layout of a yacht, officer?' Annette asked, without any hint of sarcasm.

'Not really,' I answered with a smile.

'Well, I went to get a drink on the upper deck from the main deck and the two of them were tucked out of sight of the rest of the party. I heard Josie say something like, "You should go and see her. Let her know that I'm still thinking about her even after all these years." Adam's reply was a little less enthusiastic but he seemed to be saying, "I think your plan is a bad one but I'll do it." That's about all I heard.'

There was little else that Annette could tell us about Josie and her conversation with Adam despite our questioning. It seemed that Annette hadn't figured out who they had been talking about, so we declined to fill in the blanks for her. Again, we changed tack.

'Does the name Benjamin Makepeace mean anything to you?' Wingsy asked Annette.

She paused, her lovely face tilted towards him, intelligence alive behind the bloodshot eyes. After a few seconds, she said slowly, 'I'm not entirely sure. But I do remember Jason telling me he had met an old schoolfriend the last time he was in Spain. I wasn't too sure who he'd been talking about but now you mention the name Benjamin...' Annette uncrossed and crossed her legs again before adding, 'He may have said Ben. I'm sorry. It was one of those calls he made from Spain. It was just before they called his flight; I could hear the announcements in the background at the airport. He said something about seeing an old friend and that he'd call me at Gatwick. He did call me when his flight landed, and he got home a couple of hours later, but he made no mention of Ben or whatever his name was. I'd forgotten all about it.' Annette dabbed again at her reddened eyes. 'He disappeared a few days after that. Everything just went from my mind...'

We spent another couple of hours with Annette, taking another statement from her, getting as much detail as possible to make sure we were talking about the same Adam Spencer and Josie Newman. When we finally left, it was after 10pm.

In the car, Wingsy and I sat quietly for three or four seconds before he broke first. 'Can you believe that?' he asked. 'Josie Newman was an associate of Spencer's all that time.'

'Best give Cotton a call, tell her about Newman and see if the sour-faced cow wants us to do anything else,' I said.

'Hope not,' said Wingsy. 'I could do with getting home, but with a revelation like that one she may well want something done tonight – like a visit to Susan Newman.'

'Yeah,' I said, 'I haven't had a chance to call Bill all day. I'll text him and say hello, see if he's still at work or not. Think he was late turn today. I can't remember.'

'How's it going with him?'

'OK, but our whole big romance has been one pizza together. Finding the time is proving a bit tough at the moment.'

'You do have a habit of making a mess of things.'

'It's never my fault. Well, there was that one time when I threw up on that bloke from Manchester I was seeing. To be fair to him, he was quite good about it.'

'Yeah, till you went round to see him and he'd moved back to Manchester without telling you.'

'Can you be quiet now? I'm about to ring Cotton.'

Thankfully Kim had nothing more for us, in spite of the news that Adam Spencer was the boyfriend of Josie Newman. I was grateful not to be sent to Mrs Newman's and assumed that there was a plan in place for that one. I was getting too tired to worry about it. We headed back to the nick, intending to complete and hand in our paperwork and have a word with Pierre about the interviews in the morning. Our plans changed rapidly when a very flustered-looking Catherine appeared in the doorway and said, 'Nina, Wingsy. Glad you two haven't gone home. Can you come with me?'

My heart sank. I was really tired at this point. It had been another hectic six days on duty. I'd been envisaging going home and waking up refreshed for my day off.

'What's the matter?' said Wingsy. 'Did you run up the stairs?'

She glanced over her shoulder towards Nottingham's office. 'When we got Spencer back here, he was insisting that he be interviewed tonight. The plan was to leave him until the morning as it's getting late. He declined a brief. He wouldn't stop talking about Jason Holland and Amanda Bell so Pierre went downstairs with Mark to put in an interview. They've only been going for a few minutes but I think you'll want to hear this.'

Chapter 75

Without another word, we followed her to the remote viewing room. Catherine was right. I did want to hear what Spencer was saying.

At this precise moment, I was unable to distinguish what exactly was causing the slight shake of my hands and a really unpleasant sweating in my palms as I opened the door to the viewing room. Nerves or adrenaline were both likely to produce this effect on me. Wingsy looked as if he was faring much better but I couldn't be sure about that. We took a seat, already transfixed by the pictures and words coming from the monitor on the wall before we even reached the chairs. Catherine took a seat by the door.

'Listen, it's important. Ask me what you like, but hear me out first. I have to tell you this.'

With my eyes on the screen as I slid on to the cushioned surface, I located the speaker. I'd seen enough photographs by now to know what Adam Spencer looked like. The images I'd previously seen were those of a much less worried man. The Adam Spencer I was now looking at had a worn expression, sallow skin, bloodshot eyes. I could have passed him in the street and not recognised him.

'Blackmail, yes. I'll admit to blackmail. I'll go to court and plead guilty. But murder, no. Not murder.' His voice was raised, and his eyes locked on Pierre and then Mark. I wasn't sure which one held his gaze, due to the angle of the camera, until I heard Pierre speak.

'Tell us about the blackmail, Adam.'

Adam banged his head on the table and left it there for a couple of seconds. When he straightened himself up again he said, 'It was Josie Newman's idea.' He held his hands up and added, 'But yes, I'm as much to blame. I went along with it. She had this idea to blackmail Jake Lloyd.'

As he said Lloyd's name, I felt a shiver go down my spine. I hugged my goosebumped arms.

Adam continued. 'Josie had some compromising photographs of Amanda Bell and Jake Lloyd from a few years ago. She wanted money for them, as he was doing well for himself. Problem was, as it turned out, he wasn't doing as well as we'd thought. We just assumed that he was kicking up a fuss about paying. Five grand is five grand at the end of the day. We'd sent him some sample pictures so he knew we weren't kidding about. When I went to see him to collect the money, he told me he'd burnt them.'

Adam gave a dry laugh. 'Thing was, what neither me nor Josie knew until later was that Lloyd was stalking one of your officers. I went to collect the money and we rowed. He said that he would pay the five grand but there was to be no more money. It got very heated and he told me that he "knew all about taking photographs". At the time, that meant nothing to me. He handed me five thousand pounds in a large padded envelope. I took it off him.'

Adam paused, took a sip of a drink from the plastic cup next to him and rubbed his hands over his face. With a sigh, he said, 'Later that night, I waited for him to go out, let myself in through an open window and went through some of his stuff. I found a load of photographs of a woman. It was obvious that the freak had been taking them for years, and without her knowing. I found a press cutting about a policewoman who had rescued some battered housewife, Annie Hudson. Lunatic husband had shoved an iron in her face and beaten the living daylights out of her. This WPC had got a bit of a kicking herself but saved the woman's life, keeping the bloke off the wife till more police turned up. It was quite clear it was the same woman as in the photos. Her name was Nina Foster. Do you know her?'

Credit to Pierre. 'Go on,' was all he said.

'Anyway, I took the photographs, found an address for her on the internet and posted them to her in the envelope Lloyd had given me the money in. Figured it wouldn't be too long before police came to talk to him. Thought it might shake him up a bit. You know, let him know that we were serious. Last thing I expected was that he'd confess to murdering his cousin eight years earlier.'

'What happened to the money?' asked the unseen Pierre.

'The plan was to give some to Amanda,' answered the haggard murder suspect. 'Me and Josie were just trying to help her out. You've got to believe that. We felt sorry for her. We had a good life in Spain; she was stuck here being paid to have sex with disgusting men. She's got a young son. She was doing some really sordid stuff with her kid in the house. We wanted to use some of Lloyd's money to help her and her son. And teach Lloyd a lesson.' He gave a humourless laugh and said, 'Thing was, I didn't want to give her any of Lloyd's actual cash – you know, dirty money and all that, just didn't feel right – so I called her, gave her €2,000 of my own to change into sterling and went with her to the travel agents to change it. No doubt you've got me on CCTV with her. I didn't think there'd ever be a comeback on it. But then I didn't expect her to end up dead either.'

He clenched his fists, leant his weary face towards the interviewing officers and said, 'I didn't kill Amanda Bell. It wasn't me. But I must have led him straight to her door.'

'Who, Adam? Who did you lead to her door?' asked Pierre.

'Benjamin Makepeace. He turned up in Malaga. Me and Tony had been in the papers, the Spanish ones and the ones in the UK, when our second bar opened. We even made a point of going to the press in Birmingham 'cos that's where me and

Tony met, at the children's home in Leithgate. We thought it was clever publicity. We didn't recognise Benjamin when he turned up, until he introduced himself. He came to the bar, bought us drinks, chatted to people in the bar. He wouldn't leave at the end of the night. He got a bit weird. You know, all intense and very morbid.

'Jason Holland was there that night. He'd come over for a few days. In the end, Jason took Benjamin out of the bar and tried to take him back to his own hotel. Turned out Benjamin didn't have one. He crashed on the floor in Jason's room.'

Adam put his elbows on the table and covered his face with his hands. After a few seconds of total silence, he moved his hands away and said, 'Knowing what I know now, I could have saved that old lady's life. Daphne Headingly worked at the home when we were there. After a few drinks, Benjamin started to talk about the day this kid called Peter died. He told me that he'd found Peter hanging and had seen one of the staff, Daphne Lloyd she was called back then, in the attic when he'd got there. He'd run away and told no one. I then found Peter myself, hanging by his neck. All these years and I had no idea Benjamin found Peter Woods' body before I did… I'll never forget what I saw, but I had no idea Benjamin had already seen him. To this day, he thinks he walked in on Daphne after she'd killed him. Why he didn't tell anyone, I don't know. I could tell from the way he talked, Benjamin had never got over it. He told me that he had seen her photograph in the paper – she'd won seven hundred and fifty grand on the lottery or something like that – and he'd got so angry. Then he'd seen her at Gatwick Airport when he was on his way out to Spain to visit us. He called it a "sign". She was telling someone that she'd just flown first class from a holiday in Hong Kong. He was so angry that she was living such a good life when he knew she'd murdered a small boy in her care. He ranted on and on. I couldn't get a word in to tell him the truth, and he was too drunk to listen anyway.

'Peter was an uncontrollable little boy – taking risks, ignoring orders. We'd been told the attic was unsafe and out of bounds so it would have been the first place he'd go.'

Spencer went very quiet, head hanging forward to examine his feet. The only sound I could hear was the noise of my laboured breathing.

'When I got there, what I saw… Daphne was getting Peter down, trying to get him breathing. She tried and tried. She saw me there and called for me to get help but I couldn't move. For years I thought it was my fault he died. Fucked me up no end. I would have told Benjamin all that, but he'd passed out by then and to be honest, in the morning, I didn't feel like bringing it up again.'

Adam had started talking and now he couldn't stop.

'Jason had a bit of a temper and I saw him lose it a couple of times with Benjamin. Jason used to talk to us all about his exploits with prostitutes. You know what it's like? You have a couple of drinks, you take a bit of coke and talk about stuff.

'I got talking about how I was going to see Amanda, help her out. Jason was gobbing off that he'd had sex with Amanda a few times, knew her well and once even made her eight-year-old son watch.'

Credit to Spencer: the memory of this conversation was doing him a lot more harm than the criminal justice system ever would. Another tortured soul to add to the list.

'Jason went home to England and said he was taking Benjamin back with him. Benjamin was getting on everyone's nerves. He was weird and creepy and seemed like one of those people who could go off at the deep end for no reason. We wanted him out of the way. I never saw either of them again. Jason's dead, Daphne's dead and Amanda's dead too, because I led him to her.'

I'd heard enough. Wingsy followed me out of the room. 'You alright, duchess?' he asked, concern all over his face.

Catherine opened the interview room door a few inches to allow her face through the gap. It was if she was guarding anyone else from seeing and hearing the goings-on behind her on the screen. 'Nina, did I do the right thing? I thought you'd want to know who sent you the photos. It was one of the things he was insistent on telling us this evening.'

'Yeah, thanks, Catherine,' I said. I knew it was what she wanted to hear from me. 'Glad you did. I'm heading off home now.'

'I'll come downstairs with you,' said Wingsy.

A few minutes later, we were in the car park, saying goodbye.

'You sure you're OK?' he said as we got to my car. 'I can follow you home and join you for a beer. We're days off tomorrow.'

'That's a kind offer, but I'm OK. It was the shock of finally hearing straight from the horse's mouth how those photos got to me. The stupid thing was, Wings, I was so bothered that whoever sent them did it to get Lloyd out of the way. The truth is, they were only sent to get even with Lloyd. They had nothing to do with me, and he really did just confess because he believed in his sick way that it proved how much he was looking out for me. I'm kind of taking comfort in that: none of this is about me and never was. Best news for a long time.'

'Well, as long as you're sure you don't want company, I'll see you in a couple of days.' He leaned across and gave me a peck on the cheek before striding off to his own car.

Once I'd run an eye over the back seat and the boot, I drove home. My plan was to lock myself in and hide under the bedcovers. It had been another of those days, and I was envisaging spending what was left of the evening relaxing at home. I was going to be very disappointed on every level.

Chapter 76

Bill called me as I got home. Using the last of my energy, I cradled the phone to my ear as I opened the front door. 'Hang on,' I said, 'just got to get into the lounge.' I kicked my shoes off as I went, dropping my bag at the bottom of the stairs, shrugging my jacket off all at once. The effect was that I dropped the mobile. 'Trying to do too many things at once,' I explained.

'You worked late again, then?' he asked.

'Yeah, we got Spencer in the bin for the three murders. Two down, one to go.'

'Think you've got the right one this time?'

'Definitely not, if Spencer is to be believed. He's talking but denying it. It turns out that Spencer got the photos of me by breaking into Lloyd's and sending them to me. It was all part of a complicated blackmail plot. I'll tell you about it tomorrow.'

'You want me to come over, Nin?'

'No. You've worked long hours too,' I said, feeling how tired I was and longing for sleep that I probably wouldn't get if Bill came over, however tempting that thought was. 'Think that we'll be pulling out all the stops to find Benjamin Makepeace now. There's still no sign of him.'

'Probably right under our noses the whole time. Nina, what's that noise?'

'The sound of me pouring wine. Let's be honest, I deserve it.'

I heard Bill's chuckle down the line.

'Fancy going out somewhere tomorrow night?' he asked.
I hesitated.

'Or not?' he added.

'Sorry, sorry, got distracted then. Looking out into the garden and it looks as though my shed door is open. I thought I heard banging when I was opening the wine. Course, I'd love to go out tomorrow, but with Spencer in the bin I'm going to have a really long lie-in. Can I let you know in the afternoon?' I thought I heard a sigh but, as one police officer to another, Bill, of all people, should really understand.

'It's that I'm on an early morning warrant the day after next,' he said, 'so I have to get up at 3am. Perhaps not too late?'

My love life felt as if it was slipping away. 'Sounds like a plan,' I said in a more cheerful manner than I felt.

'Well, goodnight, sweetheart. I'll speak to you tomorrow.'

'Night, Bill.'

I stood for several seconds thinking about our conversation and hoping that this wasn't the beginning of the end. Police officers had relationships all the time, got married, had children, I couldn't understand why I struggled so much. I was going to have to put more effort into this one.

The noise of the shed door smacking against the frame jolted me into putting the phone down, unlocking the back door and making my way outside to secure it. I'd never got round to putting a padlock on the shed. I had an old lawnmower and a few rusty, token tools stored there. Knowing how frequent break-ins to sheds were in the area, I guessed I'd probably had several night-time thieves sneak a peek and leave empty-handed and disappointed. The few pathetic items I had in there weren't worth stealing, and word of that had probably got round, so I never worried over the contents. It was a sturdy shed, however, and, if the local burglars could have nicked that, they probably would have.

As I got halfway across the lawn, I smelt a musty odour. There was quite a breeze blowing, sending my shed door on a non-stop shuttle between open and closed as well as causing the trees backing on to my boundary to bend and rustle. In conditions like this, there was no way I could trace the origins of the smell. The coolness of the evening stopped me from hanging around to find out. I ran the last couple of metres to the shed door, pulled the bolt across and legged it back to the kitchen.

Once inside, I banged the door shut behind me, shivering as I did so. I rubbed my arms to warm myself up before turning towards the window, where I'd abandoned my mobile phone and my untouched wine. As I reached towards the glass, I realised that two things were very wrong. Firstly, my mobile wasn't where I'd left it. Secondly, the knife-block to my right next to the sink had spaces for six steak knives and four carving knives. They were a very good set of knives, given to me for my thirtieth birthday by my great Auntie Lou. They had a twenty-five-year guarantee. One was missing. Whenever I used one, I washed and dried it, replacing it at the end of every meal. I hadn't eaten a meal in my own house for days. I most certainly hadn't eaten steak. My world went quiet.

Then, out of the corner of my eye, I saw a movement. I had seconds to decide whether to grab another knife and turn, or stay still and hope my imagination was playing tricks. It was not my mind playing tricks. This was happening. Someone was in my house, feet from me, with one of my knives. And he'd come to kill me.

I turned my head to my left as slowly as I could. My voice was a whisper; I just about heard myself speak. 'Hello, Benjamin.' I risked facing him; it seemed better than having my back to him. I knew it wouldn't stop him. I could see emptiness in his eyes as his gaze locked on to mine.

He said, 'What I hate the most is children being hurt and families breaking up.' His face was pale and the muscles in the side of his neck bulged. A sob escaped from his lips. 'She was supposed to be looking after Peter but instead she killed him.' Both of his hands moved up to the sides of his head, as if the images in his mind were causing him pain. I saw the glint of the blade in his left hand. My mind flew back to the pathologist's reports stating that the wounds were likely to have been caused by a left-handed person. At least the evidence would match. That was something.

Having turned to face him, I took a voluntary step forward. What did I think I was doing? Years of Officer Safety Training and I didn't ever recall the instructor telling us to move towards the man with the knife. My feet seemed determined to demonstrate the Home-Office-Approved Get-Yourself-Killed Manoeuvre.

I stopped myself from advancing any further. I didn't know why he'd come to kill me, but more pressing was how I was going to stop him.

'Benjamin,' I said, 'I know what really happened.'

His head snapped up, and he lowered his hands from his head. I focused on the knife. That instruction came back to me at least: all those hours practising in the gym at headquarters with a trusted colleague waving a rubber knife around. I was much fonder of that scenario. Keep your eyes on the blade, I told myself.

'Benjamin, please listen to me.' I was struggling to keep my voice even. I could sense the hysteria rising. 'Daphne, the woman at the home with Peter. She didn't kill him. Everything points to it being an accident.'

'What?'

I stole a glance at his face. His eyes were bulging. I looked back at the knife and tried to calm my heart rate. It felt impossible. The red mist had enveloped me totally. I could only see Benjamin and hear him over my own hammering heart. Nothing else existed. His fingers tightened and loosened their grip around the blade handle. I forced myself to concentrate on the knife, mainly to save my life but partially – remaining optimistic – so that I could describe the weapon to the patrol that would surely burst through the door any moment. Problem was, I couldn't see the door. I couldn't see anything but the murderer and the blade only feet from my face.

He pounded his fist on his chest, still clutching the weapon. 'A fucking accident. I don't think so. When I got there, he was, he was…'

I risked another glance at his face. His mouth was agape, saliva in the corners of his mouth, eyes staring into a historic horror. The event might have been in the past, but for Benjamin the scenes were very much alive.

'Benjamin, Daphne tried to save Peter,' was all I could manage to say.

Suddenly I was aware how dark the room had become. Perhaps it had been dark for some time and I'd only just noticed. I was having trouble making out Benjamin's frame, his sweat-soaked shirt, the bags under his eyes. Panic burst alive within me. I couldn't afford to pass out. I didn't want my name added to Operation Guard's list of victims. I wouldn't have my details on a pathologist's report.

'Benjamin. Listen. It would be easier to talk to you without the knife.' I said, propping myself against the kitchen worktop, fingers numb from gripping the counter. I was now peering at his face, prepared to take the chance because the knife was so close to his own face. Also close to mine. He'd taken a step towards me, that much was clear, but as to when he'd done it – the red mist had blurred the details. I was left with all I needed to know – I was going to die.

Makepeace stared at me, unblinking. 'Jason Holland,' he sneered through his teeth. I thought of the rotting flesh lying undiscovered until Wingsy and I found him. 'Holland had a thing for prostitutes. Did you know that?' he shouted at me. 'One of them was Amanda Bell. She had a son. Just eight years old. Her son is better off with his father. Boys need their dads. And you – I've read about you in the paper. Instead of going after Jake Lloyd, you come after me. I have to see that the right people are punished. And now, you're going to die.'

As he was saying these chilling words to me, the last words I was going to hear, he pulled a length of curtain wire from his pocket with his right hand. I knew I'd been right about the curtain wire. But smugness was superseded by fear.

'No, Benjamin,' I said, voice croaking, 'I was stalked by Jake Lloyd for years. Please understand that I've been a victim in all this too.'

'You're not a victim,' he said. 'Police officers are never victims – you ignore them like you ignored Peter's murder.'

I wanted to point out the twisted logic of this accusation coming from someone who was a murderer himself, but he was beyond rational argument, insane with hatred. I was wasting my breath. And it was possibly my last one.

My brain romped back to Officer Safety Training. What was it they told you to do in close proximity to a knife attack? Oh, yeah, that was it. Attack. Wrap yourself around the arm holding the knife as it came for you. Like hell. But right now it seemed to be my only option. I'd have to hope he hit a kidney – at least I had two of them.

'Benjamin, the knife,' I said, trying as best I could to sound like I wasn't scared out of my wits. I watched him stare down at the hand holding my kitchen steak knife, as if he wasn't sure how it had got there. I took the opportunity to slide a little to my right, away from the corner I'd been backing into. The movement refocused him. He pivoted his head in my direction. My hands went down to the kitchen drawer handle.

As he lunged the knife at me from his left side I pulled the drawer out, knowing it would come loose, and threw myself back into the ninety-degree corner of the cupboards, jarring my back as I did so. I swung the drawer and its contents up as I lurched to the side. His arm hit the wooden base of the drawer and the gas and electric bills in it spilled to the floor. But it wasn't enough to stop him coming at me. Most of the material was chipboard. By now I was in danger of ending up on the floor. Even during training, with my mate looming over me with a rubber knife, that hadn't ended well. The last thing I could let happen was to find myself on the ground.

I straightened up, put my hands on the edges of the worktops and pushed my feet off the ground. I had all my weight behind my legs as I brought my knees up to my chest and kicked out at his abdomen. The force of the kick, and the impact as he tried to pick up speed in the last couple of feet between us, had the desired effect of winding him and pushing him backwards. Unfortunately, as I flung my head back I caught my skull on the plinth around the bottom of the wall unit.

The blow stung but didn't hinder me. I was cornered. I ran for the door. Mistake. He grabbed my right hand with his, the one holding the wire. I sensed rather than felt a movement with his other hand. The blow to my stomach stopped me in my tracks for just a second until I remembered he was armed so I did the only thing I could think of – I went for the arm holding the knife. I caught a glimpse of it, processing the thought that it was covered in blood. He must have cut himself when I kicked him. That would give me an advantage.

I didn't realise I had fallen until I felt the cold ceramic tiles on my bare arms. I'd tried my best, but I was in pain and couldn't work out why. I slumped on the ground, finding breathing trickier than it had been a couple of minutes earlier, when all I could hear was my heart.

Another sound came to my ears but I couldn't put my finger on what it was. I could have sworn I heard the back door opening, but I doubted that Makepeace would leave me alive so he was hardly likely to walk away. He'd come to make me pay for Jake Lloyd's obsession with me. It was a totally insane reason to kill me and a terrible one to die for. The pain in my stomach was like no other I'd ever felt. It began somewhere in my middle but raced like a flash-fire all along my body, making any movement hurt. I was half sitting up with a view of Makepeace's knees straight in my eye-line. I couldn't lift my head to look up at him.

A shower of earth rained down on me, scattered with fragments of crockery, as Makepeace's knees fell away from my view and were replaced by his shoulders. My gaze followed the shoulders to the ends of the arms and saw that one was still holding the bloodied knife, the other the curtain wire. He must have stabbed himself and passed out. But where had the earth come from, and the other pair of feet?

A scrawny, unkempt face came into view. 'Love, love. You alright?' It looked familiar but my mind was doing funny things. I put it down to shock, but, if I wasn't mistaken, Joe Bring, the world's worst shoplifter and burglar, was in my kitchen.

'You've been stabbed,' he said, crouching to speak to me.

'No. He has,' I said, struggling for breath. I tried to point at the knife in his outstretched hand. Joe jumped up to stamp on Makepeace's wrist. A grumbling noise came from the prostrate killer as he involuntarily released the handle. The jogging-bottom-clad Joe kicked it to the far side of the kitchen.

'Gonna get you an ambulance. Where's your phone?' said Joe, bending back down. He smelt quite bad, but then he always did. My sense of smell brought me back to the severity of the situation. If I was dead, I wouldn't be repelled by Joe's scent. It got stronger as he lifted me under the arms and inched me along the ground to lean me against the oven door. 'You need to stay upright,' he told me, running towards the living room. He actually was getting some use out of those joggers – how about that?

He was back within a couple of seconds, my landline in his hand, dialling as he went through the drawers. For a moment I thought he was hunting down my valuables, until he pulled out a couple of teatowels and pressed them against my stomach. I could hear him talking, picking out words like 'stab', 'blood' and then 'officer down'. I tried to tell him that no one in the UK said 'officer down' – that was American TV shows – but I just gurgled at him and marvelled at the deep red colour my teatowels had taken on.

Joe stayed crouching down beside me for what felt like some time. But it was probably only a few minutes before I heard the sirens and the pounding of pairs of heavy boots coming for me once more. There was a certain amount of shouting which, I later found out, was largely aimed at Joe, ordering him to get away from me and get on his knees. Poor Joe. He'd saved my life and been repaid by half of the force shouting at him. A couple of uniform police officers spoke to me; I couldn't have told you if they were male, female, black or white. I just saw endless body armour and heard a ceaseless stream of talk on the radio.

Hands snapped into rubber gloves in front of me. Made me think back to Wingsy and myself finding Jason Holland's body. That felt like many years ago now.

I tried to think about what had happened. I knew they'd want a statement from me. That was what police officers did – they spoke to the witnesses, wrote it down and, by and large, got them to sign it. How else would evidence get to court? Someone was wrapping clingfilm around my stomach. That's my clingfilm, I wanted to say, but couldn't really find the strength. I decided to let it go. I had an emergency roll somewhere else. That sad, unheroic thought in mind, I passed out.

Chapter 77

6th October

Some of the next few hours I remembered in chunks, other parts not so much. I guessed I'd only been stabbed once, which seemed like good news. While it was perfectly possible to die from a single cut, I also knew of instances of multiple knife injuries not taking the life of victims. It often took the victims months to get back to normal, though, and being stabbed might well render me unable to do my job, so I'd be made redundant only an ill-health pension to live on – but I'd worry about that when I was out of hospital. For some reason, I started to find being unemployed quite funny and began to laugh. That really hurt. Someone in green told me to lie still. I think I was in the ambulance at that point, but I wasn't really sure.

When I woke up, I was propped up in a hospital bed, hooked up to several monitors and a drip. There was a great deal of bleeping coming from some of the machines but they were all drowned out by the sound of Bill snoring. He was asleep in an armchair, head to one side, dribbling on to his own shoulder. I watched him slumber until a nurse came into my view. 'Hello, Nina,' she said, scrubs rustling as she came to the side of the bed. 'I'm Charlotte, the ICU staff sister. Do you know what's happened to you?'

I tried to speak but my voice came out in a raspy knot. I heard Bill shift in his chair and looked over at him. 'Good to see you awake,' he said.

I tried to swallow, but it felt as though the last thing I'd drunk was a bucket of sand. Charlotte held a clear plastic beaker of water with a straw up to my lips. 'Only take a small sip,' she warned.

Even leaning forward a couple of centimetres to meet the straw halfway was agonising. I leaned back, worn out from such a tiny task.

'Was I stabbed?' I asked. She had bent her head level with mine to hear me.

'Yes,' she replied. 'One stab wound to your stomach.' She straightened back up to point to her own stomach, just beneath her waistband, or where one should have been if she hadn't been wearing a baggy blue top over baggy blue trousers. 'It was here. We had to knock you out for a while in case of internal bleeding or complications we couldn't see, but it all looks fine. The doctor will come and speak to you later, and some of your colleagues want to talk to you, but I've told them not to wear you out. I'll be back in a minute.'

She bustled off towards the nurse's station. I was too tired to care what she was doing if truth be told.

'Hey,' said Bill, moving his chair closer to the side of the bed. 'Are you in pain?'

'No – no, I'm not really. Probably off my tits on painkillers. I didn't imagine it, did I? Benjamin Makepeace was in my kitchen with one of my knives?' I shut my eyes, sagging back against the pillow. I felt Bill's hand on mine. He probably thought that I was trying to put a brave face on the pain, but the truth was I was totally shattered. 'I realised it was him from the photos I'd seen of him. Accent was a bit of a giveaway too.'

'Don't worry about him. Makepeace has been nicked and is being interviewed.'

I did a quick mental calculation of how long it took to get a person to custody, booked in, swabs and samples taken, clothing seized and at what point they would attempt to take his bite mark imprints. It would have taken hours. I couldn't see whether it was light outside as the window was behind me. The NHS was doing its best to block out all natural light and any hope of fresh air breaking into the building, bringing with it a hint of the time of day or weather conditions.

The sound of a man's shoes making their way towards me on the hard, shiny floor, accompanied by the clip of a woman's high heels, made me wish hard for Eric Nottingham and Catherine. I should have known better than to wish for something so carelessly as, on this occasion, it came true.

I managed a smile in their direction, pathetic as it was. Bill's hold on my hand tightened marginally. He didn't ask if I wanted him to stay, but assumed I did. He already knew me very well.

'You look pale, Catherine,' I croaked at her.

'Never mind me, how are you feeling?' she said.

'Like someone stabbed me,' I said.

This was met with awkwardness for some reason. It wasn't like everyone was unaware Makepeace had jabbed one of my steak knives into my gut. I was the one on morphine. What was their excuse for not having a grasp of all the facts?

'Nina, we couldn't have foreseen that Makepeace would come after you,' said Nottingham. 'If we'd had any idea, we'd have warned you and moved you.' He was finding it difficult to look at me as he spoke. He continued, 'He had several newspaper articles on him, some naming you and Jake Lloyd.'

Now that the DCI had got this off his chest, there was an uncomfortable pause. I concentrated on the bleeps and pings of the equipment. I was finding the noise comforting. It meant I was still alive.

Nottingham's voice broke my concentration. 'Makepeace put a lot of effort into trying to implicate others. On examination by the custody nurse last night, he was found to have a fairly recent cut, possibly self-inflicted with the knife we found in the rear of Gary Savage's van.'

Through morphine, fatigue and shock, I tried to recall who Gary Savage was and why DCI Nottingham was telling me about his van. I had an image of Wingsy and myself peering at a bloodstained knife at an early morning warrant, and the details came back to me. He was off the hook, then. At least the nick's toilets could get their final coat of paint.

'We've started the interviews but we haven't got much out of him,' Nottingham was saying. 'I have a feeling there's a great deal about Benjamin Makepeace that we've yet to get to the bottom of.'

'Can you tell us what happened last night in your kitchen?' Catherine said, stepping forward to the edge of the bed.

'Got home, opened my back door when I saw the shed door was open, went outside to shut it. When I went back into the kitchen, I saw one of the knives was missing, saw something move in the kitchen, turned to see Benjamin Makepeace. He stabbed me in the stomach. Joe Bring saved my life.' I closed my eyes again. I'd had enough. They had what they'd come for: scanty on detail but an account they could tell the CPS in case I died before they came back to take a statement. Now I wanted them gone.

Without opening my eyes again, I knew someone else had come into the room. The noise of her uniform gave her away. 'OK, you two,' said Charlotte, 'Nina needs to rest. You can come back later.' I hoped I'd remember to thank her when I woke up.

Laura and Stan were sitting next to me when I opened my eyes some time later. They didn't notice me at first but continued to chat, chairs beside one another, until Laura glanced in my direction.

'Nina,' she said. 'Am I glad to see you.' She jumped out of her chair to give me a peck on the cheek. I remained motionless; even seeing someone else move took it out of me. She stroked my face with the back of her hand.

'You certainly know how to worry me,' said Stan. 'I've spoken to your parents. Your dad will be here later but he didn't think that your mother would be up to it.'

To be fair to her, over the years, there'd been a lot of trips to one hospital or another. I was hardly surprised. It made me think of my sister. I had no idea whether I was still wearing her St Christopher. I tried to lift my hand up to feel for the necklace, but the cannula stuck in the back of my arm seemed to weigh pounds. 'Your necklace is in the locker with your other possessions,' said Stan, as if reading my mind. 'Apart from the clothing the police have taken.'

I was about to ask if they'd taken my underwear. My colleagues bagging up the knickers I'd been wearing for something like fifteen hours prior to seizure was a bit too embarrassing. Then I figured I would worry about it when I had the energy. I realised that Stan and Laura were peering intently at me as though they knew I was about to say something. I thought I'd leave my knickers out of it.

'What happened to Joe Bring?' I asked. This caused me to cough, and Laura to hold the water-straw combo out for me again.

She waited for me to take a sip before she said, 'He was arrested for ABH of Benjamin Makepeace initially, as it wasn't clear what happened. You started to explain that he'd saved you from Makepeace, so he was then further arrested on suspicion of burglary.'

I could only muster a raised eyebrow, and even then I might only have done so in my own head. Somehow I managed to convey my surprise to Laura, as she got the point.

'When it became clear that he was only in your house to help you, it was looking quite good for him... until a search of the garden indicated he'd been living in your shed.'

I smiled to myself at that. Joe Bring had always had a strange smell. It must have been the waft of him travelling on the breeze that I had smelt in my garden.

My smile must have looked odd: Laura's face held concern as she said, 'You alright? Want us to leave?'

I shook my head and she continued, 'Joe's wife threw him out about three weeks ago. He was spending the odd night with friends here and there until he decided to sleep rough in your shed. He's not saying why it was your shed, just sticking to saying it was a random choice.'

Another, slightly older memory came into my mind: of the musty smell in my house when I got back from Birmingham. It explained why I could never find my remote control. He'd broken into my house and watched my television. Joe might even have watched the DVD of Jake's interview – the DVD I wasn't supposed to have in my possession. What else did he know about my past now?

For some reason, right now this didn't seem to worry me as much as I'd have expected. It had all been in the papers anyway. Life sometimes brought the oddest situations to your door. In my case, it had brought Joe Bring in the form of a very unlikely hero. For his troubles, he'd been nicked. At least it had given him somewhere to sleep. And with any luck they'd have let him have a shower. His clothes would have been seized, too, so he'd have got some new ones. Standard issue police jogging bottoms and a sweatshirt.

Stan stood up to go in search of a canteen, leaving me and Laura alone.

'They let Joe go?' I squeaked, voice still full of holes.

'No, he was wanted for two other burglaries through DNA hits at both houses,' said Laura. 'He's been charged and remanded.'

'I owe him a lot,' I said, with a slightly improved voice.

'He wanted to go to prison this time. He was happy to have somewhere to live now that he's had to vacate your shed.'

I smiled again at this. I was still racked with fatigue and I wasn't even sure I didn't nod off again for a minute or two. I wanted to tell her that she was my friend and I was glad

346

she was here in the hospital with me, but the utterance of a simple sentence was too much for me to handle right then. I summoned the energy for another smile.

'You OK? Do you want the nurse?' she said. I was going to have to stop smiling; it clearly wasn't working. My reply was a shake of the head, as talking was beginning to hurt.

Stan reappeared with two hot drinks, handing one to Laura and resting the other on his thigh.

'Got these from the machine,' he said. 'Listened to my voicemail, too. Your dad is on his way, Nina. He's bringing your sister with him.'

Acknowledgements

So many people to thank but firstly, a massive thank you to everyone in the Myriad family but especially Candida Lacey for taking a chance on me and this book, Vicky Blunden – a more patient and generous editor you'll be hard pushed to find – and Linda McQueen for her amazing copy-editing skills and for taking the time to explain to me where I was going wrong and putting me right.

My family and friends have been very encouraging and, although I can't list them all here, I would especially like to thank Elizabeth Haynes, for encouraging me to start writing in the first place and for all her support and enthusiasm over the last eighteen months; my friend Liz Hubbard, who read an earlier draft and made some fantastic suggestions; and Andrew Goose at Studio 96, who not only read through the manuscript but has helped me with my blog and website. I'm grateful as well as technically inept.

Thank you to Jo Millington, forensic specialist (the inspiration for Freya Forbes – although I don't think I've ever subjected you to such a dreadful café experience) for your help with the ageing of blood. Your knowledge and my ignorance lost me a £5 bet. I'm grateful for your assistance.

I have to thank my friend Diane Ashworth, who has patiently listened to my tales from first draft to final publication, for offering support but mostly for just listening to me. I think that you had more faith in me than I had in myself.

Thanks to my dad, Bill. I'm not sure how you managed to remain positive throughout thirty years of policing but, without you passing that on to me, I doubt I would ever have joined the job. I might have found something else to write about, but it wouldn't have been Nina Foster or murders.

Last but by no means least, thank you to my husband, Graham. Not only did you walk the dog, do the shopping, cook the meals, clean the house and do the laundry while I embarked on edit after edit, but you never once doubted I would do it. And you read and re-read the manuscript time and time again, even after you stopped falling for me telling you to start at page one – 'No, no, I've changed loads – start at the beginning, honest.' Love you.

AUTHOR Q & A :

ABOUT LISA CUTTS :

What did you want to be when you grew up? Have you always wanted to be a writer?
I had always wanted to be a police officer. Once or twice I had the idea of writing a book but dismissed it as impossible. The thought that I could write a novel seemed a little too far-fetched but, at the age of forty, I began writing crime fiction. By that stage in my life, I had a lot of police stories and anecdotes to work with.

What do you do when you are not writing?
At the moment, I'm writing and working full-time. I don't have time for much else apart from walking our Labrador, Laughing Gravy. I try to read at least one book every month but even finding the time for that can be difficult.

What do you enjoy most about your day job?
A successful conviction. It's something positive for the victim or victim's family following a terrible tragedy. It also means that everyone on the team who worked hard on the investigation knows they've contributed to putting an offender before the court and in prison.

What is the worst aspect of your day job?
Seeing how ordinary, decent people have their lives ruined, often in an instant, by someone's actions.

How much is your writing inspired by your experience as a serving police officer?
Being a police officer gives you a glimpse into so many other people's lives and homes. The amount of people we meet is staggering, as is the diversity of those we deal with and serve. I've tried to show the humour and banter that exists in stressful situations between officers. It never means that we

aren't taking our work seriously, but laughter is definitely a coping mechanism.

Are you an avid reader of crime fiction? Who are your favourite crime authors?

My favourite author is Agatha Christie. I've read so many of her books. She was a truly amazing author. I have read a number of different crime writers over the years but I always come back to Miss Marple and Poirot.

Do you have a favourite book?

1984 by George Orwell. It's one of the few books I've read more than once. It shows a frightening world, years ahead of Orwell's time, where ordinary people are forced to behave in a certain way. With the right or wrong influences, a person can be made to accept anything as the norm. A person's mental capacity can only cope with so much pressure: we all have a breaking point, it's just a matter of finding it.

What do you look for in a novel?

It's important for me that the story keeps going. The characters are important but even if they are fascinating, if the plot is slow, it won't hold my attention. I like just about any genre of book whether it's crime, horror or sci-fi.

Do you have a favourite character in fiction?

Clinton Tyree, aka Skint, from a number of Carl Hiaasen novels. He stood up for what he believed in, although he never stood a chance, and trying probably sent him crazy.

What would your superpower be?

I know I should choose something fun, like being able to fly, but I'd want my superpower to be retribution – making people face the consequences of their actions and suffer for eternity for what they've done. As you can see, I'm not very forgiving.

What is your greatest extravagance?

A few years ago we went to New York and sailed back on the *Queen Mary II*. I wanted a cabin with a balcony. It was a great extravagance because crossing the Atlantic in April was a bit choppy so we couldn't actually use the balcony. We did, however, stand on it watching the Statue of Liberty as we cruised away. It was a fairly costly half-hour.

What's the best piece of advice you've been given about writing?

There have been so many, but it was probably Elizabeth Haynes, the author of *Into the Darkest Corner*, who said something like, 'You won't know until you try how it will work out. Have a go and see what happens.' It was her prod in the right direction that started me writing in the first place.

What tips would you give aspiring writers?

Get started. Don't put it off.

Get in touch with other writers, too. I've had nothing but fantastic support and encouragement from other Myriad authors but also from people I've met via Facebook and Twitter.

Have a blog, so that, when working on your novel or short story seems a bit too much, you can ease yourself into something a little less daunting but which can serve as a warm-up for your brain.

Keep reading – anything and everything that holds your interest.

Join a writing group. It may work for you. I prefer to write alone but it's great to have the support of others as it can be a bit lonely.

What made you decide to write the novel?
I think it was the challenge to begin with. I wanted to write an accurate police procedural, writing in custody time limits, what the law will and won't allow and what happens on a murder investigation. It was much more difficult than I thought it would be: trying to get the procedures correct without slowing down the pace was tough.

How long did it take to write?
I began in November 2011 and sent the first draft to Myriad in May 2012. The edits, well, they're a different story...

What encouraged you along the way?
I was really enjoying writing so I needed little encouragement. I had no idea if anyone else would want to read it or publish it so I found writing a total pleasure. Winning Myriad's Writer's Retreat Competition in May 2012 with an extract from *Never Forget* was a huge incentive too.

How important was research to the writing process?
I joined Kent Police in 1996 so I've had 17 years to try to get it right. There were one or two things I had to check to make sure what I was writing was factually correct, but the majority of the procedures are those that we do every working day.

Is the location based on one you know well?
Parts are based on the old police station in Dartford. It's no longer a working nick and has been knocked down. The rest is pure fiction.

In what ways did you draw on your own experiences?
Only in the practical sense of working long hours, being tired, letting family and friends down because you can't

get away from work, laughing at your colleagues and them laughing at you. I have not used any actual investigations, victims or witnesses when writing this book. That would be hugely disrespectful.

Which of your characters did you most enjoy writing?
Nina made me laugh. I'd go for a beer with her.

Are any of the characters based on people you have known?
No. The closest to a real person is Wingsy. He is an amalgamation of every decent part of every decent male detective I've ever worked with.

Did you feel a responsibility to represent police work accurately and positively?
I did. And it was difficult. Much of the work in a murder investigation is thousands of hours of paperwork. That won't ever change. It's also not particularly interesting for a reader so I tried to show that sometimes it's tedious without making it a tedious read (I hope). Showing the police in a positive light was also important. We aren't infallible; we make mistakes. Many of my friends are police officers, my husband and dad are both retired police officers. I'm proud to do the job I do.

Do you think that crime writers often misrepresent the police?
Yes, I do. However, I now have a little more sympathy and understand why that may be so. It was difficult to keep the story moving, keep it accurate and not write the 'tortured detective out to right a wrong' cliché. One scenario I've often read follows a single detective who doesn't sleep, doesn't eat but finds time to solve the murder and bring the offender to justice by themselves. It's a team effort every single time.

Should crime fiction show what crime is really like, for the offenders, the victims and the police?

Yes, I think it should, especially for the victims or their families. It's important to represent the legal system accurately but this doesn't always make a good read. I did shy away from writing anything too revealing relating to covert or sensitive investigative methods.

Will we meet any of your characters again in future books?

Never Forget is the first in the Nina Foster series. In my next book, *Remember, Remember*, she and Wingsy investigate a historic crime, and meet up with several of their old adversaries. It was just too hard to say goodbye to some of the characters from *Never Forget*. Nina also meets new characters as she makes her way through her professional police work, and her ever-changing private life.

What would you like readers to take away from the experience of reading *Never Forget*?

I tried to make it as accurate as I could and I hope that comes across. Also, please never forget that the police are only human.

MORE FROM MYRIAD EDITIONS

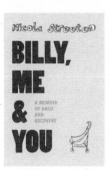

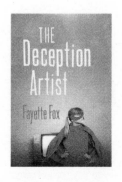

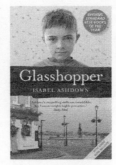

MORE FROM MYRIAD EDITIONS

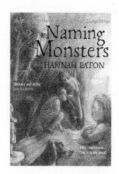

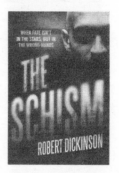

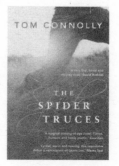

MORE FROM MYRIAD EDITIONS

www.myriadeditions.com